An Underground Conspiracy

A Between Heaven and Hell Story

Jerry B. Sanders

Leaves & Streams Books

ISBN (Paperback): 979-8-9920777-0-4
ISBN (eBook): 979-8-9920777-1-1

Cover design by Rafael Andres
Interior book design by the Aaxel Author Group

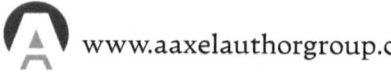 www.aaxelauthorgroup.com

This novel is entirely a work of fiction. The names, characters and incidents portrayed in it are the work of the author's imagination. Any resemblance to actual persons, living or dead, events or localities are entirely coincidental. Jerry Sanders asserts the moral right to be identified as the author of this work.

First edition

This book is dedicated to the millions of people who have been persecuted for centuries and have lost their lives simply because they were born Jews.

"The LORD spoke to Moses in the plains of Moab by the Jordan opposite Jericho, saying, "Speak to the sons of Israel and say to them, 'When you cross over the Jordan into the land of Canaan, then you shall drive out all the inhabitants of the land from before you, and destroy all their figured stones, and destroy all their molten images and demolish all their high places; and you shall take possession of the land and live in it, for I have given the land to you to possess it...But if you do not drive out the inhabitants of the land from before you, then it shall come about that those whom you let remain of them will become as pricks in your eyes and as thorns in your sides, and they shall trouble you in the land in which you live. And it shall come about that as I plan to do to them, so I will do to you. "

—Book of Numbers, Chapter 33, verses 50-56. NASB

Foreword

The ideas that form the basis for this novel are entirely fictional. This is not a history book. That should become obvious as one reads the contents; however, I must emphasize that this author does not want to cast any disparaging statements or thoughts against a race of people who have suffered enough throughout history. I chose the particular sect of Judaism because of their advancements during their existence, especially over the past thousand years. There are three sects, generally speaking, of Jews today. One is the Sephardic, and one is the Ashkenazim, which literally means "fire that spreads", and refers to its "Germania" roots. The third one is the Misrahi. The Ashkenazim can be traced back to the tenth century, according to some historians, and were from Central or Eastern European descent. Today, they are noted for their important contributions to philosophy, scholarship, literature, art, science, and music. The Sephardim Jews have been traced back to what is now Spain, as well as the Middle East and North Africa. The Misrahi Jews remained largely in Israel, as well as the Middle East and North Africa. Misrahi was not a term known in the time of this book's story but came about when Israel became a recognized state.

In America, the Ashkenazim population does not exceed three percent. However, the Ashkenazim account for 25% of our country's Nobel Prize winners in literature and 40% of Nobel Prize winners in science and economics. It is their tenacity in the face of persecution and ingenuity that guided me towards selecting their race as a basis for this fictional novel.

Obviously, this book has no factual basis, and there is no conscience intent to discredit the Ashkenazim (plural of Ashkenazi). They were chosen by the author because of their creativity more than for any other reason. Who else as a race could create the ingenious weapons and advances in science than the Ashkenazim as described in this book? We live in a world where vast numbers of people, and countries persecute the Jews for made up causes, such as, the Black Plague, believed by many during that period to have been caused by the Jews. It is my hope that the rebellious Ashkenazim depicted in this book are not taken as another misguided attempt to discredit the character of God's chosen people. There is much debate on college campuses, especially in America today, on who is guilty of terrorism. Is it Israel or is it Palestine? This book disregards those debates and simply tries to put an entertaining theory out for amusement only, and not to debate or an attempt to take sides with any nation or race of people.

This novel, *An Underground Conspiracy*, is the third and final book in the series. It is not necessary to have read the previous two books to understand the thread depicted in the following story. It is helpful to know the backstory, however, which can be summed up in the following first two books synopsize:

BOOK ONE (*Between Heaven and Hell*)

In the Middle Ages, a teen, aged 17, decides to leave his small village in England in an endeavor to overcome his poverty and illiteracy. He leaves his family to search for a better life for him and his betrothed. Soon after leaving home, he encounters men who deliver a mortal wound that only the two witches who find him can cure. The cure, however, allows demonic powers to enter, providing good and evil consequences. Having received amnesia because of his grievous wounds, he begins an extraordinary journey to find knowledge and wealth, traveling to foreign lands, meeting world leaders, gaining and losing fortunes, saving the innocent, while destroying evil.

BOOK TWO (*Servant of Duty*)

After his family dies of the Great Pestilence in 1348, Troy decides to leave England for one more try at finding someone to rid him of his demons. His journey leads him to Africa where he endures deception by Bedouins, battles with native tribes and a rogue elephant, and is forced to marry someone to save another's life. He endures a terrible shipwreck and is imprisoned and enslaved on two continents and vows to end the evil actions of ruthless people. He is a servant of duty, and, against all odds, he must seek retribution against evil men despite the dangers.

The protagonist, Troy Kensington, in the first two books, was endowed with incredible abilities due to his demonic possession, such as, near perfect memory, extraordinary abilities to self-heal, his amazing strength and fighting capabilities, extended years of life and astounding creativity. His demons protected his physical body against any who would attempt to harm Troy, because he was their human host. In this third novel, Troy must battle his adversaries, and, for the first time, he must battle those forces without the assistance from demons. He has become a mortal just like all of us.

Places mentioned in this book are the names they are known by during the period it takes place, 1362-1363 A.D. The words "gun" and "surgeon", for instance, were not known as such at the time, but would become the words we know today. One of the first evolutions of today's guns was first called hand cannons or fire lances before being called gonnes, which are featured prominently in the story. They were believed to have been invented by the Chinese in the 1200s but, perhaps, as early as the tenth century.

Is it possible to create a vast underground world where twenty thousand or more people can live for decades? In 1963, a city was discovered in the Neveşehir Province of Turkey, called Derinkuyu. The city extends to a depth of nearly three hundred feet and is believed to have held a population of perhaps twenty thousand, in addition to their livestock and food storage. The city contained wine and oil presses, stables, large storage rooms, and worship chapels. The underground city was probably populated in the 8th through the 14th centuries with Christians using it for protection from Arab Muslims. The underground complex was also connected by a tunnel to another city. Such underground habitats of lesser size were common throughout Cappadocia. Some parts of Derinkuyu were used as late as in the 20th century for a haven by Cappadocian Greeks and Armenians to escape persecution. The idea that there could be such vast underground cities as spoken of in this story is not that farfetched.

The term "electricity" was unknown in the 14th century, so the word for it, used in this book, is "sparks". While static electricity had been discovered by Thales of Miletus, a Greek, around 600 B.C., the first electric motor was not invented until 1821 by Michael Faraday. This was five hundred years after the Ashkenazim discovered electricity in this story. My book proposes that an extraordinary race of people, who have many workers of the highest intelligence whose sole job is to participate in "think tanks" to discover useful applications for their unique world, can and did discover electricity. Why could it not have happened?

The first great discoveries of medicine originated in the Middle East by Muslims. The Muslims, unlike Christians, who believe the human body was too sacred for exploratory investigations, did not live under those moral reservations. As a result, the Islamic world in Persia made great strides in surgery and treatments for many illnesses. The word doctor in the 14th century simply meant teacher and had nothing necessarily to do with medicine. The person we know of today as doctor was earlier known as a healer or "chirurgeon", which became known as a surgeon in France and England in later centuries. Chirurgeon means "the person who works with his hands or a person who heals by manual operation on the patient."

All dates are given in the normally recognized Gregorian calendar format except the first one given at the beginning of Chapter One, which provides the date it would be according to the Jewish calendar.

It is my sincere hope you enjoy the following "Winter's Tale."

Prologue

I count him braver who overcomes his desires than him who conquers his enemies. For the hardest victory is over self.
—Aristotle

Since the Great Flood, perhaps no one has lived to the age I have. Last January, I reached the age of 175 years old. There are few places in the known world I have not been to and fewer places I desire to go. For nearly 150 years of my life, I lived, possessed by demonic spirits that enabled me to achieve great wealth, reach levels of abilities, stamina, resourcefulness, youthfulness, and knowledge unheard of. Both God and Satan used me, to their cosmic amusement, to see how I would respond to experimentation by their supernatural powers and influences. Finally, after much effort and by the benevolence of Christ Himself, I was rid of the very powers that gave me those supernatural abilities and youth.

There have been occasions over the past dozen years when I desired to have back those demonic gifts, the following

1

tale included, but only for a little while. To be possessed by devils is to be damned. That has eternal consequences I do not want. Such powers in the hands of a mortal are too dangerous. If my ambitions had taken the path that so many tyrants had taken, I could have become the long anticipated Anti-Christ. Eternity is a long time to spend in the lake of fire, so I desired to be freed of my host of demons.

As I expected, when God chose to free me of Satan's fallen angels, I began the slow process of dying, which had been essentially on hold for many decades. At the age of 160, I had the countenance of one who was in their early thirties. Long, thick, light brown hair crowned my head, but now, fifteen years later, it is completely white.

Still, as I begin this story, I am strong, healthy, vigorous, and the attributes I gained in my walk with the dark side have not all left me. I can run and play with my young two-year-old son, Troy, with ease of a man in his thirties. I often teach my other son and daughter the art of hand fighting with swords and daggers. I teach them select languages from the more than a dozen I am fluent in. I give them lessons in history, mathematics, astronomy, geography, art, and the reality of God's words as I know them to be, having seen the Christ with my own eyes.

Many would give their wealth to have achieved what I have, and to live such a life for as long as I have. I know I have been blessed but, with blessings, come responsibilities. Eleven years earlier, I discovered a secret that had worldwide consequences, but no more so, than on my family and me. A secret so profound that I feared getting involved. So dangerous, so overwhelming, even though I had never feared any foe ever before. Something was being planned that would impact my family, my country, all of Europe and beyond. *Something had to be done*, I thought. To notify my king seemed too hazardous, too unbelievable for him to believe, or might initiate the wholesale destruction of millions of innocent people. I believed the public attention given to what I knew needed to be done was too risky. Already, things were in place I did not want to trigger by involving the king's soldiers. No, it needed to be done as quietly as possible, I believed, with the fewest people possible. At least, that was my belief in the beginning. I did not know that the cost of trying to solve the problem I faced would be so very expensive.

I discovered the presence of a nation bent on fulfilling an Old Testament command. My greatest concern was what I was about to do. Was it contrary to the wishes of an omnipotent and wrathful God? Would I be damned to hell because I stood in the way of his ancient commands? I didn't think I was given so much in unparalleled abilities to believe I didn't have the blessings and resolve to save much of humanity. It wouldn't be the first time I believed I was doing the Lord's work. I determined I would take my chances in doing what my conscience told me to do and defend my side of the story on Judgment Day.

As has happened too often in my long life, my single-minded focus on results had its consequences. What I will relate in this, my final tale of my exploits, may seem fantastic, unbelievable, far-fetched, even arrogant, but it is a true story of how I was able to save the world from a disastrous world war.

After I finish writing my last tale, something that will take many weeks to do, maybe months, I will lay my pen down and take a well-deserved rest. I must write it all down, for soon there will be no one else to tell what I know. In fact, I was commanded to write it down. If I had known when I began my interference in the plans of others, what I know now, I would not have begun the journey I ultimately made. Too many people I love have died in the wake of the effort to accomplish an impossible goal. My journey, to correct what I thought was a great wrong, cost me everything. Today, I am bankrupt of nearly all I held to be my most precious possessions. The story of Job tells us that he lost nearly all his wealth, health, and family before God granted it all back, plus much more. I was not so blessed.

My name is Troy Kensington. While participating in a raid eleven years earlier for ill-gotten gain, perpetrated and directed by greedy and power-hungry men, I stumbled upon a diary of sorts. At the home of Francois Mitterand Laurent, a wealthy aristocrat living not far from my home in southern England, I found the handwritten account of Laurent and many other men's plans to change the balance of power across the civilized world. In that diary, Francois gave hints of what was soon to take place by his people. The journal gave some details as to where he and others met and planned for the mutual purpose of creating a world theocracy. The journal I had discovered, and have since read dozens of times, gave only a glimpse of the enormity of what was to happen. The immense network of people involved in an unbelievable scheme to gain universal leadership over the world was soon to become known to me, and that knowledge would have comprehensive consequences well beyond my home country. Consequences that would impact the lives of as much as two hundred thousand Ashkenazim people who live in underground caverns, as well as many millions of aboveground gentiles.

I discovered where Francois met with other men who were part of the conspiracy, for I had already visited the site eleven years ago and, briefly, saw the men participating in what I expected was sordid preparations. I was too frightened of being discovered to stay longer than the quarter of an hour I was in the cavern in which they were meeting. Besides, I thought the clandestine gathering was taking place in a small cavern chosen for its secrecy. What I saw on that day was only a grain of sand on a sandy beach compared to what I was to discover on subsequent trips. Finally, to get the truth about what was happening, I had to speak with the diary's author, Francois Laurent. For me, Francois, who had made a vow of silence to protect his people, to protect a nation, meant getting information from him that was not going to be an easy task. In fact, it was the most difficult thing I have ever done. It was not easy for Francois, either.

Before confronting the Frenchman, I decided to visit the place one more time, where I last saw the men gathered for what I had yet to understand to its full implications. I still did not know who he was and what he looked like. I had only met his wife and family, who acted as if they knew nothing about what the patriarch of the family was about, and I believed they did not know. Francois was rarely at home, sometimes being away from a few weeks to several months before returning. I could not visit his house every day to find out if he had returned, so it was required I revisit the cavern again. I did so many times afterwards, but only on the outside.

Not for the first time, I reasoned it would have been better if I had never left home when I was seventeen and an ignorant peasant to find knowledge and wealth. Had I not, I probably would have died at forty, oblivious of the world's dilemmas and having to endure demonic possessions. Now, at 175 years of age, after having six wives, I still have too many sharp edges, too many dozens of men I have killed, and have survived too many attempts at being killed, I have one more quest to accomplish. This time, it would be without the protection of demons who, on numerous occasions, had destroyed men who tried to kill their host - me. What I did not know at the time I began in earnest to detect the far-reaching purpose of the Frenchman was that I had powers more formidable at my disposal than Satan's minions. God, himself, was on my side. That, however, did not give me immunity from the effects of my actions.

My sixth wife is Dania, the sixth because I had outlived all the previous ones. I met her in Egypt where I had been a slave to her father. I married her out of obligation but, in time, learned to love her deeply. When I would go and do some reconnaissance that would sometimes take days, sometimes weeks to accomplish, I would tell Dania. She asked what it was about of course, being a woman of great curiosity and motivated to always being part of what I was doing. My task was too dangerous to get her involved, at least initially, so I said I would let her know more after I returned. That, of course, did not sit well with her. She wanted to go with me, but our three little ones needed their mother with them, so she reluctantly let me go on my discovery trips.

I believe in omens. I believe that when the sun, moon, and stars were created on the fourth day of creation and were scattered about in the heavens, there would happen, thousands of years later, a celestial alignment of the stars that would commence the epoch in which I was predestined to begin. I was born for a purpose, to be what I had become, to do what I was about to do, when those stars aligned in the year 1362. A purpose that I would not act upon until I was one-and-three-quarters of a century old. My destiny was written in those young stars when the foundation of the world was laid. I was born to save a race of chosen people from annihilation. That sounds like the epitome of arrogance, I know, but read my story, and then, decide.

On a warm morning in the summer of 1362, I set out to discover more of what lay inside the secret cavern I had discovered years earlier. The lives of many people were never the same after that visit.

Chapter One

Discovery and Being Discovered

August 10, 1362 (Jewish Calendar: 11 Av 5122)

If someone can prove me wrong and show me my mistake in any thought or action, I shall gladly change. I seek the truth, which never harmed anyone.
—Marcus Aurelius

The implications of what I was facing scared me more than I had ever been before, because the potential impact on my livelihood, my life, and more importantly, my family, was enormous. If I were killed, that would be acceptable to me, since it would be a just payment for all the evil, all the killing, I have done but, if the truth got out, my death would not be the end of it. Surely, my family, all my family, would be implicated because of what I was about to do. The secret I wanted to expose, to destroy, was too large-scale for my adversaries to let anyone not connected to the intended operation be allowed to live. I feared for my family's lives, but I also feared for my countrymen and, to a lesser degree, the impacts on livelihoods of tens of millions of people across England, Europe, and Israel, among other places where I had been and still held dear to me. Even though most of my acquaintances in Mongolia, Rome, Japan, and Israel have long since died, I still hold their memories dear. I was foolish enough, or arrogant enough, to proceed as if I alone was qualified and capable of saving the current world order. Not that the current situation in the world with its despots, tyrants, and military leadership was all that great, but a one-world government of sorts had the earmarks of being potentially dangerous if the governing body was tyrannical itself. Rome gives us a good example of how a republican government will eventually turn sour. It's just the nature of people to let power be their god.

In the beginning of my exploit, the August day I left to revisit the cavern, I did not know enough about what was to happen to make an informed decision of what to do next. After all, I might have grossly misunderstood the intention of Francois' journal. Maybe he was mad, or maybe it was just wishful thinking by a handful of people to make the world a better place to live, based on their own misguided ideas. Wars are always conceived by one or a handful of ambitious men regardless of the impact it could have on the citizen masses. Maybe Francois was one of those men.

Nevertheless, I rode for several hours, retracing the route I took for the first time I visited based on the crude map drawn in the journal's pages. When I arrived at the site, nothing had changed since I was last there, and I saw no evidence I had been noticed by anyone the last time I visited, at least on the outside. Ironically, there was a light mist falling just as it had been the first time I had been to the secret entrance. I had accidentally discovered the cavern opening by observing a mouse carrying straw in its mouth when it squeezed underneath a hidden doorway in the tall rock cliff. Still, I saw no indication any traffic in or out had occurred at the doorway site.

It might occur to some to wonder why I had waited eleven years to revive my interest in the plot enough to seriously resume my investigation after such a long time. After all, if I had truly believed it to be of such importance, why would I not immediately do something to stop what I thought was madness? The day I found the secret cavern entrance and the meetings taking place within, my wife gave birth to our first child, little Catherine Adele. Suddenly, my wife and baby girl became my focus, my only focus, and everything else became secondary. World events were set aside for things closer to home. Between my new family responsibilities and my work at growing and expanding my branch of the East Asia Trading Company in London that I helped found, Francois' secret became less of a pressing obligation. After our third child was born, my mind once more drifted back to the idea that had not entirely left me but then, it began to bother me like a single buzzing mosquito does in our bedroom at night.

On this most recent visit, I spent the better part of the day riding around the area looking for signs of a corral for keeping horses or other signs that people were visiting the area on a regular basis. All I saw were wild animal tracks and an occasional single horse rider passing through the area. No signs of activity by humans could be seen leading up to the cavern entrance. The idea that there might be more than one entrance had not yet occurred to me.

My senses were heightened towards any sounds that might betray me to them. I listened to see if any noises emanated from among the rocks. I looked for tracks, scratches of horseshoes against rocks, pieces of fabric on a limb, any sign of anything that might be concealed amongst the boulders or someone spying on potential intruders. The only sound I could hear was a distant crow whose caws were muffled by the light mist falling. Confident that everything was safe to proceed, I hobbled my horse, took with me a canvas bag with items I believed I might need, including my short and long sword, and approached the hidden doorway. I again marveled at the ingenuity of how the entrance could be so indistinguishable from the surrounding rock face. Like previously, I ran my hands along the coolness of the granite, seeking a way to open the door. My eyes could not find the secret, only the pressure of my hands could hope to reveal the invisible entrance portal. Slowly walking along the shelf of rock that protruded outward from the rock face, I applied pressure until I felt the slightest give, and then, a soft sound of a click. The spring-operated doorway opened perhaps half of an inch, and cool air escaped past my nose, smelling dampness, mold, and strange fragrances I had not smelled before. The smell was not altogether distasteful. I waited to see if an arm or sword would thrust out towards me from unseen men guarding the entrance from intruders like me.

I waited for at least half an hour until I thought it safe to open the doorway wider. When I pulled the rock door open just enough to allow me to enter, I marveled at the silence and ease at which it pivoted. I would have loved to have examined it more, but that wasn't why I was there. If found, I probably would have been captured or killed immediately. Pulling that marvel of a door closed, I heard voices not far away. Several voices. Angry voices with intervening shouts in a room close by.

For a few moments, I stood just inside the room, surveying my surroundings. Unlike before when I was there, the room was less dark, because lanterns of some strange design were giving off a light that revealed a remarkable space. I say a lantern of strange design, because the light's source wasn't from a candle or oil. I could see no source that would produce such a light, except that a wire or rope was connected to it, which ran from the fixture, along the wall, and disappeared behind a wall partition. Again, there was no time to ponder the unusual aspects of light-giving appliances. I have been inside many caves before, but never have I seen one with a paved floor.

Anxious to find a place to hide in case someone came into the room suddenly for some purpose, I stood and observed the room for clues as to where I could conceal my presence if someone approached. I saw furniture of a kind I've not seen before. On the left wall, I saw cabinets, in the bottom half were boots, and the taller top half contained narrow doors with names on them. On the wall to my right were more cabinets, and they stored types of equipment that were unlike any I had ever seen. Investigating, I saw that the tall cabinets had printed on them names, and there were pictures on the doors depicting life-like images of people. Names like A. Ben Asher, C. Barzilal, G. Efron, and D. Gershon were written neatly underneath pictures showing men, women, and children, dressed in strange clothing. I opened one of the cabinets and saw it contained a garment of some kind. The other cabinets on the opposite wall contained what I guessed to be strange-looking masks and unusual knives. Knives much shorter than the two that I carry. Hanging on hooks were items that resembled devices with wood handles mounted to short pipes that must have been some form of a weapon. Months later, I would discover the tremendous bloodshed they could cause. In the middle of the room stood a row of three desks with ledgers and writing appliances on top of them. I stepped back and looked in wonder at things I had never imagined, much less had seen before.

On the opposite wall of the door from where I entered, was another heavy metal door, and that one was set into a stone wall built by an amazing artisan. The metal was covered by shiny paint. Beyond the wall, I could hear human noises, though I could not understand what was being said. It seemed to me that the room I was in, about thirty feet square, may have been a staging area for people to use when entering or leaving the cavern that lay beyond the metal door. The room and stone wall were new since the first time I had entered through the rock face. I wondered if that was due to simple improvements, or because it was believed someone, like me, had entered their secret sanctum and therefore more security was needed. The door was locked, leaving me two options. One was for me to hide in the room, as in under a desk, and risk being found out by one or more inhabitants or find a place outside and wait for someone to approach the entrance. I chose the latter as a path of least potential danger.

I returned to the outside of the cliff wall where the mist had turned into rain. For a moment, I entertained the idea of returning to my warm and dry hearth and my soft bed where I could lay next to my lovely wife. I did not allow that thought to take root, however. So, instead, I began looking among the boulders for a place where I could observe the cliff's hidden entrance, and still be unseen by anyone approaching the cliff wall. How long would I have to wait, I wondered? What if it took weeks? I did not have that kind of patience. What I really wanted was to discover Francois Laurent going in or coming out. The only clue I had as to what he looked like was from a painting I had seen in their parlor on the four occasions I had visited his home. I still enjoyed an extraordinary memory that permitted me to see the likeness of Francois with clarity. However, he could have changed much since the painting was first created, or the artist did not accurately capture his likeness.

Before searching out a good observation spot, though, I remounted my horse and rode around the site once more, looking for any detail that I might have missed earlier, that may give me the slightest clue as to what lay underneath the rocky hill around me. Whoever lived underneath, maybe a few, maybe many, had to eat, drink, breathe air, and surely, I thought, something on the surface must give a clue to the secrets below. That argument, I thought, was weak since the entrance I found was all but impossible to detect. How could riding around on my horse help me find such secretive openings or tell-tale hints to the activity of the underground inhabitants?

The rain continued and I finally dismounted and walked around looking for the slightest hint of human presence. It was possible that there was only one entrance to the cave, but logic began to convince me that there must be others, also. I was sure the occupants were as wise as they were ingenious, and they must have backup plans that included additional means of entering or exiting the extensive rock outcroppings I had been riding and walking around, if in fact the caverns were more extensive than the two rooms that I was aware of.

Then I saw it. A tale-tell clue.

I must have been two miles distance from the hidden entrance I knew about when I saw what looked like a very thin swirl of smoke rising from behind a myrtle bush that grew out from between two large boulders. It could have been my perspective of the rain hitting the boulders, but it looked out of place, and I approached it to take a closer look. What I found was a thick-walled pipe painted to blend in perfectly with the surrounding rocks. It was about a foot in diameter with a screen over the opening, I assumed to keep out rodents or other creatures from crawling down into the tube. It appeared to me that the pipe embedment was done a very long time ago. That puzzled me, because that would mean Francois and his conspirators could have been working on their plot for a very long time, also.

The thin veil of smoke had a peculiar smell, like nothing I had smelt before. It wasn't unpleasant, just peculiar. It occurred to me to stop up the pipe with mud, so someone would have to eventually come out to clear the stoppage away. I discounted the idea because it would alert the inhabitants of discovery. Then, the realization of what I was looking at first hit me. I was at least two miles away from where I heard voices on the other side of the metal door. The cavern then had to be extensive. Far more than any cave I had ever been in. It could also mean that there were many, many people underneath where I stood, and many of them could be warriors who could easily overpower me and my blades. I shook my head and thought again of my warm and dry bed. I hate being a servant to responsibilities I voluntarily place onto myself.

Rockslides. That would do it. I could cause piles of rocks from above to slide down the slope and cover the pipe, and it would be seen as a natural event. That would be a last resort. I wanted to see who might enter or exit the one rock face door I was aware of. Perhaps Francois would come out. I knew, from a recent reconnaissance, that Francois was not at home near my estate, and that might mean he was in the cavern. I rode back to the rock face containing the hidden door and, after a half an hour, I found a spot that suited my purpose of being able to see, but not be seen, and waited.

The rain had abated and, since it was late evening and my stomach informed me that it was past mealtime, I took out some cold mutton and cheese and dined, while I occasionally looked toward the secretive cave entrance door. Detachment from one's surroundings is often a man-killer. Whenever a man gets too engrossed in routine that he ignores his environment, usually because he thinks nothing could happen to him, life often gives him a wake-up call. I got mine while I was chewing on a piece of sheep gristle. Nonchalance.

I hadn't seen or heard anything prior to when I felt the tip of a sword on the back of my neck. It wasn't the first time I had been ambushed, and there was no excuse for it to happen again. I was too lax and not attentive to all the possibilities that could happen. *So, I might have to pay for my lack of wits with my life*, I thought.

"Who are you, and what are you doing here?" the quiet assailant asked.

The man spoke with a heavy accent, very reminiscent of the type I had heard before in distant travels in the far eastern parts of the world.

I said, "I'm trying to have a meal. Why do you ask and why must you sneak up behind me? I suggest you remove that blade from my neck, or you will find one against your own."

"Stand up," the voice said. When I turned around, I saw a large man, maybe in his fifties, and a younger man, most probably his son by the looks of him. He was perhaps twenty. Both were well built, light in complexion, with dark eyes and dark hair. The younger man held his sword pointed at my throat. He stood too close, and I could have easily disarmed him, but I wanted information, so I stood my ground, waiting to see where things would go.

The older man said to the younger one, "You know what to do. Do it."

That statement was said, not in accented English, but in Hebrew. I learned that language much earlier in my life when I served as a monk intern in a forest enclave many miles from my home today.

I said to both, in Hebrew, "If you are thinking of killing me, I would advise you to reconsider. I have taken the life of many men more capable and more dangerous than either of you by the looks of how you hold your sword, your stance, and the condition of your weapons."

It wasn't a boast; it was simply a fact, because my gift lay in the taking of men's lives. I have killed dozens and, though most of them were in self-defense, I had no qualms in doing what was necessary in my quest to save my country and, by extension, my family and me. Also, I shocked them by stating my advice in their native tongue.

They looked at each other, and the young man lowered his sword, and his father said, "How did you learn my language; you are not Jewish?"

"I spent many months learning it, and I spent a lot of time in Acre a long time ago. Now, tell me, why did you wish to kill me?"

"Father, do not tell him anything. Our orders are to kill anyone who we suspect as spies."

"I know what our orders are. We won't kill him but, instead, bring him to the rabbi for questioning. Take his swords."

Like I told him, I could have killed them both and not exert myself, despite my age. I wouldn't, though, as I wanted more information. In retrospect, I should have killed them both.

"I don't believe I will let you take my swords, but I will go with you, and find out why you think I'm a spy, as if you are important enough for me to spy on you."

The boy hesitated, looked at his father, then motioned me down the rocky slope. When we got to the flat area at the bottom of the hill I had perched upon, the father said, "We will have to blindfold you so that you can't discover how we get inside."

That little piece of information told me that they were cave dwellers, and that they believed it was possible for me, once inside and I knew my way around, I could find my way out at a future time. Otherwise, they could just kill me inside their environment and not worry about me returning. So, I agreed to the blindfold, knowing that would have no effect on my retracing our steps in the future, but I would not tell them that.

We walked in a different direction than where I knew the familiar rock face entrance was, I had discovered previously, thus proving they had multiple entrances and exits that emphasized the cavern had to be very large. We had walked nearly a half hour when we finally stopped. I heard a slight noise of rock sliding on rock and felt a breath of cool, stale air move across my mask. While I stood there waiting on the signal to move again, I took satisfaction in my amazing senses in case I never exited the cave again. The air and the mask prevented me from cataloguing aromas properly, but my ears picked up sounds within the unknown compartment in front of me, as well as the distant sound of thunder moving off to the east as it accompanied the rain to destinations yet to be dampened. Crows were having a meeting, or a meal, not far away, oblivious to my situation. A man behind me blew his nose on the rock shelf nearby. I heard the phlegm hit the granite with a splat. Far off, I could hear a woodpecker searching for bugs beneath tree bark. Those were the last sounds of the outside world I heard before I was pushed forward into another, secret, world.

Chapter Two

Imprisoned

It is no advantage to be near the light if the eyes are closed.
—Saint Augustine

Once inside, I heard a door grind its way closed behind me. I was led to a chair where I was told to sit. The father removed my blindfold, and I had a chance to look at my surroundings which, not surprisingly, looked very much like the one I had seen at the other entrance I had discovered originally. Only this time, there were others present. Three men and one woman sat at desks, who were staring at me as if I were a new species of humans. By their faces, I could tell they were not happy I was there. They stared at the father and son with dislike as if they had violated an important covenant covering the difference between what was acceptable and what was not supposed to be.

The father went to a set of wooden handles near a metal door leading out of the room, and pulled a lever, then another. No one spoke, as if it weren't allowed, so I took it upon myself to break the silence.

"My name is Troy. What is your name young man?" I asked the son.

"My name is Amos, and my father is Hezron."

"Quiet," spoke one of the men sitting at a desk. "Don't say anything until the rabbi gets here. You know the rules."

Nothing else was said over the next quarter of an hour, and it gave me time to consider the pressure acting upon my bladder. That would need attention before much longer.

In due time, the metal door opened, and a man of perhaps seventy entered, along with eight other men who were young, strongly built, dressed alike in brown clothing, and held either swords or spears ready to use them. In what I thought was in politeness, I stood up to greet the man. Sitting while greeting someone, I believed, was rude. This idea was not part of the philosophy of my subterranean hosts, because I was forcibly pushed back down in the chair by one of the large soldiers or bodyguards.

The rabbi asked why I still wore swords on my hips.

I said, "Because I told them they could not have my swords and, for them to take them, meant I would have to kill them."

Rabbi looked at the guards. He had a frown on his face as if he smelt someone's night jar. One man grabbed my arms from behind, and two more roughly removed my swords. My swords are not just two pieces of sharp metal with handles. They are my friends and having them taken, did not sit well with me. I attempted to rise again, whereby I was pushed back down once more.

I said, "Sir, we are not going to be friends if you continue to treat me like I'm the enemy."

A bold and brash statement, but I wanted him to understand that I was someone to be treated with respect; otherwise, they would find me a formidable enemy. There were at least ten armed men in the room, too many for me to overcome, but I could put up some serious battle if I felt threatened, and I began to feel threatened.

"Why were you spying on us?" The elderly man said, who I assumed was the rabbi I had heard mentioned.

"I was eating a meal after a long ride. I wasn't spying on anyone. I hadn't seen anyone to spy upon. Who are you that you should fear being spied upon?"

"Let me warn you; I will be asking the questions, and you will answer them or suffer the consequences. Do you understand what I am telling you?"

"I am fully aware of what you are saying, and I would like to be treated a little more courteously if you don't mind."

The rabbi was surprised at my statement and looked around at the people in the room and smirked. There are few things I detest more in the world than smirking men. If there weren't swords and spears pointed at me, I would have slapped the old man across his smirk. It was one of those times to be cautious and bide my time, rather than hastily do something with potentially severe consequences on my well-being.

"You are clearly not of Jewish heritage. How do you know our language?"

"I served for eleven months as a monk intern copying biblical texts. That is where I first learned Hebrew. I also spent many months based out of the city of Acre in the Kingdom of Jerusalem. I fought against the Saracens there, and escorted pilgrims on the way to the holiest city in Israel, Jerusalem. I am a friend of Jews and Christians."

"Ah, so you must be a Templar. Is that correct?"

"I was, and proud of it. I am not the enemy of Jews. You are not my enemy, either. I just wanted to eat my meal peacefully."

"Take him below and lock him up. I will talk more with him later." And then, nothing more was said.

My swords had been taken away from me, including my long sword, one of two blades I called "Blind Justice", because it did my bidding and claimed lives based on a justice system it was blind to. I passed judgment on those I fought, and my sword was unbiased against anyone whose blood it shed. God knows it was used only to protect others or to defend my life. God's justice is perfect, and my sword was used to exact judgment on those unfortunate people I felt deserved both mine and God's wrath.

I was blindfolded again, and then escorted out of the room. We walked through passageways, turning often either left or right until we reached a doorway that opened into a small compartment. I could feel the closeness of the walls, though I couldn't see them. In a few moments, I felt the compartment moving downward. I reached for my blindfold to remove it to observe the wonder of what was happening, but a strong hand knocked my hands away. I don't know how many men were in the moving room with me, but I guessed four of them. It was obvious that I was not to be allowed to witness my surroundings or attempt at escape.

Eventually, the compartment stopped going down, a door was opened, and I was led out and down another hall. I heard metal against metal, and a door was opened, and I was pushed inside. When I removed my mask, I saw that I was in a confined cell. I was in an underground dungeon. I had spent many months in prison cells before in various countries, and now, I found myself in a dungeon in my own country, a half day's ride from my home. I was both humiliated and angry. I thought it was time to give up on displaying the nice person attitude I had been portraying, and seriously start looking for a way to get out of the place. But then, I was there to disrupt or stop the conspiracy that I believed was taking place by the very men who had put me in that cell. I certainly did not know the extent of what was going on, because Francois' journal gave no details, but I knew the ultimate goal, which was to take control of our government somehow. How that was to be done, I had no idea, and being in prison without swords greatly hampered my ability to dispense my form of justice.

It was not completely dark, because there was a lamp burning in the hall's ceiling. The light, like others I had seen in the cavern, gave off no odor of oil or wax. I was in one of eight cells. A hall separated the eight into four on each side. I was alone in my cell. There was another man across the hall from me and another at the far end, also across the hall. I stared at the man across the aisle, and he was equally curious about me.

"You look like an outsider," the curious man said.

"Don't talk to him," the other man down the hall shouted. "You know we aren't supposed to talk to outsiders without authorization. You know what they will do to us if they catch either of us talking to him."

"I'm a general. I have the clearance to do what I want and talk to who I want," said the man across the hall.

"My name is Troy, son of Finn. What is your name?" I said to him, hoping to get what information out of him I could.

"I'm General Eliab, son of Ammihud."

"I'm curious as to why a general is in a dungeon cell like an outsider such as me."

The general sighed, backed up and sat on a raised cot as if his story might take a while to tell.

He said in quite good English, "No matter how important you are, no matter how high you climb, there is always someone more important and more powerful than you. I report to the highest general in our colony's army. Unfortunately for me, he has a beautiful wife that I coveted. Unfortunately for her, she coveted me, as well. We were caught in bed together. Tomorrow, I will be stoned to death for breaking the seventh and tenth commandments. It didn't help that we were caught on the sabbath, either."

"I see. What will happen to the wife?"

"Oh, she is dead. Her husband ran a knife across her beautiful neck. It wasn't about sex with us. Well, not just sex. We truly loved each other."

His plight saddened me, but I found a possible avenue for information from a man sentenced to die. He had nothing to lose by telling me what I needed to know. That is, if he wasn't still a true patriot to the cause and to his people.

"I'm sorry to hear about your problems but, truthfully, I have my own problems to worry about. Do you think I will be stoned to death, also? Or worse?"

"Troy, being stoned is the least of your worries. You are not the first outsider who has been questioned. None has ever found their freedom again, and all have been questioned during imaginative torture to ensure the accuracy of their answers. Oh, you will die, but it will not be until you are begging to die."

That was not the kind of news that I had hoped for. I was a resourceful person, but things did not look very hopeful. I was in a prison cell within a larger underground prison.

"You are of the nation of Israel, aren't you? Doesn't that mean 'Thou shall not murder?' I haven't done anything to your people to warrant killing. I was just outside eating some cold meat and cheese when I was confronted and brought to your cave. I'm not your enemy am I, just because I'm a gentile?"

He laughed and shook his head. "Oh, we are Jews alright. Ashkenazim Jews to be specific. We call ourselves that now to differentiate us from the above ground Jews. We are God's chosen people, alright. Are you a Christian? Well, the God we serve is a God of wrath, not love like what you people believe. And that is why I will be stoned to death tomorrow. I've seen it done before, many times. I've even taken part in it, and I'm not looking forward to my turn to die. No, you will be killed, not because you are a gentile, but because you are from above."

"I have a lot of questions, but let's start with these. Why am I a threat to your world simply because I am from aboveground? How long have you been living in this underground cavern? Why do you need an army, and how many are there of you living like hibernating bears?"

The general said nothing for a while. He scratched his head and his right arm pit while he pondered whether he should confide in me. Then he finally said, "Our people fled the old country, originally, after the Bar Kochba war, twelve hundred years ago, but went underground only about three hundred years ago because of unrelenting persecution. Our forefathers have never forgotten that God commanded his people to take control of the land promised to them. So, we have an army that trains and grows larger every year so that one day, we can fulfill God's command to conquer and control the land promised to Moses and Joshua. Our leaders are not concerned that the land promised to our forefathers did or did not include the world outside our hidden doorway you call England. You, Troy, are a threat because you have discovered we exist; therefore, you cannot be allowed to live or leave. You will never be permitted to go home again. Never."

"General!" Said the voice coming from down the hall. "You must know you are speaking treasonous words to the outsider! If I'm asked, I will have to tell what you have said."

"I'm going to die tomorrow, and my new friend here will certainly die shortly after me, so what's the harm in what I say?"

"Wait, are you telling me that you have an army here, underground, that plans on attacking my people and taking over our kingdom?"

"Yes, of course that is what we are going to do. Well, they are after I'm dead."

I said, "What if I could get us both out of this prison cell? Is it possible to find our way out of this cave to the outside?"

I was ashamed of what I had just said, because I was then thinking more about personal freedom than accomplishing the reasons I was in the cave to start with. I justified my thinking by believing I needed to be free to gather answers, rather than being imprisoned like a common thief. I wanted to accomplish my goal from a position of strength, rather than a weak one, not as one that would be given a death sentence in a day or two.

Eliab asked, "You think you can get us both out of these cells? How can you do that without a key?"

"If we get out of this room, then what? Can you get us to where we can find our way out of the cavern?"

I had been imprisoned many times, and I have had the

need to open those and other types of locks for various reasons, especially in the years I was a pirate and learned never to go anywhere without a stiff piece of wire embedded in my boot sole. In fact, I had one in each of my soles. My time pirating in the far east working for a powerful woman pirate, I had become very adept in opening locks with a bent wire. It was never a question of if; it was always a question of how long. My only concern was if the patriot down the hall betrayed us.

"I can open this door and yours. I just need to know if you will help me find our way out of these caverns. Once we are free, then, we must talk about what happens afterwards."

"Okay, I'm with you. Get me out and I'm your man. I know a way we might escape to the above ground, but my people will never stop trying to hunt us down. I've got nothing to lose by at least attempting freedom, but you will have to pay for the consequences."

"Hey, Eliab, what are you doing?" came the question from the man down the hall.

"I'll take the chance at consequences. What can we do with this problem?" I asked the general, indicating the other man's objections.

"Get me out of this cell, and I'll have a quick talk with him."

So, in just a short time with little effort, I had removed my stiff wire, bent it in just the right way and had my cell door open. In the time it took the general to put his boots on, I had his door open, also.

The general walked swiftly down the hall to the other man's cell. The man's attitude changed, after persuasion, and he begged, "Please, take me with you. Let me out and I'll do anything you tell me. If you won't take me with you, I'll tell the rabbi everything you both said."

I heard voices outside the prison door, and then, the sound of a lever turning.

"General," I hissed, they're coming in!"

I stood behind the opening door and two men walked in carrying trays of food. As soon as they stepped inside, I slammed the door closed. At the same time as I closed the door, the general was there, and hurled himself into one of the men, the largest of the two, and I attacked the other, and both of us fell hard onto the floor. It appeared that one of the men was a kitchen worker, from the looks of his soiled apron, and the other was a guard. I easily grasped the kitchen man and pushed him into what was my cell while the general put the other into what was his former confinement. General Eliab removed a short sword and a set of keys from the guard, who did not protest, but glared at us with an angry look.

"Do you see any advantage in bringing the belligerent man with us?" I asked the general.

"Well, except for the fact that he is a sparky, no, there is no reason to bring him. Doubtful we will need his expertise, but just in case, to keep him from saying anything to other guards and we can't kill him."

"What's a sparky? Never mind, you can tell me later. We must get out of here. We will take him with us in case he's needed, but only as long as we can depend on him."

Using a key from the guard, I unlocked the door of the cell that housed the one who had admonished the general for telling secrets. I found out his name was Pagiel.

"Pagiel," I said, "if you betray us, as my last free-will act, I will ram a sword through your eye into your brain."

Of course, I still had to find a sword to do that, since the general held the only weapon, we possessed.

It was a new and uncomfortable world for me. Ordinarily, I would elect to escape during the dark of night but, because I was in the deep bowels of the earth, there was no distinction between night and day. It was either artificial light or natural darkness, depending on where lights were shining, or where there were none.

I let Eliab lead the way, since I assumed he knew our surroundings, and kept Pagiel between us to watch him. Eliab was invested in our freedom, since his life would be forfeit if we were caught, but I had reservations about the sparky, not knowing his crime. The general opened the prison rooms' door, then looked left and right down the wide hallway leading away in both directions. He saw men and some women in both routes. I had been blindfolded when I was brought down from above and, for the first time, I was able to notice the construction of the walls and floor. The walls were of mudbrick, hand laid, and some floors appeared to be natural bedrock in some locations, smooth, but slightly uneven, in others, the floors were manmade pavement. It must have taken a considerable amount of time and effort to create the underground world those Jews had made for themselves. Only later would I find out the extent of that world.

It was also the first time I studied the general. I guessed he was between thirty-five and forty, but it was hard to tell since everyone underground, I had seen thus far, was pale and seemed in dire need of sunlight. He was several inches shorter than me, but it was apparent he, which is typical of most soldiers, worked at building strength in his muscles. I wouldn't call him handsome, but his face had a kind of simple

31

appeal. Long black hair, dark eyes, beardless, full lips, and startling white teeth. As would be expected of a general, he seemed to be adept at being a leader.

The general said, "To our left is a break room where I can see several people gathered. On the other side of the wall in front of us is a kitchen serving this floor and the two floors above us. On the other side of the kitchen is a mechanical room. Down the hall to the right is the lift that brought you down from above. It's too dangerous to use since many soldiers use it. Next to it are the stairs in the event the sparks are not working. We need to get to the stairs. It will be an hour at most before the lights go out because of the mandatory outage. You two walk ahead of me towards the stairs as if you are prisoners and I'm your guard.

I began a mental notation of the many questions coming to mind about all he was saying, but there was not time to hold an information meeting until we were somewhere safe. His plan seemed workable, so I walked side by side with Pagiel while Eliab poked us with his short sword. I was at the mercy of two men I did not yet fully trust. My wife Dania and my children often came to mind, and I missed them. Maybe it was irresponsible of me to have left them for an impossible mission. Too late to worry about that now. I had no idea whether I would still be alive by tomorrow. It was impossible for me to even know when today became tomorrow in the hole in the earth I was desperately trying to exit. My life had suddenly become a priority, and thoughts of saving my country were temporarily set aside, becoming a distant second.

We were walking down the hall to where the lift and the stairs were when two brown-suited soldiers turned the corner towards us. They were armed with a club that they wore on one side of their hips and a medium size sword on the other. They were at least twenty feet in front of us. Eliab told us to keep walking and do or say nothing, just keep walking as if everything was alright.

"Greetings, general," one of the men said. "I didn't know you had been released. Who are these men?"

"Major Reuben. I've been given a reprieve, but only after being reduced in rank to a private. My new duties include taking these prisoners to work in the mine on 'C' level."

"Poor men. I wouldn't wish that on any man. Sorry to hear you are a private after so many years of admirable service. I respected your leadership, sir."

An altercation was prevented by the quick thinking of the general, and we proceeded to the stairs.

"We must hurry before the power goes out for the quiet period."

The long climb up toward the surface began. Twenty-four steps to a floor. Eliab stopped after five floors, even though the stairs continued upwards, and eased open the door. The door opened onto a very large room with multiple parallel iron rails on the ground leading in both directions. On some of the tracks sat large metal compartments or boxes whose iron wheels sat on the parallel tracks that allowed the movement of the steel containers. Some were stationary, but some were being pushed by men covered in black dust as if they were mining coal.

"Why did we stop here?" I asked Eliab.

"I'm not sure this is a good idea," complained Pagiel. "If we get caught, we're dead. What are we going to do now?"

"If I were a betting man, I'd bet I will kill you before we

find our freedom," Eliab said, and I smiled for the first time since entering the cavern system.

"Don't worry," Pagiel said, "we will get free of the underground. It's what happens after getting out of here that concerns me."

"This is mining level 'A'. My sister's husband is in command of this operation. He has connections and we are friends of sorts. This level is mined for metals like silver, copper, gold, and some precious stones, such as, diamonds, chrysolite, amethysts, chalcedony, and more. Ore is sent to a crusher down those tracks, and what metals and stones are found, are brought to an assay office for further extraction and refinement on the treasury level. That's the noise you hear; it's from the crusher. We don't have to worry about being caught here. Even if the workers had any incentive to care about what was going on around them, my brother-in-law would help us. Valuable metals and stones discovered are for use in buying what we can't grow or raise below ground, as well as for such things as building materials, spices, clothing, and especially, products used in the making of weaponry. This operation works non-stop, no worries about lights-out. Now let's go."

Pagiel said, "We need to find something to eat soon. I'm starving."

"I must agree with Pagiel this time. And something to drink, also."

We walked down a wide tunnel with rooms built into the walls on one side. Some had dirty glass windows in front revealing people working at desks. At one of the larger rooms, we stopped and went inside. Sitting behind a desk was a tall man who looked to be in his thirties, thin body, and thinning hair. He had a long dark beard and wore things over his eyes to enable him to see better. Just another marvel I saw in the underground world I was in. When he looked up from the book he was writing in, his face showed a sequence of surprise, pleasure, and disappointment. He seemed to be happy to see his wife's brother but, obviously, not his companions.

"Eliab," the startled man said, "have you been released from prison, or did you escape? And who are these men?"

"Joram, we don't have time to go into the details. We need your help in getting us some food, drink, and a way to the surface. Also, if you can find some weapons, that would be great too. Will you help us? For my sister's sake?"

"You know what would happen to me if I got caught helping you? And you know what would happen to Delilah after that?"

"I'm aware of it. Will you help us or not? We don't have much time before all floors will be flooded with soldiers looking for us."

He sighed his frustration and said, "Wait here," Joram said, and left us in his office.

"I wish I had stayed in my cell," Pagiel said again. "I would have already eaten by now."

Eliab and I ignored him, but he and I both knew, at some point, we would have to deal with his whining. Half an hour went by and Joram hadn't returned, and I began to worry if maybe he was going to contact the authorities, when he opened the door, carrying a box of supplies. The box contained bread, cheese, skins of water, and two daggers, old, but usable.

"Delilah knows I'm helping you and I won't tell you what she said about it. She's angry that you have put us and our children in jeopardy, but she also knows you are just trying to save your life. If asked, we will deny we ever saw you. Please, take these things and go."

Eliab had a short sword that he had taken from the prison guard. I took one of the daggers, and asked Pagiel if he knew how to use one. I did not want him to have one, but could hardly refuse his own self-protection, even though I had strong reservations whether he could use it without harming himself. He took one and slipped it into his boot. It gave me a reason to watch him more carefully.

"Go where?" Eliab asked. "We need your help to get us aboveground. I know you know people from treasury who come and go to spend the gold and stones you harvest down here. Do this for us, and you'll never see me again. If not for me, for Delilah."

"Do you know what you are asking? If word got out about us, our whole way of life, our goals, our secrets, and our purpose for being would be jeopardized?! Your life and my life aren't worth that revelation."

"Listen, Joram, I am to be stoned to death and, probably, Troy here, as well, for being accused of being a spy. I've given my life to being a soldier for the cause. You don't need to lecture me on duty. The truth is, I no longer believe in the cause. I've seen hundreds already who have died for that very reason. What we were promised two thousand years ago is no longer feasible if, in fact, it ever was. We are no longer entitled...."

"Shut up, Eliab! You must not speak such treasonous words, especially in front of an outsider!"

"Joram, I'm not asking again. If you don't help us right now, I am dragging you with me, and you will be counted as one of us. If you help us, I promise you will not be implicated in our escape. I will swear it was all my idea. Now, we are running out of time."

"I don't like it. Our nation's future is bigger and more important than my life. I won't help you."

"You leave me no choice then."

Eliab walked over to a dusty lever painted red and put his hand on it as if to pull down.

"No! Alright, alright, I'll do what I can to help. You've lost your mind, Eliab. This is the last time I will help you, and I don't want to ever see you again after this. Come with me."

We took the stairs again and went up three floors to what he said was the treasury level and told us to wait at the stair landing for his return, but Eliab didn't trust him and insisted he go with him. Pagiel and I waited for word from them on when we could follow.

The treasury department had its own hidden doorway to the outside. That door was locked from the inside, and a code had to be entered for it to be opened from either direction. Only the top two managers of the treasury floor knew what that code was. I don't know what lie Joram said to the assistant manager or what bribe he gave, but the door was opened for the three of us to exit into my world. By the time we exited the hidden doorway, the sun had set, and it was nearly dark, and I did not know where we were relative to the entrance, I had discovered but, according to the stars, we needed to travel north, so we walked on in hopes of finding refuge away from the insiders who would surely come looking for us.

Chapter Three

Flight!

You must remember that no one lives a life free from pain and suffering.
—Sophocles

We walked north for about two hours before it got too dark to safely walk among the boulders and cliffs. We ate a meal that Joram had given us but built no fires for fear of discovery. We talked very little, also for fear of being overheard; and, when it was necessary to speak, it was in whispers. There was much on my mind and many questions to be asked, and I was disheartened about myself because, once I was captured, all I wanted to do was escape. My intent was to foil the progress of men intent over doing harm to my country and my family. I found myself placing my family and myself over the duty I felt to save a country. I needed much more information before I could develop any kind of plan. If I could enlist Eliab, if he would agree to join me, I would have a much better chance of infiltrating and foiling the plans of those desperate men. I began to wish for my powers as a demon-possessed warrior that I used to be, but that was crazy even to think about. God removed the demons from me and God, I figured, could help me even more than my long-possessed demons. That is, if God chose to help me.

When the sun began to smudge the clouds in a pink blush as it slowly rose above the eastern horizon, we also rose and continued our journey north. It was the first time in his life for Pagiel to be aboveground and witness a sunrise, and only the second time for Eliab. Pagiel was filled with wonder, so much so, that he shut up his complaining for a while, though, the humidity and mosquitoes did come as an unwelcome surprise to him. I wanted to ask Eliab the questions that crowded my thinking, but I didn't want to ask them in the presence of Pagiel, so we walked on, mostly in silence.

At mid-morning, we arrived at the place I had tethered my horse, but it was gone. I assumed the insiders did something with the horse to prevent any suspicion of the whereabouts of its owner that would cause people to look for me nearby.

"We must walk to my home, but that will take until dark. There, we will be safe and can eat and drink and rest." *And plan our next move*, I thought, but did not say. We walked for hours, resting occasionally, because neither of the insiders were used to much walking, and their muscles cramped, and their shoes rubbed blisters on their feet. The weather was somewhat cool, compared to what it could be in August, and, now and then, a light mist fell, something Eliab and Pagiel had never felt in their life. Everything was a wonder for them, and I had to answer dozens of questions, all the while I seethed with questions of my own. I held grave doubts as to what to do with Pagiel, and began questioning him about his background, why he was in prison, and why it was important for him to want to escape with us. As I look back on this day, I am amazed how much Pagiel had come to mean to me, how much he matured once given his freedom.

"Pagiel, tell me about yourself, your background, talents, why you were in prison, and what will you do next," I asked him.

"I'm a nobody, so there isn't much to tell you. I'm my parents' only child in a culture that desires many children. My father is a hard man, who hates me because I'm not hard and mean like him. My mother wanted a daughter, but she got me, and raised me like a daughter, which made my father hate me that much more. Me being much smarter than he only made things worse. He's a hard man who oversees other hard men. I'm an embarrassment to him, and he threw me out of our home years ago. I have worked in our farm fields, livestock chambers cleaning the filth, and worked in mines of various sorts before an overseer discovered my ability to calculate sums rapidly, remember sequences and codes without having to write them down, and design varying systems using sparking skills, especially in weapon development. I never fell into the normal structured system of determining my status as a student, worker, or a member of the military, because I was forced out of my home before my place in society was determined. Where I went wrong was having a conscience. Where men wanted me to design things that would kill, I wanted to develop medicines that would heal. I was imprisoned for a while to think about my future. Then you came along, and I saw a chance to escape my moral dilemma by running away. I don't know how to use this dagger you gave me, nor do I want to learn. Here, you can have it."

I walked on for a while thinking about what he said. I

saw potential in his knowledge that could help me in seeking how to stop Francois Laurent and his people but wondered if his ideology would be a help or a hindrance. I thought about Francois, too. Evidently, Francois was an Ashkenazi Jew, as well. I began to discover he was one of a network of aboveground spies and contacts used to further the cause of the underground nation of Israel's refugees, whose purpose I was only just then beginning to grasp.

An hour before dark, we entered my forest, part of the five-thousand-acre estate I owned with my wife Dania. In the distance I could hear my wolf hounds barking at something. Maybe the kids were playing with them, or they had found a deer to harass. By the time we reached the clearing where our castle sat, I caught sight of my three children playing some game that required them to yell and run and scare all animal life for a mile in every direction. When they saw me, they yelled even more and ran towards us.

Catherine Adele, whom we called Kat, was eleven years old, and Jaleel, whom we call Jay, was nine years old, was pushing his little brother Troy, two years old, in a wagon. It was late for them to be outside, and they should have already been preparing for bed by that time, but they are a wild bunch and as hard to coral as are our barn cats. Dania was standing at one of our back doors with her hands on her hips. She finally lifted one arm and waved to us after recognizing it was really me with two strangers with no horses, and not vagabonds who some time passed through looking for handouts.

After hugging each of my children and chiding them for still being outside and acting like stray hooligans, we reached where Dania was standing with a bewildered look on her face. I introduced them and said they would be staying with us for a while and asked her if she would please get the cook to find something for us to eat. By the look in my eyes and the way I set my mouth, she understood that I would explain later about my companions and me. She had not expected me to be back so soon and deduced that something had changed my plans. Dania was gifted with extraordinary common sense, and we were able to speak volumes just with our eyes and facial expressions. She and I had experienced many adversaries and challenges previously in foreign lands. Those experiences were complicated, since I was still possessed with multiple demons, and those unique experiences helped form the basis for our amazing compatibility in our extraordinary life together. Oddly enough, I had married her because I didn't know what else to do with her, not out of love for her, but for convenience. Since then, I long ago learned to love her with all my heart.

The three of us ate a quiet meal together late that evening. Dania had gone to bed and eagerly awaited me to join her. The questions I wanted answered would have to wait until the next morning, since my guests were very tired and travel sore. My wolfhounds were enamored with them and their smells, and I finally had to call them away for being nuisances.

"We have much to talk about in the morning, my friends," I told them when we finished our meal. "Let's get some rest and talk about the future after breakfast tomorrow." The two men looked at each other, and I believed they were assessing each other's willingness to betray their people by telling me, an outsider, more secrets they had held as sacred since birth. Secrets they swore to uphold throughout their lives or suffer the pain of death.

I had no doubt that the underworld people, the Jews known as Ashkenazim, who I had stumbled upon, would eventually look for us, would expend all necessary effort to search out, find, and kill or capture all three of us. Sooner or later, I was sure they would come to my castle and, if they found me and/or my guests, it would go bad for my family, also. I knew we had to leave for a more private location within the next two days, three at the most. I understood that my family and I would not be safe until I brought about my ultimate quest of neutralizing the Jews of their plans to a conclusion. How long would that take? Weeks, months, years? I was naïve enough to believe I alone could stop a nation bound and determined to fulfill their destiny. I had, at that point, not a clue what lay ahead, how vast a network they had, and how dogmatic the Ashkenazim were to their cause. I came to understand that I was the most naïve man in the world to believe I could change the unchangeable.

Our roosters woke me long before the sun hinted about showing its face over the high hills to our east. I arose, kissed my wife, and went downstairs. Our cook, Maude, was just taking out pans in preparation to begin the morning meal for my family, the rest of our servants and now, my two guests. She was helped by a woman and her husband who once had tried to kill me but, because of his conscience, instead, saved me from a slow death. I took a chance in hiring him and his wife, and it turned out to be a good thing for us, as well as for them. Or so I thought.

Since my guests were still not up, I went out to our stables. I had lost a good horse, a courser, and I wanted to make sure three of my remaining horses were ready to take Eliab, Pagiel, and me, somewhere safe until a plan could be formed.

When I got back to the kitchen, Eliab and Pagiel were up, as were Catherine Adele and Jaleel, who were curious about our guests, probably because we seldom had overnight guests. Soon, Dania came into the kitchen carrying little Troy. We ate a good meal of eggs, ham, and biscuits with freshly churned butter served with apple cider. Of course, Eliab and Pagiel, though surely tempted by its' smell, did not eat the ham since it came from an unclean animal. When breakfast was over, I invited Eliab and Pagiel over to the stables to talk and to plan our trip away from my home, so as not to endanger my family. It was time for some uninterrupted answers to many questions.

Eliab had been trained in how to ride a horse as part of his duties as a soldier, but Pagiel had never sat on one, and had only seen drawings of them before he saw the real, live animals in my corral. At first, he was afraid of the large horses, just as he had been afraid of my wolfhounds, having never seen a dog before, either. Teaching Pagiel how to saddle a horse and ride would be part of the day's lessons but, first, some questions had to be broached.

"Before you answer my questions, know that any secrecy you have been sworn to, is now void. You are fugitives condemned to death, and you can never go back to your former world, neither you nor Pagiel. Your secrecy has been forever compromised by escaping with me, so don't hold back on your answers. Instead, tell me all I need to know, so adequate plans can be prepared."

I could see the turmoil in Eliab's facial expression and by the way he stared at the ground, avoiding looking at me. All his life, as a common citizen, then, especially as a soldier, the secrecy of his people was foremost in their culture. To be found out could be the end of his people's lifestyle, maybe even their lives, not just his. At least that is what they were told all their lives. Clearly, it was difficult for him to switch his allegiance from his people to fully answering my questions as an outsider. Pagiel looked at us, also clearly uncomfortable. They had answers I needed to know, also, and I would get them, or I no longer had use for either of them. Even if they foolishly wanted to return, I could not allow it. They knew where I lived.

"I have no wife or children," Eliab said, "so I have no pressing reason to go back. This new world out here is now mine, and my allegiance to the people who judged me and sentenced me to death is over, and I no longer feel the obligation to remain quiet. I will tell you whatever you ask, and, in return, I only ask that you help me adjust to my new world."

"I will do what I can to help you with that. We barely know each other, and how we will adapt to a relationship is yet to be seen, but I will help you. I owe you my life for assisting me in the escape. Now, I need information. Some years ago, I discovered a journal written by a man whose home is not far away from here. Apparently, he has two homes, one nearby and one underground. Through that journal, I discovered how to enter your world, and it is why I stood watch at the doorway I had found, waiting for one of your people to emerge. In that journal, it spoke of a conspiracy of your people to overthrow my country and alluded to the same being done in other countries, as well. I wish to know all you know relative to that conspiracy if, in fact, the journal was not the ramblings of a deranged man lost in his own delusion. Let's begin by you telling me how many of you live below."

Eliab rested his arms on the corral fence and stared at one of my horses munching on grain as he thought about the question and the many that would most assuredly follow.

"There is a census taken every two years to determine that question. However, our leadership has ways of knowing the current population regularly. It is very important for my government to know such information for planning purposes. A little over a year ago, our numbers were something over twenty-two thousand, three hundred. That information is given out to all citizens, but that number was just in our colony."

"What do you mean, your colony? What is a colony and how many colonies are there, and do you know where those colonies are?"

My interest and excitement of my discovery began to build. It was like discovering a lost continent, a new world, and twenty-two thousand people living underground?! How was that even possible? I was trying to be patient, but questions were flooding into my mind. I looked at Pagiel, who sat on a wooden barrel a few feet away, unsure about his future and whether he wanted to hear what was being confessed. I got the uncomfortable feeling he wished he was still in the prison cell serving his time. Unlike in the prison, he no longer admonished Eliab for telling secrets. He understood his new dilemma and the forever loss of his past life.

"We belong to the Britannia colony. There are others, six besides ours. There is a larger one, larger than ours, in Burgandy near Charolais. There is a small one near Rouen in Norman France that will be connected by a tunnel with our colony eventually. There is another west of Toledo in Castile, another one south of Milan, one in Adrianople in Byzantium, and the largest one of all, the one that dictates every facet of our lives, is in Armenia. It is the oldest, established shortly after the Bar Kokhba war, sixty-five years after the temple was destroyed in Jerusalem. Our people fought their last battle then, and the Romans defeated us and caused our final dispersal west. Rather than be persecuted, as was our fate for hundreds of years, our forefathers believed it best to go underground and establish a colony, or colonies, and build a dynasty that would one day take back our homeland that God promised to Abraham thousands of years ago. No one could blame us anymore for diseases, atrocities, or heresies if we lived in our own world, away from the prejudiced gentiles in your world. Rabbi Horam Getz, in a secret meeting that took place just after the dispersion, directed a hundred devout men and their families to leave Israel and find sanctuary in the mountain country of Armenia. It was there, after years of persecution by the Seljuks, in what is now Turkey, that my ancestors found a cave system, expanded it, and began the expansion west to where we are today."

I listened in stunned awe as Eliab told me about the amazing expansion of his people to the west and their determination to survive, despite living in a hostile world, a world that they had once shared with people who hated them.

"You mean, Eliab, that there are possibly a hundred thousand, or more, of your people living underground from here to Israel?"

"That is correct but understand that we were never to stay underground. The goal is to rise up and take the lands our spiritual leadership said rightly belonged to us."

"But from what I have read," I told him, "God told Moses and Joshua to take the land from the Mediterranean Sea to the Euphrates River. There was no mention of England, France, and Germania. Does your people plan on taking this area in addition to the Holy Land of promise, all of it from England to Persia?"

"The plan is to take control of all territory from here to beyond the Jordan River, beyond Moab to the Euphrates River. All of it. My people believe, or at least the Armenian Priests believe, that it is what Adonai really intended by his decree: 'When you cross over the Jordan into the land of Canaan, then you shall drive out all the inhabitants of the land from before you, and destroy all their figured stones, and destroy all their molten images and demolish all their high places; and you shall take possession of the land and live in it, for I have given the land to you to possess it.' The priests and rabbis see the world from here to Moab full of idols, as they were in Moses' day, and those pagans who worship such idols must be destroyed. We are taught that Adonai's peoples are destined to replace the inhabitants that Satan has corrupted, with the Ashkenazim. God warned the Jews in the Torah that if his people did not drive out the pagan inhabitants of the land, then, 'It shall come about that those who remain will become as pricks in your eyes and as thorns in your sides, and they shall trouble you in the land in which you live.' Then Adonai said, 'It shall come about that as I plan to do to them, so I will do to you.' That is why we are persecuted so heavily. Because my ancestors did not do what Adonai said, and so, Adonai is allowing us to be punished. The priests and rabbis are going beyond the area first given to us by expanding the area far west and destroying every pagan nation in between to please Adonai. I have not read the Torah; I've only listened to what has been explained to us by our teachers and rabbis."

I wanted to take some time to let all that he said soak into my mind, but there was so much more to know. From what Eliab told me, it would be imperative that the three of us must be found by the Ashkenazim to not let such information get out to the outside world. No expense or effort would be spared to find us. We were in extreme danger, and so was my family.

"Eliab, I don't think I can fully grasp the importance of what you have just told me. Is there a timetable that you know of when this takeover will begin?"

"I'm a general, Troy, but I'm not high enough in the chain of command to know that. That information will come out of the Armenian colony. It's possible that each colony chief rabbi knows something about the timing because it is generally believed that we are very close to achieving the final preparations. One of the deciding features of the decision to go ahead was the completion of the connecting tunnel from our colony to the one in Rouen. That passageway has been under construction for maybe fifty years. The tunnel was recently finished. I don't know the schedule to begin the attack, but it will happen soon. The tunnel is important, because it will allow the quick dispersant of our armies and supplies under the land and sea rather than having to depend on slow ships traveling across the channel between Britania and the mainland of France, which can be dependent upon the weather. The thrust and timing are very critical, and it is expected that domination of our armies over kingdoms will be a matter of a few weeks or even in a few days. The movement will be great, fast, and so surprising that no army will be able to respond in time to defeat us. We won't win because of our overwhelming numbers, but mostly because of our surprise attack and advanced weaponry. This battle plan has been in the making for centuries by patient people who died before ever being able to see the outcome. Only the people at the highest levels know all the details. I'm a soldier, and even the highest generals don't know what the highest rabbis know. It seems most propitious that you have discovered our plans on the eve of my people's quest."

"The rabbi that questioned me and put me in the prison cell, is he the rabbi responsible for your colony?"

"No. There are dozens of rabbis, maybe forty or fifty in our colony. There is one rabbi for every five hundred or so people. The army has always done what the rabbi dictates, because Adonai supposedly speaks through priests, not generals."

"Now."

I turned around to look at Pagiel, who still sat on a wooden barrel containing oats, staring at the ground between his feet.

"What did you say Pagiel?"

"I said we need to leave now. I never told you the real reason why I was in prison. I was there to await trial for sorcery, which is forbidden by our religion. I can sometimes see things happening now and in the future, and I see a dozen riders, perhaps more, who have left our colony and are headed towards us on swift horses. They have your horse too, and they are allowing it to return to its home. They are following it to where we are. They will be here in about an hour."

I looked at Eliab, and he shrugged his shoulders as if he believed it was possible Pagiel was right.

"Pagiel," I said, "run to the house and tell Dania to get the children ready and tell the cook to prepare food enough for us for five days. Tell her we must leave now and do not delay, as we have less than an hour to leave. Eliab, help me saddle six horses!"

The Jews of the Britannia Colony were cleaver people and, knowing what I now knew, I knew they would be ruthless when they found us. They would simply kill us if we were lucky and do so much more to us if we weren't. My legs and arms were tingling with fear for my family as we hastened to get the horses ready to ride. My single-minded focus just might kill us all. I had been naïve enough to think they might only be after Eliab, Pagiel, and me. I came to the sudden conclusion in the corral, I could no longer take a chance they would not harm my family, especially if they believed I had told them about their plans for warfare.

In just over half an hour, we were riding at a gallop down our entrance drive towards the road that would take us to London, where I hoped we could reside in our townhome, out of danger from the people heading our way, at least I assumed so. I told everyone as we rode northeast to London, where we were going. Normally, it would take as much as five days to arrive, but I hoped to get there in three days or less. Kat and Jay were each on a horse of their own and, since they had ridden from the time, they were two years old, they could ride as well as most adults. Troy was within a wraparound next to Dania's bosom, and we rode at a trot. Pagiel, never having ridden before, held on to the saddle pommel with both hands, hoping he would not fall off. The terror on his face would have been comical if our situation wasn't so dire.

We had ridden for two or three hours when I heard Pagiel shout, "Stop!" It angered me when he insisted, but we stopped long enough to talk.

He said, taking in deep breaths, more out of fear of the

ride rather than from exertion, "They have left your castle. Six riders are going to area farms to search for us, and six, no, seven, riders are riding to London on the same road we are on. They killed your servants after they revealed where we are going. I'm sorry."

My servants, dead! They were more than just servants to my children, Dania, and me. They were our friends, too. "Okay," I said, angrier than I had ever been. Had I still been possessed by demons, I would have stayed and waited for the riders to approach and let them play havoc on the Jews chasing us. For ten years, my husband-and-wife servant couple served us faithfully, and the cook even longer. What would or did happen to their children, I wondered? If I were alone, I would have been seriously tempted to wait for them, regardless of being demon-less, but my first duty was to my wife and children. "I know of a cave where we can go and stay for a few days while we make plans on what to do next. It would be foolish for Eliab and me to take on the seven riders alone."

Eleven years earlier, I had searched for and found the hiding place where the wife of a good neighbor had been taken, while the person responsible for the abduction waited for a ransom to be collected. We would now go there, just long enough to plan how to combat the immediate threat. Riding through the forest, we arrived at the location next to the river Wye. The skeletons of the two men I had killed remained in the cave. The cavern wasn't large, but large enough for the seven of us to be out of the weather for a few days. Then the crushing reality of what had and what might happen hit me, and I cursed myself for being too rash in my plans to begin with.

"I can't stay here, Dania. Those men will arrive in London, and eventually find out where my office is, and may very well harm my daughter and son there. I can't let that happen."

My daughter, Connie, was the president of the East Asia Trading Company that I had helped establish long ago and was the owner/manager of the English office in London. She and younger brother, Carl, were both the only survivors of the Black Pestilence among my seven children and wife, Anna.

Dania was not happy, believing my allegiance was now with her and our children, but I loved my other children as much as mine with Dania. I understood her concern, but I had to try to protect them and worry about the consequences of what I would do later. I turned to Pagiel. I hardly knew him, but I had no one else to trust if I took Eliab with me, and I wanted his help in case I had to kill the seven men headed to London.

"Eliab, will you come with me? It will be a hard ride and very dangerous. It's up to you. Pagiel, will you stay here and help my family? I will return, if possible, as soon as I deal with the threat."

Eliab agreed to go with me, and Pagiel stayed behind with my family. I believed Dania would be the one protecting Pagiel, but at least he was there to give assistance with what she might need. I did not know Eliab's capabilities, but I knew he must be smart and had risen to become a general in the army by being good at what he did. I had come to believe the Ashkenazim were good at developing, planning, and training by what I had witnessed so far, and I was confident they would not promote a man to such a high position unless he was capable in the areas, I needed him to be proficient in, especially in fighting. Before leaving Goodrich Castle, I had retrieved my favorite of the two swords I christened as "Blind Justice," my short sword, and some others, of lesser quality, for my two companions.

It was midday, but we had no time to stop and eat lunch, only when we were riding did, we eat. The Jews who were after us had a half day head start, and we had to overcome that so that we could arrive in London before them. That was assuming Pagiel was indeed a seer. I knew of some shortcuts we could take, but that would require fording some narrow rivers, rather than using bridges. We rode hard until I could feel my horse begin to lag; then, we walked both horses for a spell while we ate a meal; then, rode hard again. When night fell, we alternated, riding fast; then, dismounted and walked our horses until they caught their wind. We repeated that the next day and night. Eliab's butt became very sore having never ridden as much as I had. He did not complain, but I could see him adding padding to the saddle. He was saddle-sore, indicated by the way he walked when we did dismount. At no time did we just sit and rest. I wished for Pagiel to be with us, so that he could give us an update on where our pursuers might be. I also wished for a miracle from God, since I could expect none from the devil, who had often in the past helped me fight my battles in return for using my body as a host.

Two days and two nights without sleep began to tell on both of us. By early afternoon on the third day, I could smell London's vile street gutters that were filled with rotten food, sour ale, and human and animal waste. Not long after, I could see some of the taller buildings and, in a little while, we were near the Tower of London, which was very close to my office warehouse. Connie and Carl should be there. At least I had hoped they would be, and it would not be necessary for me to go looking for them. The three days we rode towards the capital city, I mulled over plans for how I would protect my children. Each plan I came up with, I discarded as unfeasible.

Carl was, by then, thirty-eight years old. I had trained him in the art of hand fighting, taught to me by a Mongol guide, as well as in sword fighting, and he would be a great asset. I had also trained Connie, as I had all my children, all eighteen of them before Kat and Jay, but I was reluctant to put my daughter in harm's way. I wondered if Carl had trained his children as I had trained him. If so, that would be a bonus for us. I no longer had friends in London as I once did that could come to our aid in a fight to the death. With the three of us men, I believed we had a good chance of defeating the Jews, although I did not know the quality of their skills.

We arrived at my London office very tired, dirty, and road sore, but I could tell when we entered the main office that we had arrived before our antagonists. It looked as though business was as usual. Connie saw us and, with a great look of surprise, ran over and hugged my neck. It had been half a year since I had last seen her. She was approaching forty years old but looked not a day older than thirty. It was strange, and due only to my many decades of being nurtured, like a gardener cultivates his crop, like my demons took care of me as their host, that I looked perhaps as young as my daughter despite being more than a hundred and thirty years older than her. My hair is white because of the traumatic experience I had, seeing a divine specter in an alley in Cairo. If I were to dye my hair the color it once was, a light brown like the color of a dead oak leaf, I could pass for Carl's younger brother.

"Poppa! So good to see you. Why have you come, and come looking like you are, and who is your friend?"

"Before I say anything, where is your brother? Is he here today?"

"He had a meeting with a distributor but should be back any time now. Come, let's go to my office and talk. How about something to drink?"

We went into her office and closed the door, and Eliab and I sat down heavily, glad to rest, if only for a moment. An aid brought us some drink, which was soothing to our dry and parched throats.

"Connie, we have a serious dilemma. There are several men, we think seven of them, who are on their way here to question you, and probably Carl, also, about Eliab and my whereabouts. They will stop at nothing to find out that information. They have already killed George, his wife, maybe their children, I don't know, and our cook. I have endangered you and Carl just by being here, and I'm very sorry. We are here to see to it that no harm comes to you or your brother or your families."

It was then that Carl knocked on the door and entered. After our hugs and greetings, I told him what I had told his sister.

"They will be here soon," I said. "They believe the existence of their very culture and way of life is in jeopardy. They will stop at nothing to ensure word of their existence does not get around, and that means finding Eliab and me. Because they will think you might have heard something from us, they will try to eliminate you just to ensure nothing about them has spread. Eliab was one of them. He helped me escape after I was found spying at their cavern entrance. There is much I don't know about what takes place belowground, and I haven't had the chance to quiz Eliab as much as I would like.

So, with all that said, we must prepare for their arrival. We can talk more about what has brought this catastrophe upon us and yourselves but, first, we must see what our fighting assets are. Carl, can you still wield a sword and fight like you used to?"

"Of course, I can. You taught me well, and I could use the practice. One of my sons, my only child now, Gerald, is tall, strong, and nearly as good as me. He will want to join us."

"Don't forget about me," Connie said. "If you discount me, I will be furious. True, I haven't fought in a real battle, but I have been trained by the best fighter in the world. You, Poppa."

"Okay," I said, "with Gerald, that makes five of us. That should be more than enough to take care of the seven on the way. I believe that the only solution to dealing with them is by killing them. I know that no argument will change their mind; they are on a do or die mission. They have already killed my servants to silence any knowledge of their existence, and that is reason enough for me to pass sentence on them. If either of you are not okay with defending yourself to the death, then let me know now. Again, let me say that I am terribly sorry for having put you in this position. I had no idea of the storm I was going to stir up."

"I'm in," said Carl. "I will fight to the end to help save my family, and that includes you, Poppa. No need to apologize to us."

"Okay, then, thank you. Carl, go find Gerald, and both of you join us at our townhome. Connie, what will you tell your husband? His life is endangered, also, so both of you must come to the planning meeting."

"I won't tell him anything, except that I am meeting you

at your London home. That's all he needs to know for now. I will tell him all of it later. I will not bring him with me, since he is in ill health, having never fully recovered from the plague."

"Connie, inform your assistant that, when asked, they are to tell any strangers looking for you or Carl that both of you are at my home with me and a friend of mine. Their willingness to inform them of where we are, should be enough to send them on their way to where we will be waiting for them. We are tired, but they will be, also, and the three of you are fresh, so we have a very good chance of defeating them."

While Eliab and I rode to my townhome, I asked him if he thought that ridding us of the seven would end the search for him and me. He thought not. He believed it would just be a temporary end to the current problem. Sadly, I had to agree with his assessment. I was discouraged and frustrated by that idea. It had been years since I had fought a death battle and, to be truthful, I was looking forward to another fight. The idea that it was only a brief solution to a prominent problem left me not only sad, but angry with myself for having started an uncontrollable storm. The imminent battle was probably just the beginning of a war. A war that had international consequences.

The trail we had embarked upon would become littered with dead bodies; not only those of the enemy, but also those of my family and friends. What we were going to do over the next several weeks was going to be as difficult as stuffing six feral cats into a feed sack.

Chapter Four

The First of Several
Battles to the Death

The child who is not embraced by the village will burn it down to feel its warmth.
—African Proverb

Behind my three-story townhome, as was the case for other homes on our street, we kept a stable large enough to accommodate six horses and a carriage. While away, there was seldom more than one horse in it at any one time. We had one servant, Lizzie, who stayed and maintained our home year-round, and she was occasionally assisted by her daughter. I informed her that, if a group of men inquired of our whereabouts, she should tell them we were behind our home in the stables seeing to our horses.

It was evening when we first arrived in London and, by the time we gathered at the stables behind our townhome, it was dark. I did not know if our Jewish followers would attempt to attack us at night or wait until morning but, in either case, we had to be prepared. It could be that they would not even arrive until days later, but I wanted everyone to be together with me and ready for whenever they arrived. Once they came, there would be no time to retrieve help, believing they were focused solely on the task to eliminate Eliab and me without delay.

As a group, we talked about strategy and how we five would defend against the seven. Eliab did not know who the seven were, nor did he know their skill level. He said those tasked for policing in their underground world were trained well, though, they had never, to his knowledge, been in an actual fighting situation that would be to the death. A fight to the death was the only scenario we could imagine that would happen in the next few hours or days. They were brave and skilled, but untested, and some might find real fighting, with real swords, distasteful and be too afraid to engage fully. We could only hope. Neither Eliab, Carl, Connie, nor Gerald had ever been in a fight to the death either, however, they had no choice but fight as aggressively as they could, because death was the only outcome for them if they didn't. I was a warrior having fought in many shield walls and knew the smell and feel of death and mayhem.

We also talked about what would happen after our confrontation with the seven. Surely, there would be more coming after us. What then? Eliab said he thought they would be relentless in searching for us. Seven could be followed by twenty, thirty, or whatever it took to erase any possibility of being found out. They weren't as worried about me, since I did not fully understand the history of the colony and its purpose, but Eliab and Pagiel did. They had to die no matter the cost or the effort. Eliab eventually, although without enthusiasm, volunteered to turn himself over to those seeking our whereabouts, however, it wouldn't end there, because they would also have to find Pagiel, and never could the Jews know for sure what was said to us. No, we were compromised by what we already knew, even though what we knew was only the tip of a long spear. Eliab and Pagiel's death would eventually lead to my family's and my death. I had stirred up a hornets' nest, and there was no putting the hornets back in it. I had bitten off more than I could possibly chew. I needed more help than the four who would stand beside me when the fighting began. I either needed several vast armies or the help from one true God.

At midnight, I urged everyone to go inside and sleep, and I would take the first watch. After three hours, I would wake Carl to relieve me. I thought how great it would be if Pagiel was with us to know when they would come, since I had already come to believe he was truly gifted with special prophetic insight. For three hours, I prayed, schemed, brooded and fought against sleep over what had happened and what could happen. While I did that, I sharpened my swords and practiced parries and thrusts I had used often in battle, even though I was impossibly weary. I did not worry about the impending fight, as I had confidence in our skills. I only worried about what would happen next to my family and their future. What would my father think about what I had become? He wanted me to be a tinsmith like him. Had I followed his advice, I would have died over a hundred years ago, and I would have died poor and illiterate like my father. I was a victim of destiny and had no options other than to be what I am, and to be sitting up in my parlor sharpening swords and waiting until the moment when they could spill blood.

I was awakened the next morning when Connie shook my arm.

"They are here," she said. "They just rode up but have not yet approached the front door. They are out on the street looking the house over."

I slept hard and was still groggy when I put my boots on. The sun indicated it was mid-morning already. I should not have slept so long, but that was Connie's doing, knowing how tired I was. I grabbed my swords and raced downstairs. Justice was about to be dispensed once again by a blind and just judge. The other four members of my justice league were in the back yard. Eliab was rubbing his face as if he had just been awakened. We were sufficiently rested, and I wondered if our antagonists were tired from riding all night. I hoped so. I longed for three or four eggs and some of our cook's biscuits that were the size of cat heads, but that would have to wait until after much blood soaked into our back yard. I hoped it wouldn't be our blood.

We waited at our predetermined places. The servant was instructed to send them back to the stables and, through a rear window, I could see them coming towards the back door. As had been planned, Connie, Carl, and Gerald were hidden behind bales of hay in the stable out of sight. One by one, the dark riders came out of the back door, giving me a chance to take notice of each: their size, tiredness in their faces and whether they looked excited, pleased, or afraid.

Unfortunately, I was not wearing chainmail like I used to wear in battle. I did have on leather jerkins, as did Connie, Carl, and Gerald who had been trained to wear such clothing in the years I spent teaching them how to fight, knowing one day the fight might be a real one. A battle where they would have to defend themselves, or their family, against the forces of evil where death was the only outcome. Such a possibility was always present, especially in the world we then lived in, post pestilence days, where survivors were desperate for food that was scarce. Only Eliab was without any protection other than his sword.

One man, I guessed him to be the leader, was tall and well-built, and I saw no fright in his face, only weariness and resolve. I would go after him first. One by one, they strode up to us and formed a line facing us. Not all of them were smiling, in fact, only the leader was. I know what they saw in my face. They saw determination and confidence and not a little anger.

"So, Eliab," began the tall leader, smiling as if what was about to happen was going to be easy. The idea he would most probably die in just a few moments never entered his mind. He said, "We have found you and your friend. You are a traitor, as well as a fornicator. For those reasons, you have been sentenced to die. You can come back with us for the execution of your sentence for crimes committed, or you can die right here at the point of my sword. As for your friend, he is sentenced to death for being a spy. Regardless, you both will die, as well as the rest of you. As for me, I'd rather you both die right here, right now. It would be such an inconvenience if we must tie you on a horse, feed you on the way, and worry about you trying to escape. So, why don't we just settle the debt to us now?"

After saying those arrogant words, he withdrew his sword, and the others did the same. I drew out Blind Justice in my right hand and, in my left, I held its little brother, my short sword. Smaller, but just as deadly.

I said through clenched teeth, "I'll give each of you this one chance to leave and never come back or die right here, right now. Your choice."

When I spoke those words, Connie, Carl, and Gerald left their hiding spot behind the hay bales and attacked the men from behind. I ran to meet the arrogant leader, and Eliab attacked another. It was a melee, eleven men and one woman, all equally determined people. The leader was momentarily stunned when he heard the shouts of those behind him. That shock for him proved to be fatal. Before he could compose himself, in that moment, he turned his head back toward me, I slashed my long sword down onto the base of his neck followed by a thrust with my short sword into his exposed stomach above his belt. As quickly as I withdrew my blades, I attacked one of the two that were fighting with Eliab. In the briefest of moments, I looked for Connie. I saw her parrying and thrusting and using foot work just like I had taught her, and it made me proud. The man I fought next, was good, but I saw fright in his face, and we both knew he would die soon, and so he did. Two lay dead near my feet. I looked for the next one to fight. Connie's right arm had been cut and was bleeding, but Gerald looked to be in the most trouble, so I killed his attacker next. I told Connie to step away and, with one swift downward stroke of my sword, I cut the right hand off her adversary. I told her to finish him and, in the next few moments, Eliab and Carl had killed their opponents.

We looked around at the seven dead men laying on the ground. Two of them were still breathing but wouldn't be for long. Shortly, their spirits were gathered to their forefathers.

Each of us had a minor cut or bruise, Connie's cut the deepest, but it wasn't a bad one. It would leave a small scar as a reminder of the battle. Her smile showed me she was proud of herself, but she was not nearly as proud as I was of her. I hugged her for a long time and told her how much

I appreciated her help and loyalty to me in my time of need. I thanked all of them for their great job in a cause that was greater than the one the attackers were sworn to. Getting rid of seven dead bodies would not be so easy, though. Killing people in London was not an easy thing to explain away. There were the police in the city, who might want answers about why we had seven dead men in the backyard. We had great excuses but were not yet at liberty to explain to a skeptical kingdom without time-consuming effort. That kind of time, I did not have. The seven bodies were drug into the corral out of sight of the neighbors. We agreed that, when night fell, we would put them in my carriage and take them away. Where, I had not yet devised.

Lizzie, my house servant, saw what had gone on in the backyard and was quite shaken. I told her to trust me that they were bad men who had killed my servants at Goodrich Castle, and were intent on killing us and any, such as herself, that were in their way. She calmed down enough to prepare us lunch with the help of her teenage daughter, Sophie. While we ate, little was spoken about the fight itself. I think we each thought it would be inappropriate somehow to speak ill of the dead. We knew the men were simply following commands of their superior. They may have wives, children, sisters, or brothers where they came from and would be missed. The consequences of what we had done lay heavy on each of our conscious. Taking another person's life is never easy, at least for most people. I wanted to leave to see if Dania and my children were alright, but I decided to wait until the next morning. I couldn't ask anyone to dispose of the dead without me. Eliab reminded us that Jewish law required they be buried and not left to the weather or foraging animals in accordance with their custom. I wasn't so particular as he was about how they were to be disposed of.

When the meal was over, we were still full of the fire in our veins that comes about when a person gets extremely excited. I invited everyone into the parlor and closed the door and warned Lizzie to stay away from the door until we exited. It was time to talk about what we were up to. All five of us were now part of the solution I wanted to discover, whether they wanted to or not. Connie, Carl, and Gerald had wagered their life on what we were up against, and they deserved to know the details as much as me. I began by telling them about my capture, incarceration, and escape. I told them about how I had found a journal a neighbor had written, leading me to believe some terrible and secret program was taking place near my estate, and I felt obligated to investigate. I told them I had discovered an entrance eleven years earlier but did not pursue looking into the conspiracy until the previous week. I told them that there were a hundred, maybe two hundred, thousand or more Ashkenazim Jews living underground in colonies from England to Armenia, and that their goal was to take control of the world from here to Persia. Of those, there could be as many as sixty or seventy thousand who were soldiers, trained and ready to be unleashed on the unsuspecting people living above ground.

I saw incredulity written on their faces. They were shaking their heads, not in disbelief or doubt, but in the audacity of what the Ashkenazim were attempting to do. Their bewilderment was the same as it had been for me.

"Shouldn't we go to the king?" Connie asked. "I mean, it is his responsibility to protect his kingdom, not yours, and he can contact the rulers of the other countries. They have armies at their disposal and could do something, couldn't they?"

Eliab said, "First, you must understand the mindset of my people. This has been in the planning for centuries. We have research and development departments in each underground colony that have been developing weapons which have unbelievable power. In fact, the only reason the seven men we fought this morning didn't bring some of those weapons is because they did not want to risk exposure of their use to the world. Not before it's time. Also, it is a fundamental belief of my people that what they are doing is God's will. We believe God commanded his chosen race to take control of the land he gave them. Also, we have spies everywhere in towns, cities, as palace courtiers in several nations, for instance. To prepare for an attack against my world would be impossible to conceal. Entrances and exits of the colonies are invisible unless you know exactly where they are. Our people would die fighting for what they think is their right to rule the world. I'm here, alive, today only because, had I not left with Troy, I would be dead already. I would have died, not for a cause, however, but because I loved someone. No, an assault across all fronts would be more disastrous than the crusades. Having been harshly ruled by Rome once, has put such a bad taste in the mouths of my ancestors that our race has sworn to never allow ourselves to be ruled by oppressive rulers again like Augustus, Tiberius, Nero, and Herod who slaughtered my people like they were imperfect sheep. Their goal is a global theocracy ruled by priests and rabbis with Adonai as the supreme ruler. A week ago, that was my mantra, too. It was until I was sentenced to death."

"What, then, is the solution?" Connie asked.

My daughter Connie was strong willed, brilliant, very organized, and a born leader, and that is why she was the president of my company. I had given her that position twelve years earlier, and she was doing an outstanding job. She was lovely, and that was a bonus among her other traits. She had married well, at least I thought at first, but discovered her husband had a weak character and was too easily influenced by Connie's strong personality to be a good leader or an independent thinker. They had four children, but all of them died from the pestilence, and the same disease had left its permanent mark on her husband, Alfred, who seemed to be constantly sick following recovery from the black death. He was lucky to have Connie. She was devoted to her husband, but I think, secretly, she was tired of his being weak and indecisive. She was tall like me, and quickly learned anything she set her mind upon, including the ability to speak several languages. Though she was strong-willed, she had a sensitive heart that caused her to love animals, little children, defenseless people, and me. Her dark hair and height made her favor me in some respects, but her loveliness came from her mother, Anna. When I look at her, I can't help but think of my wonderful dead wife who meant so much to me.

I said, "First, let's obtain as much information as we can from Eliab before we even try to suggest solutions."

A disturbing thought came to me during that discussion. What if these underground Jews were indeed doing God's will? What if what I was trying to do to stop the Jews was not what God wanted? If it wasn't, then there would be no way possible to defeat his chosen nation. I believed the Ashkenazim were a brilliant people, able to overtake the world if that is what they really wanted. Israel had, for thousands of years, fought determinedly and effectively against their enemies and, when they fought within the will of God, they never lost. Who was I to think I could thwart the Creator? Those thoughts haunted me that day and many days and nights afterwards. That day, however, more facts were needed from Eliab.

One question I wanted answered first was, "Explain to us the primary purpose of the army in which you are, or were, a general. Is it to participate in the overthrow of world governments or monarchies, or is the army simply a force to keep criminals in line within your communities?"

Eliab explained, "Armies were created within a few years after the first disbursement, which was in Armenia. As colonies grew in the expansion west, armies were put in place at each of them. It has long been the goal of our race to fulfill God's command to go and conquer, so the armies grew and were trained in the eventual hope of following our perceived destiny. As time went by, it became obvious that we needed more of us and better training and weaponry to reach our goal. Time and again, before our people went underground, we were beat down, taken prisoners, and dispersed by such powerful people as the Persians, Babylonians, Syrians, and Romans. It was agreed upon by our ancestors that no longer would we fight unless we were assured of success, assured our lineage would continue and grow stronger and more powerful. This was to preserve our race. To emerge from our underground world prematurely, before we were sure of success, would destroy our hope for victory and ruin all future optimism of winning our cause. It has become increasingly obvious to our leadership that we now have the numbers, the unwavering dedication of determined people, and the advanced weaponry to achieve the thousands of years old hope of doing what Adonai commanded us. To further answer your question, the army does not do day-to-day investigation of crimes or crime prevention. That is done by departments of law enforcement but, in our world, there is very little crime. To break our laws would bring too great a shame on the person and their families."

I asked him, "You have described weapons as secret, powerful, and advanced. What kind of weapons are you talking about?"

I could see hesitation in his face and in his manner. I knew the subject was sensitive and off-limits to outsiders, but he was no longer an insider, he was a new citizen of the aboveground world in which he earned a place with us by partaking in the killing of the kind of people who had enforced secrecy upon him all his life. That was emphasized by the seven bodies that still lie in the backyard. It was time to tell all or lose his rightful place among us, we who had stood beside him in protecting his right to live among us.

"I can't tell you all that has been created because I don't know it all. What I have mentioned before about secret weapons is only for those to know at the highest levels in our leadership. I don't know if the weapon or weapons are in our colony or the Armenian colony or in somewhere in between or in all of them. What is rumored within our army, something the non-soldier is not permitted to know, is that they can destroy hundreds of people at once, or they can destroy stone walls with ease. Swords are still our basic hand-to-hand tools in battle, and what we use to train with the most. However, we also have handheld devices that use gun powder to propel pieces of lead or small round stones great distances, and can pass through shields, as well as bodies wearing chain mail.

These I have seen and handled. They are deadly. The only problem is that the quantity of them may not be sufficient to distribute to all soldiers. When the number is sufficient, and it is one of the deciding measurements of our readiness, then, it will be time for armies to exit our underground habitation and fulfill our destiny. That is, at least, what our priests and rabbis tell us."

Carl asked, "Eliab, do you have a guess as to how long before there will be enough of these special weapons to distribute to the armies, so that this takeover that you have described, begins?"

My son Carl was the oldest boy by my wife Anna, and the only son to survive the black pestilence. He was well-built and tall like his sister and me and resembled his mother more than me. He was intelligent too, but his true gift lay in his ability to relate to people. He was ideal for negotiating business deals with our customers, those who would purchase and distribute goods we imported from the far east, such as, China, India, and Mongolia. He was not ambitious enough to seek power and glory and did not care that his sister was the president of the company. He was simply a very talented people-person and loved dealing with the distributors personally. I envied him that ability, since I was far from being the type of person who could deal with the vagaries of people's personalities. I prefer to give them one chance to say yes or forget them. Take it or leave it. Carl helped make the company very successful. His ability to relate to people did not mean he had a pliable or weak character; in fact, he was the opposite. He was very humble, but brave, and his strength and broad shoulders could easily intimidate any man who made the mistake of thinking him weak or trying to demean or threaten his family or his company. Carl's wife and two of his children died from the pestilence and, prior to that, two had died in childbirth. Only Gerald remained alive. I was proud to call Carl my son.

"I don't have enough information to answer your question, Carl, with certainty. The commanding general in my colony believes that we have everything needed to initiate the plans. I don't know if that is something he is guessing, or if he knows for sure. The significant point is that, after hundreds of years, we are finally at the point where the greatest battle of God's people in history begins, and there is no army in the world that can stop what will happen."

Connie said, "Tell us about the extent of your cavern. How can it be so big that there can be as many people as you say there is in your colony?"

He smiled, took a long breath, and said, "Originally, our people searched until they found the caverns that already existed that would suit their initial purposes. These discoveries begin as natural wonders that are miles long and hundreds of feet deep, in places where there are underground rivers already existing. That gives us the starting point for centuries of expansion. There is no need to dispose of the spoil above ground. The excess stone removed from one area is used to build up other areas needing leveling, or walls built. Large caverns within the system permit multiple floor levels for living areas and functioning departments, as well as deep pits, that provide us with large gathering rooms. Excavations have been going on for about four hundred years in my colony alone. They never cease. There is always a need for more rooms as populations grow and for storage of food, medicine, powder, and weapons, as well as classrooms, dormitories, hospitals, recreation rooms, kitchens, stables, and such, as are required to make our world not only livable, but comfortable and enjoyable."

"Didn't you tell me that there is a tunnel being built towards Europe?" I asked him.

"That is true. The tunnel is to make it easy to send armies back and forth and improve time of information exchange with the Rouen colony. Crossing the channel between countries can be dangerous during certain times and, when the time comes for the gathering of armies, rapidity of travel will be important to our leaders. The tunnel is no longer being built from both directions but is now complete, I'm told. It had been under construction for many years. At least fifty years. Our elders tried to learn from what happened to the Romans. They came to England a thousand years ago in the expansion of their empire, and it turned out to be too remote for adequate support for the armies, because of the distance from their supply source, Rome. This tunnel will help in eliminating the problem the Romans faced.

"But wouldn't that take a thousand or more years for men using hammers and chisels against rock to accomplish that?" Gerald asked.

Gerald is my only remaining grandchild, born from the eighteen children my wives and I produced. Eighteen that I had a hand in raising anyway. I did not know him well since I spent much of my time at my beloved Goodrich Castle or working in the office when I was in London. He was a good-looking young man and quiet. I think he will be more like his Aunt Connie than his dad. He was broad shouldered and had shoulder-length blond hair that reminded me of his grandmother Anna. I knew him to be uninterested in books and more interested in adventure and exploring. He was not one to boast or stand out in a crowd, desiring to watch and listen, rather than make a spectacle of himself. He was adventurous and I suppose he was like me in that respect. He had a quiet demeanor, but that hid a determination and inner strength that could serve him well if we could somehow overcome our problems with the Ashkenazim.

"Yes, Gerald, it would take a long time if we used hammers and chisels. If it was human strength alone by which we were doing it. Do not think of me as arrogant when I say to you, our people are far more advanced than you above-grounders here in England or those in Europe. I saw the evidence of that for myself riding from our colony to this dirty city. We have machines that do the digging for us that are operated by steam and some by other means. Our scientists have learned to heat water in steel drums to create steam that is used in driving drills and large hammers. Steam is also used for other machines, as well, even some weapons. The two tunnels from the two colonies have met somewhere below the middle of the channel. Communication between colonies will now be much more rapid, as will the advance of our armies and efficient transport of supplies."

I asked, "How is your leadership organized? Is it like in the days before the temple was destroyed? Do you have Pharisees, Sadducees, and priests still?"

"As then, we are governed by the Sanhedrin, made up of the High Priest and six Chief Priests. The Halakha, or our law, is established and overseen by this governing body. It dictates how we live and our policies, it governs the armies, and it is even responsible for choosing a new chief and a high priest when one is needed. The Sanhedrin decides when the time is right for the war to commence. It decides if new colonies are needed and, as the highest court, it settles disputes that come up from time to time. There has been the occasional priest who has rebelled against the Sanhedrin's constraints, or it had to put down a minor rebellious uprising led by an errant elder. We still have Pharisees, and each rabbi in the colonies is a member of that order, and the Pharisees are under the constraining hand of the Sanhedrin. There are no longer Sadducees or Essenes as there were before the temple in Jerusalem was destroyed. There is one High Priest who leads the Sanhedrin. He is like a king or emperor in your world. It is he who controls the actions of all the Ashkenazim. He is the one you must overcome to be successful in stopping the plans to take control of your world. Maybe as many as two hundred thousand, or more, men, women, and children. That includes hundreds, maybe thousands, of spies, aboveground contacts, agents, and suppliers in a network from London to Jerusalem. To my knowledge, there are about seven hundred and fifty thousand Sephardic Jews who exist in the aboveground world, and even they have no idea we exist below the ground they walk upon."

"Who is the Sephardic and why are there the two sects of Jews?"

"The Sephardic Jews are essentially the Jews who are not with us. Most of them today live in or have journeyed away from the Castilian Peninsula, but both Ashkenazi and Sephardic originally were products of the Jewish diaspora after the Bar Kokhba war. The Sephardic chose to stay and live among the nations of the world. The Sephardic are not governed by our Sanhedrin. They are not governed by any central organization. They just exist in small groups worshipping at one of thousands of synagogues around the world. What makes us stronger is the Ashkenazim are organized, centrally governed, and are driven by an ancient command to go and take control. You could consider us more Orthodox, since we have many roots going back to the days of Abraham, our forefather."

"Eliab," I said, "my discovery of your existence began with a journal I found written by a man named Francois Laurent. His journal was not very descriptive of what was going on but did lead me to get a glimpse of what you have been telling us. He lives with his family not far from my castle home. He evidently lives part of the time aboveground, and I firmly believe his family has no idea of what he does when he leaves his home, sometimes for many weeks. I think he is part of the planning group. Do you know who he is and, if so, could he be a valuable person to talk to?"

"I know of him, though we have never personally met. He is a member of a think-group which gathers information from a network of spies, evaluates the knowledge they gather, and makes recommendations on how to use the information relative to our overall purpose. I believe there are about a dozen men who make up the analysis group in our colony. His group gives the rabbis and topmost generals information to keep us apprised of current and local intelligence. I have participated in several of the meetings he was part of. He is very organized and intelligent. His real name isn't Francois Laurent, as you may have surmised; it's Eliasaph. He was a spy in France in the Gascony region until he moved to England and became part of the analysis group here some years back. I know this because I was one of the men who imprisoned the person he replaced. That person was stoned to death. Wrongdoing can be a harsh penalty in our world. I have never wanted a family, because I have become somewhat unhappy with the local leadership and didn't want to bring up a family in such a climate. To answer your question, do I think he would be helpful in your, also, mine now, cause? Yes, of course, but getting information from him would be very difficult. He would die before giving you details. We both know, however, there are different ways of dying."

Connie said, "I'm curious as to how you can sustain your enormous population, who live almost entirely underground, and still be unnoticed? How do you grow food? Do you keep horses for transportation purposes, or animals for food, and do you do crop sowing and harvesting? Is it possible to grow food underground in the quantities needed by so many people and without sunlight?"

"Ah, that is our best kept secret! To plant, grow, and harvest food aboveground would be the simplest, but could not be done long term without being discovered. In the beginning, our history teachers tell us, we did purchase food from farmers with the precious stones we discovered in our mines. As our population grew, we had to abandon that way, because it became too dangerous for our existence. We, from the beginning, have had research scientists and people of extraordinary talents who experiment, and they have devised many imaginative means of growing food, in addition to developing hand tools, more efficient work methods, fertilizer, and methodology, such as, steam machines and, of course, very deadly weaponry. Plant-based food can be grown without soil, using water only. The water is not drinking quality water but has ingredients developed and added to the water by our scientists from such things as fungi and animal and human waste. This had been made possible by underground rivers that flow from the outside into our world and carry with it tiny water-laden organisms that we have multiplied and used as a growth enhancer. We can grow anything you can grow, and grow it year-round, regardless of the weather and conditions. Farming isn't my area of expertise, but we are all taught what other departments do. As far as meat goes, we can grow lots of fish and water-based creatures like frogs, shrimp, crabs, and the like, even oysters. All food we grow is of course Kosher. In your aboveground world, I know from my schooling that you eat venison, beef, and mutton. You also eat pork, which is not permitted for us, since it is considered dirty or non-kosher."

"So, you have never eaten beef or venison or the meat of any animal? Never eaten cheese or chicken eggs?"

"Oh, yes," he smiled and said, "we raise lots of chickens in various parts of the many spaces that are either natural areas or where we have hewn them out of the underground rocks. There are always lights in their spaces which promote laying. The older chickens, who are at the end of their two-year highest-level laying cycle, are eaten. Their waste is used in modifying the water that improves growing of vegetables and other smaller plants, like grapes for making wine. In the larger, natural cavernous rooms where the plants are grown, we have hives for bees that visit the flowers and where we get our excellent honey. Our scientists have developed miniature fruit trees, as well as figs. Apple trees are grown for the purpose of making juice to supplement drinking water or wine. But no, we have little space for growing large animals for meat. There are a few, such as me, who have tasted the meat of animals like cows, when it was brought in by spies or those whose job is outside reconnaissance or security, such as the two who found you outside our cavern. Some experimentation is ongoing, however, in growing smaller versions of larger animals, such as sheep, feeding them plant waste, but such areas are limited so far."

He continued, "I know precious little about this new world I've become an inhabitant of. Only what I've seen in the past few days and what we are taught in school. We are taught about the governments that relate to our colonies, the people's customs, and their languages, so that we will be familiar with them when we do leave the world, we have lived in for centuries to take what is believed to be rightfully ours. In our colony, we are taught English, because we exist under England's territory. In the Milan colony, they are taught the Italian language for the same reason. We hear about all of what you do; it's just that we haven't experienced them. I've never felt cold, never seen rain, until recently, or snow, never seen leaves turn gold-like, which our teachers tell us that you have seen all your lives. I had never seen a sunrise or sunset until a few days ago. I think I could never go back to my world and be truly happy."

"We know a day ends when the lights are dimmed in some areas, or they are turned off completely in others by a mandatory reduction of light levels for promoting rest during the dark periods and to mimic the world above us as much as possible. We have grown up knowing only what we experience and know no hardship in what the world below deprives us of. In fact, we are taught that we live in a better world, because it is governed by godly and moral people who know what is best for us. Whereas kings and sheriffs, we are taught, are often corrupted by greed and power and without a moral base to live by. We learn that, in your world, there are storms that destroy, plagues and disease that kill, snow and ice that freeze people to death. None of that happens in our safe, insulated world."

Carl said, "You are correct that we do have those negatives you mentioned but, as far as people are concerned, surely there are some you know who are corrupt? People are prone to depravity in all races and nations of the world. I mean, you, yourself, did a crime deemed worthy of death. Aren't your people prone to lying, stealing, and other terrible crimes that the Ten Commandments tells us, especially you Jews, that we are not to do?"

"Yes, we are not immune to sin. It is why we have prisons and law overseers. It is just that we are told it is much worse in the world above. Maybe we were misinformed. I suppose it could be that we are told of the great evil above to make us more satisfied with our situation. Occasionally, a dissatisfied man wanting to gain some power, or recognition, will stir up an uprising about our perceived plight, but they are put down immediately, because we have one set of unilateral laws from Adonai, and our leaders do not have conflicting opponents. It is not allowed."

"Is there much of a problem with people escaping?" Connie asked Eliab.

"Every day, there is a head count of every single person by floors and departments. Everyone must be accounted for. There are levels of overseers who make sure that no one in their area of responsibility is missed, and they report to others higher up the ladder. The confirmation that all is well, and everyone is accounted for, is passed on to the army and the rabbinical leadership for their approval. If anyone is not accounted for, they are hunted down and found. Most of the time, they are in a different part of the underground complex. Maybe a young person got lost, which is very easy to do, or an elderly person fell or got sick or even died in a solitary place. I know of no one who has ever escaped and was not found and either brought back or killed. So far, Pagiel, Troy, and I have been the only ones who have not been found that I'm aware of, but it is still very early in the hunt. Every effort will be expended to find us. I believe it will take a miracle to remain undetected for any length of time. If necessary, hundreds will be sent out to find us. There is no exception to the rule that all people must be accounted for. Our secret must be maintained. The longer we are outside, the more likely what we know will be told to others, and those others must be silenced, as well as the three of us. I'm sorry it is that way. We should never have left the cavern. I was being selfish when I agreed to help Troy escape. He and his family, all of you, will most likely pay for that sin. I guess I just wanted a small taste of freedom outdoors, despite the penalty it will bring. They can only kill me once, though."

Connie asked, "What do you do with people who die? I was under the impression that Jewish bodies are not to be destroyed by fire. Aren't your dead supposed to be buried, since the human body is a sacred vessel of the Lord?"

"You are correct. Our rabbis teach us that only pagans burn the bodies of the dead. Our Talmud dictates we must honor the body because, before death, it housed the spirit that communicates with Adonai. Therefore, we must bury, or store, the body with ceremony. When a loved one dies, their bodies are placed in a tomb carved into a rock wall within a burial chamber. After one year and a day, the bodies are removed from that tomb where it will be free to house another person's body who recently died. The decayed bodies' bones are placed in stone ossuaries belonging to family members. The bones are stacked in the ossuaries, which are in a space-saving arrangement, housing several people's bones of the same family. The stone boxes are then stacked inside vertical chambers for storage. There are multiple chambers throughout our cavern system. We live a long time in our world, though. It is not uncommon for us to live to be one hundred years old or even older."

A somewhat disturbing idea crossed my mind during our conversations. Could it be that their sovereign theocratic government might be better than what existed in my aboveground world today? Our above ground world was full of crime, hate, crippling diseases, high mortality birth rates, widespread poverty, crop failures, extremely low literacy, dangers of all kinds, punishing taxes, and deadly natural disasters. Maybe it would be a mistake to stop the Ashkenazi. Somehow, my sense of what I thought was right was being violated though, and I didn't want the decision made for me. I needed more information about them than I knew at that time to make a knowledgeable comparison or assessment.

"Okay," I said, after a pause while we all reflected on Eliab's words. "I would like to hear more about Eliab's world, but it will be dark before long, and we must dispose of the bodies. I must leave in the morning to check on Dania and my children and bring them back here. We can learn more about the cavern or colony later but now, let's spend some time discussing what we can do next and what are our options for stopping an impending world war, if anything. I'd like to hear from each of you. Connie let's start with you. Have you any thoughts on what we should do next?"

She drained the last of her water and set her glass down while she let the last few hours race through her mind. "Several things disturb me. This idea of world domination by your people, Eliab, has, of course, far-reaching impacts, including those of us here in London. I'm most disturbed that my family and me will be hunted down and probably killed in the next few hours, days, or weeks. That means, to me, that I must hire guards to protect us, maybe permanently. It seems that our lives, however long they may last, will be changed. The thought makes me angry, but I can deal with it, because something will have to be done to erase the danger. I know my father can think of something. He always has. As for me, I don't know what can be done to end this danger. The only thing I can think of doing right now that might help is to speak with Francois to get more information from him and, if necessary, forcefully convince him and his leaders to leave us alone, even though I doubt it would do any good. I don't know what else can be done."

"Carl," I asked, "any thoughts?"

"The only choice I see is to run. We can be on a ship tomorrow or at least in the next few days, but it will mean leaving our friends, our work, our world, and our hopes behind."

"Gerald?"

"I can't think of a solution. I will do or go anywhere you think best. I don't have so many roots here that I can't leave. I promise to help in any way I can."

"Eliab, you are in the best position to know how to stop the wave of people who are, even at this moment, looking for us, but that is only our first problem. The bigger issue is how to stop your people, the people you once were a part of, from killing and taking control of cities and nations across the world. Those are people who only want to be left alone and live their own lives without being told how they must live."

Eliab said, "Troy, Carl, Connie, Gerald, I'm sorry about what has happened. If I knew my return to my people would prevent harm to all of you, I would gladly endure the stones. The facts are facts, though. There is no telling them we are sorry; it's too late. Even if it takes every soldier from our world to search, they will find us and kill us. I know they will do whatever is necessary, kill as many as it takes, to prevent knowledge of their plans from spreading throughout the aboveground nations. Reasoning and begging won't stop them from destroying us and all our families and closest friends. To do what must be done means we must buy some time. Your, our, escape may very well hasten the day when our people will rise and begin the war against your world. All directives for all the Ashkenazim, who live in colonies from here to Israel, comes down from the High Priest in Armenia. Each colony has a counsel of rabbis who are subject to the High Priest, who is, in turn subject to most of the Sanhedrin. I think, if there is one man who can call off the wolves chasing us, it would be the High Priest. He can be overruled by the Sanhedrin, but he is a strong personality and not without much influence. It will take some time to get to him, and it will take some time for the wolves to stop following us, even if we can get the priest to call them off. As far as the idea of destruction of all my people, the Britannia colony, specifically, I cannot allow that to happen. I have no problem in killing those individuals who are attempting to kill me or you. However, if you decide to blow up or somehow destroy my world, I can't join you in that."

To them all, especially to Eliab, I said, "Let me make

myself clear. I will kill every one of the people in your colony and in every colony that exists, or die trying, if it means saving my family. With that said, it is not my wish to kill anyone, except those who are trying to kill me or Dania or any of my children, whether it be Connie, Carl, Kat, Jay, Troy, or Gerald. My suggestion, at this point, based on my limited understanding of our situation, is for us to remove ourselves from England at the earliest opportunity. All of us should set sail as soon as possible. My first thoughts are for Dania and the children and any of you that wish to, to go to Gascony where my company has an office. It is the founding office of the East Asia Trading Company. From there, I want to travel to Armenia where I will somehow find and talk to the High Priest and convince him to leave my family, and you, Eliab, and, hopefully, Pagiel, also, alone. If the High Priest does not help us, he will regret not doing so. I don't know if I will be able to convince him that taking over the world can't happen, regardless of their centuries-old mission to do just that. Details for all of this will have to be worked out along the way but, first, we must leave the country. If Eliab is correct, those seven in the backyard will be replaced by succeeding groups of men until we are all dead. Connie, hiring guards will not only be very costly, but will only work for a short time until more men are sent than you can effectively defend against. Again, I'm sorry for putting all of you into the position we find ourselves."

"Any further comments or questions for now?" I asked.

"What is the next thing you want to do?" Carl asked.

"We will dispose of the bodies tonight and, at first light in the morning, I'm going to retrieve Dania and the children. I will bring them back here, so we can depart for the continent as soon as possible. Let's plan on leaving here, assuming there is a ship available, within a week at the latest. Connie, if you or Carl can, tomorrow, find us a ship and book passage for the eleven of us. It will take a few days for me to reach the cave where Dania, Pagiel, and the kids are in and a few days to return, so see if you can find a ship that will leave in a week. Remember, others from the underground cavern could arrive in the city in a matter of days, so be very careful and limit as much presence as possible in the office. I will do my best to return before they arrive. Appoint whomever you wish to take control of the company. Just know that they might have to be in charge for as long as a year. Now, Carl, Gerald, and Eliab, help me start loading the bodies in my carriage. We will take them out of the city and dispose of them a little before midnight.

I have been in many fights, some against single opponents and, many times, with multiple ones in battles and shield walls with snarling men trying to stick a sword or spear into my belly or face. I was never afraid. I was too excited and too sure of myself to be afraid. That night when our meeting broke up and the uncertain future stared its ugly face at me, I was very afraid. Never had I been so frightened before in my life. I was pessimistic about our ability to stop the inevitable. My small family was all that I had left after my 175 years of living. Eight family members and two new acquaintances. They, along with me, could be dead within a week and, when judgment day came, and I stood before our Creator, I would have to explain my actions for what I had done. My only excuse was that I thought I was doing the right thing. I was the sole decider of what I thought was the right thing. "Depart from me," God will say to me "I never knew you." At my lowest point, behind the stables, I vomited. That was enough to get my attention. The ten people going east with me were my responsibility, and it was time to act like a man born to lead. There was no time to feel sick and sorry for myself. I would let my depression and sadness become anger and determination. I did better with anger. That's how I got things done when I was at my angriest.

Chapter Five

Plans to Leave England

Why should you waste your energy feeling angry towards the world,
as if the world would even pay attention.
—Marcus Aurelius

It took two trips to carry all the dead men out of the city to a marshland that lay along the Thames River. On some of the rare days I took leave of working in my London office, I, and, sometimes with my boys, would go to the marsh and hunt ducks, geese, and marsh hens with bows and arrows I had made for each of us. I knew where the deepest holes were, and it was there we placed the dead bodies. Their own swords were used to pen them to the bottom of the hole. It was distasteful for all of us, especially for Eliab, who wasn't sure it was proper. He didn't know any of them by name, but two of them, their leader being one; their faces, he recognized. He knew they were just doing their job, and I hoped his will to keep his freedom and help us in our cause was not weakening.

To my utter astonishment, and delight, after our return

for the second load of bodies, Dania, our three children, and Pagiel, were sitting in our parlor. Lizzie was serving them food and drink. When we saw there were lights on, Carl, Gerald, Eliab, and I went inside to see why. Dania was always unpredictable, and it wasn't the first time her presence surprised me. She was an independent thinker, a trait that often alternately angered and pleased me.

After we all laughed uneasily about the little reunion, I asked, "What in the world possessed you to endanger you and the children, and Pagiel, to travel here. Didn't I tell you to remain hidden until I came back for you? Didn't I..."

She did not let me finish my fussing. "Troy, listen to me. We took the chance because we would run out of food by the time you got back to us but, mostly, because Pagiel insisted that we needed to find you. He swears that more men have left their cavern and are looking to join up with the six that are searching the nearby farms for you; then, they will all most assuredly come here to London. He says we need to leave London as soon as possible. Pagiel believes that there will be at least twenty of them combined, who will arrive here soon, including those who killed our servants and were following us when we left our home. At least until they meet up with them, those who just left the cavern do not know where we are, but the seven who were close behind us probably do, since our servants must have told them or maybe our neighbors. What are we going to do, Troy?"

Little Troy was asleep with a piece of ham in his fist, and Kat and Jay were nodding their heads, trying to stay awake, but sleep was winning the battle. Everyone looked at me for an answer, and the only one that seemed feasible was for us to leave the city as soon as transportation could be arranged.

Either to another city or, as I had originally believed, to another country.

"Okay, everyone," I said, "Gerald, if you would help me with the three men out back, we will take them to the marsh. The rest of you get some sleep. First thing in the morning, we will try to find a ship, any ship, leaving for Europe or even Africa. Connie has left to retrieve her husband, and they will pack a few things to bring and join us in the morning. The rest of you, be ready to go tomorrow or at any moment. We can purchase what items we need once we arrive at a safe place. We don't have long. It is late summer, so travel conditions are good, and there should be several ships coming and going this time of year. At least one of them should be available for us to take. So, go and get some sleep, if you can."

Gerald and I disposed of the last three bodies and then we returned to the house hours after midnight, tired and ready for some sleep. Sleep, however, would evade me, because of the tension and anxiety I felt for what we must do in the hours that lay ahead and the decisions that fell upon my tired shoulders. I hoped it would not be required for us to have to battle the twenty men coming to silence us. I doubted the five of us could overcome the twenty. From the time I settled in next to my soft and lovely wife until daylight, I spent much of it praying like I hadn't in a long time. I beseeched the Lord for his guidance and for wisdom. I did not sleep at all and, in the darkest part of the night, the hour before dawn, ghosts from my past paid me a visit, as they often did. I, like Paul on the way to Damascus, had seen the Lord Jesus with my own eyes when he exorcised the group of demons that had long held my body as their domain. I was no longer a piece in a celestial game between God and Satan. The outcome was never in doubt, because God never loses but, still, I was tossed around by each to test my mettle. Finally, I was judged acceptable in God's eyes, and he chose to free me of my demons. I hoped that meant I was in his favor, and he would grant me protection, along with my family and friends, so I prayed and asked God for help.

In the morning, Lizzie labored over the stove, with her daughter's assistance, making breakfast for us all. She was confused about everything and wondered why we had all gathered at once and all of us seemed tense and worried. Of course, the seven dead men that had been in the backyard just added to her dismay. The food was good, and it woke us up and helped me think a little more clearly. While we waited for Connie and Alfred to arrive, Carl, Eliab, Gerald, and I went down to the shipping wharves to begin investigating ships that could take us away from our danger. Dania hinted that I should take her and the children to Egypt and let her stay with her parents. She argued that the assassins following us would never find them there. It was a good idea, and maybe it would come to that, but I had no idea if her parents were still alive and hesitated in taking the chance. I wished I had done what she asked. I admit that the desire to have my demons came to me again. The desire to have their supernatural protection would seep into my thinking until it occurred to me what was happening. Then, I would shove the dangerous thoughts aside in favor of praying to God for help. I hoped God understood the weakness of my faith and would fill me with peace and wisdom.

Eliab was ever on my mind, also. I searched his face and speech for assurance from him concerning his dedication to our escape and defense against those from his world who were just as dedicated to killing us. Was he carrying doubt around with him, even as he helped us organize and prepare to leave our home? Would he betray us in the false hope of saving his life in exchange for a safe return to the only world he knew? I still did not trust him fully. In fact, I trusted Pagiel more than Eliab on that day we walked the wooden wharves in search of an escape ship. He would bear watching and I would warn my family to do the same. His comment to us that he would not allow the destruction of his people concerned me since I, too, would not allow the destruction or servitude of my people, meaning my family and my country. Maybe, at some point, there would have to be a confrontation. Until then, I would look for signs of him trying to undermine our efforts to stop the madness of domination, if ever domination was possible.

The sun had risen from the direction we wanted to go, but the clouds hung low, and the suggestion of the sun was visible only for a little while before a soft pewter-gray blanket was pulled over it, barring the light and its heat from us. The bottom of the clouds turned red, indicating that the weather would most probably turn stormy in the next few hours. The seagulls circling and squawking overhead were oblivious to the impending weather and the distraught men below them who were seeking escape. Northern Gannets sailed towards us on six-foot-wide wings, heading to calmer water. Their discordant hoarse calls could be heard over the gasping wind. The familiar smell of rotten fish and barnacles was strong, but the smell reminded me of the many times I went to sea and reveled in the independence I felt with the wind blowing in my face, and the feel of salt spray against my skin. I have many cabinets in my memories that are filled with the smell and feel of the seas.

It was still early, and the quay had only a few people scurrying about getting their fishing boats ready for the day's work. Some street vendors were setting up their carts to sell bread, dried fish, breakfast fare, cheese, ale, seasonal fruit, some vegetables, and various articles of coarse clothing that were suitable for sailors to wear. Already, sailors too old to go to sea anymore sat on wooden benches or barrels too old, like the men, to be of use anymore. Benches and barrels were as rugged as the faces of the men who sat on them. The old men all had long white beards, and they talked of the old days and their adventures, the storms they survived, the amount of rum they drank, the captains they hated, the women they had bedded, and the booty they had taken. All of them wishing they were fifteen again and were walking up that gang plank once more like they did so long ago when their muscles were strong and vibrant. Pigeons, their heads bobbing back and forth, hung about their feet in hopes of bits of food tossed in their direction. The grass across the boardwalk was alive with buzzing grasshoppers leaping from weed to weed like frogs jumping across lily pads. Fishing boats were lined up between the larger ships, and some fishermen were preparing their boats for another attempt to catch a few fish for their families to eat, maybe an extra one or two to sell before the weather turned nasty. Between some of the boats were the collected flotsam brought in by wind-driven wavelets: melon rinds, pieces of wood, and some stuff only God knew what it was. The previous day's rain left puddles and, in one of them, a skinny momma cat and her three kittens lapped at it to quiet their starving stomachs. They were skinny because the rats were too big for them to catch. All along the quay were posts rising above the wood walkway. On most of them, sat a gull and the top foot or so of all the posts were painted white from years of birds depositing their guano.

I studied the ships at anchor to evaluate, first, their sea worthiness and how the captain maintained his boat, but, also, to assess their readiness to begin their journey to other parts of the world. This was not an easy task for those unfamiliar with sea life, but, for me, it was like reading a good book. There were very few ships of such a size that could safely negotiate the channel between England and the continent or beyond to places like Africa or the far east. Eliab and Pagiel had never seen a ship until that day, Gerald knew a little about them, but Carl and I understood the ships, their cargo, and the hardened men who sailed the world's seas to exotic places.

One of the ships was carrying cargo of wool, cloth, salt, timber, and pottery. We saw seamen pushing carts of the products up the gang planks, or bundles were lifted by pulleys from yard arms overhanging the adjacent docks. I asked one of the sailors where they were headed, and he said Genoa in the kingdom of Italy. They planned to leave the next evening.

"Are you visiting ports along the way?" I asked.

The man could have passed for a thousand other sailors I had seen in my life. He had faded and worn clothing that smelled of sweat, salt, and dead things. His face's skin was like the skin of a warthog I once saw in Africa. Sea life is hard, but there was no other life in the world for them. They craved the freedom of the sea and the uniformity of life and the occasional dangers they faced. All they needed to be satisfied was enough money to buy rum and an hour with ladies of pleasure in the occasional port of call. The ports of call that ship would visit were unknown to him, and we needed to ask the captain or first mate.

I wanted to be able to leave that day, but the next day could work. Maybe it would if destiny was on our side. Carl, knowing many of the sea-going captains because they are the ones delivering cargo from the eastern ports like Constantinople and Venice, and so it was on that ship, the *Sea Lady*. We found the captain talking to the first mate by the capstan, the winch support used to lift the anchor from the sea floor, giving him instructions on how to more effectively work the seamen to get them to work faster. The mate nodded his head as if to agree with his superior, but, if I wasn't mistaken, they had that conversation many times before with little result. Only ships of war had the needed discipline for the men to do what they were commanded to do, unless the captain was of the cruel sort, and, of course, many were. Captains are absolute sovereign on their ships. They have the right to bestow praise, rum, and lucre upon his men as he chooses, and the right to pass judgment on them leading to a beating or hanging.

Carl called the captain by name, and he was in turn recognized by the captain. Captain Bartholemew McDougal, who went by the moniker Cap Dougal. Carl inquired into the ship's destinations, and if there was a possibility of accommodating eleven paying passengers. As was the custom of many merchant captains who did not own their ship, but only piloted it for the benefit of the owner or owners. Any paying passengers, well, those coins could be pocketed, and it would never be reported to the owners. Cargo had manifests; people did not.

Carl found out the ship was going to Honfluer, Bayonne, and then, to Gascony where it would pick up a cargo of wine. From there, they will sail to Marseilles, Genoa, and then, towards Rome, docking at Centumcellae.

I was tempted to disembark at Honfluer, since it was not far from there to Rouen. I believed that those following us, if they ever concluded we had sailed from England, would never suspect we would go anywhere near Rouen, a place Eliab said was home to one of the colonies. In a way, Rouen was a twin of the Britania colony, since they were to be connected, to my astonishment, with each other by a very long tunnel. I had a few days to decide on which port of call to disembark; the immediate concern was to leave. Leave my home country and begin the most difficult of all my quests. Another trail to follow; another trial to endure. I was glad to have a group of people this time to act as advisors. Someone to alert me if my ideas were too bold or too foolish.

With an assurance from the captain that we would be allowed passage on his ship, we gathered back at my townhome to reconvene and talk more about what the next steps were to be. Connie had arrived by the time we got back to my home with a few belongings and her husband with her. I was shocked to see his frail body. I had not seen him in more than a year, and various sicknesses had taken their toll on his body, weakened by the pestilence. I did not dislike Alfred, nor did he dislike me, but there was never any closeness between us. We had nothing in common, except Connie and their children, and the children were all now dead. Connie loved him and that was enough for me, but I feared that the travel ahead of us would not mix well with his health.

"It is very important, Connie," I began our meeting with this warning, "that Lizzie, Sophie, your assistant, and all the other workers in the office, that no one knows where we are going. They must not know we will be boarding a ship. They must believe we intend to remain in England. Just to be sure, think, has anyone mentioned in the presence of others outside this room where we are going?"

Everyone shook their heads. No one admitted to saying anything to anyone, but I could not bet my life, our lives, that Lizzie may not have overheard something. "Dania," I said, "please tell Lizzie that we are going to leave for one of our castles in Colchester and will not be back for at least a month. Maybe much longer. Connie, if you would tell your assistant the same thing before we must leave."

"I didn't know we had a castle in Colchester," Dania said.

"We don't, but our pursuers don't know that. Yet."

Outside, the expected tempest arrived, and large drops of rain pelted our windows on the west side of the house, and the wind blew debris against the glass, making pinging sounds like pebbles dropping on stone. I hoped the storm would not delay tomorrow's departure. If the storm abated just a little, I would visit the captain that evening to determine the sailing status.

"Carl and Connie, we must bring enough silver and gold with us to survive on our journey for at least six months. Can you get that much coinage without causing anyone's suspicion? I'll have to do the same. I have some hidden is a safe place, but to support my family, Pagiel, and Eliab, it will mean we must live frugally. Above all, we can't bring too much baggage with us without arousing questions from neighbors, friends, and coworkers."

A noon meal was served to all of us. Little was said about the impending trip so as not to alert Lizzie and Sophie. After lunch, we returned to the parlor for more discussions. I had Kat and Jay play outside in the stables, because they both loved horses, so that they would not know we were talking about leaving nor where we were thinking about going. Dania watched over Troy as he toddled about and played on the floor with some toys.

Connie asked, "At what port do you think we should disembark?"

"That's up for discussion among us," I said. "I am thinking we should initially leave the ship in Honfluer or Bayonne. Bayonne might be best, since it is only a two-day ride south to Boïos to where the home office of the East Asia Trading Company is, in the event we need resources. However, I don't believe we should stay there in case our pursuers somehow connect us with that office. The options between here and Rome are Honfluer, Bayonne, Marseilles, and Genoa before arriving in Centumcellae near Rome. Keep in mind that, from any of those ports, we can investigate a departure by way of another ship to anyplace in the east. We can go as far as India, if you think it better, but I would want to know why you think it would be better."

Eliab said, "I do not know where any of those places are, except Rouen, where you say it is near Honfluer, so I leave the destination choice up to you above-grounders who have more knowledge than I about the land east of here."

Pagiel nodded his head in agreement with what Eliab said. I studied Eliab throughout the meeting, trying to get a reading on him. I made a mental note to pull Pagiel aside and ask him if he had any concerns about Eliab and his decision to be part of our cause completely. To see if he had some kind of fresh supernatural reading about Eliab.

I asked the group, "Do any of the rest of you have thoughts on where we should go? It doesn't have to be any of the ports I just mentioned."

Dania again brought up Cairo as a possible location to stay for a while. I felt uneasy because I did not want to go to northern Africa, to my shame. I held too many unhappy memories of that part of the world, but I left it open as an option. Connie favored Rome, since it was also a major office location for our office, and it would be closer to Armenia in our pursuit of a meeting with the High Priest. Carl thought Rome was a better option, also. I asked Alfred his opinion, but he had none and was not happy at all about leaving his comfortable home. In the end, I called for a vote to see how the wind was blowing, and Rome was chosen as the best place for us to spend as much as six months away from our home. Truth be told, it might be that we could never go home again, so Rome it was, to Dania's disappointment.

We spent the rest of the afternoon until shortly before sunset talking about details and how we should proceed beyond Rome. I asked Carl to visit the captain about the schedule of departure. Also, traveling to Rome meant paying him at least twice what sailing to Bayonne would cost us. At least, in Rome, I could draw on resources from the bank there, as I had done on previous occasions. It also meant many days aboard a small deck and enduring potential storms and sea sicknesses. Outside, a storm was still sending down rain, but the wind had dissipated considerably.

"Sir Troy," Pagiel said. We all turned and looked at him because he rarely said anything. Also, it was the first time he acknowledged me as a knight. "They will be here tomorrow night."

Chapter Six

Departure

There shall not be found among you anyone who makes his son or his daughter pass through the fire, one who uses divination, one who practices witchcraft, or one who interprets omens, or a sorcerer.
—*Deuteronomy 18:10*

The darkness of the day had descended on us early because of the tempest, and Dania was lighting more candles when Carl came in from visiting with the captain.

"Cap Dougal will take us to Centumcellae. It's no problem but, of course, he does want more silver. The bad news is the storm damaged some rigging and some of the sails before they were furled down. He won't attend to the damage until morning's light. It could take all day, and he might miss the strong westerly wind that has blown since the storm. Most likely, he will depend on the river current to deliver the ship to the North Sea. He is thinking we can leave the morning after."

"That can't happen. While you were out, Pagiel told us that our pursuers will arrive tomorrow night. It's possible that we could bring all our gear to the ship and stow it and be prepared to stay there until the ship sails. It is also possible that those looking for us would not discover our whereabouts that night or the next day, but we can't bet our lives on that. That is cutting things too closely. Carl, you, and I will meet the ship at daylight and give assistance to the men aboard. I, at least, have rigged many a ship and will do what I can to make the ship ready for embarkation before tomorrow night. Gerald, you can be a big help, also, if you don't mind coming with us. Eliab, why don't you come, also, and learn how to repair ship rigging? It would be a good learning experience for you. Pagiel, if you would, stay and make sure nothing happens to my family."

When everyone went to bed to try and get some sleep before a busy day following, I got Pagiel's attention and asked him to go out to the stables with me. We each carried lamps of oil to light the way and endured the slackening rain on our trip. I went about like I was checking on the horses' tac, but horses weren't my concern at that moment.

"Pagiel, what do you think our chances are?"

I saw a faint smile and he had a look of contentment as if he felt like he had value for the first time in his life. He wasn't a pariah around me and my family. In fact, we depended upon his gift of sight. He had already saved us once. I hoped he could save us again. I did not look upon him as a sorcerer but viewed him as a prophet. That was splitting hairs, but I justified my thoughts as appropriate in that we needed him.

He said, "In the fifth book of the Torah, the Book of Deuteronomy, in the eighteenth chapter, it says no one shall use divination, no one will practice witchcraft, no one shall be a sorcerer. God says it is a detestable thing to be sorcerer, and he commands his people to drive them from their midst. For me, for all of us underground, to be driven out means to be stoned to death, because we are not allowed to become part of your world. You have accepted me, despite who or what I am. Thank you for that. I can't help what I was born. I can see things before they happen. Our people have many prophets in our history. Most of them, like Isaiah, Daniel, and Moses are well respected, but I am a damnation and must be killed. I can't see everything that will happen, and my sight isn't perfect, but I know that they will arrive tomorrow night, and they will kill you if you are found, however they will not find you, not tomorrow, but I cannot see too far into the future. Days, sometimes weeks, but usually not many months and, very rarely, a year. I can see Eliab is torn and you do not have to be a sorcerer to see that. I know you can tell as much. He holds a high office in our army, and to be a general takes years of training, and his purpose was driven into him relentlessly. He wants to be a good general and he wants his freedom, also. The two dogs fighting in him gives him torment. He can't sleep because of it. I can't tell you for sure which of his dogs will win. I can only tell you that he will leave with us tomorrow evening without protest. I can also tell you that he will give us away. We will be safe for now, but they will find us in Rome because of Eliab's treachery."

He will give us away! I wanted to go into the house at that moment and run my short sword into his heart. I don't know why I didn't. Forever after, I wished I had. I guess I was becoming soft in my old age by taking the path of least resistance. I weighed my family and Eliab on a scale and let the scale tip towards Eliab, but I swore to myself that, if I saw the slightest hint of him betraying us, I would not hesitate to cut his throat. From that day onward, Eliab was on my mind and in my sight. I owed him my freedom from the cavern, and I suppose I felt I should return what favor I could until he no longer deserved my favor.

"I don't suppose you can see if we end this contest between us and our pursuers, and we live through it?" I asked him.

"I see a gauzy-like veil and, on the other side of it, I see struggles and bitterness and pain. I see the hurt in your heart for what will happen. There are battles that will take place, and I see blood and death, lots of it. I believe you, we, will accomplish the goal we are after, but not without great costs. The details are yet too unclear to know for sure. It is yet too distant. Keep a watch out for Gerald and Carl. Before we reach the safety of another country, they will be faced with serious dangers."

I marveled at his insight. I had seen enough of his prophecies come true to believe what he had just told me, and it made my blood turn cold. Whose blood and whose death could he be seeing? What will Gerald and Carl do or see that will endanger them and maybe us? I had long ago stopped being afraid of death, but I was concerned about my family. Would they survive this mess I had gotten us into? No need to fret, I told myself. Whatever happens, happens. If it came to it, I would die with a sword in my hand doing my best to protect those I loved. At the top of my worry list was Pagiel's statement that we would be found out in Rome, and Carl and his son would be endangered. Endangered was not the same as harmed or killed, I convinced myself. I vowed to do my best to prove those prophecies to be wrong. Can the future be changed, I wondered? It was not until later that I would become aware that, sometimes, Pagiel saw more than he wanted to divulge. He feared telling me about what gave me the most pain.

Carl, Gerald, Eliab, and I boarded the *Sea Lady* just as the sun's light rose above the Thames' distant horizon. The captain was having his breakfast on deck because the late August heat, coupled with the very humid air, had already made his cabin uncomfortable. We urged him to permit us to help in the rigging repairs, because we were very interested in leaving that evening. He was dubious of our ability to help and, since I was the only one with experience among our group, he was justified in his feeling. I knew Carl and Gerald were capable of learning quickly, and they were strong and had an incentive to do good and fast work.

The main and fore topgallant sails had to be replaced; each having been torn by the storm's wind. The main topsail yard arm, too, had its end broken and needed replacing. Rigging on the main and mizzen masts also had to be replaced with new ropes. The carpenter set about doing the repairs on the yard arms, and Gerald gave him help, while the crew, Eliab, and I, helped in taking down the torn sails, bringing the new ones from below deck, hoisting them into their proper place, and helped in replacing the damaged rigging. The bowsprit, too, was damaged and the carpenter's helper worked at repairs. The ship could have sailed without doing any of the restorations, but the captain, a merchant seaman with much experience, was of the type who could not rest until the ship was in perfect condition before sailing. A day or two of loss was of no concern for him. I spent two years as a pirate, and it was my experience that we, and other privateers, were not so picky about perfection. Speed and maneuverability were our primary concerns, and appearances were less important.

The wind began to pick up from the west when the last of the repairs were finished. Gerald had already summoned

Connie, Alfred, Pagiel, Dania, and the children, with our supplies, and they were onboard when the repairs were finished. A half-hour after the wind had turned favorable, the crew removed the tie-down ropes from the seagull's roost posts, and we slowly drifted in the current away from the pier. The sun had set by the time we left the dock. We slowly moved out into the current of the Thames that was gently flowing east toward the channel and, so far, we had not encountered the next group of our pursuers.

I, and all my companions, were on deck as we slid from the docks, letting the breeze pull us towards the middle of the river. I tried to let peace find its way into my mind, wanting it to push out the stress and anxiety that had so buffeted me these last weeks. We had at least the comfortable feeling that we had left before our pursuers arrived. I was physically and emotionally exhausted, and I hoped the open sea would restore calm to my tormented soul once more. I looked around at my family and companions and felt the weight of responsibility for them. They looked to me for protection and guidance. I felt so inadequate that evening, drifting out across the green waters of the Thames contaminated with rubbish. I got us into the situation we were in, and it was my duty to get us out of it. That responsibility also included getting them out of it without any of them being harmed.

I asked Carl, "Where is Gerald? I don't see him on deck. Do you think that he is below?"

"I saw him not long ago, maybe an hour. I better check."

The storm had cleared the air considerably and the sky was devoid of clouds, the sun already having disappeared below the red and gold horizon. The last vestige of the tempest was the light westerly breeze that pushed us away and downstream that would eventually deliver us to the vast channel between England and Europe, the North Sea. The breeze dispelled the heat and removed any mosquitos, making it a pleasant evening. The tentative peace I had felt was suddenly destroyed when Carl came back upon the deck.

"He's not down there. Not below deck nor on top, either! I don't know where he is unless he left the ship, for some reason and did not return."

"For heaven's sake!" I exclaimed with more bitterness than I should have. My peace was too suddenly, and violently, ruined by more disquieting news.

"You sure? You checked thoroughly?"

Of course, he did, and I knew it when I asked.

"Okay, Carl. Let's go find him."

We bid Dania, Connie, and the others goodbye with instructions that, if we could not join them downriver later, we would catch up with them in Honfluer. If we weren't there within a week, to proceed on to Rome, as vessels going that way allowed. The captain would not return to the dock we had left, because the Thames was not wide enough for tacking upstream and, besides, he was not willing to undergo that effort. He had already been paid his passenger fees, leaving him no incentive to do our bidding. We convinced him to get as close to the southern shore as possible; then, Carl and I went overboard for the short swim to the bank.

We stood panting on the bank and rested our heaving breasts for a short while, and then, took off on a run back towards the city's wharves. We had not drifted far before it was discovered Gerald was missing, so we didn't have too far to run. After reaching the place where the *Sea Lady* had docked, we did not see Gerald anywhere. Gerald was young and still a bit immature, but he would never leave without telling one of us that he had changed his mind about leaving England.

"I don't know Carl. I don't see him. Let's begin at my house. Maybe he left something there that he wanted to retrieve."

It was six blocks from the wharves to where my townhouse sat, next to a wide, tree-lined boulevard. It was perhaps fifty feet higher in elevation than the river, and that alone kept it normally clear of the often-harsh smells that usually accompany the docks, like dead fish, rotten vegetables, soured wheat, and other odors common to seaports everywhere.

Working on the assumption that foul play could have happened, before we were in sight of my house, we became more cautious in advancing. It was well that we did. In front of the house were several men and their horses. The men were near the front steps. It was dark, but lights from inside the house revealed what appeared to be three men, maybe four, some sitting on the front porch, some standing near the bottom step. That could mean there were a dozen or more in my house. It could also mean that they were elsewhere so as not to draw too much attention from the neighbors, but was Gerald in the house, also? My guess was that he was, along with Lizzie and her daughter, and the Ashkenazim were in the process of getting information out of them. Damaging information. We had very little time to delay.

Carl and I went down to an alley that ran behind our row of homes. The alley separated our houses from the stables behind them. When we reached the back of my house, we crept alongside the east side of it, hidden by the dark and by shrubs planted next to the house. Arriving at a tall window that revealed the interior of my parlor, we could see Gerald, Lizzie, and Sophie sitting on a sofa in front of my desk. One soldier was sitting in a chair that had been pulled up in front of the three sitting on the sofa. Another man stood behind him watching them, maybe participating in the interrogation. Gerald's nose was bleeding, he had a bruise on the left side of his face and his hands were tied behind his back. The women were whimpering. The ladies did not know where we were going, so they could not tell the soldiers, but Gerald knew. I hoped he was brave enough for a little while longer.

Carl said, "Poppa, maybe we should go get the police. We could use some help here."

"Carl," I said, a little bit exasperated. "The police don't even carry swords. All they have are clubs. Do you think these soldiers, who have orders to kill us or bring us back to their leaders for execution, will let a few men carrying a stick stop them? No, we will have to get Gerald and the ladies out of there on our own and do it now. They have orders to kill or capture us, so we ourselves will do what is required to rescue Gerald."

"There is a door in the back of the house that leads into the cellar. From the cellar, a set of stairs goes up to the kitchen. That's where we will enter the house. The door is locked, but I know where the key is."

When we got into the cellar, I lit an oil lamp kept down there for use when stocking shelves with preserved vegetables.

"Once you are in the kitchen, Carl, go from there into the dining room. The other opening into that room is across the foyer from the door leading into the parlor. Once you are at the dining room doorway, call out, in Hebrew, "Sir, we have a problem out here." Probably only one man from the parlor will go out to investigate. When that man exits my parlor, I will kill him and drag him away before he has a chance to call out in alarm."

That was the plan until new obstacles were discovered.

As silently as the stair treads allowed, we crept up them to the door that led into the kitchen. Slowly, ever so slowly, I began the process of opening the door. I held my breath, as if that would reduce the sound the door hinges would make. When the opening was perhaps one inch wide, I could hear and see two men sitting at the kitchen's work island, snacking on my food! For several moments, I stared at them, trying to let reason win the battle in my head over insult and anger. What could I do to them where they would not cry out for the others to come to their aid?

I closed the door, but did not latch it, and told Carl there were two men in the kitchen. They were two significant obstacles that had to be overcome, somehow. I begged God for a break. I could not remember the last time something went the way I wanted it to go. *Now was a great time to change that trend*, I thought.

I motioned for Carl to ease back down the steps. At the bottom, I told him what I thought we should do under the new circumstances. When Carl had stationed himself under the steps, not far from the top, I called out, in Hebrew, "I need some help down here," but not so loud that anyone in the parlor could hear.

I had no idea if the men in the kitchen would think it was impossible for anyone from their group to be in the cellar. It was my hope there had been enough confusion when all of them forced their way into my home that they might believe it possible for one of their fellow soldiers to be down on the floor below.

The door at the top of the stairs opened, letting light shine down from the kitchen.

"Who's down there?" Called a man at the top.

"It's me, I think one of the ones we are after is down here hiding behind some shelves. Help me move them."

The foolish always rush in. He made it down four steps when Carl grabbed his right foot from under the steps, sending the man tumbling down to the bottom where I met him with my dagger. The noise made by the falling comrade caused the other soldier in the kitchen to investigate what all the noise was about.

"What's going on down there?"

I said, "I fell down the stairs and I think I broke my ankle. Help me get up, will you?"

By the time he got to the fourth step, Carl grabbed his foot and down he went, also, into the hereafter, courtesy of my dagger. We waited for things to settle for a short while to see if any from the parlor investigated, but no one did. Carl retraced his path up the steps, and I was right behind him. The door was still open when we got to the top, and we could see the kitchen was empty of soldiers. Quietly, Carl went to the doorway leading from the kitchen into the dining room. I took up my position outside the parlor door.

Carl called out, "Sir, there is something happening in the back of the house, that you need to see." He did not know many words in Hebrew, but he knew enough to get that message to the men in the parlor. I doubt his accent was very convincing, but the words were enough to investigate.

The moment the investigator stepped far enough beyond the door, I grabbed him with my right arm and, with my left hand, placed it on his mouth. I removed my right arm just long enough to sever his windpipe, stopping any chance of him crying out. I dragged him into the kitchen.

"Sir, you need to come see this," I said. In a few moments, the soldier who had been slapping Gerald around and intimidating the two women was dead. So far, no one from the front porch had come inside. Carl entered the parlor and freed Gerald's hands.

In the kitchen, I said to them, "We have to leave now."

We went back down the steps to the door exiting the cellar and over to the stables.

"Lizzie, Sophie, you must go now. Go wherever you feel safe. Maybe to Sophie's house. Stay there and do not return here for at least a month. Do you understand me?"

From my stables, we procured three of the horses we had arrived on a few days earlier. We walked them down the alley far enough that no one in front of the house could hear us leave the area.

We rode east as fast as we could in the darkness. A half-moon was overhead, but passing clouds often obscured it. We rode towards Rochester, and once there, we would then ride north to Grain, which lay alongside the river's southern bank. Grain was a small town near the confluence of the Thames and the North Sea. Cap Dougal, captain of the *Sea Lady*, would not be able to unfurl sails on his ship because of the narrow river in the darkness, but relied upon the current to bring him to the channel. It was my belief, and my hope, that, if we rode fast enough, we would make it to Grain before he could arrive. If so, we could reboard the ship with my family, Eliab, and Pagiel.

On the long ride, about thirty miles overland, Gerald explained why he was captured by the Ashkenazim. He had left the ship to make a quick trip back to my townhouse, because he had forgotten his dagger. His sword, he had at his side, but the dagger was still in the upstairs bedroom at our house in which he slept. He had no sooner retrieved the dagger and reached the foyer than the soldiers burst into the door. He swore he had not revealed any information about our destination.

We reached Rochester two hours before the sun rose. The merchant port lay in a bay off the Thames River, but too far for any ship to see anyone hailing them from the docks, so we rode north towards Grain. There, we hired a fisherman, giving him our three horses in ample payment, to take us out onto the river where we waited in hopes the Sea Lady would sail by soon. The Thames River, which is really an estuary from London to the sea, has a current speed of no more than ten miles an hour, depending on whether the tide is going east or west. London is only about thirty miles as a seagull would fly from the sea but, because of its meandering through the country, it is closer to sixty-five miles by water. Also, obstacles, like having to avoid tidal beaches, and a bridge or two that would have to be raised to clear, the ship would take close to nine hours to arrive near Grain. The ship should sail near our location about nine hours after leaving the London dock, at the most. Maybe eight hours at the earliest. That would mean the ship could have already passed by. If my luck, bad luck that had been hitching a ride on my shoulders for the past weeks, had not changed, it meant we did miss the boat. It was going to be close.

Finally, a break came our way. We had been in the fisherman's boat no more than a half-hour when we spotted a ship coming our way. It was the Sea Lady!

Chapter Seven

More Bad News!

In peace, a wise man makes preparations for war.
—Horace

Dania, Connie, and the children slept that night in a small cabin on the 'tween deck away from the coarse seamen, while the rest of us bedded down on the weather deck where there was at least a breeze to keep us cool and away from the foul odor of sweaty men, night jars, and cargo. Subsequent nights, unless it was bad weather, the children and ladies also slept on deck with us.

Two days after reaching the North Sea's channel, we sailed into the port city of Honfluer. We stayed there two days while the captain took on supplies and off-loaded some of the cargo while taking on other stores. On the outgoing tide of August 24th, we sailed back out into the channel and began the journey along the coast of Normandy and then, south towards the Kingdoms of Leon and Castile where the seas grew rougher as the days passed. Eliab and Pagiel were very afraid of the sea, especially when its waters grew more turbulent with rolling waves. They were sick much of the time. I had some medicine that I had brought with me, which I gave to my small children, but there wasn't much leftover for the two men.

We continued to sail south and, in one of those rare moments I was alone on the foremast deck, and, when the seas weren't too bad, I had time to stare out at sea, ruffled by foamy wavelets, and contemplate the past and future, and I let my mind wander where it wished. I loved the sea life. There is no feeling of freedom like being on the sea and seeing no land in any direction. For the passengers, like Eliab and Pagiel, who never learned to swim, sailing on top of water thousands of feet deep, was daunting for them. I tried to develop a workable plan on what to do next but, in truth, my mind could not devise a way out of our predicament. It was easier to let my thoughts revert to past days at sea. Some were great, and some were about shipwrecks I had experienced. Most of my sea memories were pleasant, and they made me smile, which is something I had not done much of lately.

While I was staring out seaward, watching the slow descent of the sun as it made its way west, and seeing a few gulls returning towards land, Eliab approached me and broke my meditation. I sighed with disappointment that my peace was over for the evening.

"What do you think is out there? It looks as if you are you searching the horizon for something?"

"No, not looking for anything. My eyes are looking out there at the sea, the water that seems to go on forever, but what I'm really looking at are memories that move across my mind's eyes. To my knowledge, no one has gone in that direction, far beyond the western horizon, and found out what is there. Some went west, but eventually, came back and said there was nothing but more water. Endless expanses of water. Some have sailed that direction and have never returned, and that has led to many speculations about what lies out there. Some believe that there is land beyond where giants roam here and there, seeking human prey to devour those who have washed up on their shores. Others believe that a land of dragons exists, snake-like creatures that spew fire from their mouths and can fly like eagles, and still others say that there is a land where people from other worlds travel to and from their home planet. They believe they have vessels that can fly into space amongst the stars, to other worlds, and these space beings are setting up life here on our planet. At some point, they think the powerful creatures from those other worlds will come east and take over all of us."

"But what do you think is out there, Troy?"

I had thought about that question many times and had come to my own conclusion. "Many years ago, I was shipwrecked upon the great islands known as the Japans. I think, if we sailed west long enough, we would eventually arrive at the eastern shore of the Japans. The earth is round and, if we keep sailing west, we will eventually arrive back where we started."

"Maybe," Eliab suggested, "there are other lands out there that have never been discovered. I would like to go to those lands if that is so and find the peace I long for. Even if I were the only person there, it would be like the Garden of Eden for me. A paradise where there is no one to tell me what I should do or think, no one wanting to kill me."

We both looked out across the great waters and thought our own thoughts until Pagiel approached us.

"Sir Troy, I'm sorry to bother you, but I thought you would like to know what my mind saw. I believe the soldiers who came to London have discovered four of their numbers had been killed. Lizzie and Sophie, unfortunately, have returned to your house, and were questioned by the remaining soldiers. They told those questioning them that we had gone to Colchester. They couldn't find us there or anyone who even knew you. They returned to find Lizzie and her daughter still there, and they were beaten severely for lying to them. After suffering so much, Lizzie said she might have heard us talk about getting on a boat. They now know we left England, but do not yet know where, but are seeking answers from those who live near the wharves and the sea captains who were still at port."

I was suddenly consumed by a mixture of grief and anger that once could have been lethal to all the people near me. It was the kind of feelings my demons fed upon and would lash out to harm those they thought might be harmful to me, and that meant anyone standing in the same area I stood. My anger was directed towards the people who would harm gentle and innocent women like Lizzie and her daughter, and anger at myself for what I had spawned by being so arrogant. I emphatically told Lizzie to stay away for at least a month. Why did they go back so soon? Never had I felt so helpless in my life. I seethed within and spent all the self-control I had to not lash out with curses and do harm to myself. Others were looking at me, and my shame burned in my face, and I could not let my children see me act like a deranged child, so I calmed down enough to ask Pagiel if he thought Lizzie was dead.

"She and her daughter are not yet dead. Some of my people are still with them in your house. They are a loose end, though, that will have to be tied up. They will not live long, I think."

I could no longer hold in my anger. I grabbed a belay pin from the pin rail and banged it down on the taffrail, leaving a dent in the oak, and cursed the evil that followed me like a shadow, and then, threw the pin as far as I could out to sea. I would have given my soul to be standing outside my townhouse at that moment with my swords in my hands. God's revenge would be as sweet as honey in my mouth when I spilt their wretched blood. We did well by leaving, but five of my servants were now dead, or would be soon. I swore that many of their kind would pay for the cost of their evil. I wondered if I were once more being tested. Could it possibly be that God was angry with me for going against his chosen nation? Maybe I wasn't doing God's business of revenge for him, but I was so angry at that moment that I didn't care. If he wanted my soul in payment for what I was about to do, then, I would give it up for the chance to kill at least one of those who were relentlessly hunting us down like they were after a rabid dog who was killing their sheep. If Francois Laurent was in my grasp at that moment, I would have sent his lifeless body over the rail and his soul to Hades.

Dania would have no part in me getting off at the next port and returning to England. I begged her to let me go while the rest of them continued to a safe harbor. Her crying and pleading wore me down, and I promised I would continue with them, but every quiet moment I had, I killed the pursuers in my mind. "Vengeance is mine, sayeth the Lord." I begged God to let me be the one to exact that revenge in his name.

That night, I had a vision. It wasn't the first time I had a vision, but it came when I needed one the most. My visions could not be confused with dreams. Dreams are too nebulous and too easily forgotten as for what they were, a fantasy tale created independently by the brain. They were not as specific or numerous as Pagiel's sight. My visions were like I was standing there awake, and though I could not speak, I could see clearly what I was to do, though not how to do it. It was a profound experience because the sight that I could see, even with my eyes closed, told me I was to do whatever was necessary to stop God's own people from the misguided plan they were about to release upon the unsuspecting world. The vision was a substantiation that I had been appointed, just as David had, to slay a Goliath. I awoke the next morning refreshed, my grief and anger gone. I was in God's will. I had been given a directive to pursue the gigantic underground snake and remove its head. I hadn't been tested; God had already done that with my legion of demons he personally removed. He just wanted me to be in a mental and physical place where I would have given my most precious possession, my soul, to carry out his purpose for me. He was making sure I was fit for his kingdom. This was why I was born and had lived so long, to be alive and physically capable at that point in history in 1362. I was told in my vision, that I would receive no compensation for what I was to do, nor would fame accompany my efforts. If there was glory to be given, it was to him, and not me. So be it, I thought, I would rather sit next to my swift and bubbling brook in my forest than have a fame that might take me away from its peace.

Chapter Eight

Rome

The gates of Hell are open night and day; smooth the descent, and easy is the way; but, to return, and view the cheerful skies; in this, the task and might labor lies.
— Virgil

I said nothing about my vision to Eliab and Pagiel and confided only with Dania. She was born into a Muslim family and was taught the tenets of that belief system all her life. We had, by then, been married for nearly twelve years and, though I tried to convince her of my faith, and though she had witnessed two miracles involving divine figures, she would still not fully embrace my Christian faith. So, while I explained to her my vision, I could tell she was unconvinced with what I had seen. She only wanted safety for herself and her family, and how I ensured our safety was of no concern to her, so long as I knew.

Eight days after leaving Honfluer, we arrived at the weather-protected port of Bayonne in Gascony. The ship was to stay there for four, maybe five days, if the wine delivery wasn't delayed, so all eleven of us disembarked, choosing to stay in a place whose floor didn't rock when the wind blew. It was the latter part of September, and the weather had cooled, and the terrain was beautiful. We all loved the scenery, and Eliab and Pagiel were stricken by the beauty of the world above, hidden from them all their lives. Pagiel, especially, was elated, and his demeanor improved drastically. Alfred, Connie's ill husband, seemed to improve, also. Kat and Jay, even Troy, were able to run, unfettered, as they had been by the closeness of the deck aboard the *Sea Lady*. Everyone's spirit was improved, except for mine. The weight of what must be done was heavy on my spirit.

We rented a house outside the city for the few days we would be in port. On the second afternoon, Connie asked me to walk with her.

"Poppa," she began after we had been walking a while on a rugged path high above the harbor, and overlooking the houses below, "tell me what's bothering you. I know you and, when things weigh on your soul, you get like this. I know you are worried about us, but do you know things you haven't told us? If so, I need to know. I want to help you, but I need to know how I can help you."

The afternoon had warmed up since the day before. The sky was clear and blue just like Connie's eyes. She was so much like me and putting her in danger burdened me as we walked the dusty trail that wound through patches of trees, among meadows decorated with colorful wildflowers. The locusts buzzing and flitting from weed to weed seemed to make the day seem even warmer. If Connie's mother, Anna, was looking down upon us, if such things were possible, she would be very unhappy with me for putting her daughter and son in such jeopardy.

"Connie, I know that what we are doing is the right thing. However, I don't know how exactly we are to get out of this fix I got us into, but I do know enough to feel we will be successful. I also know that there will be obstacles ahead of us, and maybe some of us will not survive the effort, but I know we must do what we must to stop the madness that will assuredly one day take place. People will have to die, we will have to shed blood, but it will be worth it in the end, at least for the survivors. Eliab, Carl, Gerald, and I will have to draw swords. I know for certain we will, but it must be done. The only thing I know for certain is that we must confront the High Priest to stop those relentlessly pursuing us. If we can stop the taking over the unsuspecting nations aboveground, that is a plus, but I'm mainly concerned about the safety of my family. That means the High Priest must be convinced by any means possible, either by words or by blood."

"Poppa," she said with that familiar insistence of hers I had witnessed all her life. Her eyebrows almost touched as she scowled at me. She had been a strong-willed young girl growing up, and she still was. "Do not think for one moment, because I'm a woman, that you won't use me to help you in this fight! If you leave me out of your plans, I will be immensely angry with you. I will not be a babysitter for your wife and children. Not even for my poor husband, while you and Carl and Gerald will be putting your life in jeopardy for us."

"I promise you that you will be part of what I have in mind. Still, I wish for Dania and the kids to be safe, and I'm not sure Pagiel can be of any help in protecting them, and I know Alfred's illness will not allow him to help. We will see when the time comes, but I think it best that we start working on improving and refining our fighting skills like we used to do years ago. The fighting will be deadly, I'm sure of it, so we must be at our peak efficiency to take on our new enemy. There will be danger when we arrive in Rome. Pagiel says we will be discovered, and we may have to deal with Eliab there, also. Don't tell the others what I've just told you, I don't want them to worry, but be alert, especially when we arrive in Centumcellae."

We walked on for another mile or so, and then turned around. We spoke of what was and what could be. I always loved talking to her because she knew me and offered good advice. Her confidence and common sense were more like my first wife, Veronica, than Anna or Dania. I suppose it was because she was more me than her mother. I got another twinge of pain realizing how I had endangered her. Ever since she was a little girl, she and I had a closeness stronger than my other children. We always seemed to know what each other was thinking and feeling.

That very afternoon, we began sparing with wooden sticks at first, which would, before we left Bayonne, be replaced with real swords. Since I had more fighting experience than all of them combined, I was the teacher. I taught them skills that not only involved fighting with swords but, also, the use of feet and hands to augment the use of blades. I saw great potential in all my students, especially Carl and Connie, and I knew that not many men that we would encounter, could out-fight us. However, we were only five of us, not counting Pagiel, who was not the warrior type. He did participate in the sparing, because he was just not gifted with the ability to fight in deadly confrontations. The daily practices continued after boarding the ship once we left Bayonne. We sailed for another twenty-three days before reaching Marseilles and, by then, the children and the two underworld escapees were weary of the confinements of the ship. Much cargo was off-loaded at the port, and much was brought on, as well. The cargo exchange took four days to accomplish, and it gave us time to stretch our legs and walk among the forests and hills on land, whose surface was stable. Pagiel and Eliab had started to lose their pale pallor, though their skin did burn easily at first.

We would be in Rome within two weeks, and that thought began to weigh on my mind since, if Pagiel was correct, trouble would once again be an imminent threat to all of us. The weeks we spent on the ship gave me some time to spend with my youngest children, telling them stories of my past adventures, and giving them general instructions on behavior, as well as teaching them about history, literature, science, and mathematics. The older two already knew how to read and write, but I wanted them to have a well-rounded education that most children their age were denied, especially for girls like Kat. The constraints of the ship allowed me to get to know Eliab and Pagiel better, as well. I studied them closely for signs of unhappiness, frustrations, anger issues, or lack of desire to participate in family discussions or indications of aloofness. It would not be unnatural for them if their once strong devotion to their own people caused them to want to return to the only world they knew. To their own kind. Eliab grew sullener while Pagiel seemed to blossom and grew closer to my young children, participating in their childish games and telling them made up stories.

Each day I quizzed Pagiel to see if he had any insight as to what was going on with our England-based pursuers, or what might happen at the next port, or any potential actions of

Eliab that could betray us. He assured me that the remaining men who had followed us to London had discovered our departure was by ship. After discovering which ship we left on, they were able to know exactly which ports we would visit, simply by interrogating sailors and captains at the local pubs. They knew, then, where we would most probably end our journey, at least initially, in the city of Centumcellae, only a short overland journey from Rome. How they would get that information out to others on the continent, he did not know for sure. Knowing long before our arrival in Rome may somehow provide these industrious and very advanced people with time to notify their spies in the Roman area. How they could do it in that timeframe was beyond my ability to fathom, but everything I had seen about these Ashkenazim thus far caused me to believe it was possible they would or could be waiting for us when we arrived at port. Pagiel remained confident that we would be discovered in Rome, and Eliab had some part in our discovery, whether by intention or by accident, it was unclear to him.

On the long journey between Bayonne and Marseilles, Alfred became listless and, for three days prior to our arrival at port, he had eaten nothing and only drank a little water. I feared for his life, but there was nothing I could do, despite my extensive medical training I had received from Islamic professors of medicine. Under our circumstances, we could only work at keeping him comfortable, which on a rocking and heaving ship, was nearly impossible. We found a villa available to us to rent over the four days we were in Marseilles, a major port within the County of Provence. It was a beautiful area and would have been a joyful experience for us had it not been for Alfred's declining health and, of course, for the reasons we were there in the first place. I visited some shops and found certain medicinal herbs I wanted, and walked through nearby forests to find others I knew would be effective in treating pain. For a time, he felt better and even smiled and conversed often with Connie during the day. However, on the third day, he fell into a sleep that he would not awake from. I knew the symptoms and knew he would not survive. Connie knew it, also. When the day came, we were to set sail again, Alfred still had not revived. Connie was faced with the decision to stay and tend to her dying husband or bring him with us and let his fate have its way on the next voyage. She was torn about what to do. Alfred was the last of her family, all her children had died, and it was eating her soul to lose the father of her children, the love of her life. In the end, we carried him to the ship since it was not feasible for Connie and her husband to remain behind. She would be all alone when he was dead in an unfamiliar place. On the second day at sea, he died. Connie was devastated and wept bitterly when his weighted body slid out from under a canvas blanket into the sea. I never like burials at sea. I didn't like to think of bodies of those I cared about being eaten by sea creatures.

On the third day after leaving Marseilles, we docked in Genoa, a port in the Kingdom of Italy, a city I despised. I had once been sold into slavery at that port and wanted no part in being there and did not wish to spend any silver or time walking the dirty streets of that city, known widely for its reputation of being a large slave marketplace. We only stayed at the port overnight, and I elected not to go ashore, though everyone else did, for a chance to escape the confines of the ship. Had I not been sold into slavery in that port, I would never have met Dania, so my dislike of Genoa was tempered with that fact.

It only took three more days to arrive at Centumcellae, on the 27th of October, and those days went by quickly. We knew our lives would be in danger there. There, or in the city of Rome. My guess was that there would somehow be spies at the dock watching ships discharging passengers, and we would be easily recognized as the escapees. I still marveled at how word could possibly get to the Jews who were looking for us so quickly. Regardless of how, I knew it was going to happen. I thought of trying to disguise ourselves so that we wouldn't be recognized but, in the end, I believed that would not fool such people, who had thus far shown they were not fools.

We disembarked the ship before midday and, as I had done many times in my past, went to nearby stables and rented horses and a carriage for Dania and the children. Eliab, Pagiel, and I were alert to any suspicious men who could be possible spies. We saw a few that could be, but it wasn't possible to be sure. It was a two-day ride to the ancient city built on seven hills, and it was very possible we could be ambushed along the way, but Pagiel assured me that nothing would happen to us in route. Nothing would happen to us until Rome. So, why did we go to Rome knowing, or at least we believed, we would be discovered in that city? I believed then, knowing where they would be, would be an advantage for us as much as it would be for them. We would be on alert and ready to defend ourselves. We had time to plan and prepare. I was overconfident enough to believe we had the skills to overcome them, if their numbers weren't more than a dozen. I was also anxious for the chance to get them off our trail by simply killing our pursuers. No one knew what we looked like, except for Eliab. Traveling as a group, the number of us was our giveaway. That meant they had to either discover us getting off the ship or find us traveling from the port to Rome as a group. In a very short time, Connie, Carl, Gerald, Eliab, and I would be leaving and going east to Armenia. Dania, probably Pagiel too, and the children would, hopefully, be lost in the large population of the ancient city. My immediate concern was to find a safe place for them to stay while we were gone. However, neither Dania nor Pagiel could speak the local language, and it would be difficult for them to blend into the background without being noticed eventually. I sincerely hoped that before then, our mission would be successfully completed.

We ate a midday meal in the port city before leaving east for Rome, a city I had been to many times, and it held sad, as well as very happy, memories for me. I met my first wife, Veronica, there, and where an original cofounder of our East Asia Trading Company had his office. Not far from that city, demons, using my hands as the perpetrator, took the life of a very good man and a priest of God, Father Mathias. Bittersweet memories. When we finished eating, we found the old Roman stone paved road leading to the once home of the most powerful men in the world and, where now, the leader of the universal church lived and oversaw the bride of Christ. I had met a former bishop of Rome, Pope Innocent III, and I gave some thought to try and gain admission to the current Pope, but he, Pope Innocent VI, had just died a few weeks earlier on September 12th. He was replaced by Urban V, and we left Rome before he was installed as pope. I gave a lot of thought to talking to him, even if it meant staying in Rome longer than I wanted, about how there was a vast number of people who were determined to try and usurp, not only him, but all the rulers of the world from England to the Holy Land. *Maybe I would still try and convince him of the danger he and much of the world were in*, I thought, but, first, I needed to gather more information before I approached powerful rulers with armies.

I knew the manager of the East Asia Trading Company who was stationed in Rome, since the principles of the company met every five years in either Rome or Boïos, and there was a bank in that city, too, that I could draw money from. I left my family and friends to seek out the manager. I met with Antonio Severino, and explained to him that the London office was being managed by a diminished crew for the time being, but there should be no long-term impact on business. I asked him for a co-signature on a draft at the bank where I could withdraw what I thought should be enough funds for expenses over the next six months. Antonio had a villa on a remote lake, which served as his summer home. He and his wife had left it for the season just weeks before, and he offered to let us stay there while they were back in the city. Its remoteness would be a great place for Dania and the children to remain while they waited for the rest of us to return from Armenia. Most importantly, I was able to get references for men who were trained in the art of fighting for pay. Mercenaries really. Since he was the manager of a large and very profitable company, he used such men frequently and some were at his office daily, serving as hired guards. I asked him to find four such men who would be guardians at the villa to protect Dania, the children, and Pagiel, if he chose to stay with my family, while the rest of us were away. I believed they could also be useful if a fight took place with our pursuers, which I suspected would happen imminently.

Late that afternoon, with my newly acquired funds and four guards with me, I returned to the inn where the rest of my companions were staying. I questioned the guards at length, checked their weapons and their condition, asked about their experiences as guards, and asked if they could acquire additional help, if needed, to get some idea of their usefulness. In the end, I was reasonably confident they would be beneficial if it came to a fight. They were not a pretty group of men but looks were the least of my criterion. I wanted ugly and ruthless men alongside of me when it came to fighting, and when it came to protecting my family in my absence. Over the next few months, they became more than just hired killers; they became friends.

That evening, we dined in a pub and discussed our departure the next day to the villa. We talked about where we would go after departing Rome, how we would get to Armenia, and what we would do once we got there. Our new guards ate at the same pub, but at a different table. I watched them during our meal to see if they got drunk or acted out of line, as mercenaries are apt to do. If I saw them act in a way that didn't meet my view of the kind of person who would guard my children and wife, I would have dismissed them on the spot. They did laugh and drank a quantity of honeyed mead, but never did they get rowdy or drunk, and that gave me a tremendous sense of ease. The easiness I felt at the pub, however, before the day ended, had evaporated, and was replaced with more disappointment and fury.

When the pub began to get crowded after dark, we left it, and returned to our rooms for an early bedtime, so that we could leave for the villa before sunrise the next morning. Dania put Troy down on a pallet in our room, and she tucked in Kat and Jay on another raised bed nearby. We were about to lie down, too, when I heard a knock on our door. When I opened the door, with a short sword in my hand, I found it was Pagiel. Kat and Jay had taken to calling him Pagie, which seemed to please him greatly, like he was part of my family now.

"Sir Troy," he began, visibly shaken. "Can I talk to you now?"

I followed him downstairs and found a quiet corner in the small lobby of the inn. My heart was racing, knowing what he was about to say would not be good news.

"Sir, they have found us. They found us the moment we got off the ship in Centumcellae. When we got off, remember, Eliab was wearing part of his army uniform, enough that it identified him and, by association, us as well. He did that on purpose."

"How many of them are there?" I asked.

"Only four right now. They followed us here. They are outside, somewhere close."

"Only four of them?" For only a moment, I was relieved and excited. Four would be easy to overcome, but Pagie wasn't through with telling me about his vision.

"Four right now, but they will be joined by ten others, maybe eleven. I can't tell for sure. They will be here in two days. Eliab knows where we are going, the villa, and that is where they will attack us, where it is quiet and secluded. Killing all of us won't alert anyone in the city. Eliab will first kill me, and then he will join them."

"Kill you?! Why would Eliab do that? He fought with us and killed his own people not long ago. We fed him and gave him shelter as if he was one of us. Also, he is one of your people."

"He is doing this because he has been promised by those

following us that, in exchange for his assistance in capturing us, his punishment for his crime will be dropped, and he will be allowed back into the good graces of our nation. Maybe even a promotion."

"But kill you? Why?"

"I know too much. All of us must be killed anyway, but me especially, because I can see things that give them away. I must be killed first, and as soon as possible. Tonight."

"Okay Pagie, we are not going to let that happen. Go back to your room, get your things, and come right back here. You are going to sleep in the same room we are in tonight. In the morning, on the road out of Rome, we will confront Eliab and stop his craziness. Be back here as soon as you can."

While he was gone, I told Dania we were going to have company in our room that night and told her what he had said to me. I doubted either of us would sleep that night. How right I was! A quarter of an hour went by, and he had not returned. It couldn't take that long to get his few belongings and come back to our room, which was on the same floor. I put on my trousers, boots, and swords, and went down the hall to his room. The door was closed, so I opened it and pushed the door inwards, but it wouldn't swing all the way, because the door was hitting something. I went through the door sideways and heard a moan coming from just inside the room. I bent down, and, in the very dim light from the moon shining through his window, I saw Pagie lying on the floor, and I felt warm blood on my right knee as I knelt.

"Pagie," I pleaded, "hang in there, my friend, I will take care of you."

With difficulty, I picked him up and carried him down the hall to our room and locked the door behind us. With oil lamps lit, I examined him. He had two stab wounds in his back and was bleeding badly. In my medicine bag I normally carried with me on trips, I took out powder I used to stem the flow of blood; leaves, and herbs I would make a poultice with, a needle and thread to close the wounds, and I would use a bottle of opium for cleansing the contaminated dagger wound and for pain. I had come to rely upon Pagiel and, even, to like the quiet, humble, and respectful man. He had changed drastically since I first met him in the underground dungeon. My children loved him, because he liked to play with them and told them stories that he made up as he spoke. When I first met him, I had a dislike for him and an appreciation for Eliab. Now, it was just the opposite. How ironic things had become. After applying the poultice, I sewed the wounds closed and wrapped bandages tight around his chest and back. Then, I prayed for his recovery.

Back two months earlier, I had sat between boulders and ate an afternoon snack watching the nearly hidden vent pipe release smoke from an underground cavern. Since that day, my world has endured a continuous decline, I thought as I sewed his wounds closed. When would things stop going so badly, I wondered, or would things never stop going badly? I was angry and frustrated with myself and life in general. I prayed to God for guidance and wondered when my recent vision would prove to be authentic and begin to reveal that God, in fact, was on our side.

Even before daylight came, I went down the hall and awakened Carl and Gerald and told them we needed to go into the city for some needed supplies. I awoke Connie, and told her what had happened, and asked her to arouse the guards and have them remain outside our room. She was to remain in our room with Dania and the children until we returned. I checked on Pagiel and changed his bandages. He had a high fever, which was normal. The flesh around the wounds was an angry red. I gave him some more opium to help deaden the pain. I worried that he wouldn't make it. In fact, I kept remembering Pagiel saying Eliab was going to kill him. If it were within my abilities, I would not let that happen. In fact, it was I who was going to kill Eliab, or at least that is what I wanted.

In villages and smaller cities, those who wanted to buy swords, axes, spear points, and such weapons went to blacksmiths to find them, because they were the makers of such items. In cities the size of Rome and, since Rome had a history of war, fighting both offensively and defensively, there were some shops that sold various kinds of implements of war. That's where we went to early the next morning.

I felt reasonably confident in leaving my family behind, since they were well guarded, and I had come to believe Pagie's ability to foretell what was about to happen. Since it would be another day or two before our pursuers would arrive in numbers, we made our way to one weaponry sales shop I knew of, from previous visits, but would nevertheless be hasty about it.

When we entered the shop, it was like it would be if Kat or Jay had entered a store that sold only candy and sweet breads. So many weapons to choose from and my smile never left my face while I temporarily forgot my woes and stared at and handled the cold steel implements of death. I don't enjoy killing but, if I must fight, I want well-made and deadly weapons in my hands to make sure it was my enemy that was bleeding and dying, rather than me. Of course, they had short and long swords and daggers and plenty of them. In addition to the varieties of blades, I saw war-hammers, sickles, battle axes, maces, scythes, mauls, add-chains, halberds, pikes, and spears. They also had what I most wanted, bows and arrows. I was surprised to find they also had hand-bombs, a ball bigger than my fist with a wick that, once it was ignited and exploded, would decimate every person within thirty feet of the explosion. I bought four of them. Also, four bow and arrow sets, four daggers, six spears, three swords, and three axes. If we survived the fight with the fifteen or so we would encounter in two days, I was certain there would be more fighting to come once we arrived in Armenia. The thought that I, or one of my children, would die in the fighting did not enter my mind. When I envisioned the fight, I saw only my enemy bleeding at my feet. It wasn't confidence or arrogance; it was all I allowed my mind to think about. I would know soon enough.

With our weapons stowed away on our mounts, we hurried back to the inn to gather up my family and companions and head towards the remote villa. There was much preparation and practicing with our hand weapons to do in a short timeframe. When we arrived at the inn, I took the four mercenary guards aside and warned them about what would take place in one or two days. I wanted to see if they would leave then, rather than run when the fighting started, to see if they were worth their pay. When I finished telling them how many were coming for us, and when, they each looked at the others, smiled, nodded their heads, and said they were eager to do what they had trained all their lives for. Carlos, Luca, Enzo, and Cosimo were going to be put to the test, and I felt sure they would be valuable assets for us. In the following weeks, they became more than just hired fighters to me. I recalled the fight we had with the seven men behind my townhouse. The men who we had fought had been trained in fighting but were not very formidable. I hoped the same could be said for the fifteen we would next encounter. None of the ones we had fought were battle tested, and I doubted the next group would be, either. Still, we had to fight intelligently with forethought.

I had the guards carry Pagiel downstairs after I checked on his wounds. The flesh was corrupted and still red, and a clear liquid seeped from the two sword cuts but did not leak blood. We left the inn just before the noon hour. Dania, Troy, Kat, and Jay rode in a wagon, with Pagiel laying in the back with our supplies of food, clothing, and weapons. Carlos and Luca rode a hundred yards ahead; Enzo and Cosimo, a hundred yards behind us. We did not stop to eat a meal but rode as quickly as the wounded patient in the back of the wagon could safely endure. I wanted to arrive at the location Antonio had given me before it got too dark to look at the surrounding area for signs of danger.

After passing by the last house on the northeastern side of Rome, we rode through miles of forest. The terrain became more rugged, and some of the valleys dropped off suddenly from the road we traveled. Just as the sun had set, we saw the southern shore of the lake Antonio told me about. A half-mile later, we came upon a large house with tall, white marble columns supporting the second-floor balcony. Down below the well cared for lawn was the shore of the lake. Next to the lake was a gazebo and, below it, were two boats lying upside down and tied up to a small dock. Trees grew tall and thick on three sides of the villa, and gardens consisting of manicured shrubs and large patches of mostly dead flowers were accented with marble statues standing among private sitting areas. The large garden filled the spaces between the house and the forest on two sides, and a smaller one on the south side between the house and the stables. The lake was about one hundred yards distance from the wide front porch. It was obvious that the grounds were maintained at least weekly during the summer months. It was approaching November when we arrived, and it was possible that the gardener had not been gone for very long.

Once the wagon was unloaded and the horses put away in the stables, I went into the villa and into a downstairs bedroom nearest the foyer to check on Pagie. His forehead was beaded with sweat, because his fever was still battling against the bad blood the sword blades had caused. I put my hand on his fevered hand to give him some comfort. He motioned to me to bend down so that he could whisper something to me.

He said, "Tomorrow night, they will be here, but they will not attack us until the next morning. There will be sixteen of them with Eliab as one of them."

"Thank you for your help, Pagie. We couldn't hope to defeat them if it weren't for your insight."

"Lord," he whispered and swallowed, and his dry lips showed he needed water. After I gave him some, he went on, "You will prevail in your fight with them, but it will not be without consequences."

"Consequences?" I asked. "What do you mean by consequences, Pagie? What's going to happen?"

"I'll say no more now. Let me rest, please."

I had no time to push him for more answers, or to brood

over what might happen, and it was obvious he was suffering and needed the rest. Before it got too dark to see, Carl and I looked over as much of the ground as we could, so that we could get the layout in our memories. It would allow us to have a basis from which to formulate a plan. In particular, I wanted to see what trees would be good for hiding in or around, what bushes that could conceal us, what manmade structures would be good to serve as protection or serve as some secret place we could attack from. Before retiring for the night, I checked on Pagiel once more, but he was asleep.

The next morning, Carl, Connie, Gerald, and I practiced with our bow and arrows to refresh our long-ago skills. I had begun teaching my children how to shoot arrows and fight and hunt from the age of eight years old. I was always the warrior because that was where I was most proficient. I was more talented at killing people than any other skill I possessed. My medical skills saved quite a few people, but it was the taking of lives where I was most adept. During the sleepless night before, I gave our situation hours of thought and, by morning, I had developed a basic plan that I shared with the others, the guards included, at breakfast. My effort in trying to formulate a plan battled for equal time with my thoughts about what Pagiel had said. There were going to be consequences. Was he afraid of telling me what he saw? Was someone, maybe one of my family, going to die tomorrow? I couldn't bear to think about it.

I told everyone at breakfast, "All preparations must be completed before sunset today. Our pursuers must not see us doing any defensive work. Anything we do or prepare for must be a surprise to them when they attack. Pagiel thinks there will be sixteen of them. There are seven of us. We must have the upper hand over them if we are to prevail. Now, does anyone have concerns they wish to discuss? Anyone who wants to leave? I'm open to ideas. Everyone has an equal say in what we do today. Tomorrow morning, there will no longer be time to do anything else but fight for our lives. We will have to fight and kill or be killed. If it is at all possible, I would like to take at least one of them hostage. They have information that might could help our cause."

Connie said, "Poppa, do you have a plan? If so, let us know what it is before we decide on what we are to do. We don't all have to stay here or leave together. Maybe if we split up and go in different directions, at least for the next few weeks, then we can meet up again somewhere next month, maybe. Unless you have a workable plan."

"I have a plan," I said.

Chapter Nine

A Fight for Our Lives

Anyone can become angry, that is easy. But to be angry with the right person, and to the right degree, and at the right time and for the right reason and in the right way — that is not within everybody's power and is not easy.
—*Aristotle*

According to Pagiel's vision, we would not be attacked before morning of the next day, so we had a full day for our preparations if that were so. I placed Gerald and myself on the west side of the villa, or the right side looking from the lake, and near the dead-end road that led to the villa. I told Connie she would be on the south side of the house, behind it, hiding in the stable. With her on that side would be Luca and Cosimo behind the stables. I stationed Carl, Carlos, and Enzo hiding on the east side. In front of the villa was the lake, and I was reasonably sure they wouldn't come to us from the waterside. During the day, we identified large trees, and some fallen trees, also, that could serve as hiding places. We prepared brush piles, too, which would effectively shield us from detection, places we could use as blinds to attack our adversaries from. Carl, Connie,

143

Gerald, and I would each have bows with six arrows. Our four mercenary friends, I hoped, would finish off any we happened to wound, or would, themselves, make proactive attacks on the unsuspecting enemy.

Pagiel said they would arrive that evening or night, but not attack us until the next morning. I had seen enough of his soothsaying to believe he was right, so I suspected they probably arrived in time to find out where the house was, and then, retreated to a safe place to camp and spend the night before attacking us in daylight the next day. At least, that was what I would do if I were them. I strongly considered attacking them at their camp, taking the fight to them, figuring the surprise may be the wisest way to go. I concluded, however, that if we hid and waited for them to arrive at our encampment, we would be able to defeat them with no casualties. It was perhaps the biggest mistake of my life in not doing what my conscience told me to do. We must live with our mistakes. Sometimes, we also die from our mistakes.

About two hours before daylight the next morning, we left the villa and went to the places we had arranged the previous day. I climbed a large oak tree with huge, low hanging limbs for a place to observe what would happen below me. The tree was about twenty-five yards from the clearing where the villa sat and was about fifty yards from the road that led to the estate. Gerald was about ninety to a hundred yards to my right. When I approached the tree, I startled two birds that had roosted there during the night, and they fluttered to another tree and stayed there until closer to daylight. The morning was chilly, and I tucked my head as far into my cloak as I could, to keep my neck warmer. Thankfully, there were no mosquitoes because the chill and a slight breeze kept them away. I felt a spider cross my hand as I steadied myself on my perch. That nearly made me fall out of the tree because I loathe spiders. I would rather fight in a shield wall than have a spider touch me.

In a little while, I heard the first chirp of an early awakened bird, and I saw that, beyond the roof of the villa, the sky had gotten less dark. Soon, it will be daylight. While I was looking at the changing light to the east, I heard something step on leaves behind me. I tensed and very slowly began easing my bow up. I grasped the string with two fingers, one on each side of the arrow already nocked on the bow string. The sound became noticeably closer, and I could tell it was more than one person. They were just a few steps behind me when they stopped. I was disappointed that they had gotten so close before I discovered their presence. Could they have seen me? I cursed my stupid luck. That would ruin our surprise. Worse, they would have the advantage over me. The steps started up again until they were directly under where I sat! No, they didn't know I was above them, or they would have already attacked. I saw darker shapes than the surrounding ground and brush. They stepped beyond the tree, and I could make out in the dim light that it was a doe and two yearlings. I felt a bit embarrassed because I got so tense over three deer, and then, smiled at my foolishness, but was also greatly relieved it was only deer. A few more peaceful moments were mine to enjoy before fighting would commence.

The deer emerged from the woods and began cropping the short grass of the villa's lawn. An early rising squirrel emerged from the hole it used as a den and climbed down the large limb I was leaning against. He stared at me for a several moments before scampering away. Many birds were now awake and chittered and chattered happily in the trees and brush all around me. I was watching the deer browse on the grass when I heard other sounds, noises that weren't from the forest waking up. I slowly turned my head to the left and saw dark shadows coming from the road that were obviously not deer. They were on foot and were walking just inside the tree line. The lighter color of the road's backdrop allowed them to be seen. They were very quiet, but now and then, one or more stepped on newly fallen crunchy leaves or twigs. When they got near the clearing where the lawn began, they all stopped. I could just make out one man, the leader, I assumed, making gestures with his arms. Maybe a third of the men went straight ahead, crossing the lawn that would take them in front of the villa. *A bold move*, I thought. Never would I have sent them across the clearing where they could be seen. Evidently, they didn't know we were alerted to their arrival's timing. Eliab, of all people, should have known.

The rest of the group came in my direction, silently walking about ten feet inside the forest line. I smiled when one man stopped about forty yards from me and knelt near the clearings edge. Another stopped nearly even with my tree, and another passed beyond where I was waiting, and, after walking about forty yards further, he stopped. The others kept going. The three men I could see all knelt near the forest edge and waited. I assumed they were to wait on some signal before proceeding to the house and attack as a group.

The sun began to cast more light around our part of the world as it rose on the other side of the villa. It had yet to rise above the horizon, but I could make out some details of the two men nearest me. The closest to me was mostly hidden by a myrtle bush. I put two spare arrows in my mouth for the readiness of rearming my bow quickly. My right hand was feeling the tension of the bow string. When King Edward III fought his successful battles at Crecy and Poitiers, he had bowmen who could pull back their bowstrings with one hundred pounds of pulling pressure. They could easily kill the enemy at one hundred yards. My bow, according to the shopman who sold it to me, had a pull weight of seventy to seventy-five pounds, easily capable of killing the man forty-five yards from me, assuming my aim was accurate. While I was picturing in my mind the shot, I heard a man moan loudly to my right. I hoped it was because Gerald had shot one of the men, rather than Gerald had been found and killed. The moan caused the three men in front of me to stand, and the one nearest me was now clearly visible. Since they were looking south, I could not draw my bow back, fearing my movement would be seen. In a few moments the furthest man turned back towards the villa, and I pulled my arrow back, judged the distance and let loose. The arrow struck the man just inches below his shoulder, and I saw the bloody arrow land beyond him. He fell without uttering a sound. I could then see the man to my right, looking in the direction of the man I had shot, maybe trying to discover the reason for the slight noise he heard from his friend falling. My second arrow flew at him while he was still confused about what he had heard. The arrow hit him in the chest, and he fell, and the sound of his cry alerted the man in front of me.

The third man looked around to see if he could see where death was coming from, and he spotted me removing another arrow from my mouth and placing it on the bow string. I saw him pull something up that was hanging on his chest and point it towards me. I was pulling the taught bow string back when I heard a loud explosion and saw smoke leap from whatever he was holding. Instantly, I heard something hit a limb hard just inches from my face, and the impact blew bark off and pieces hit against my face. I vaguely remembered feeling blood run down my left cheek into my beard.

I saw the man fumbling with the object he had pointed at me, an object I had never seen before, as if he were preparing it again to send another deadly object towards me. That gave me time to pull back my arrow and shoot. In my haste to shoot, the arrow hit him low in the stomach. A wound that would kill him but would take hours to do so. If the men had been waiting on a signal, the loud explosion must have superseded it. Their presence was known by everyone by then, and secrecy was no longer possible. I quickly climbed down and ran to the fallen man who had already begun calling for help. My dagger through his neck silenced him.

When I withdrew my dagger, I heard yelling and more explosions and the sound of blades against blades. With my bow armed with another arrow, I raced towards where Gerald had built a blind out of cut brush against a fallen log. I passed one man lying dead with an arrow sticking out of his back. Gerald was bleeding from his left shoulder but, with his right arm, he was fighting a man who was desperately trying to defend himself. I saved Gerald the trouble by running my sword through the frightened man. He had used his explosive device to shoot Gerald, but his aim had not been accurate enough to be deadly.

There were at least eleven more men somewhere, besides the five Gerald and I had killed. I worried about Connie and Carl and hoped the four mercenaries had been successful in taking the brunt of the attack. As fast as my nervous legs could carry me, I raced towards the stables where Connie had been hiding. Her location would allow her to ambush any man who would try to attack from the rear of the house. I found her fighting one man, both were wielding swords, each trying to kill the other. Not far from the stable lean-to, a man lay with an arrow sticking out of his side. He was not dead yet, but looked as though he would be soon. The man Connie was fighting had an arrow sticking out of his left shoulder, and that greatly limited his ability to fight my daughter. I was confident she could defend herself from the wounded soldier. Out of the corner of my eye, I saw another man lying on the ground and four men fighting with swords. My mercenaries looked to be having no difficulty in their fight, so I raced to the east side of the villa to see if Carl needed help.

I had heard explosions come from that side of the house earlier and I feared that whatever the things were that the enemy was discharging, may have harmed my son or my hired men. It occurred to me, when I raced towards where Carl was supposed to be, that I should have left one of the hired fighters outside Dania and the children's door. I wished at that moment we had more men. I wished too, that I had taught Dania how to fight, even though she was never interested in learning. I wished I had sent her and the children to Egypt. There was no time to dwell on what I should have done, because I saw Carl fighting two men in a desperate fight to survive. Carlos and Enzo were also fighting, but against one man each.

I ran as fast as I could to engage one of the men Carl was fighting. I could have used my bow, but I dropped it, wanting to fight close enough to see the man's eyes. With my short sword in my left hand and Blind Justice in my right, I swung them at such a speed that my opponent backed up, so fast that he tripped over a fallen branch. I killed him, and then, gave Carl the rest he needed by engaging and killing the man he was fighting. By then, my wrath had been stirred up such that I shoved my sword into his belly up to the hilt, and I felt his warm blood cover my hand. I saw Carlos had been injured and was bleeding badly, but was bravely fighting a defensive battle, barely able to hang on. He was slowly being driven backwards. The fire in my blood was at such a level that I charged after the man who would, at any moment, defeat Carlos. He saw me coming. I was like a runaway stallion racing at him. He turned to face me with eyes bulging wildly. With one parry of his sword with Blind Justice, I ran my short sword into his stomach and, when he fell, I cut his throat with my long sword. When I looked up, the fight was over. Carlos had been hit by a projectile fired at him, as Gerald had been. At least three of the devices that had been used to shoot lead balls at us had failed to ignite the powder, probably because of the dampness of the morning, and some had missed their targets because of haste.

They were all dead, or about to die. At least that is what I thought. We were all very tired and bloody, either from our wounds or from the blood of our opponents. In the few moments I had to reflect on the battle, I concluded that, if the Ashkenazim hoped to take over nations, they must do it either by cunning or by their secret weapons, because they were not of the caliber of warriors I had so often fought before. Living underground for centuries, and sparring only with each other, had led to an army of combatants, rather than warriors, and had a false sense of proficiency. That might be a good thing for us, but I had grave concerns about those things that they were using to shoot lead at us and what other weapons they might have.

We gathered up their weapons and other items they had that may be useful to us. I sent two of my mercenaries to search out their campground that they used the night before, to see if other useful items could be found, such as horses we could sell, or documents that might give us some idea of what they were ordered to do. The disposing of the bodies could wait.

Gerald did a body count and told me he had found fourteen dead enemies. The last of the wounded had died. I made certain that no one survived and that could report back to their superiors that we still lived.

Fourteen? The number didn't add up, if Pagiel was correct. There were supposed to be sixteen. "Has anyone seen Eliab?" I asked, as I stood on the front steps before going inside the house to check on Dania, the children, and Pagiel. Maybe two had escaped. Once inside the door, I heard a scream come from the upstairs level. I got that feeling I sometimes get when something alarming has just happened. My legs, chest, arms, and face began to tingle. Something bad had just happened, and for a moment, I thought of Pagiel's prediction that there would be consequences. I guessed I was about to find out what they were. On my shaking legs, I began to move towards the stairs when I saw Kat racing down the curved staircase that led from the upper floor where Dania, the children and I slept last night, and where the scream came from. She ran to me and wrapped her arms around my neck, sobbing. It was so unlike her to cry like that, it being very rare that she showed her emotions. It was difficult for her to get enough breath because she was crying so hard and deeply. I began consoling her and started to ask what had happened when I looked up and saw Eliab standing on the balcony that overlooked the foyer. He was standing sideways next to the handrail and was looking down at me, and in his right hand was a sword covered in blood.

I pushed Kat away from my chest and said to her, "Kat, you must go outside and find Carl or Connie. Stay with them while I talk to Eliab. Please go. I will join you in a little while."

While I was talking to Kat, Eliab was slowly descending the stairs, still carrying his blooded sword, the tip of which was dragging the marble treads as he took deliberate and slow steps. He had a demented and evil look on his face. I could hear Troy crying upstairs. I was relieved, because that was an indication he was still alive and breathing. When Eliab got to the bottom of the stairs, he took up a position about fifteen feet in front of me, as if a physical confrontation was about to take place. It was a bold and confident stance, which was odd, because he knew he was no match for me with a sword.

"Eliab, why are you doing this? I helped you with your freedom. If it weren't for me, you would be dead now. We fought and killed together. We gave you food and drink and a place to live. You were one of us, with what I thought was a common goal of defeating tyranny. What has changed? Why do you hate us now, and where are Dania and my boys?"

He sneered at me. Oh, I can't describe how much I hated that sneer more than all the ones I had seen before. I slowly began moving my right hand towards Blind Justice when he spoke.

"Troy, I'm sorry things have worked out this way. I truly am. I had no idea that when we left our underground world, I would miss it so much. There is too much confusion, death, and chaos in your world. The rain, the humidity, seasickness, insects, cold nights, and hot days. All these things I loathe.

The rabbi told us you aboveground people would act violently against us. I discovered the truth in his words when I let you talk me into taking part in the killing of seven of my countrymen. I have prayed to God for forgiveness, and I hope he has. You should do the same. I have also prayed you would join us in our endeavor to take what God had given us centuries ago. You could go with me back to my world. You could be a general. All your family could go with me, and I could convince them to spare all of you if you would just join us. You can't possibly win this fight, you know it. If you don't return with me, you will all die. I can promise you that. Nothing can possibly help save you, except that I help you. Tell me you will join us, or I will kill you today, right now. What will you do?"

"Eliab, where is my family?"

He took a deep breath and let it out slowly and said, "I guess there is nothing I can say to convince you to join us, can I? Too bad, as you could be a great asset for us. Oh, wait, you aren't Jewish, are you? No matter. I know you won't help us anyway. You have too much pride, so I will just have to kill you now."

As he spoke, he slowly raised his sword and put it into his left hand and, with his right, he grasped an object I had seen outside, but had not paid much attention to it under the delicate circumstances I was in. A small rope was hooped around his neck, and the end of the loop was attached to the hilt of a short wooden handle. On top of the handle sat a short metal pipe maybe a foot long with what looked like a tab on top and a trigger on the bottom. He pulled back the tab, never taking his eyes off me.

"For the last time, Troy. Say you will join me, or choose to die right..."

His sentence was never finished. A few inches below his chin and a little to the right of center of his chest, the tip of an arrow suddenly emerged, dripping warm blood on the cool marble floor of the foyer. Eliab's eyes opened so wide that it looked as if they might pop out of his skull. He looked down at the thing sticking out of his chest. He looked bewildered, as if wondering where that thing came from, and then, he looked at me. He dropped his sword, slowly sunk to his knees, and then, collapsed face down on the floor. I looked beyond where Eliab had been standing and saw Connie in the entrance to the great room that was beyond the foyer. She stood with a bow in her left hand. When the point of the arrow exited Eliab's chest, his reflexes pulled on the trigger of the object he was pointing at me. A loud explosion took place like I had heard outside coming from the man who tried to kill me while I was still in my tree. I saw smoke exit the end of the small pipe he was holding, but I didn't see the lead ball that the explosion sent towards me. I felt it, though. The ball missed my body but plowed a small furrow across my left cheek and jaw. Connie's arrow not only killed Eliab but caused his aim to move just enough to only wound, but not kill me.

I looked at Connie and nodded thank you.

"Connie, go check on Pagiel. See if he still lives. I'm going to check on Dania and the boys."

I cannot describe those moments when I turned to go up the stairs. I remember them clearly, though. It's just that what I felt, there are no words for them in any language I know. I did not race up the stairs; I could not. My trembling legs would not allow that. It took all my concentration to remain upright on legs I could barely feel. I did not want to go anyway. The longer it took to get to the top, the longer my family may still be alive. I expected the worst and I tried to prepare myself for the worst. I paused outside the open door into our room. I heard no other noise coming from it. Only the sound of Troy whimpering in the room next door. I would see him later, I told myself, first, I must see Dania and Jaleel. I must make sure they are alright before I check on Troy. I would first hold them and tell them how much I loved them. I stepped through the door and looked inside the room, and I saw what I expected to see, but did not want to see.

To my horror, lying on the floor, in front of the window that looked out onto a beautiful and peaceful view of a well-kept garden, was my wife, my Dania. Her eyes were wide open, and she looked like she had just laid down for a nap but thought of something before she tried to sleep. Laying a few feet from her was Jaleel, my little eight-year-old son who looked just like his mother. I walked over to them and knelt beside them for one last time. I leaned against the window and put Dania's head in my lap and stroked her hair, making sure her shiny dark hair hung just right; then, closed her eyes with my fingertips. I pulled my little son up onto Dania's lap, and we all sat there together. The warmth of their bodies slowly turned cold; their spirits having left for their final resting place in eternity. I silently wept. The pain of my loss hurt far more than the new scar on my face. All the good memories we shared together raced into my mind, vying for space for me to think and dwell upon. The three of us sat on the floor in another man's home far from our own. We sat together one last time. If we had attacked the enemy at their campsite, this wouldn't have happened. It was my fault my wife and son were dead. My mistake had killed them. I would have to bear the heavy load of guilt for the rest of my life.

I got very angry. Not at Eliab, but at myself. Again, I considered falling on my sword, but I could not do that to Connie and Carl. And Troy. I no longer really cared about the Ashkenazim. I had spent too much currency on them. *What was I to do now?* I thought. I stayed sitting there for a long while. Troy finally quieted down next door and probably went to sleep. After a while, Connie came upstairs and, behind her, were Carl and Gerald. They removed my son, then, my wife, and carried them downstairs. They said nothing, I did not protest, and I did not get up. My sins had caught up to me. I believed in my wounded heart that God was punishing me for what I had done in my life and for what I was going to do. Even though I believed the vision I had, it had even convinced me I was doing his will, yet, I believed, as I sat brooding, he would not allow the killing of his people without consequences. Pagiel had been right. Oh, there had been consequences.

Finally, when my legs went to sleep, I had to get up and face the rest of the day. I did not have the luxury of doing nothing. I looked at the crimson blood that pooled on the floor that was slowly drying. Antonio would not like that on his bedroom floor, I absentmindedly thought. First, I went next door to look in on Troy, but he was not on his pallet. Connie must have seen to him, God bless her. I went downstairs on weak and wobbly legs. I saw my four guards standing by the front door, and they looked solemn because they knew what had happened but were too afraid to say anything. They had become like my family, too. Spilling of blood together creates a strong and an unnatural bond between fighting men. Connie and Carl were not there, but wounded Gerald stood with them. There was also another man standing among my men, one I did not recognize. *He must be a hostage,* I thought.

He would account for the last of the sixteen men Pagiel said would come, the first bit of good news, the kind of news that was the stingiest of all. The stranger would also bear the brunt of my anguish.

"Who do we have here?" I asked no one in particular.

"We caught him trying to sneak off and he begged for his life," Cosimo said. "Clearly, he isn't much of a fighter."

"What is your name?" I asked him. Rage boiled up to the surface and I wanted to slap him down, and then, beat him to death with my fists, but common sense prevailed, and I waited for him to answer.

"My real name is Eliasaph, but you might know me as Francois Mitterand Laurent. I appeal to your sense of morality and spare my life."

Chapter Ten

Retribution Against Francois

*I count him braver who overcomes his desires than him who conquers
his enemies. For the hardest victory is over self*
—Aristotle

I am writing this story in my lonely parlor at Goodrich
Castle where I do all my correspondence. Paintings of all
my wives and children hang above me on the walls like a
memorial to the dead because they are no longer in this life. In
the next few paragraphs, it might seem to anyone who reads
this, my last winter story, as being callous and cruel. Maybe
you would be correct. Up until I saw my dead wife and son
lying in each of their own pools of blood, I was not such a
person. Connie and Carl would attest to that. The sight of my
family lying in my lap, dead, triggered in me a change. Like a
great demonic moth emerging from a horrendous chrysalis, a
monster was set free, not unlike the demons that once were
released from within me when I was threatened by danger.
I was like the legendary Kraken freed from the constraints
that had held him in the depths of the sea by Poseidon. For a

while, at least, I was simply a willing human tool in the hands of a wrathful God who wanted justice against his people who, once again, rebelled against his authority. Now, I had become something men fear. It would take a long while to emerge from the rage and hatred's black veil covering my heart.

When the man standing in front of me in the foyer told me his name, a thousand thoughts came into my head. The first thing I thought about was revenge. Francois would be a perfect target to take my vengeance out on. Rational thinking, though, prevailed and I knew I needed information from him. Once I got that, then, I would kill him, and it would not be an easy death. He appealed to my sense of morality, and I spared him. I wanted to laugh out loud. He and his ilk had murdered a woman and her child, and he asked me to appeal to my morality. Not going to happen.

The evening of the day we battled our enemy, and prevailed, we buried Dania and Jaleel near the shore of the lake. I dug the hole myself. I laid Dania down inside the cold, damp hole upon a thick blanket. I placed Jaleel, I couldn't call him Jay anymore, it seemed too contrite or disrespectful, against Dania's bosom. I placed her arm around her son who looked so like her. I laid them facing towards the water and placed a silken sheet over them both. I put a note in her cold, stiff hand telling her of my love. Dania loved the water. Until she married me, and we left Egypt, she had never seen a body of water larger than her bathtub. My four guards, Connie, Carl, Gerald, even Pagiel, and I stood next to the grave's edge and looked down upon them one last time. I wanted to say a few words, but I knew, if I did, I would begin crying and I swore I would never cry again. Monsters don't cry; they just get even. As it had in uncountable times in the past, ever since the day it swallowed Abel, the cursed ground opened its hungry mouth to receive two more bodies. From dust, they came from, and, to dust, they shall return. Will the ground ever say to us, "Enough, I've had enough, give me no more of your dead offerings?" Finally, Connie said a few things, words that I cannot remember because I wasn't listening. I was thinking of glory days when my wife and I laughed together at nonsensical things. When we would spread a blanket on the leaves among primeval trees and make love together in the forest near our home. When it came time to shovel dirt upon their peaceful faces, I turned away and let the others do that deed. I had a man to interrogate, and he would not like what I was about to do to him.

My hostage was in the small house that the gardener stayed in when he was working the grounds. He was bound tight and was not able to escape. Attached to the house was a shed with various garden implements. I gathered a few of them that would make handy motivation tools when I questioned Francois. They would get his attention.

"Cosimo," I asked before we went inside the house, "are you squeamish? Does the sight of blood make you sick? Because, if it does, before I start convincing our hostage he needs to talk, you might want to leave."

He only shrugged, so I would let him decide on when he wanted to leave, and I was sure he would.

"Cosimo, strip all his clothes off and tie his hands to that beam up there and tie his ankles, one to that table and the other to that post. Then, I think you should leave. Wait outside and don't let anyone enter. If anyone comes in, I will hold you responsible. Understand?"

"Now, Francois, I hope you don't mind that I call you that

name, since it is Francois that got me started on this path to hell that I stupidly followed. You know what that place called hell is, don't you, Francois? I'm sure you do since you are a Jew. Although you probably know it as Sheol or Hades, depending on whether you prefer Hebrew or Greek. Well, before this day is through, you most probably will see it firsthand, and you can ask the devil what name he calls it by."

His face was very red. I didn't know if it was because of anger or simply embarrassment since he stood spread-legged stark naked. I guessed he was maybe sixty years old, maybe sixty-five. He was in good condition and appeared healthy, with good teeth and a full head of hair that was streaked with a few strands of white. I was glad he was healthy. He would last longer. I would hate for him to die so easily.

"Francois, inside your throat is a box, and that is where we create sounds when we talk. It allows us to sing, make laughing sounds, and to communicate. It is used to tell our family we love them or tell our enemies we want to kill them. It is also where screams come from. I have heard of men who screamed so loud, for so long, that the box ruptured. It actually ruptured. They were no longer able to talk or utter a sound afterwards. To be honest, I don't know if voice boxes can rupture. Maybe it is because the pain is so great that their minds permanently lose the ability to form words any longer. Either way, most probably that will happen to you. I hope so because screaming people annoy me. Before I begin my interrogation, I want to give you a chance to tell me everything I want to know. In fact, I want you to go with me to the Armenian colony where I wish to talk with your High Priest. He is the face of my enemy. I want you as part of the team that will convince him to call off the plan to take over lands that do not belong to your nation, nor does God want you to take it over. Will you help me? Will you answer all my questions? At first, you will refuse, of course; then, as the pain gets worse, you will start lying. Men can be so obstinate. If you lie to me, well, you won't like what I will do to you then. So, what will it be?"

I must give Francois credit. He was brave enough to give me a sneer. Oh, that was good, I thought; that is how I wanted it to begin!

He arrogantly said, "I have sworn, as has everyone among my people, that we would never give an outsider information about what we are to do. It would be treason and cowardly to say anything. You can do whatever you think you must do, but I will not help you. I will die before I say anything to you."

I backhanded him hard against his soft mouth, then said, "That's good, Francois. That is exactly what I hoped you would say. Dying is easy. It is how you will die that you must fear. I will give you a little background first before we begin. I have lived with the Mongols in the far east and seen their means of interrogation, and I have witnessed what certain tribes of Africa do to people they don't like. You can't imagine the pain one feels when their skin is removed in sheets. I have learned the art of asking questions while convincing bad boys like you to cooperate. Of course, even if you spill your guts with me right now, even before we begin, I must exact some torment on you simply because your people are responsible for the deaths of my family and several of my servants. Also, when I return to England, I promise I will visit your estate where I will do terrible things to your wife, your daughter, and your granddaughter. Your property, and all that you own, will become mine to do with as I wish."

That promise did cause his face to lose some of its resolve, but he still wasn't convinced I was the monster I really was. His mind could not conceive of what I had become.

"Okay, then, last chance before we begin the long journey to your change of heart. You will, of course, change your mind no matter how tough you think you are. I suppose I will at least tell you some of the things I'm going to do to you, so you can better make an informed decision on helping me. I will state some things, but they will not necessarily be all that I will do. I will remove the fingers on your right hand, so that you can't wield a sword against me or my family anymore. Your right hand is the predominant hand, isn't it? No matter, I will take the fingers off your left hand, as well, just to be sure. I will do that whether you answer me or not because you must pay your debt to me. I will also do something to you that I have never personally done myself, but I have heard it is often used in Japan against someone who hesitates in telling what the inquisitor wishes to know. Now, listen closely Francois because this could be your future very soon. I will make a cage that fits over your head and rests on your shoulders. Inside this cage, I will place two very hungry and large rats. These rats will begin eating the easy, fleshy parts of your head at first: lips, nose, ears, and eyes. I will first stuff a rag in your mouth, so you won't scare the rats and I won't have to hear the screams before either your voice box ruptures, or your mind stops working. Eventually, you will either tell me what I wish to know, or you will be insane, or you will be dead. Then, I will tie your naked body against a tree by the edge of the woods and let the crows peck at what's left of your head, and the wolves will come and eat other parts of you until there is nothing left of you and your soul will be in Sheol. Your body, or what is left of it, will stay tied to the tree to rot. Somewhere in the middle of all that will be when your sound box in your throat will have given out, or your mind will have turned to porridge, and you will no longer scream, thankfully. How does that sound to you, Francois? Are you ready? I am."

About three-fourths of the way through my spiel, Francois lost control of his bladder and bowels. I reckoned I was getting to him by then.

"Just to let you know," I continued, "I have made these threats before to other obstinate men. Sadly, I've never had to do many of those things. People have always been able to see in my face, the resolve in it, and they knew I would do exactly as I have said. Will you be one of those? I'd rather you answer my questions because, otherwise, we both are in for a long night, and I hate getting my clothes so messy."

I saw the set of his jaw, the clinch of his teeth relaxed just the slightest amount. The lines above his eyebrows dropped at the corners almost imperceptibly, but enough that gave me some hope he would help, and I would not be forced to do all those terrible things I threatened. Oh, but I would do it without remorse and, in fact, I would be a little disappointed if I couldn't give him some amount of pain to lessen the pain that ached in my heart and mind.

I picked up the gardener's pruning shears in preparation for removing his fingers and walked over to him, placing his thumb between the shears' blades.

"Francois," I said when my hatred subsided just for a moment, "I do not wish to destroy your people. You all can live above or below ground in contentment; I don't care. I just want two things. One, I want you and your kind, from England to Jerusalem, to leave my family and me alone. I do not want to hide or look behind me for the rest of my days, waiting for your breed to ambush me. Secondly, I want you and all the Ashkenazim to give up this insane idea of domination of people and lands God did not ordain for you to control, in fact, does not want you to control. Going through with your plans is in direct contradiction of what Jehovah, or Adonai, has said in the Torah."

"How would you know what the Torah says, you pagan?"

I removed the shears long enough to tell him, "I have read the Torah many times, you arrogant swine. I've read the holy book from Genesis to Malachi, the thirty-nine books you recognize as having been written by the prophets. Tell me, Francois, have you read the Torah? Have you read Deuteronomy? Have you read Joshua? I have many times, and I can quote them to you."

By the way he looked at me, I could tell he had not, and I was bewildered as to why. Why would he not know it almost by heart? I was a monk apprentice for eleven months and, during that time, I copied the Torah, as well as all sixty-six books in the Old and New Testament and, with my ability to remember nearly everything I read or saw, I knew most of it by heart.

"Only the rabbis are allowed to read the holy words of the Torah," he said. "Those first five books of the prophets are sacred to my people. Our creator's names are in the books written by the holy prophets, and it is forbidden for us to not only speak his name, but to read them, as well. Pagans like you do not care about respect and have no qualms about speaking the name of YHWH."

His impudence earned him another backhand across his mouth. Light was beginning to reveal itself in my mind.

Just as the early church did not allow the common people to read Scripture, only the priests could and, so, only the church leadership knew what the Bible said. The people were at the whim of many corrupt men calling themselves priests. These underground Ashkenazim, like Francois, were just as ignorant of what the Bible actually said. It was time for a Bible lesson. Changes in a nation sometimes begin with the education of one person. Marcus Aurelius once told his students, "If someone can prove me wrong and show me my mistake in any thought or action, I shall gladly change. I seek truth, which never harmed anyone." I have lived my life by that axiom, but I was having a difficult time convincing Francois that, sometimes, change is necessary, even preferred. He was obstinate and filled with a false sense of pride. His pride would be the death of him.

"Francois, let me give you a little Bible lesson. Moses wrote in the book of Deuteronomy, 'When you go over the Jordan, and dwell in the land which the LORD your God gives you to inherit, and when he gives you rest from all your enemies round about, you will dwell in safety.' Notice it says the Jordan. Furthermore, that same book states, 'Every place the soles of your feet shall tread, shall be yours, from the wilderness and Lebanon, from the river Euphrates, even unto the uttermost sea shall your coast be.' That coast, Francois, is the Mediterranean Sea, and the Euphrates is many miles east of the Jordan. God did not give your people England nor any part of Europe. You and all the Ashkenazim have no right to the ground your naked feet are standing on. You and your kind have been fed a lie for these past centuries by the same kind of people the Pharisees were back in the days of Jesus. That sect just wanted power and praise. You are fighting a fight you can't win, because you are defying God in your misguided efforts. Because of your ignorance of God's commands, I am about to cause you more pain than you can imagine."

Francois still hung by his hands from an overhead beam. I could see his hands were turning purple from lack of blood circulation. All around his feet were liquid feces and urine. Under other circumstances, I would have felt pity for the man, but the memory of Dania's head laying in my lap and the sight of Jaleel's dead hand in mine, did not permit any remorse to exist in my mind. A part of me wanted the kind of help someone like Francois could give us in our quest, but an even larger part of me wanted him to remain obstinate and tell me nothing, so that I could enact judgment on him. My transformation into a remorseless and amoral person was changing me into someone worse than I was when I had actual demons within me.

I put one of his fingers back in between the shears, about to sever it. I wasn't sure he had heard anything I said, but he had. "How can I know for sure what you are telling me? You could say anything to get me to tell you what you want. And why would our rabbis lie to us? Dozens of rabbis over the long history of our people and across the land from England to Israel have all said we must take what God has given us."

"Yes, you should have taken what God gave you when your people came out of Egypt. That was nearly three thousand years ago. You didn't because your people were lazy and cowardly and were afraid of the powerful people in the land flowing with milk and honey. They intentionally defied the commandments of God. Today, you will not win God's favor by taking what he never told you to take. I can prove what I have said is true by reading the prophets to you. I always bring a copy of the New Covenant with me everywhere I go, but I don't have a Torah with me, but I know where I can find one. If I got a copy of the Old Covenant, would you accept it as the truth? Would it convince you of what I have been telling you? If so, would you then help me convince the High Priest to stop pursuing us and the madness he endorses?"

I could see Francois was weighing having his manhood cut off in addition to other pieces of body parts removed, with believing what he was told all his life was wrong. A mental battle was waging war in his head. And in me, also. Part of me still wanted him to refuse to answer my questions, so that I could effectively kill him, but the part of me that wanted the Ashkenazim to leave me and my family alone, convinced me to use rational thinking and try to gain his assistance.

"I can't think. I need some time to digest what you have said. I don't mind dying for what I believe to be true. I would even endure the torture you've mentioned instead of betraying my people. If we are wrong and you can prove we are wrong, I will help you. Please let me down and let me clean myself up; then, show me your proof."

I believed, in the depths of my heart, he was just buying time, but I had to give him the benefit of my doubts, at least for a while. "I will get you that proof tomorrow. I think you should know that I want the information you can give us, but you should also know that doing the things I have mentioned would be no hardship on my part, and the reason is, Eliab, one of your generals killed my wife and my son today. The very man who told me many of your hallowed secrets. I must hold you responsible for those murders since Eliab is now dead. You understand that I must take an eye for an eye? Isn't that what the prophets tell us?"

He said nothing; only nodded. I opened the door and told Cosimo to untie Francois and watch over him. "Get Luca and Enzo to relieve you and, if you must, let Carl or me know if more help is needed. Tie his hands together, and then, his body against the post after he cleans himself up. Under no circumstances is he to leave this room unless I tell you, personally, that he can."

When I left Cosimo, and walked out of the guest house, it was dark, and a light, cool mist was falling. I could only find my way to the main house from the light shining from within. I paused outside the front door and let the water drip from my beard onto the porch's stone floor. The water was dripping red from the blood that had seeped into my beard. The weight of the day pulled at my heart, and I sat down and, despite my will not to cry, I wept bitterly. I was so angry and so very sad. The two emotions broke me down, and I wanted to take revenge on someone or something. I knew that wasn't a rational thing to do, and I willed myself to calm my shattered nerves before I went inside and talked to Carl, Connie, and especially Kat and Troy. I had to act like a man and be a father to them. I had to set pride and my personal emotions aside for the sake of my family. I had made enough mistakes in raising them to convince me to not let me make more mistakes that night.

When I went inside, everyone was sitting around the large table in the kitchen. I smelled a soup of some kind being prepared on the large brick oven. Connie was stirring two steaming pots, and I smelled bread being made, also. If my heart hadn't been hurting so much, I would have smiled at the scene with family and friends altogether in one room. Pagiel was also at the table and, for the first time that afternoon,

I fully registered that he had been spared by Eliab's sword when he attacked my wife and son. I sat down at the table, and Gerald set a cup of water in front of me. I hadn't realized how thirsty I was. I drank two more cups of water before I said anything. No one else spoke a word, either. I think they were afraid to say anything until they could assess my mood. My mood was very dark, too.

Finally, shaking off my petulant temperament, I got up from the table and spoke.

"All of this, all the deaths, all the wounds you have suffered, all the displacement from your comfortable homes, has all been the result of my imprudence. For that, I'm sorry, but I can't change any of that now. The fact remains that we must stop what the High Priest and his Ashkenazim people plan to do. In a couple days or so, I will leave for Armenia in hopes of putting a stop to their madness. To stop them is also to stop their pursuit of us. I will go alone if need be and, hopefully, Francois will be going, also. None of you are obliged to go with me. You can stay here for as long as you wish, probably until next spring anyway. I have put you in enough pain and inconvenience already. No need to tell me of your plans tonight, but you should decide by tomorrow night. I plan to leave soon after.

Only small talk was made during the meal if any words were spoken at all. That made me angry, too. Why couldn't they talk like family and friends are supposed to talk? I felt like a pariah. Kat sat next to me and silently wept. She ate very little, mostly stirring her soup, lost in her own thoughts. Her mother and her playmate brother were both gone and thus her world was violently changed. Troy was asleep upstairs. My whole world was upside down also; so different than it was only three months ago. *Dear God help me*, I thought.

After our solemn dinner, I checked on Cosimo and Francois and made sure he would be relieved in a couple hours. I brought both some soup and bread. When I went to my room, both Kat and Troy were in my bed, both asleep. I laid down on the floor next to where they slept and tried to sleep myself. I was so very tired, but my mind wasn't ready to turn off. I saw Dania in my lap and Jaleel lying next to us. I saw Eliab's wide eyes staring at me when an arrow emerged from his chest. Fighting, dying, men moaning, blades clashing, sounds of explosions, Francois fowling himself. All those things played out in my mind's eye repeatedly, and I could not stop them. A long time after midnight, I finally slept.

I woke with a start when I heard a knock on the door. The gray dawn of the day shone through the window when I opened the door. It was Connie.

"I'm taking Catherine Adele and Troy, and we will be leaving for England this morning."

I started to protest, but she stopped me.

"You know you can't bring them to Armenia. You must let me take them back to England and take care of them. I don't want to stay here, so far from home. Our company needs me, and I need the company's work to keep me sane. I will take care of your children as if they were my very own. You know it's the right thing to do. I can protect them if I must hire an army. If I haven't heard from you in three months' time, I am going to King Edward and tell him what has happened and what will happen. I will leave it up to him to take care of the situation in England. I just wanted you to know. Also, I want to bring Luca with us."

"Luca? Why him? Of course, you need some kind of

protection and help with the children. I should have thought of that myself, but why Luca?"

"Luca can read, for one thing. Something the other three can't do or do well. Also, he has all his teeth, he has been kind to me, he has no family to go back to, and he likes the children."

"I see," I said. I had some thoughts about what other reasons might be but kept them to myself. "Yes, Luca is a good choice, but would he agree to go all the way to England with you, him not knowing the English language?"

"I will teach him our language on the way. Thankfully, I know his language well from frequent business dealings with the Roman home office. I think he will learn it readily enough. I have already asked him if he would help us return to England, and he has agreed. Another reason I want him to go is that I wish for him to prepare and train a group of guardians for our company and your children and me, in the event more of the Jews come looking for us."

"Good thoughts, Connie. I'm proud of you and your ability to see things that need taking care of when my mind is bogged down in grief and thoughts of what to do next."

I hugged her and watched her walk away, so pleased she was a born leader. I couldn't drag my young children on the crazy journey I was on. I wondered if it was wise, though, to return to England yet. Surely, more Ashkenazim would show up at the office. She would need an army to protect her but, in my tired mind, I believed I would resolve the danger once I met with the High Priest. I was that naïve.

The first thing I did after going downstairs was to peek into Pagiel's room to make sure he was still all right. His breathing was normal, so I left his room and went out to the guest house. Luca was outside the door relieving himself when I walked up. He sheepishly smiled and said there were no incidents or problems during the night. Francois slept fitfully, sitting up next to the post he was tied to. I promised to bring them some food shortly and went back outside. Before going back into the villa, I went down to the lake where Dania and Jaleel slept, waiting for judgment day to arrive. I knelt and removed a few leaves that had fallen on the fresh dirt covering their bodies and spoke silent words to them both. They were not the first of my family to die, but they were the first to die because of my mistakes. Not just because of my actions, they died, but they died violently and that tore at my heart and soul. Larks and other songbirds sang a chorus of music to accompany my thoughts. A single tear dropped and watered the hallowed and fresh turned soil. I promised both that I would make sure those who were ultimately responsible for their deaths would pay dearly for their crimes. I was not innocent of their deaths, and I would have to pay my debt, also. I would pay by blaming myself for the rest of my pitiful life.

When I entered the kitchen, everyone was stirring around setting the table, helping with plates, knives, forks, and doing busy work as if nothing had happened. Life was beginning again for them. It was a new day, the first day in their new future. It was as it should be. I would carry my own burden close to me and try not to have them help carry it.

I replaced the bandages on Gerald and Carlos' wounds from the day before, as well as Pagiel's. Pagiel's wound was healing properly, and it no longer had signs of corruption. Gerald and Carlos's wounds were very painful to them, having been made worse by the digging I had to do in their flesh to remove the lead ball inside them. Unless blood disorders became an issue, they would survive the wounds, I was sure.

Luca was still with Francois, and would soon be leaving us, but the others, Carl, Gerald, and the three other mercenaries, volunteered to go with me to Armenia. I had not yet asked Pagiel what he wanted to do. I wanted him with us, but his stab wounds were still grievous, and I hated to be so selfish as to jeopardize his health further. Even though the rest of them also had wounds of varying degrees, they still said they would go and do what I thought was needed. The details of what was needed, though, I had yet no idea.

Chapter Eleven

A Trip to a Synagogue

Truth is not what you want it to be, it is what it is, and you must bend to its power or live a lie
—Miyanmoto Musashi

The last of the fourteen dead Jews had been weighted down with stones, placed in the skiff, rowed out to the middle of the small lake, and dumped overboard. They would become turtle food. It was hard not to hate them; they were only doing what they were sworn to do, and they weren't the ones who killed my wife and son. There was one body that I wouldn't allow to be buried in the lake. Eliab did not deserve to be buried with the others, and I had him stripped of all his clothes, brought well inside the forest, and tied standing upright against a tree. I wanted the ravages of animals and time to slowly rid the world of the man who changed my life so drastically. My anguish knew no bounds.

While Connie prepared for her and the children to leave, some of the men finished disposing of our attackers, and made repairs to damages done to the villa in the battle and cleaned the floors of blood. I saddled two horses for Francois and me to ride to Rome. I did not trust him not to either kill himself or run away, so I tied his feet to the stirrups and his stirrups to the pommel of my saddle as we left mid-morning for the two-and-a-half-hour ride back to Rome. I had told him I knew where I could find a Torah to prove to him that he and his people had been lied to by generations of rabbis. I knew of a Jewish synagogue that once was in Rome from previous trips, and I hoped it would still be there.

On the road to the city, I told Francois about how I discovered his journal in his library that mentioned his people and their plan, about my visits with his wife concerning devil worshipping in my forest, and what I had read in Scripture concerning the Jew's promised land. Francois spoke very little, maybe out of anger with me, or himself, for betraying his people with that journal, or his distrust of what I was saying. My inference of me finding his journal was strongly made so that he would understand that all that was happening was, in a large part, due to him. He was the one who created the journal and did not protect it properly from eyes that weren't allowed to see it.

From previous discussions with Eliab and Pagiel, I learned that he and the people in his English colony spoke primarily Hebrew, but all the Ashkenazim of each colony learned the language spoken by the people under which their colony existed. Francois could speak Hebrew and English and because, he formerly lived in Normandy, French, also. One attribute I appreciated about the Ashkenazim was their intelligence. Their ability to speak multiple languages, their dedication to a common goal, and their ingenuity were remarkable. Three things that also made them a dangerous adversary.

It was fortunate that the synagogue was still where I had remembered it to be. It was also fortunate that it was Wednesday, rather than the sabbath, and the rabbi was present and available to talk to us. I explained that the man with me (I had removed the bindings from his hands just for the meeting) was a devout Jew but had not had the opportunity to read the Torah or any part of the writings of the ancient prophets. In fact, his rabbis forbid the reading of the prophets for fear they would read out loud the name of God. Not even to speak the name, YHWH, which Christians knew as Yahweh.

The rabbi seemed to understand the conservative stance the Ashkenazi rabbis took in not saying the name in any form. That was typical of all Jews, but he saw no reason to forbid them to read the prophets. Jews must be able to understand God's purpose for them, which can only come by the study of the old writings. The rabbi we spoke to, Rabbi Eliakim, said he didn't know what the rabbis called God where he came from, but he uses the name Adonai, meaning "My Lord", in place of God's name.

"Rabbi," I said, "one point my friend here, Eliasaph, would most like to know is what areas constitute the land promised by Adonai to the descendants of Abraham, Isaac, and Jacob, the land Moses and Joshua were to take.

"The land promised to Abraham is the land of Canaan," the rabbi began. He said, "Here, I can show you where it is on a map of the land."

Rabbi Eliakim walked over to shelves holding parchment scrolls and pulled out one that was an old yellowed-with-age map on scraped parchment skin that he slowly unrolled. Outlined by a bold line to give definition to the area was the vast area that Abraham was promised millennia ago. The map showed the western boundary beginning from Cairo, south to Abu Simbel in Egypt, north to above Syria to Armenia, and east to Persia and the Persian Sea.

I looked at Francois' face to see if I could see comprehension or apprehension. The rabbi spoke to us in Hebrew, and I knew Francois could understand what was being said. The look on his face was one of astonishment. The wrinkle of his forehead and the half-closed eyes told me he was feeling a profound disappointment, because he was being told his whole world had been all a lie. The set of his mouth, his lips forced together in thin lines revealed his growing anger. He wanted the lie to be true. He wanted it so much so, I was sure, he didn't care if it was a lie.

"Rabbi," I said, "would you read in the holy scripture where it describes the area?"

As I knew he would, he read aloud several passages from the Torah in Genesis, Deuteronomy, and Joshua that described the area we could see on the old map.

"Are there any other lands that some Jewish rabbis might think could be included in this area? For instance, could there be any land in the Kingdom of Italy, any of the Holy Roman Empire and beyond? Could there possibly be part of the land promised to Abraham and his descendants that is not described in Scripture? Is it possible that the originators of the Talmud could somehow have interpreted the area to be different than what was described in the verses you just read?"

"No, there are no other lands besides what you see on this map that Adonai promised to give to the people of Israel. Sadly, very little of that land was ever conquered and, today, we don't even have Jerusalem or a temple anymore. We are a rebellious people and, too often, as a nation, we follow other gods created by man and, because of that, we have been dispersed to all parts of the world. Here I am in Rome, rather than in Israel. We are not really a nation anymore but, someday, I know we will once again have a temple on the holy mount Moriah where Abraham was to offer Isaac as a sacrifice. Maybe next year, maybe a thousand years from now, but, one day, we will."

"Eliasaph, do you have any questions for the rabbi? Did you understand what he told us?

He asked, "Do you think Adonai would bless his chosen people, or punish us if we tried to take over lands by force that are not part of this area we were promised?"

"It is not difficult for me to answer your question but may be difficult for you to accept. The prophets speak a great deal about our ancestors who went against great odds and won the battles, but Adonai gave instructions that our people were to go against the enemy in those events, because they worshipped foreign gods, or they, such as the Canaanites, wanted to annihilate Israel. In cases where Adonai did not command his people to make war, and our fathers attacked, even with odds on their sides, they were devastated. I have read the prophets from Moses to Malachi. I know the sacred text almost by heart, and I know of no lands Adonai wanted his chosen people to acquire other than the land promised to Abraham. If the papal states, which Rome is a part of, for instance, were attacked by a large army of Jews, I believe they would not succeed. However, I must add this clarification. The Holy Roman Empire, which extends east to the Baltic Sea and west nearly to the coast of the great ocean, cannot be categorized as a pagan state. If it were, then perhaps Adonai would not punish his chosen for brashly invading the territory. To take over nations that are not the enemy of Adonai, I think, would have very grave consequences for the invaders. Adonai's wrath is a terrible thing to fall under. You know of plans to do such a thing?"

Giving a slight chuckle as if to dismiss the idea, to remove any alarm about what he might think, I said, "No, rabbi, no such invasion will happen. It's just that Eliasaph has overheard a band of young and bored zealots, who like to beat the war drums and pound their chests about taking control of lands, simply to impress their women friends. The idea is too incredulous to even think about. I just wanted my friend to hear what a learned man, such as yourself, had to say about people, even those from God's chosen race, who do not really care about God's will but, rather, desire to seek fortune, power, and fame."

"Anything else Eliasaph?"

"No. I think not."

I knew that look on Francois' face. I have seen it many times in many countries. I've seen it in my children's faces when they were denied their favorite treat. When a person's greatest hope is suddenly and irrevocably taken away, they have that look. In Francois' case, he had been an important operative in a program that would have global consequences and would, if successful, make him a historical figure among his nation. That future for him dissolved as the rabbi said the same thing I had already described. Everything he knew in life, his very purpose for his existence, suddenly disappeared.

I thanked the rabbi and dropped a few coins in the alms box, and we left to return to the villa. It was an awkward ride back since Francois was in a dark mood. Nevertheless, I had no time for a brooding prisoner. Since I still did not trust him, he was still constrained by bindings, so that he could not escape. I let three quarters of an hour pass by with him sulking and letting him digest his future, but that was all the time I could afford to give him.

"Francois, you've heard the truth. You've been lied to by your High Priest, so what are you going to do? Are you going to help us, or will I have to kill you very, very slowly?"

"I would like to go back to my colony and confront my rabbi there to get his opinion of what I have just heard. I want to bring back a copy of the Torah with me and show him what I have been shown. If you take me back home, I promise I will convince him to leave you and your family alone. You won't have to worry about attacks from us anymore."

"That's nice of you to offer that, Francois, but this idea, this goal of your people, is bigger than me and my family. It is bigger than you are, also. It must be stopped from England to Armenia. You can give me no guarantees that your rabbi will believe what you tell him, or care what you think. Most probably, you will be killed within an hour of revealing what you have learned. No, Francois, you will help me stop the mass killing of innocent people by your own people, who have been deluded by centuries of lies. It is imperative you help me stop what your High Priest is doing and what he and his people are about to do. God will help me, even if you don't, and, if you don't help, you will not only have to endure what I will do, but you will also have to give an account to God when I'm finished with you. I suggest you stop feeling sorry for yourself and join us to stop a global disaster. It will be a disaster, not only for the people you will be trying to overcome, but also for you own people, who will suffer the wrath of an unforgiving God."

We rode on for another quarter hour and I began to grow angry, so angry I wanted to thrust my sword through his neck and waste no more time trying to convince him of his folly. Besides, the torture I was going to put him through would be very time-consuming. When the fifteen people we had killed did not show up in a day or two, those who sent them most probably send another group out to look for us. We needed to escape Rome by the next day, and I was growing increasingly anxious to leave. I desperately wanted the help Francois could give us if he could cast aside his years of indoctrination.

"Francois, we are running out of time. I need to know if you will help us and, when I say help us, I mean do whatever it takes to stop your High Priest's armies from invading Europe and England, as well as leaving my family and me alone. What is it going to be?"

"I don't seem to have much of a choice. Be tortured to death or help you."

"You aren't getting the point of the trip we just made to the synagogue. Your people are absolutely wrong in the path they are taking. You and your people have been duped. Not only will they fail, but they will die by the tens of thousands in the attempt to go against the will of your God, something no self-respecting Jew would ever do."

We rode on another hundred yards, and I was about to prod him again when he spoke.

"I will help you. You must understand how hard this is for me. My whole life seems to have been a mistake. All my dreams, my status as a leader, my reputation, everything will be wiped away."

"Don't look at it that way. Your reputation as a leader of a failed mission will be replaced with one as a man who helped save his people from annihilation. I would take that exchange any day."

"Are you still going to cut my fingers off anyway?"

I nearly smiled at his question but caught myself in time. "If you agree to help us in all we ask of you in our quest to end this madness and, if you tell me that you will help before we reach yon sycamore tree, then, I will not take off your fingers."

He sighed deeply and confirmed that he would help. His shoulders looked as if a huge weight had been placed on them.

"Okay," I said, "agreeing to help us means you will not try to escape from me because, if you do, there will not be a second chance when I catch up to you, and everything that I said I would do, I will do, no matter how much you beg me not to."

We rode on for a while, and then, he looked at me and nodded his head.

"Do you give me your solemn word to not run away and to help us? Do you swear on the name of your God whom you serve?"

Again, he nodded his head. Still, I would not trust him for a long time. Proof is in the practice of it.

When we arrived back at the villa, Connie had the wagon packed and ready to leave with my two little children. They were just waiting on my return to say goodbye but, before I could see them off, I had to discern what I should do about Pagiel. He was sitting in a wooden chair on the front porch. He was still pale, but some color was coming back.

"Pagiel, let's talk a bit. What do you want to do, my friend? Connie, Luca, and the children will be returning to England today, while the rest of us will be journeying on towards Armenia. Each has made their own mind up as to what they wished to do. I haven't heard what your wish is. Honestly, I wish you would go with us, because I need your insight, but you would be better off going with Connie and continue your healing along the way. I don't know what we will run into in the next weeks or months ahead of us. Maybe you do, or will know, but capture and death are likely outcomes, in my opinion, so you must decide today whom you will travel with."

I could see the anguish and battle going on in his mind, because it was reflected in his face. His eyebrows sagged and tried to meet in the middle. His lips had a slight tremble, and the corners of his eyes turned downward as he tried to describe his thoughts with words.

"Lord, I'm not a warrior as you and the others are. I cannot fight and I barely know which end of a sword to hold. My only talent, if that is what you want to call it, is seeing what might happen tomorrow, or next week. If that can salvage a win for you, I will go with you and be of what service I can. If you want to know what I would rather do, then, of course, it would be to go with your children. They, too, may be able to profit from my insight into the future. I will submit to your decision for me. I owe you my life and my future."

In my mind, I was still severely depressed with grief, tormented by what to do next since I did not have a plan, angry with the situation we were enduring and then, another disappointment hearing Pagiel did not want to travel with us. He was right, of course. Logic said he should travel back to England with Connie, rather than face the hardships and the danger ahead of us. Still, I wanted every edge I could get, and he had given me such edges in previous weeks. Anger and greed blinded my judgment. I would rather Connie and my other children be safer than me, even though Carl and Gerald would suffer the same fate as me, most likely.

"Of course, Pagiel, you should go with the children back to England. You can be of great service to them. I am forever grateful for what you have done for me and the others with your abilities. Thank you for your help, and I'm sorry you had to be so grievously wounded on my account. I hope you will continue to be of service to Connie long after your arrival back in London."

With that said, Pagiel gathered up a few things he had with him, tied them up inside a cloth bundle, walked over to the wagon, and set himself down opposite Kat.

Connie sat in the front wagon seat holding Troy in her lap, and Kat and Pagiel were in the back with what supplies they had. Luca had not yet climbed up and taken the reins, so I asked him to come with me for a few moments. Out of earshot of anyone besides the two of us, I gave him some parting advice.

"Luca, you are tasked   with transporting three people who mean more to me than my own breath, my own heartbeat. Connie trusts you, and it was her idea for you to assist her on the way home. Therefore, I must trust you, as well. There is a lot of responsibility placed on you now, more than you realize. I am obliged to tell you that, when I get back to England, and find my family is not, or that they have been harmed in any way by you or by your negligence, I will hunt you down if it takes the rest of my life and exact a special punishment. Do you understand what I am telling you, Luca? Don't just nod your head. I want to hear the words come out of your mouth."

"Yes, lord, I understand, and I give you my blood oath that I will protect them with my life."

I placed a sizable bag of silver in his hand for payment covering the past weeks, and for the weeks it would take to get back to London. I was placing a great deal of trust in a man I did not know very well. When you fight to the death against an enemy, though, you somehow get to know their character. I felt some level of confidence that he would honor his oath.

Chapter Twelve

Return to Centumcellae and the New Mercenaries

Anyone who has the power to make you believe absurdities has the power to make you commit atrocities.
— Voltaire

We spent the next two days after Connie and her group left, finishing up with repairs to the villa caused by the battle, and bringing the horses we captured to Rome to sell, but Gerald and Carlos mostly rested from their wounds. The money we received from the sale of the horses was divided up amongst Carl, Gerald, and the men. I made Francois help us with our labors in place of the wounded men. He was sullen most of the day, and I had little hope that he wouldn't try to escape at the first opportunity, even though I threatened him with severe punishment if he tried.

Before Pagiel left with the others, I quizzed him to see if he had any insight as to what might happen concerning those returning to England, as well as those of us soon to be leaving for Armenia. He did, at least to some extent. He saw clearly that there would be some difficulty in leaving Centumcellae for both groups but, what the difficulty was, he was unsure of. I knew there would be danger, but what kind, I asked him. He reluctantly admitted that not all of us would survive, but he could not or would not tell me who wouldn't survive. I asked him if the quest we were on would be successful. He told me that he was sure that, in the end, the journey would be successful, but he would not say more, except that not everyone would survive.

"All I can tell you, all that I know for sure," he said, "is that you will survive and return to England. I can see you back there in your castle. I see there are others, some I don't know who they are, who will also return with you, but I can't see their faces, only a blur. I can see you, not so much by your face, but by your personal being. You are a strong and singular personality, and I can always make you out specifically because of your aura. There are weeks between now and when you arrive at your destination and, being that far ahead, I can't be sure of the entire outcome. There will be problems along the way for both of us, and you must be prepared for what lies ahead. I see death ahead even before you get to Armenia. I see your sword covered in blood once again. You must watch Francois very closely, because he will do whatever he can to thwart your efforts. You would be better served if you killed him today. Before you leave here tomorrow, I beg you to kill him. He will be a source of anguish for you if you don't."

I was disturbed and disappointed in what he said. I like definitive information, not muddied by a lack of details. There was also another question that had bothered me for the past two days. Pagiel had told me that we would survive the battle with the enemy at the villa, but there would be consequences. There certainly was but, if he knew what those consequences were, then, why didn't he tell me, so that I could have better protected my wife and son, and if so, was it possible to change the circumstances or outcome of what he saw?

"Yes, I assumed you would one day get around to asking me that question. I saw in my vision your countenance more than I saw the death of your wife and son. I saw your grief and anger because it was so vivid in my mind. I could not see who would die, but I knew there were going to be the deaths of someone very close to you. I did not know if it would be Connie or Carl or Dania or your children. If I had known specifically, I would have told you. I feared to say more than I did, because I believed it would have distracted you from what needed to be done to protect all of us. Sometimes, my visions are more specific than at other times, and I do not know the reason for that, unless my own emotions get in the way of what I see. I'm very sorry that I couldn't be more specific. You've no idea what your children have come to mean to me. If I had been free of my wounds, I would have stood outside their door and offered my dreadfully little help to protect them. It was a combination of my wounds and being unsure exactly what was going to happen that resulted in their deaths. All my life, I have forcibly ignored or brushed aside my visions, because I knew they were evil in the eyes of my people. I believe, now that I am free, my sight will improve as I nurture them, rather than disregard them. I would not blame you if you harbored ill will towards me for not giving you a better idea of what was going to happen. I wish I could have done more to help you. I am deeply ashamed of my people and what they have done and are hoping to do."

"I don't blame you, Pagiel. All the blame for all that's happened belongs to me. You have been a great asset, and I will be very unhappy to see you leave. I look forward to seeing you again in London. Take care of yourself and my family."

With that conversation over and my final farewell to Connie, Kat, little two-year-old Troy, and Luca given, they rode down the narrow road, back towards Rome. I watched them until they disappeared around a curve in the road. I hoped Pagiel was right, and that I would see them all again when my nightmare quest was over, if it is ever over.

While I was watching my family depart, Enzo approached me and said, "Lord, I thought that, since Luca is leaving us and Carlos and Gerald are wounded, maybe we could use another man or two. We have warrior friends, like us, who are honorable and capable, and who might be interested in joining us on this venture. They could use the work since they have families to support. If you think we might could use more, I will ride back to Rome and inquire if they are available, if you wish."

"We do need more now that we are without Connie's, Eliab's, and Luca's swords and, as you say, Carlos and Gerald will be of little help for a couple more weeks. See if you can find five men who would be willing to join us. They must be dependable and willing to face unknown dangers. It's possible they will not all make it back to their families. Let them also know, however, that, if they die on this mission, I will see to it their families are taken care of. They must also be ready to leave by mid-day, day after tomorrow."

With Enzo gone to look for more men, and Carlos and Gerald laid up with their wounds, Carl, Cosimo, Francois, and I finished taking care of getting the villa back in order and preparing food for our journey. Francois was confined to the guest house at night, which was bolted from the outside and guarded by the convalescing men. I missed Connie and Kat so much and, especially, Dania and Jaleel. It was so quiet around the house and grounds, too, as we worked without all their voices, teasing, and laughing. I wondered if I could ever be happy or even content again. Maybe I was getting tired of living.

Enzo arrived back at the villa late that evening and said he found five eager men who he knew well who were willing to join our mission and would meet us on the road going from Rome to Centumcellae around noon, two days hence. Carlos and Cosimo said they knew them well, also, and vouched for their worthiness.

At a meager dinner that night, we talked about a plan, as if one could be devised, because I had none and none of the others did, either. I foolishly permitted Francois to join us, and he kept silent during the meal, offering no help. What we knew for sure was that we would search for a ship or ships heading east that would eventually get us to, or near, Armenia. Anything beyond the port at Armenia was unknown, and I trusted some guidance from Francois in helping us locate an entrance, which must assuredly be hidden, that would lead us to a meeting with the High Priest. It was a naïve belief, I knew, to think the High Priest would easily give up on their centuries' old thinking of taking control of the nations from England to Israel just because I asked them to. The books of Deuteronomy and Joshua, among others, states that not only are the Jews to invade the lands promised to them, but they must also kill every man, woman, and child, as well as their livestock. I just could not allow that to happen, since it was my unalterable sense of duty to not let something so despicable happen to the innocent.

The sun had risen that morning, on the morning of our departure, by the time we began our ride back towards Rome. Francois was tethered to Enzo's saddle. I asked him how he was feeling, but he said nothing.

"Francois," I said, "I'm getting a little bit fed up with your attitude. You swore you would help us to save your worthless neck, and I demand nothing less than your full cooperation. That cooperation includes you acting like a mature individual, who has become a valuable part of this expedition. That means, when I speak to you, you will respond with an answer or comment. A flick of my dagger point can remove one of your eyes before you can blink. Do you want me to start there? Now, I insist you act like a man and not like a sulking child. You have seen the proof that you, your High Priest, and your people are wrong and will be condemned if you stay on the path you have sworn to take. I'm saving you from that torment, so be grateful and happy you are with us. Now, let me ask you again, how are you feeling this morning?"

"I am feeling well, if not a little unhappy about my circumstances."

"I can understand your feelings but, still, I am trying to save countless lives, including your and your families' lives. Remember that as we travel to Armenia. I'm doing you a favor and risking mine and my family's lives in doing so."

"Now, tell me this. What were those things your people used to fire lead balls at us? Eliab had one of them, also, and its explosion sent a ball across my face leaving a scar that will never go away."

He offered me a smile, the first one I had seen since meeting him. Anger again rose in me, but I forced it back down for the sake of getting needed information. "Those are schioppis or gonnes. They use powder to propel the lead ball at amazing speeds and are accurate within fifty feet or so, if aimed properly. A flint striking metal operated by a trigger is used to ignite the powder in a small pan that causes the explosion you heard, sending the ball towards its target. My people developed them a century ago. Additionally, we have much larger versions, arquebuses, that require wheels to transport and can shoot heavy steel balls more than a mile with devastating destruction. We also have other, far more destructive weapons, that have been designed by our scientists to easily assault stone walls and destroy masses of people."

He spoke about those things with obvious pride. I knew the Ashkenazim to be imaginative and brilliant people and, unfortunately, they used their intelligence to focus on evil too often, rather than the good of the people. At least it seemed that way from what little I knew of them. Centuries of being isolated in their own world allowed them to devise advanced weaponry, but what else did they develop?

"Items that excel in killing are admirable when it comes to defending your people, but I'm sorry that you will use it for offensive killing. The God I know, the Christ who preaches that we are to love one another, says we should not dwell on such things. Even Adonai says Thou Shalt Not Murder. Killing people who have done you no harm seems like a contradiction in your faith. Yes, I know that Adonai sent your ancestors into the promised land and ordered them to destroy all who lived there, every man, woman, and child, but that was because they worshiped other gods and because he commanded Moses and Joshua to do so, to prevent the Jews from being swayed towards worshiping Baal and other gods made of stone and wood. Since Adonai has not ordered your people to

195

kill everyone in England or the Holy Roman Empire, you are going to destroy your own selves. How many times am I going to have to remind you of the lunacy of what your people are about?"

"I hear what you are saying and I'm trying to soak it in."

"Another question I have concerns Pagiel. When I first met him, he said he worked in the spark department, indicating it was important, and had to do with how things function underground. I think it must have something to do with the lights I saw that were not lit by candles or oil. He also indicated that was how something he called a lift operated. What did he mean by sparks; what is it?"

Again, he wore that smug look that didn't sit well with me.

"Sir, sparking is one more advancement we have that the rest of the world has not caught up to and probably won't for centuries. Our scientists have developed a power source even more powerful than steam. Through coils of copper configured in such a way that allows it to be rotated by underground rivers, it generates power that can be distributed anywhere we want, through copper wires created in our own smelters. I'm not a scientist, and so, I don't know how it works, but you can be sure it is very effective and deadly if used improperly. It is useful for many operations. Lights can be powered by the output of the coils, run lifts upwards and downwards, it operates all sorts of equipment, such as those used to excavate tunnels rapidly in addition to those powered by steam, and we use it to send messages instantly across the expanse of our colony, to name just a few conveniences it gives us. The design of the equipment is a closely kept secret that no one above ground, not even a Sephardic Jew, must know. For me to even mention its capabilities is treason."

"I appreciate the information, and I have no desire to tell anyone your secrets, but only to protect innocent people. Tell me what you know of the Armenian colony. Have you been there? How can we find an entrance to their colony? Where is it located?"

The battle in his mind was obvious by the look on his face. He still struggled with uttering treasonous talk that betrayed his beloved people, but he also knew the consequences of not telling me what I wanted. Although I knew he would most probably hold back some information he thought he could keep secret from me, he also knew he had to tell me enough, so that I wouldn't begin cutting off parts of his body. I knew he had no doubts that I would do as I had told him.

"I have not been to Armenia. I have been to two other colonies besides ours as part of my duties, but not to Armenia. I have known men who have, so I know some things about it above what we are taught in school as we grew up. I know about where the primary entrance lies in relation to the closest city. As far as how to find the entrance exactly, I do not know. I know the High Priest's name and some things about the council of elders, or Chief Priests, who assist the High Priest in governing and planning. They are the ones who set regulations on how we govern our individual colonies and the laws we operate over and above what the Torah says. You may know of the Talmud and Mishna, which has been part of the Jewish nation since Moses' day. The Armenian colony provides all colonies with interpretations that are in addition to the Talmud and Mishna."

"What is the High Priest's name, and is he appointed for life, or for a year, as in the old days of your history?"

"He is appointed for life or until removed by the Chief

Priests over unsuitable actions. His name is Yoseph, and he has been in that position for the last fifteen or sixteen years. He is a brilliant and powerful man beloved by the council and their colony. He will not be easily convinced to stop the plans that have been in place and dictated to us for many decades. In fact, he wants to be the High Priest that fulfills our destiny and is driven to do so. No, he will not be easy to deter, and he will not be easy to even gain an audience, with you being an outsider. The fact you are an outsider means you will not be permitted to leave even if you gain entrance to see the High Priest. You and your friends will die, I'm sure of it. Maybe he will kill me, also, but it would be worth it if you die before my eyes."

I didn't know if I should laugh or slap him off his horse, so I didn't do either. I would not permit his attitude to worsen what was already a bad day for me. I would somehow, in some way, settle my debt with the French Jew before we went separate ways. That, I vowed to myself, and to his and my God.

We continued riding south and west on the road that would take us to Rome, and we had already reached some of the outlying hovels. There were other questions I wanted to ask Francois, but they would have to wait when we had a little more privacy than the increasingly congested outlying regions allowed. Pigs, sheep, goats, geese, and two-wheeled carts pulled by donkeys began to crowd us, and we had to weave in and out of shouting people, as well as bleating, honking, and braying animals. The sounds of the city made conversation too difficult. We stopped at an outdoor market, and picked up more supplies that we would eat while waiting for a ship and, once on the ship, if we could find one soon. There would be twelve of us traveling, and that meant a lot of food was needed for so many hungry men. I feared for the rapidity my funds were being drained after giving so much of it to Connie for her and her contingent traveling home, as well as giving Luca his wages. I also needed to give some to the three mercenaries that had served me in the past weeks, so I stopped once again at the East Asia Trading Company, thanked the director for the use of his villa, and had Antonio give me another draft letter. He had not expected me back so soon, but I said we had pressing business that needed attending to.

The shipping season, I knew, would be slowing down soon, meaning fewer ships would be available. I hoped to find a dependable looking ship going in our direction with a sober and capable-looking captain, quickly. The sooner we could get to Armenia and confront Yoseph, the sooner we could resolve the impossible task ahead of us. Or the sooner we would die. Antonio was very familiar with cargo shipments going to and from Constantinople, so he gave me names of reputable ships and their captains we could seek out that would be going in the direction we hoped to go. The company owned two such ships, but they were not in port in the timeframe we needed them, so we had to depend on intuition. Ships going towards Constantinople should not be difficult to find, since it was a busy market port but, going from there to Armenia, those ships would not be so easy to find, since the Turkish people had a reputation of being insolent and hard to negotiate with, and European merchant captains tended to stay away from those ports.

At an inn and pub on the western outskirts of the city, we found our new mercenaries. Enzo introduced us to Branca, Mattia, Luigi, Ferrante, and Benetto. It occurred to me that it would be difficult for Carl and me, the only two of us not wounded, to defend ourselves against those five, plus Enzo, should they wish to take the funds I had stashed in my saddle bags, rather than go far away on a dangerous trip. I figured, if we made it onto a ship, I would then feel safer about the crowd we were travelling with. It was enough to keep an eye on Francois' whereabouts besides having to worry about my hired warriors taking my money and, possibly, our lives. I trusted Enzo, but not the latest mercenaries who joined us just yet.

On the second day after leaving Rome, we reached the port city of Centumcellae on the blue water coast of the Mediterranean Sea in the midafternoon. Since Carl was more adept in speaking with sea captains, I sent him to look for a ship going east. Also, I was still in no mood to listen to belligerent seamen. I would have just as soon thrown them overboard if they said one thing that grated on me which, at the time, would be a lot of things. We sat in a pub washing down the dust of the trail with honeyed mead and ale while we waited for him to return with news. I watched carefully how much the new men would drink, since the drink was free to them, paid for by me. If they got drunk, they would not travel with me. I couldn't depend on a man addicted to drink. Francois, though, did not drink mead or ale or rum but, in the absence of wine, drank cider.

Maybe an hour went by before Carl came into the pub. He sat down at my table and called for a drink from the man behind a greasy, dark-stained bar.

"Well," I asked, "find anything?"

"There are two ships that can work for us. One is leaving for Constantinople in two days. Another is sailing to Acre with a shipload of pilgrims going to the Holy Land. It leaves tomorrow. Both ships have room for paying guests if we have enough silver to make it worth the captain's effort.

Interesting. Getting to Acre straight from Rome could get us nearer to our destination sooner, I believed; however, it meant a long ride from there to Armenia.

"Do we have any other options, Carl?"

"I think we should take the ship to Constantinople. That same ship leaves from there and sails to Myra, and then, to Antioch before going to Tripoli and Cairo. Antioch is not far from Armenia. For that distance and, for the twelve of us, it will take a lot of silver. I guessed the captain to be close to seventy years old, and he obviously wants to fatten his retirement fund."

I gave Carl enough coins to allow the twelve of us to sail to Antioch, and we reserved rooms at the inn for the next two nights before we would sail on the second day of December 1362. Every day could be our last day on earth. I always tried to keep that in mind. Pagiel said some of us would die on this trip, and that my blade would once again shed blood. I took some comfort in his words that I would return to London. I hoped that Carl and Gerald would, as well. I did not fear the days ahead, because I did not fear death. I only feared returning to my castle bedroom and finding it empty.

Chapter Thirteen

More Misfortune

They ravage, they slaughter, they seize by false pretenses, and all this they hail as the construction of empire. And when in their wake nothing remains but a desert, they call that peace.
—Tacitus

We had two nights and a day free until the ship would leave port, so we rested from our travels that first evening and went to bed early. As is typical of me, when there was so much unknown ahead of me, I slept little. Before the midnight hour arrived, I had finally put my boots on, and went outside for a stroll to see if I could clear my mind of the past three days but, instead of clearing my mind, it got considerably more confusing.

It was a very dark night, and only a few city oil lights burned along the docks. I walked on past the last ship, and above, darkened clouds skittered past, and occasionally revealed a nearly full moon. The ships and boats tied up to the wharves creaked, wood against wood. Two cats nearby screeched as they coupled, oblivious to me. I walked on to where the wooden walkway became a dirt or sand trail, and a narrow strip of grass separated the path from a sandy beach. My mind fixed on nothing but finding my way through, or around, occasional obstacles. The trail continued north along the water's shore, and, in the distance, lightning danced east to west, sometimes from the dark sky towards the ground. The distance was so great, though, that I heard no thunder. All was quiet save for crickets, tree frogs, and whispering wavelets. Every now and then, an owl hooted, and another answered its call. I stood on the beach trying to discern how I would convince the High Priest of the irrational stand he and his people were committed to. A desire to destroy tens of thousands, possibly hundreds of thousands, of innocent people. They were mad, and I had to convince the deluded High Priest they were. It would most likely be easier to convince the two coupling cats to get a room in an inn. The worst thing about crazy people is that they don't know they are crazy. Crazy, sometimes, is a matter of perspective.

The lightning struck again and, that time, I heard faint rumbles of thunder. The storm was moving my way. Between lighting flashes and the approaching thunder, I could hear the soothing, eternal lapping of waves washing clean the sand on the shore. Peaks of the waves glistened from the moon's subdued light.

"You would do well to tell your son to go home immediately."

The sound startled me out of my trance. I looked towards the direction the sound came from and, not more than ten feet behind me, sat a very old woman in front of a small fire. It was impossible that I could not have heard her arrive and build a fire, but there she was, dressed all in black, like the darkness she appeared from. With a very white scrawny hand, she used a stick to stir the few branches burning in the fire, embers rising and blinking out. She was wearing a hood, preventing me from seeing her face, only the movement of that one thin hand. I could feel the hairs on the back of my neck tingle, because of the realization that something unnatural was happening. Though I'm very familiar with such things, I never get used to them.

I said, "Who are you and what do you mean about my son? Is he in danger?"

Beyond her, the lightning was branching into several bolts, some towards the ground and some sideways, disappearing into clouds, lighting them up from within by their brightness. In just two excited breaths, the sound caused by the flashes arrived with a crack and more rumbles, louder this time. The flash of lightning revealed the old woman had stood up and was facing me, though I could still not see her face. She was taller than I had thought, and no longer did I think of her being old. Only the bottom half of her face could be seen, and her skin looked as white as fresh fallen snow.

"So that you will know that you are not alone, know this. A man with a gold tooth will save your life. You must follow a dog with no tail. When you find a trident tree, you will have found what you are looking for."

"Who are you, what are you talking about, and what did you mean about Carl?"

The lightning flashed so close above me, the sound arrived at the same time, and I instinctively ducked my head. I turned to face the snow-white woman and force her to tell me what she knew about my mission, but she was gone, and so was the small fire she was tending. I called out to her. Over and over, I called out to her until Carl shook me awake.

"I'm sorry son. I had a disturbing dream."

As I spoke those words to him, lightning flashed a bright light into our room and, immediately, the sound of thunder rattled the windowpanes in response to the spectacular light displays going on outside. Rain pelted the windowpanes, and the storm made me think of what I saw in my dream on the beach. Maybe it wasn't a dream after all.

We had another day and a night, at least, to wait in the city until our ship would sail, so we, as a group, met in a quiet corner in a pub, and tried to develop creative ways to infiltrate an underground world, and then, overcome the zealous thousands of dedicated men we would have to face who would surely try to kill us. The only clue we had, if a clue it was, was to find a tailless dog to follow. That seemed to become more of a ridiculous thought the more I thought about it. The thought of a man with a golden tooth was pushed aside in my mind as also being of little consequence, considering the immense obstacles that lay ahead that we knew about.

I wrestled with what I would say to Carl to convince him that I needed to send him home. He would balk, I knew it. It was only a dream, maybe, but it seemed real enough that I would make him find another ship for him to go back to England.

While I thought about the arguments I would use to speak to my son, I sent him and Carlos, after our midday meal, and to look for a few more supplies we would need on the journey east. I thought having Carlos with him would be some protection for the short time they would be gone. I did not believe the enemy could yet know we were in the city. Another of many bad decisions I have made. Two hours later,

Carlos returned by himself, and it was obvious that he had been beaten.

"Lord," Carlos spoke, even as blood trickled out of the corner of his mouth, "we were attacked by a group of men and brought to someone named Asa outside the city. I'm sorry, but there were too many of them for us to overcome."

I was both furious and alarmed that we had once again been found, and our enemy had the advantage. I had to get Carl back, at all costs, but it wasn't just Carl they wanted. They wanted to kill all of us. I was running out of ideas and luck, if ever I had an ounce of luck these last few months. The apparition the night before told me to send Carl home as soon as possible. I had ignored that warning. It was only hours after I was given the warning, not days! Why had I sent Carl with Carlos? I should have erred on the side of caution. I'd seen enough such visions to believe that it was telling me the truth. No matter: I would get him back safely. *Regardless of what the barriers were*, I swore in my mind, *I would get him back safely*. The Ashkenazim were intelligent, and even ruthless, for sure, but so was I.

"What do they want from us?" I asked.

"They know we have Francois, and they want him back, in trade for Lord Carl. An hour before sunset, you are to take Francois to a broken-down dock on the north side of the city where the trade can take place. They said you are to bring Carl's son and Francois and no one else when you come."

"How many of them did you see?"

"Eight of them, no more than that, all of them dressed in dark brown clothing, carrying swords and those things they shot at us back at the villa. They all looked like they were made from the same mold, same height, weight, and features.

207

Before they sent me away with these instructions, they felt it necessary to pound on me for a while for the sake of emphasis. If I get the chance again, I will do some pounding myself."

"Okay," I told them, "I know where the dock is. There are trees not far inland with lots of underbrush amongst them. I want four of you to leave now and go into those trees opposite the dock, and five of you to ride north as far as you can, but still stay in sight of the dock. Find a place to hide, but don't remain together. Mill about like you are doing something other than observing the dock area. The rest of you will go with me with Francois to meet the men holding Carl. Know that their goal is to kill all of us first, and to retrieve Francois secondly. We will have little leverage with Francois since he is a secondary target. I think they will attempt to make the trade to ensure retrieval of Francois, if only to find out what we know, and then, they will have the numbers to attack us. Our advantage is that they may not know how many of us we are. I need not tell you that we must get Carl back safely, and that you must do whatever it takes to help me get him back."

I, too, had those weapons they called gonnes, taken from the dead outside the villa. I put two of them in my waistband, as did Gerald. He was still suffering from his wound, but could easily use a gonne, if not his sword. I hoped it wouldn't come to that but, in my heart, I knew there was an impending fight ahead of us. Blood was going to be spilled; maybe it would be mine but, for sure, there would be theirs, as well. Nothing would stand in the way of me getting my son back. My anger was at an alarming level and, though I tried to quell my hatred, I was finding it hard to do so. One of my most important fighting axioms was to never fight angrily, for such was to fight stupidly, without caution. I had fought many men who were so angry with me, so filled with hateful determination, that they made mistakes that I took advantage of. I spent the next three hours attempting to calm my spirit and prayed to God for some form of peace and assistance in the impending fight. Even then, it seemed ironic to me to pray for help when my focus was to kill the men who took my son. Nevertheless, I knew God was watching, and I needed all the help I could get, both natural and supernatural. If God was merciful, as I believed he was, I would get my son back unharmed.

I did not know where Connie and the children were. We left only two days after they did. Could it be that they were still in the city? Could they have been seen by the same Jews who took Carl? The thought of them finding Connie and my children sent another surge of anger and worry through me. Would this torment ever let up, I wondered? I wished I had never found that journal that began this impossible trip I was foundering upon. If anything happened to Carl, Francois would be held accountable.

At the appointed time, Gerald, Francois, and I set out towards the site of the broken-down dock I had seen the night of my dream, or vision, or whatever it was. I recalled the flashes of lightning that revealed it, the surrounding terrain, and the woman tending a fire. I still wasn't sure there ever was a woman there, but I was sure of where the dock lay broken, suffering from age and disregard. I believed that if the dock was real, then so was the vision of the old woman.

I asked Francois if he, indeed, wanted to return to his people knowing what he knew now about the error his people were dedicated to.

"Shouldn't you stay with us, and help us educate the High Priest why this madness must stop? You heard what the rabbi said the other day. Nowhere in the Torah or the Talmud does it speak of taking land outside of the area around Israel. Don't continue with a program that will destroy your people. Will you stay with us and demand Carl's release?"

The man said nothing. He still wasn't convinced; he was too much a part of an institution bent on power. It was at that point that I knew in my heart there was no turning Francois away from his lifelong course. He was dead set on rejoining and supporting his people in their stupid goal of domination. Never would I be able to trust his help.

Well before we reached the dock area, I saw them. All dressed in dark brown clothing. It looked like at least a dozen men, and among them was Carl. The closer we approached, the more I could see Carl had been ill-treated. My fury spiked again.

We stopped short of the gathering of brown clad men by about fifty yards.

"Release Carl now and I will release Francois," I shouted.

As soon as I spoke those words, I saw a man in front perform a series of hand signals. They were followed by Francois kicking the heels of his feet into the sides of his horse, bolting away before I had a chance to stop him. I held up my hand as a signal for my men nearby to hold until I saw what the men holding Carl would do, but it wasn't long before they showed their hand.

The same man who performed the hand signals took out his gonne and pointed it at Carl's head.

I shouted "NO" at him. Panicking, I kicked my horse in the flanks and raced towards the group and, as I did so, my men charged from the forest, as well as those who waited beyond, north of the enemy group. A few moments of fear, dread, and enormous, unbridled anger and trepidation washed over me as I raced to defend my son. It was a series of surreal moments that lapsed as I raced those fifty yards, hoping against hope that I could arrive before that man pulled the trigger that would end my son's life. My hands were turning numb with fear. All anger had been replaced with a dreadful apprehension of what might happen. Please God, don't let this happen.

Halfway to where Carl sat on his horse, I saw the men who were behind the leader move into a line in front of him and prepared to meet me. Then, I heard a small explosion and, with the darkening sky as a backdrop, saw fire and smoke spew out of the gonne the man held. I saw, with horror, Carl jerk sideways and fall off his horse. From my right, I saw my men approaching and, from behind them, I saw the others racing toward us from the north. The enemy in front of me withdrew their cursed iron weapons and pointed them towards me, but the shouts of my men racing in their direction distracted them and rather than fire at me, they turned to flee but were instead met by my men from behind. The sea was to their left and my men on their front and side, and me behind. Some gonnes went off, but to no avail. They panicked and so were their horses. My men's swords swept down upon them and would have killed every one of them, except I shouted for them to spare two; Francois and the man who killed my son. A sword would be too kind to both. I had fought in so many battles, not only in shield walls, but some also I met headlong after racing across a field to meet the enemy in wild melee, blade against blade, shield against shield, all against overwrought and hungry-for-blood opponents, wielding my sword furiously at the men just as eagerly trying to kill me. I knew the feeling intimately that comes over a man faced with the enemy only inches away. Blood lust takes over and reason and sanity are replaced by one desire, which is to kill the man in front of you. That is how I felt about Francois and Carl's killer. I would kill them, and then, I would ask God why he let my son die.

My men took the two away from me to guard while Gerald and I picked up Carl's body and placed it on a horse. A small hole was visible just above his left eye. A hole the size of my little finger. In the back of his head the hole was much larger, large enough for his life to drain out quickly. Gerald wept and I wanted to, but I was too angry to cry. That would happen later when the enormity settled in on me and I was alone. My servants, my wife, Jaleel, and now, my son, Carl, were all dead. Payback was going to be historical, I vowed to myself, beginning with our two captives.

I'm hesitant to describe in detail what I did to the man who pulled the trigger that ended a life much better than his. He at first begged me to spare his life, and then, he begged for me to kill him quickly after, little by little, I removed the things that make us look like humans. I have since begged my God to forgive me for what I did. No human should have done what I did to another, animal, or man. In the end, he was dead, but no more dead than my son, and that made me sad. I wanted his death to be more dead than dead. I wanted God, if he cared for me at all anymore, to bring the man back to life, so that I could kill him again.

Francois, I decided, could no longer be trusted to help, or not attempt to run away. He had to die, and he too could not die a death that was too easy. He had served his purpose, I surmised. In a civil society, men must be found guilty by a judicial system and hanged. We were no longer in a civilized society. He was largely to blame for Carl's death and must beg for his life. I would not do what I promised to do to him that I had sworn in the servant's house behind the villa. It would take too long. My blood lust was mostly sated after the dismemberment of Carl's killer, and now, it was just time to execute an evil man. I had given him enough chances to regret his ideology and actions. No more chances for him.

"Francois, you are responsible for the deaths of my family, and I hereby sentence you to death."

After those few words, I slapped the hip of one horse and Gerald slapped the flank of another. They both bolted away in opposite directions. In between the horses was Francois, each leg tied to one of the horses. It did not take long for him to die, but what time there was, was very painful. We left the two parts of him lying on the forest floor for the elements and animals to have their way with him. I promised Francois that, when I returned to England, his estate would be forfeited to Gerald, and his family evicted to find their way in the world on their own.

"Vengeance is mine, sayeth the Lord."

And mine, too.

Chapter Fourteen

An Angry Maelstrom

No man alive can say, this shall not happen to me.
—Menander

No man or woman born, coward or brave, can shun his destiny.
—Homer

The next morning, we boarded a ship that would take us to Constantinople, then, on to Antioch and, from there, we would make our way to Armenia. My men looked at me as if I were a cold, inhuman creature. They had never seen anyone who acted as I had. They feared me but, at the same time, they respected my resolve and my focus on the task at hand. They were aware of the enormity and importance of what we were doing, and they also knew, to fix the problem, required difficult actions. Carlos, Enzo, and Cosimo had been with me long enough to know I was fair with those loyal to me, but deadly to those who weren't. The new men received a fast education on who I was. They may have been afraid to proceed with me on the dangerous road ahead, but they were also too afraid to leave me. Often, out of the corner of my eyes, I saw them staring at me as if I had lost my grasp of what human decency was. Maybe they wished they had never fallen in with me, since bad luck and death were following us like a puppy following a little boy. Often, they talked among themselves quietly so that I could not hear what was being said. I figured I was the topic of their discussions.

The difference between them and me was that I did not care if I lived. I was going to sacrifice myself to do whatever I saw was necessary to fix the problem. The men, even Gerald, were young and vigorous enough, and naïve enough, to think life was still worth living. My heart was too damaged to believe that. The distant thoughts of Catherine Adele and little Troy, still alive, did little to salve my painful soul. I felt that my losses exceeded my assets, and I'm deeply ashamed of that way of thinking today as I pen these words. I lay awake that night, after we, I, executed the two men, and fantasized about still having my demons and how I would use their enormous supernatural power to exact retribution on my enemies for all that they had done to me. The truth was that I never could summon the demons for my own behalf; they just reacted to all who threatened their host body. Still, I visualized their help in getting even with the men responsible for my pain.

No longer was I on a mission to save the world. I was on a mission to exact revenge. If the two got the same results, so much the better.

We sailed on the ebbing tide on a chilly December morning. The wind was favorable and the skies clear when we left the wharf and turned south to reach the deep blue of the Mediterranean Sea. The weather, beginning in December, can be unpredictable. Temperatures were moderate, but storms could be violent. Once, on that sea, I spent eight days on a raft after our ship overturned, dumping a little girl and me overboard. She subsequently died of exposure and lack of water to drink. Those thoughts were on my mind as I kept a weather eye out for bad weather, when off to the starboard side of the ship, I saw darkening skies on the western horizon. I had been shipwrecked twice and had been in many other storms, and I groaned to see another storm brewing. Bad luck was knocking on my door once again, I brooded, so, I opened the door and let it in.

I warned my men to go below because a big blow was about to take place. Gerald and Carlos, still recovering from wounds, were getting better, and I believed by the time we arrived in Armenia, would be well enough to face whatever we were going to face, assuming we arrived there. As anticipated, the wind racing ahead of the rain, thunder, and lightning, struck with force, and continued to build over the next hour when the rain squalls arrived and pummeled the ship. When there was a storm, I preferred to be on the main deck, rather than on the lower decks, because I wanted to see and face the danger, rather than let it approach unseen and worry over what might happen. I tied myself to the capstan, between the spokes used to hoist an anchor. The captain was tied to the tiller's stanchion, so he could keep the ship facing into the wind. The captain shouted at his first mate, urging him to give the seamen orders that could be heard above the sound of the howling wind.

"Clue up the fore, main, and mizzen sails and stow them! Leave the topgallant sails on the fore and main masts! We need them up to slow the rocking of the ship in the wind!"

Sailors climbed up the shrouds to the top masts and furled the lower sails onto the yard arms, tying them up while the wind and rain beat against them, as if trying to blow them off their perches. The wind was growing in intensity every moment. Sailors were swinging wildly in the wind-battered rigging. One of the men fell and, if he hadn't grabbed the top stay on the way down, he would have crashed on the weather deck or the sea. All the sailors were dressed in oilskins, but I wasn't, and I could not get any wetter than I was. I had sea legs because of the years I had spent as a captain of a pirate ship but, still, the footing was difficult for anyone not tied down as I was. I held onto the lifeline as much as I could. The bow rose up as the heaving rollers rolled under the ship. Then the bow would hang for a moment and then slide down into the troughs, up and down like a seesaw. When the bow hit the bottom of the trough, it shook the ship as if it had hit a rock. The waves broke over the deck, washing away everything that hadn't been tied down, into the sea. I watched as the main topgallant yard arm fell downward but kept above us only by a single rope holding it overhead. The seamen had already descended by then and were on the weather deck, ready to obey orders from the captain. The foremast's top ten feet broke off carrying its top yardarm with it, both falling into the sea, when the ship rolled to starboard. The captain, still tied to the helm as he struggled to keep the ship lying-in into the wind. A huge wave washed over the deck and brought a wooden barrel that hadn't been tied down and struck the captain. It looked as if he had been knocked out. He lay limp against his rope, and the tiller was swinging out of control.

The wind appeared ceaseless, and I feared we would founder if someone didn't take control of the tiller. The sailors, believing no more orders were coming from the captain, left and went into the fo'c'sle to get out of the storm.

I slowly made my way with much difficulty to the capstan. I managed to reach the captain and saw he was bleeding from a wound on the right side of his head. He was still alive, but would be unconscious, I figured, for quite a while. A wave washed across the deck and nearly took me with it, filling my mouth with saltwater, so I tied myself again to the stanchion. I managed, with great effort, to lie-in the ship to keep us from being turned completely on our beam. If the wind and waves came at us from abeam, we most likely would turn over. Lightning struck all around us and, as I feared it would, it struck the main mast. The lightning gouged a deep and long scar down much of the length of the mast, but did not set it on fire, as the ceaseless waves did not permit it. However, the deck surface for a space of five feet around the mast was blown away, slinging pieces of wood in every direction. The mainmast swayed dangerously at the mercy of the wind. If the wind didn't fall away soon, I thought, the mast would snap and, as soon as those thoughts entered my mind, it snapped eight feet below the weather deck. Over the ship rail the mast went leeward, and it was still connected by rigging that would normally attach the main and top sails to the yard arms. The weight of the mast hanging overboard was acting like a large sea anchor in the churning waves. If the mast wasn't cut away, I was sure, it would soon pull the ship over where it couldn't be righted again, and we would most likely sink. Being on the leeward side of the ship just made the situation more dangerous, acting with the wind to roll us over on the larboard side. No one on deck was conscious, except me.

Still, the maelstrom tormented the ship but, if we were to survive, I had to untie myself and attempt to cut the ropes holding the mast and mid yardarm. When I untied myself, I laboriously made my way to an axe hanging upon the foremast, which still remained upright for the moment. I began chopping at the ropes that ran over the taffrail and connected to the mast. The topsail yardarm banged against the side of the ship and could easily have broken my arm if I misjudged the timing of its swinging. I swung the axe once, twice, and a wave pushed me several feet toward the aft before I managed to catch myself on the taffrail prior to being washed overboard. The ship was rolling dangerously over with the mast and yard arm acting to pull the ship over and down. I crawled, mostly slid, on the wet and sloping deck, water sometimes up to my stomach, staying low as I could until I reached the taut ropes still holding the main mast. Unfortunately, the axe had been ripped from my hands when the waves sent me across the deck. By that time, a seaman saw what I was doing and came out to help me. I pulled my dagger and began to cut the ropes. It was slow because of their thickness. I cut and the sailor chopped with an axe he had retrieved. When we finally cut the last of the ropes, the mast fell away, and the ship became more upright, except that the wind was still blowing in force against the hull on the windward side, precariously pushing us over with every gust. The sailor managed to get to the helm and turned the ship back into the wind. Rain and waves, carried by the wind, continually blew from west to east across the deck.

The captain regained consciousness, and, though groggy and bleeding, he was awake enough that he took the tiller back. I tied myself to the mizzen mast and observed the captain to see if he could effectively operate the tiller. The other seamen came out of the fo'c'sle thinking they needed to be seen on deck and awaiting orders, rather than cowering in their bunks. I noticed the time between lightning and thunder was growing longer, and figured the storm was beginning to pass us by. To confirm that, I noticed the wind began, just barely perceptible, to grow quieter. It would howl the rest of the day, but the real danger was over. There would be much damage to repair, but it seemed the ship would not sink, though I figured it would take many hours to pump out the flooded hull. Wave after wave flooding over the weather deck allowed much of the seawater to drain down into the bowels of the ship through the main hatch. From the direction the storm came, I saw a lighter band of sky promising that the storm would soon be over. The only fortunate thing about the storm was that no land could be seen in any direction. That meant we would not founder on rocks where the ship would be broken apart, drowning all of us.

When the worst of the storm had blown itself out, my companions came up on the weather deck. They had been tossed around violently in their cabins until they managed to tie themselves to something. They were sore and bruised but had no broken bones.

By the time the storm ended, we had reached the southern end of Greece. The sky had become blue and beautiful when we sailed by the island of Serifos. While we labored at repairs, the ship limped by the island. Greek mythology says that island is where Perseus and his mother, Danae, washed up on its shore after Perseus' grandfather placed them in a wooden chest and set it adrift in the sea. Perseus, according to the myths, after becoming an adult, returned to that same island with the head of Medusa and turned the king of the island into stone for trying to marry his mother by force.

It would normally have taken us seventeen days to arrive in Constantinople but, because of being blown off course, damage to the ship, and having to layover for additional repairs at Syracuse on the island of Sicily, we were delayed another two weeks, arriving on the seventh of January. Branca, Mattia, Luigi, Ferrante, and Benetto, my newest mercenaries, had, after the storm, begun to grumble about the dangers of our mission. Even Carlos, Cosimo, and Enzo's patience was getting thin. I shrugged it off, though, believing that, with their line of livelihood, such discomforts come with the job. I admit I was not a fun person to be around anymore, being sullen and grouchy all the time. They were getting paid, so I judged they should man up and do what they were paid to do.

It wasn't the first time I had been to Constantinople. I had begun my journey to wealth and adventure in that city many decades earlier. It had changed a lot since I was last there, and my Muslim friend and former cellmate, who once was a resident, had long since died, and I no longer had the desire to learn under learned professors, as I had the last time I was there. I only had one focus now, and it didn't have anything to do with that ancient city. I was just anxious to be on my way again to Antioch and then a confrontation with Yoseph. For a time, I mulled over sending my companions back home, and I would go on alone. What could ten men do that one couldn't, under the circumstances?

We found another ship a few days after arriving in port that would take us to Antioch on its way to other, more exotic, ports. When the world seems to close in and I feel God and man has abandoned me, I like to find a secluded spot and meditate on my situation. I was tired of being in proximity with the nine men with me, even though one was my grandson,

I needed to get away and find some peace. While waiting on a ship going towards our destination, which was difficult that time of year, I rode my horse up into the hills and found a quiet place overlooking the sea below and to the south, sat down and reflected on all that had happened. The ancient city of Constantinople sat on an isthmus separating the Black Sea from the Mediterranean. It was beautiful from my vantage point, but I missed my little fast running stream behind my castle where I often went to ponder the complexities of life. My attitude towards life had changed dramatically over the past months, and I recognized I was becoming a bitter old man, something I despised in old men.

When I was seventeen, the girl I was to marry when I returned to my village after finding my purpose in life, told me that I was impetuous. She thought I was a fool to leave the known for the unknown, the safe place for the dangerous places of the world. Guinevere. I should never have left her. When I returned from my travels nine years later, she was married and had two children and soon to have another. I had the idealization of youth, something that fades away with age. As a youth, I worked as a helper to my father who made utensils from tin, until the call to go and see came upon me in such force that I had to leave. That long, very long, road led me to the high hill overlooking the sea, and I brooded over all the decisions I made that led me there. Arrogance mostly, thinking I, Troy Kensington, could save a world that many would say wasn't worth saving. I am a hopeless servant of duty, though. I have no other choice but to fulfill, or make the attempt to fulfill, the self-imposed obligations my mind creates. All my long life I have resided uncomfortably between heaven and hell.

In two days, we would leave for Antioch, and the only clue as to what to do next centered around a tailless dog. If I weren't so depressed at the time, I would have laughed out loud at that thought. The wind on the hilltop where I sat was cold and strong from the sea, and it carried with it the smell of brine and the cries of seagulls, which flew well below where I rested. I sat in wonder at the scene below me and soaked in the peace it gave. A thousand chimneys spewed forth dark columns of smoke into the blue sky. The gray/blue sea far below soothed my tormented soul, because the sea had always been a source of comfort to me. I absorbed the feeling of freedom, and the smell of the saltwater mixed with the rich earth upon which I sat. There was another feeling, though. A terrible and ominous feeling settled upon me. Somewhere beyond the placid scene below, the presence of evil and danger lay, and it frightened me. My intense and traumatic grief I felt over the recent loss of my wife and two of my sons was being crowded out by the encroaching thoughts of doom that lay ahead where a strong possibility of my own death may occur. The weight of what we were doing was too much for me. Suddenly, I felt very old and tired, and just wanted to go to sleep and not wake up, but just cease to exist. No hell, no heaven, no in between, nothing. If only it were that simple.

I rubbed my hands together to warm them against the chill of the wind. As I had done thousands of times before, I looked at the scars that remained in each palm. The scars bore the marks of stigmata. I had an intense reaction in a dark alley in Cairo after seeing a vision of a man I can only believe was Christ himself. The vision left me blind for a few days and, in an instant, turned my hair snow white, which is the color it remains today. My hands bore the scars of crucifixion, even though I had not endured that torment. The scars remind me of my past as a carrier of demons and my quest to rid myself of them for well over a century. Since I was seventeen, I have been on one quest after another. Uncannily, I have survived them all, either because of my demons, God, or both, I've never known who it was that saved me. I do believe I was born for a unique purpose. I am a small arrow in God's quiver of tools that he uses to accomplish his complex plan, and I know it is impossible to thwart those plans. I have decided to go along with them for as long as my destiny allows me to draw a breath.

On the ride back to the city and the inn where my companions waited, I again entertained the idea of sending them away. There was no need to sacrifice another life for my ill-fated quest to accomplish an impossible task. It made no difference if I died; no ripple in the cosmic web if I did. If Gerald died, and I lived through the task ahead, I swore I would never return home. Never see Connie, Catherine Adele, Troy, or Goodrich Castle again, or my secret spot in the forest. I would simply wander about the world, or live in a cave somewhere, a pilgrim seeking forgiveness for my grievous sins. On the ride back down into the city, I spotted riders a half mile away that I would swear were men following me, keeping me in sight. I thought about confronting them and settling a debt they owed me, but I just rode on. The Ashkenazim were a boil on my butt that wouldn't go away. It would bother me until it was lanced.

When I returned to the inn, I found Gerald and the others taking refreshment, laughing, and acting as though nothing was awry in the world. By my count, forty-one people had already died since we escaped from the Ashkenazi underground world. Some of them were my family, some good friends, most of them were those who wanted all of us dead. I saw no reason for laughter, and I made a scene when I walked up to their table and said some harsh words. Gerald, whose father was only recently killed by a lead ball passing through his brain, was the object of my harshest words. At the end of my bitter diatribe, I told all of them to pack their belongings and go home. I would somehow finish what I started or die trying. There was no longer any need to jeopardize their lives or add their names to the long list already started. I let my anger override my sense of reason, but what was said was said, and I walked out of the inn, down the street, and found a bench to sit on to watch the comings and goings of fishing boats. Never had I felt so sorry for myself as that day. The weight of so many deaths on my conscience was overwhelming.

I sat on that bench watching nets being mended, fish unloaded, men voiding themselves over the sides of their boats, gulls squabbling, people shouting at each other, and passing women selling their bodies for a few coins when Gerald and Cosimo sat down beside me. Neither of them said anything for a while. We watched the scenes before us, they trying to put words to their thoughts.

Finally, Gerald said, "I'm sorry, Poppa. I meant no respect to the memory of my father or your wife and son. I feel as bad about the death of my father as you do, probably more so. In a fleeting moment in a feeble attempt to forget the horror of the previous weeks, I let myself think that life was still going on and even worth living. I'm going with you to avenge my father's cruel death. You will not be able to stop me. Someone must pay for what they took from me, from us, and I want to be there when the payment comes due. Forgive me my one moment of escape from our reality."

Cosimo said, "The same goes for the rest of us. We are in this to the end, whatever end that might be. If you will still allow it, we are at your service. I beg you to allow us to finish what we started."

"What about the new men? Do they still think it's too dangerous? Are they willing to do what it takes? I don't want any half-hearted men fighting beside me."

"They just like to grumble. Ignore them. They are good men and will do what must be done and will follow you into the pit of hell if you ask them. It's their nature to complain. They aren't afraid of dying in a fight, they are afraid of drowning at sea."

"Let's get it done then," I said.

Chapter Fifteen

A Tailless Dog

I am dragged along by a strange new force. Desire and reason are pulling in different directions. I see the right way and approve of it but follow the wrong.
—Ovid

Two weeks after leaving Constantinople, we arrived at Antioch. Favorable weather kept the grumbling of my men to a minimum, for which I was thankful. I had become more reliant upon Cosimo without even recognizing his assistance. Not until our conversation two weeks earlier on the bench near Constantinople's wharves, did I begin to recognize his leadership value and potential. Gerald was too immature to do more than follow orders. He had not come close to reaching his father's abilities; perhaps, if he lived, he would become like his father. I hoped so. Cosimo, at thirty-four years, or about that, since he didn't know his exact age, was powerful, a very good fighter, and was good at giving orders, as well as taking them. I began to take more notice of him and viewed him as being more than simply a hired man. I hoped, if time allowed, he might become a friend, as well, since I had so few of them.

The Ashkenazim knew we were going to Rome and knew when we docked in Centumcellae and at Constantinople, so I had no hopes of landing in Antioch without them knowing. How they knew was still beyond my understanding. I instructed everyone to be on the lookout for Jewish spies and to cover up their weaponry with their cloaks. I put on a hooded cloak that I hoped would hide my long white hair. However, it would only be a temporary ruse. Sooner or later, they would discover us, clever as they were.

We got into Antioch in the midafternoon. We picked up our gear and walked the gangplank down to the wharves our ship was tied up against. All of us looked about us to see if it were possible to spot those we knew would be there. At the far end of the wharves, where the boardwalk ended and where a stone path led into the city's business street, there was a commotion. Four men were laughing and making gestures with their hands in obscene ways. Standing amid the men, was a woman, a young girl, who was crying and pleading with the men to leave her alone, or at least that was how I interpreted her reactions to the crude men's gestures. There were many people on the wharves, and the business street was busy with people shopping or strolling along the quay. Some people had stopped and were looking at the scene, but no one was attempting to stop the men confronting the poor girl, probably because the men were big and brutish and well-armed.

Never being one who liked the weak being harassed by the strong, I dropped my gear, pulled my sword, and approached the men callously badgering a young woman. I ignored Gerald's plea to ignore the scene, disappointed that he would want me to disregard what was happening. That was something I would have to discuss with him later.

When I got close to one of the men, I tapped him on his shoulder with my sword blade. When he turned around to see who it was that was interfering, I placed the sword point into that little hollow spot where the neck connects with the chest.

"All of you, leave the woman alone, or I will push the point of my sword into this ugly man's neck."

The other three men looked at each other and grinned. They were about to exchange one form of fun for another kind, the one where they assault a white-haired old man, and then, get back to the woman. My companions had arrived by that time, but I gestured to them to stay away. I wanted to teach four insolent men a lesson in etiquette and humiliate them at the same time.

"You men should move along now before you start something you can't finish. If you don't, I will have to embarrass you in front of dozens of people. Now, move away from the lady before I introduce you to my sword blade. He hasn't killed anyone yet today."

I was still holding the point of Blind Justice against the man's hairy neck when his three companions pulled their swords and began making a move towards me. Cosimo cried out to let them assist me, but I said they were to stand down. The three hesitated when they heard Cosimo, and the thought entered their little minds that, after they took care of me, they just might have to deal with the big men behind me. I would be no problem, they believed, but the nine behind me just might.

"Don't worry children," I told the three hesitant men, "they won't harm you. You just need to worry about me. Now, leave or face me, and I'm not in a mood to ignore what you are doing, your attitude, or your kind of thinking that makes assaulting a defenseless young girl okay."

I pushed the point of my sword just enough to draw blood from the man's neck. He raised both of his arms high and said to the other three. "Let's all leave. This man is crazy; he will shove that thing into my neck if you try anything. He'll do it."

I'm sure the man at the end of my sword could see his future in my eyes. They sheathed their swords, and I let them walk away. I was disappointed there wasn't going to be a fight. Probably just as well. The lady, or girl, was standing alone, shaking; she was so frightened. She came to her wits and started speaking rapidly in a foreign tongue to me, not surprisingly because by her skin tone, features, and her dress, she looked to be from India. She was just over five feet tall and with her clothes and all, she couldn't weigh over one hundred pounds.

"I do not understand you, little miss. Can you understand what I am saying? Are you alright?"

She said, "Oh, oh, I can speak England! A little beet. Thank you helping me, lord man, from bad men! I okay now. I stand here right now, just good that bad men go. They bad and more bad. I not wish they do that for me."

"Uh-huh," I said. "What is your name? My name is Troy."

"My name Eesha. Thank you, lord Troy."

"Eesha, why are you here? Are you alone? Those men will not bother you anymore, but maybe you should return to your family where you would be safer."

"My lord, I live India. I don't live here. I work for Madame. She wife of ambassador to my home. We on trip to go to England home of Madame. Her and me. Not others, just her and me. I servant girl to Madame. She, my help. No one help me now."

"Where is your Madame now, Eesha?"

"She dead."

"What? She died? When? What happened?"

"Night last before morning, we talk; her bosom grabbed her hand, and she make bad noise and fell on floor. She dead. I cry. I run to hotel man, and he tell me go home. I no not how go home. I lost, lord Troy."

I felt sorry for the young girl, but didn't want another problem to take care of, although I couldn't let her just hang around the wharves with no money or idea of what to do next. I told my companions I needed to talk to the hotel manager or owner to sort out what to do with the girl's mistress. While they looked for a pub, I escorted Eesha to the hotel they had stayed in where I demanded to speak to the manager or owner. I recognized quickly that the man was one of those that recognized a profit when he saw one. He had oily hair and oily speech that smacked of deceit and predatory cunning. Eesha's mistress was from a wealthy family, and she would be traveling with expensive attire, as well as money. I demanded we see the room where the lady had stayed and see her belongings.

When we entered the room, the lady was still there, lying on the floor. By the looks of her, it was evident that there was no exterior harm done to her, and probably Eesha was correct that her heart must have stopped beating.

"Where is the lady's baggage?" I asked the manager.

"Uh, it has been removed to determine if there are enough valuables to pay for the two nights they stayed here. She owes us for the rooms and meals so, of course, I expected to sell the items to recover the expenses."

"Let me see the baggage now," I demanded, "and remove

her body immediately. See to it she is buried in the local cemetery."

"That will cost also, lord."

"I want you to worry more about showing me her belongings than about expenses."

We went back downstairs to the lobby. The manager was not happy and protested all the way to the stairs. I ignored him. He opened a door behind the front desk. On the floor was a large sea chest and a canvas bag.

"Eesha," I said, "did you and your mistress have any other chests or bags with you other than what you see here?"

"Oh, no. No more we have than what my eyes see now."

"Do you know what is in the chest and the bag?"

"Lord, I put inside things. Eesha put them in, I know."

"Look inside and see if anything is missing from either of them."

She opened the canvas bag and evidently it contained her belongings. A pair of shoes and a couple of silken dresses were all I noticed. She opened the chest, and I saw that it was filled with very formal and costly gowns, shoes, ribbons, hats, an umbrella, and purses. I lifted one of the purses and saw that it was heavy with coins. I looked at the manager with a scowl, and he just shrugged his shoulders.

After letting the man have the mistress' clothing and accessories and the chest as payment for the hotel expenses, I gave him sufficient coinage from one of the purses to pay for the burial of the body. Before leaving the hotel, I wrote a note explaining to the mistress's husband how she had died, where she died, and where she was going to be buried. I gave the manager more coins to pay for the letter that would probably take many months to arrive back to India if it ever reached him, even if the man sent the letter. To make the manager understand how he was now obligated to execute what I had told him, I promised to check on him in a couple of weeks to see if all I asked for was completed properly. I think he understood the consequences of not obeying my instructions. I put the bags of coins in Eesha's canvas bag, and we returned to find my companions in a nearby pub. Now, what was I going to do with her? I had no other logical choice but to bring her with me until we could find a place where she could live. What a predicament we both were in.

We spent the evening acquiring horses and supplies. Rather than stay in an inn, we rode out of the city, north, towards Armenia. Eesha rode with Gerald on his horse. I was anxious to meet whatever fate lay ahead. In another six weeks, as Connie had promised, she would tell King Edward of England what the Ashkenazim were going to do. I wanted to be home by then, and I wanted to be able to tell her that there was no longer a danger to England. To meet that deadline, I knew, was impossible, unless the danger could be eliminated in the next few days. Of course, that would not happen.

We rode until the sun set and made camp on a hill overlooking the sea far below us. We knew we were being followed, after seeing two men who were not being cautious and did not care if we saw them. There were only two of them, which caused me not to have grave concerns. However, I ordered two of the men at a time to stand watch, in case the followers took it upon themselves to destroy their enemy on their own.

On the ride to that first night's camp, I took a chance to quiz Cosimo to get a little deeper into his life, so that I could know him better. It helps to know the person you are fighting next to, the one who you hope will guard your back.

"Cosimo, have you ever been in love, ever thought about getting married?"

"I have and I am," he replied.

"What do you mean?"

"I am in love, and I am married. I have five children because of that love."

Shocked at that revelation, I said, "Why haven't you told me you were married, and why are you putting your life in jeopardy if you have a family back home?"

"I used to be a blacksmith. I pounded on iron for years. It's a hard job and will make an old man out of you before long. Breathing smoke all day, every day, was starting to make me sick, too. The more I pounded iron into horseshoes, swords, farm implements, and door hinges, the more I wanted to do something else. I could barely support my growing family. The children needed clothes, shoes, food, and we all needed shelter. I heard fighting for the wealthy paid more, so I put my apron and hammer down and took up the sword. My father was a great fighter, a knight, in fact, and he taught me as a youth how to fight and defend myself. My wife wasn't happy I left our meager home to shed blood to make a living, but I had to go and see if I could earn a more decent living for all of us. Since then, I have fought for pay and, when the opportunity came up to join you, I took a chance that I could earn enough silver to support my family for a little while longer."

I rode on for a bit, letting the enormity of what he was saying sink in. I felt the weight of responsibility for placing him, the breadwinner of the family, in harm's way. I almost wished I hadn't learned how much he depended on me for income and safekeeping.

"Cosimo, now, I feel bad about taking you on this

impossible trip when the outcome is so unknown and the journey so dangerous. Why don't I pay you for your help thus far, and you return to your wife?"

"You should know me by now, Lord. I never leave a job half done. I'm in this until you are safely on your way home yourself."

"Something I've noticed about you. The fights we've had with the Ashkenazim at the villa and on the beach at Centumcellae, the men plundered the dead bodies for anything of value, but you walked away from that. It was your right to take from those who tried to kill you. It's the rules of battle. Why didn't you?"

"I'm a Jew. I won't loot another Jew's dead body."

It was impossible to describe my thoughts when Cosimo told me that. The chill I was feeling wasn't from the north breeze blowing onto my face. Instead, the chill came from inside me, and I felt the flush in my face that must have turned it red. I wished I had interrogated him before I ever hired him as an accessory in killing his Israeli brothers.

"Cosimo, I'm speechless. You still want to pursue this quest we are on when you know you are fighting against your own people?"

"They are Jews, but they aren't my people, Lord. My people live above ground, they work hard, earning a living by farming, banking, and making things with their hands. They worship Adonai, and they don't kill people for an ideology that has no merit. It's because of the people like we are fighting that has given the Jew a bad name among the gentiles. It is why the Jew is blamed for the black pestilence, for every other natural disaster, and for killing your Jesus. I know what the Torah says. I've been taught the truth by trustworthy rabbis, and I know Francois was dead wrong. I need to be part of this attempt to stop them. No, I must go with you, and I will do whatever I can to help stop their madness. If our God allows it, when this effort is over, I will go home to my wife and family with a conscience unsoiled by what I had to do."

We rode on for a while, each of us absorbed in our own thoughts. My mind was a battle ground of conflicting thoughts. I hoped the newly found out news would not affect my actions when the fight that must take place occurred. I could not allow Cosimo to die on my watch.

Wanting to lighten the mood some, I asked him, "How old are your children?"

"The oldest, Nico, he is twelve. Looks just like me. Renzo is ten, Cecilia is eight, I think, Zora is six, and little Concetta is two. Zora looks just like her mother, Bianca."

"Sounds like you have a wonderful family, Cosimo. When we are back in Rome, I would love to meet them and tell them what a great dad they have."

He laughed and we rode on, both of us hoping the day would come when I could meet his family.

I took the first watch that first night with Benetto, each of us at a point where we could cover the two easiest accesses to our encampment. Our enemy relied heavily on their advanced weaponry and inadequate training and suffered, not only as fighters, but as planners. Not having been a part of the real world where men such as myself had learned by life and death experiences, they depended on untested judgments or had learned from books about fighting on the battlefield. The same kind of reasoning that had gotten about three dozen of them killed so far. I hoped our fighting acumen would continue to keep us safe. My own logic told me that the odds of continued successes could not last indefinitely. The deaths of three of my family bore that out.

After five days, we arrived at the first town of any size, Tarsus, on the 2nd of February 1363. Eesha was very tired of horses by then, having never ridden one more than a mile or so at a time before. At least horses weren't sacred to her like cows were. Tarsus was an important trade center lying next to the Cydrus River. I guessed, by the size and substantial outer wall that encircled the city, there must have been at least twenty thousand inhabitants. From my reading of history books, I knew it was the city where Mark Antony and Cleopatra first met, where Alexander the Great was nearly killed and, of course, was the birthplace of the Apostle Paul. So much of its history had to do with the mythical gods but, on the day, we arrived, none could be found; just barking dogs. Within the city's fortified walls was a very large Catholic church, or it was at least Catholic at one time in its history. Islamic influence around the city was noticeably extensive. From there, we would begin our search for a way into the primary Ashkenazim colony system of underground Jews and meet our primary nemesis, High Priest Yoseph. I knew it would be impossible to find the openings without help; they were too well hidden. I was relying upon the vision I had that mentioned following a tailless dog to a trident tree. I had not mentioned the dog to any of my companions yet, being a little embarrassed to say I was looking for a dog with no tail to lead us to our long-sought destination. It sounded too foolish, yet it was the only clue I had hopes of relying upon. It was a large city, and I found that there were lots of dogs, one had only three legs. I wondered how many there were that had no tails. The first full day there, I saw that there were several cats that had no tail, but I saw no dogs that were tailless.

We stayed in the city long enough to visit the Catholic Church in hopes they could give us an idea as to what to do with Eesha. It was not possible she could join us in our search for cavern openings; it was too dangerous. The church building was still the place of worship for what few Catholics who remained in the increasingly Islamic predominance of the growing city. The building was not as large and magnificent as the cathedrals I have seen in Europe and England but, still, it was an impressive and beautiful example of Roman Gothic design. The priest was probably in his late sixties, Father Romero, and was willing to look after Eesha in hopes he could proselytize her into accepting Catholicism, and, for a contribution to the benevolence fund. The major obstacle for her is that none of the nuns, nor the priest, spoke Bengali. Nor did they speak English. Father Romero promised to inquire among the city's large population if anyone knew her language. It being a significant merchant port city, I had no doubts there were a few who could. India was made up of a population that spoke perhaps a hundred and twenty languages, but Hindi and Bengali were the two most widely spoken.

"Eesha," I said to her before leaving her in their capable hands, "these people will help you to adjust in your new environment. They are good and kind people and will take good care of you. I will have to be away for a little while, but I will be back before long to check on how you are doing. I would not leave you here if I thought you were in danger of harm. Will you be okay while I'm gone?"

"Oh, Master Troy, be it okay with me. I speak kindly of

you. Me give much thank you. Me forward looking when you stand here again sometime. Come see me quickly, I say please. Do no harm for yourself, Okay?"

"Uh-huh," I said and left the church to find my waiting companions. I thought to myself, *the nuns will have an interesting, even entertaining, time with her.*

Gerald said, "Poppa, it might be a good idea that I stay here with Eesha to make sure she gets settled in alright. What do you think?"

"Uh-huh," I said with a "you-got-to-be-kidding-me-look. There was enough derision from my men, and their accompanying chuckles to make him feel he needed to come with us.

Each day we searched, closely, different areas in the broad expanse of wilderness. We investigated the rocky foothills, primarily, where I suspected the openings might be, because that is where they were in England. Days went by with no success. I looked for rising smoke from vents, from cliff walls, that might hide a hidden doorway, or brush that could conceal an opening, but we found none. Each day that we left our camps, we were followed, so our search did not go unnoticed. Cosimo suggested we attempt to capture one of the men following us and force him to tell us about a way into their underground caverns. I worried that the two would become twenty at any time. How did they know who we were? They must know why we were there. It must have only been curiosity on their part that we still lived. It was possible they wanted to see if we, who were diligently looking for an entrance, could find one. I suspected they could send a thousand men at us at any time. They were acting like cats playing with mice, and we were the mice.

I worried that time was slipping away from us. Every day reduced my limited funds a little more, and every day brought us closer to the day Connie promised to reveal our secret when she would inform the King Edward of the Jew's ominous plan. I had reservations that he would believe her, even receive her, but, if he did, it could set off a series of events that I did not want to happen. England and France were at war, like they always seemed to be, so I doubted King Edward would talk to the King of France, Jean Le Bon. I knew trying to set a deadline on our quest would be foolish and dangerous, also. The problem was I knew Armageddon was imminent. One problem at a time, I tried to pound into my head.

Each day, we covered a different area that had rocky outcroppings that could easily conceal openings but, if they were there, we couldn't identify them. On the eighth day, while we were passing through a small village north and east of Tarsus that probably didn't contain more than two dozen inhabitants living in mud brick houses, I saw a black and white spotted dog get up from a sunny spot in the dusty street it had been sleeping in. I watched him stretch, shake the dust off, and walk north towards the edge of the village. Occasionally, he would turn his head and look at us, as if beckoning. The south end of that dog showed that it had no tail. I was still hesitant to believe it could be of any help, but it was worth following. I said nothing to my companions, I just followed the animal as it continued to walk past the last mud brick home towards the bleak and arid wilderness beyond. Then, it turned east, seeming to aimlessly walk just to be walking. Gerald finally asked where I was going. I told him I was interested in seeing where the dog was going. You might imagine the look he gave me.

For an hour we rode. Reaching a patch of forest, and then, along an animal trail to part of the foothills we had not inspected before. The trail became broader, joined, and ran alongside a narrow stream flowing away from us. Still, the dog walked on. Now and then, he turned his head and looked at us like he wanted to be sure we were still behind him, that we hadn't given up. The underbrush around the trees began to thin out as we came upon a stretch of rocks that looked as if they had been pushed up out of the ground long ago by a great force from below. The ground consisted of packed earth for a while, and then, became flat, solid rock. Great boulders jutted outward creating many openings, or small caves, but none were big enough for a man to enter without crouching. When the dog stopped, laid down, and put his head on his paws, I looked up, and ahead just yards away, I saw a tall conifer tree. It was unusual in that halfway up its trunk, two arms, or branches, forked off making it appear to be three trees at the top.

A trident tree.

If the vision I had was true, and I no longer doubted it was, then we had found the location of at least one entrance to the underground world of the primary Ashkenazi habitation. Somewhere under those rocks, the High Priest presided over a nation of Jews. The man who held our lives and the lives of many, many others in his hands. All we had to do was lie in wait and watch. Sooner or later, someone would enter or exit from the entrance. Turns out, we didn't have to wait long.

Not from a cave entrance, but from the dense undergrowth nearby, dozens of men, some on horses, many more on foot, emerged. In just a few moments, we were surrounded by them. A hundred maybe, but probably a lot more. Swords and gonnes pointed at us and, with that many, there was no way they could all miss.

One of the mounted riders rode forward and said, "Troy, we've been expecting you."

Chapter Sixteen

The Long-Awaited Confrontation with the High Priest

It is dangerous to be right in matters where established men are wrong.
—Voltaire

My companions and I were forced to dismount, and hoods were placed over our heads. A rope was tied to my neck, and the same rope went around each of the other's necks, also, so that we must have looked like a human centipede. Each of our hands were tied behind our backs. We were led for perhaps fifty yards, told to wait, and then led through an opening leading to the underground. The only way I could tell we were leaving our world of sunshine was the change in temperature around us. After leaving the chilled air aboveground, we found it was warmer and more comfortable once below where the weather and temperature never changes. We walked for a long time, sometimes going down a series of steps, often turning either right or left. I could hear the hum of something far off, and sometimes, it was a hissing sound. We approached a room where we heard muted clanging of metal against metal, like a forge where a giant blacksmith pounded out metal objects. Sometimes, people passed by murmuring in Hebrew their surprise at seeing us. More than once, we were shoved, accidentally or on purpose, I did not know, by passersby. The hoods we wore were thick, but I could still recognize when we went from a dark area into one with light. More than once, one of us stumbled because of the change in floor elevation. At first, I smelled mold and earth, but that gave way to smells of oil, wax, sawdust, food cooking, and smoke, even incense. Occasionally, we passed by what I believed to be an eating establishment, because a myriad of food smells reminded me that I was hungry. At last, we were led into a compartment and told to stand still. In a moment, the compartment began dropping. I counted to thirty-five slowly, and the room we were in stopped, a soft sliding sound and a door was opened.

We entered a hall that was colder than all the rest of the areas we were led through and told to stop. Five of us had our ropes removed and were pushed into a room, and then, an iron door closed behind us. Nearby, the other five were likewise pushed into a neighboring room.

From the moment we were surrounded, I began blaming myself for this final humiliation of leading all of us into captivity. I knew we were being followed by our enemy, but I was too focused on reaching a goal to think about defense, like a wild hog is lured into a trap by bait inside. I wished I had sent out a scout ahead of us. I wanted to come face to face with the High Priest too strongly to think of ways to avoid getting caught. There would be no way to escape from such a deep level in the earth with thousands of soldiers making sure we didn't go anywhere unnoticed. I imagined I could feel the thoughts of my men accusing me of our capture. There would be no escaping this cell like I did with Eliab's help in England. We would be too closely monitored.

Once in our prison cell, we were permitted to remove our hoods and constraints. Gerald, Carlos, Mattia, Luigi, and I were in a room consisting of four shaped-stone walls and a floor of natural, slightly uneven, stone. One wall, the one we entered, had an iron door with a small opening about a foot square in it to permit viewing by those who imprisoned us. There were no benches or other furniture. A wooden bucket in one corner was obviously our latrine. A light of some origin, maybe by way of sparks, was just outside the view port, which allowed us to see very little inside our confinement. It was one of the most miserable prison cells I have been in, and I had been in many.

I could hear the men in the room next to us talking but could not make out what they said. The stone wall between us prevented us from being able to communicate without shouting. I studied the door and its locking mechanism. As always, I still had a stiff wire in my boot heel for the purpose of opening locks when keys were not available. The lock in the door was not a normal padlock kind, it was inset into the door. I would give it a try at some point, but I could not tell if there were guards outside our door, or not. I needed a vision from God, because I could not imagine a way out of this mess on my own.

There was no way of telling the passing of time. I don't know if it was an hour or five hours before the door was opened, and food and water were delivered to us. The food was in a bucket and smelled of goat cheese, milk, and unleavened bread, making a distasteful, lumpy soup. It was unsavory to me, to say the least. I managed to get down one swallow and let the men have the rest. A clay pot contained water that was at least cold and sweet.

It must have been the next day, after we had slept on the hard floor for some time, when the door opened, and someone asked in Hebrew if one of us was a man named Troy. A hood was once again placed on my head, my hands shackled behind my back with iron cuffs rather than a rope, and I was led out, where I walked between at least one man in front and one man behind me, but there could have been more than that. It was clear they were not taking any chances with me, knowing I had escaped one of their prison cells in England. We walked for some time, took another lift that brought us up to another level, and through many halls and turns, hearing and sensing many sounds and smells before I was stopped. For just a moment, I stood there; then, shoved forward, and told to sit down. While my hands remained bound behind me, they removed my hood. A door behind me was closed.

The room was bright with light, and it took me some time to adjust my eyes to the brightness. Across the room sat a man in a beautiful purple robe embroidered with gold thread on black cloth accents, creating scenes depicting trees, sheep, shepherds, and grape vines winding around the settings. A beautiful snow-white, silken scarf was around his neck and draped down his body to his waist. On his head was a crimson red hat that stood high upon his head. The regal man sat in a gilded chair that matched the grandeur of his clothes. Obviously, he was the High Priest. The very man I wanted to see. The man who held my destiny in his hands. He was younger than I thought he would be, maybe fifty years at the most, his hair still black, matching his dark and foreboding staring eyes. On each side of him sat three other men, similarly dressed, but not quite as fine as the High Priest. I reckoned them to be Chief Priests, his subordinates.

They all were staring at me. I figured they wanted a good look at the man who had caused them so much trouble over recent months. The intensity of their stares, the wrinkled brows, the pursed lips, almost made me want to laugh. I couldn't think of a worse time to laugh, though, so I didn't. If hate were water, I was floating on an ocean. Hate was what I was seeing in those unflinching eyes. Their dark eyebrows almost touched as they sent eye-darts at me. I carried with me my own baggage of hate, as well. I said nothing, letting them start the conversation. I could have predicted what they would say.

"Troy, the gentile who has traveled from Brittania just to be captured by us, who has caused us so much trouble, and has traveled so far in a hopeless hope to thwart our providence. You have been an irritating thorn in our side these last few months. I think we can finally remove that thorn. Now, you are helpless and in our custody at last. You have cost the lives of many of our people, disrupted our peace, and you are attempting to stop what can't be stopped, while tarnishing our reputation at the same time. Too much time and resources have been expended because of you. I need not tell you that we can't let you continue your tiring efforts to stop what Adonai has ordained. You and your companions are the last to know the secrets you are trying to reveal to the world. When you die, your foolish acts of rebellion will be over, and we can get back to doing what we, as a chosen nation, have been appointed to do. Rest assured, my deranged prisoner, we will go forward with the plans to fulfill our ancient intention, but you will not live to see it fulfilled."

I said, "Do you not know what the Torah says? Do you, as High Priest, not know exactly what Scripture says? Do you not know that God never gave you England or any land between there and here? Do you not know that to add or take away from God's word is blasphemy?"

I would have said more, but I was hit hard in the back of my head with a gloved fist.

"Now, now. Let the man talk. Just this once. You are a fool and an irritation. Of course, I know what the Torah says. How else could I become High Priest? I know exactly where the promised land lies. I know it doesn't say anything about England, France, or the so-called Holy Roman Empire. That's all beside the point, you gentile dog. We have been persecuted since pharaoh kept us as slaves thousands of years ago, tormented by Roman emperors, and by pathetic and frightened gentiles across the world. What we plan to take is extra payment for all that persecution brought upon us. Land that is over and above the land promised to us in the Holy Scripture. Call it usuary if you wish, interest payment due us for our suffering. If it weren't for people like you, we would not be living underground like animals and would not have to claim land not belonging to us. We will not be forced to wear yellow badges to show that we are Jews like our aboveground brethren are compelled. Jews are required by caliphates and European despots in your vile world to wear the badges of shame as if we are an inferior people. The fact is, we are the superior race."

I replied, "God has given me a vision too, priest. He told me that you are in defiance and will fail in this plan of yours.

You will not only fail, but you will be punished for adding to his holy word. God has said, 'woe unto the person who adds to his word.'"

Once again, I was hit in the back of the head.

"No matter," the High Priest said. "You have simply been a minor annoyance to us, and, for that, you must pay for your deeds. All of you. The rabbi you talked to in Rome for what he might have heard from you, and the rabbi in the English Colony for allowing you to escape with two of our people, they are both dead, thanks to you. Bring her in."

A guard standing near the back corner of the room, opened a door and, in a moment, led a woman in.

"Connie?!"

"Poppa!"

My daughter was ordered to sit in a chair placed in front of the High Priest, twenty feet in front of me. I tried to stand up but was forced back down by the two men standing behind me. I tried to remove my hands from the shackles, but it was no use; it was impossible. My mind and my gut were churning in a soup of anger, anguish, helplessness, and blame! How can it be that she was there in that room? I had believed she was safely back in London!

"Are you okay and where are Kat and Troy," I asked.

"Don't worry about them," the High Priest said. "They are fine. We don't harm children; they are our future. In fact, we won't harm your daughter, Connie, either. They will remain with us and become part of our community. I can't say the same for you and the other men you brought with you. I'm afraid we can't let you live and spoil what we have going here. Just a little bit of leaven can spoil the dough. As far as the Jew, Pagiel, well, we will have to decide what to do with him later, but I dare say that he is guilty of treason, among many other sins, and will die."

"Do what you want with me, I don't care anymore. I'm the cause of us being here. My men, my grandson, let them live. Gerald is just a child himself. He can do you no harm."

"Are you actually begging me?" the priest mocked.

My face flushed with heat that sprung from rage or embarrassment or both. I swallowed my pride long enough to beg for the first time in my long life, even though I knew it was of little use.

The priest said, "Pride! It was the first ever sin, you know. Satan was so in love with himself, so filled with thoughts of his own importance and beauty, he was exiled from heaven. Here you are, so filled with pride, it hurts your feelings to beg. Well, we all have some of that, don't we? I'm glad to see how contrite you are, but I'm afraid it will do you no good. All ten of you will die, and it won't be an easy death, either. Did you give Eliasaph, or should I say Francois, an easy, painless death? Or, my old friend Asa, on the shore at Centumcellae?"

I could see rage building in his face as he relayed the deaths of the two men who were directly responsible for the death of Carl. I attempted to rise again. If I could have a half-dozen heart beats of freedom, I could cross the twenty or so feet between us and, even though my hands were tied behind me, my mouth could do a great deal of damage to the priest before I was pulled away. The guards must have anticipated my thoughts because they each placed hands on my shoulders. "*God help me, please,*" I begged him in my mind.

"Take him back to his cell," the priest ordered.

Unfettered, Connie jumped up, ran to me, and put her

arms around my neck. "Wait for Luca," she whispered in my ear before she was drug away by two other guards.

Luca! I had forgotten about him. He must still be alive and free! Did the priest not know he was still alive? Connie must have meant for me not to do anything foolish that would get me, and my men, killed sooner than planned. In my fevered mind, I grasped at a thread of hope of achieving freedom once more. Maybe even a chance to put my hands around the throat of the High Priest. I have faced so many men in my life who were despicable enemies, but none were as dangerous and ominous as that so-called man of God.

Once again, the black hood was placed over my head and with a strong hand on each of my arms, I was led back to where my companions sat in dark and damp prison cells. I longed to have my hands free and the comforting feeling of a dagger or sword in my hand again but wishing wasn't putting steel in my hand nor shackles loosed from my wrists.

I never have prayed enough. I have, just like the twelve apostles, seen the risen Christ with my own eyes, on at least two occasions. Sadly, I let my life get so filled with going and doing and living that I allowed the sight of his holy face fade into the background in my busy mind. Sometimes, in the quiet moments before sleep comes or while sitting by my favorite spot next to a fast-running stream, the amazing visual sensation comes back to me. Ater I was shoved back into my cell, I gathered the other four in my room, and I led us in a prayer. Gerald and the others, I doubted, were believers in God, but no matter, I prayed a long prayer of contrition, asking for forgiveness for my arrogance and my failures to lead the perfect life I was commanded to lead. I prayed for another chance for freedom, if not for me, at least for those who followed me on my fool's errand. I thought of the vision that I interpreted to believe I was part of God's plan to stop his nation from making a mistake. Maybe I was putting ideas in God's mind that were not his, but mine. I asked my Maker to help us, to grant us freedom, to spoil the High Priest's plan to cause chaos and havoc in the world, and to let us all find peace in our own place in the world. I prayed I would have the chance to see Catherine Adele and Troy grow up and to see Connie content again. I had lost so much, caused so much pain for others and for myself. I promised God, if he spared my family and friends, I would live out the rest of my life, however long that was, minding my own business.

With no idea of the passing of time, I estimated that we were in the prison room for two additional days when I heard the door to the room next to us open. It wasn't time for food, so I rose and looked out our door's small window and saw my five hoodless companions, all tied together, being led out.

"Cosimo, Branca, Ferrante, Benetto, Enzo, stay strong, have faith," I said to them as they were led down the hall by ten soldiers. In just a few moments, our door was opened, and we were led out. This time, hoods were also not placed over our heads, just our hands were tied with ropes. I supposed that was because it no longer mattered what we saw, since we would not be returning from wherever we were being led. That meant we were on our final journey. Our time had come to pay for our deeds. Only a divine miracle could save us now. My thoughts turned to Luca. Was it possible he could help us?

After taking the lift, an amazing fete that still intrigued me, we walked down many corridors, the five of us arrived at a large room where my five other companions awaited us. The room we were in held cabinets, storage boxes, sacks of all sizes and shapes, wheeled carts, crates of food and drink, and all kinds of equipment, the likes of which I had never seen before. Maps and written information were attached to wood pedestals, information I would also love to examine had I not been on my way to being executed. Inside the room, Yoseph, the High Priest was present, as well as the six Chief Priests. Also with them was Connie. All of them were there to witness our executions. I did not see Catherine Adele or Troy. I wanted badly to see them once more, hug them one more time, but was glad they would not see my death.

We were warned to say nothing. Our hands had been tied behind our backs since we left our prison cells. Two soldiers held on to each rope affixed to our hands. That meant there were more than twenty soldiers in the room. They were not taking any chances with us. The High Priest said something to one soldier, who then walked over to a lever, pulled it down, and a large door began a slow slide to the right, allowing daylight to enter our room, and the sweet smell of fresh air rushed in to replace the stench of deceit and folly I had been breathing for the last two days.

When we emerged from the cavern, twenty more men with horses met us. The sun was high and bright, hurting our eyes, unaccustomed to the precious sight of the sun above. The High and Chief Priests mounted a horse, and Connie was forced to mount one, as well. Her hands were also tied together, and the rope led from her hands to a waiting and mounted soldier. No words were said by anyone. The only sounds were the distant bark of a dog and the chirps from a choir of sparrows in the nearby bushes. Off to my right, sitting high up on a giant boulder, sat a tailless dog watching us. We were not in the open by any means, but in a smallish arena surrounded by large boulders obscured to the world around us. The curious could not have seen us get organized for the death march.

We emerged from a narrow opening in the rocks and walked across a narrow valley with high cliffs on both sides. My companions and I walked for maybe half an hour when we emerged into a larger canyon, maybe fifty yards across. The Jews had found the perfect place to stay hidden from the curious outside world. Connie was forced to ride next to the High Priest, and I could not get a chance to talk to her, but I saw she looked back often to see how we were doing. I could tell she had been crying a lot and that broke my heart.

I looked towards the top of the stacks of boulders all around us, hoping for some hint of relief, maybe Luca or some person or persons who might could see our plight and sound an alarm, but I saw nothing by a few crows passing overhead. A few crows and one dog sitting up on his haunches. I remembered Pagiel saying I would survive to return to England, but I could not see how that was possible at that moment. Maybe he was wrong this time.

The soldiers dismounted and went about carrying out instructions they must have been given previously, because few words were spoken. I saw ten horses lined up and, across from them, about twenty feet, ten more, and then, I knew what our deaths were to be. We were to be killed just as Francois had been. I don't know exactly how they knew we killed him, but his remains must have been enough to figure it out. Now, I wished I had buried the man's body. Another mistake. My anger at him had turned around to bite me weeks later.

Between forty-five and fifty soldiers surrounded us, in addition to the priests and Connie. Time and hope were running out. I was about to join the billions of other people who had died before me. My life was just another grain of sand on a gigantic beach. I reckoned life would still go on for those who still lived and precious few would mourn my passing. Death becomes more personal when it is your turn. Many pictures passed through my mind of people I loved and many faces of people I had killed. I never felt any remorse for those my blades had killed, as if their deaths were not as important as my own. Well, we all must die sometime, even me.

With a loud voice, the High Priest spoke: "To the gentile pagan who is known as Troy, you and your companions have been found guilty of treasonous actions, murder, and blasphemy. These horrific acts are judged to be worthy of death. As High Priest, supported and attested to by the council of Chief Priests of the nation of Adonai, we pronounce you guilty of all charges and now your execution will begin. Any last words from the leader of this coven of evil men?"

"Soldiers," I began, "your priests are lying to you. What they are telling you is in defiance of your God's commands and, if you continue to do their bidding, you will perish, as will your friends and family. I implore you to stop being their pawns in this madness."

The priest chuckled, and the soldiers looked at each other, wondering if what I said had any merit to it. No one would make the first move, so that meant no one would disobey their God's emissary, the High Priest, and his minions. It was so quiet then. I only heard the squeaking leather of saddles made by horses tired of standing still. That and a lone dog barking high up on the cliff.

"Okay, we have heard enough. It's time to begin the

execution. Just as you murdered Eliasaph, you will be executed. May Adonai have mercy on your..."

I waited for the word "soul" to emerge from his mouth, but he was stunned to see what I had just heard. A new sound. I heard a soft thump behind me; then, another. I turned to see arrows sticking out of the two men holding the rope around my neck. The priests were too stunned for long moments before they could react and, in the meantime, more arrows were falling, slicing through the air, shushing as arrow feathers parted the still air. Whump, whump, whump. Soldiers tried to mount their horses, the horses pulling against their reigns, panicking over the smell of blood. I saw something small and black fall from the sky, and, in a moment, a loud explosion sent pieces of iron balls into the flesh of a group of soldiers. Another one fell, then, another. Men, a dozen, maybe two dozen, scrambled down the boulders towards us; men I had never seen before. One of them ran up to me, cut the rope binding my hands and handed me a sword. That was all I needed, the feel of steel in my hands again. It was retribution time.

I yelled at those who appeared to be our saviors to capture the priests, but do not kill them. The soldiers, though, were given no quarter. They had been warned. I saw one take out his gonne, and I ran my sword through his side, yanked it out, and ran towards another. By then, my companions were free and armed, and the killing did not stop until all soldiers were dead, except for three or four who had escaped on horseback.

Luca said, "Don't worry about those who escaped. Three of my men are at the cave opening; they will take care of them."

"Luca!" I grasped both of his shoulders with my hands and touched his forehead with mine. "Luca, you have much to tell me, my brother but, for now, I thank you for saving all of us. I owe you for saving our lives. Now, will you help me get the rest of my children back?"

I found Connie amongst the killing field; she was holding a sword given to her by someone, or one she took from a dead soldier. Blood dripped from the tip and fell into the dry sand at her feet. She and two others of our saviors were guarding the priests. The High Priest was cowering and had lost control of his bladder. His purple robe was soiled. I hugged her long and deeply; then, asked her if she knew where Kat and Troy were.

"Yes, I know. We were kept in the same room while the priests figured out what to do with us, but where is Carl?"

"He's dead, Connie. He was taken by a group of Ashkenazim who wanted to trade him for Francois but, instead, they killed him. What about Pagiel? Is he alive? Is he here?"

"Carl. Dead. My last brother! I hate these murderers, Poppa! Won't they ever leave us alone? Pagie? He at least was alive the last time I saw him, but that was a week ago. He is, or was, somewhere in the caverns. I don't know where, probably in a prison cell. What are you going to do with these so-called priests? I vote that we kill them today, right now, and then, let's go home."

That was a good question and suggestion. I wanted to kill them, too, but I wondered if God would be angry with me for killing his priests, even though they were deluded. I had to think about that but, somehow, they had to be the key to stopping the centuries old plan they had devised. Also, they might be useful as a means of bargaining with the rest of the Ashkenazim.

I looked at the dead men, forty-two of them, and several

horses killed by the bomb blasts, arrows, and swords, and I wondered who the two dozen rescuers were who I had never seen before. I looked for Luca and saw him standing next to Connie with his arm around her shoulders. That was another question I had for him, but that would come later.

"Luca, who are all these men you brought?"

"That heavy bag of coins you gave me back at the villa was used to hire them. I found them in Antioch and Aleppo. They are experienced fighting men and hungry for coin. The hand-bombs were those you bought in Rome but did not use. I gave the men what silver I had and promised them more when we rescued you. They are good fighting men, although we don't communicate well."

He grinned when he said they were promised more.

"They will have plenty of chances for plunder, starting with those laying on the ground, as well as the priests who have plenty of gold hanging on them. Catherine Adele and Troy are still in the caverns. Connie knows where they are, and I think we can use the High Priest as a ticket to get them out. Pagiel, too, needs rescuing."

I don't know how they knew so soon, but a few buzzards were already gathering overhead for a buffet no buzzard could refuse.

"Luca, how did you avoid being captured along with Connie and the rest, and how were you so sure my men and I were captured that you hired two dozen mercenaries to free us?"

"I wasn't entirely sure about you and your companions. I suspected it, because the city seemed to be crawling with the Ashkenazim, but I hired the mercenaries mostly to help me free Connie and the children, and Pagiel also, if possible. I had followed the band of men escorting Connie and the kids to their cavern, so I knew where they were being held. After seeing where they went into the mountain, I left to hire the men you see here. While scouting the area, hoping we could see people exiting the cavern, we saw you and the others being led outside, apparently to be executed."

"When we were in Centumcellae, we found an inn near the wharves to stay in until we found a ship. I left Connie and the children at the inn while I went out to get some supplies, look for ships that might be heading west, and to talk to sea captains. After finding one that would do, that would get us closer to our desired destination, I returned to the inn to join your family. I had not yet reached the inn when I saw Connie and the others being led outside by a dozen armed men. They had not seen me, and I doubted they knew I was nearby. I followed them until they boarded a sleek ship that appeared to be as fast as it was sleek. I was worried they might leave immediately, and I would have no way of following. It's a long way from Centumcellae to Antioch. The gods, or your God, was with me, though, lord. At first, it seemed the ship belonged to the Ashkenazim, since they walked onto the ship as if they owned it, and never walked off again before it sailed. Lucky for us, the wind and tide were contrary to embarking, because they stayed tied up to the wharves overnight, and did not leave until the next morning when wind and tide were satisfactory. That night, late, after everyone had eaten and was thinking about bedding down, I approached the ship. By then, I had purchased different clothing, so I wouldn't look like a fighting man, more like a businessman actually, my swords hidden under my new cloak. I quietly talked to the captain about paying him to take me, also, when the ship left port. He said the ship was chartered by a group of men escorting a woman and her children, and his ship wasn't available for other passengers. It took some negotiating skills that I didn't know I had to convince him to bring me along. I paid him handsomely and, at the same time, promised him much business in the future if he allowed me as a passenger. I promised him, also, that I would stay out of sight of everyone, and the others would not even know I was on board. That was a promise I knew was necessary, anyway."

"I got mighty hungry and thirsty along the way, with food given to me only when it was convenient and was very tired of staying cooped up in a very small cabin for the duration of the voyage. We arrived, not at Antioch, as I thought we would, but at the port in Tarsus. When we docked, I hurriedly left the ship and waited near the end of the gang plank, waiting for Connie to appear. Then, I saw her walking towards me carrying Troy, with a man on each side of her and Kat behind them. I had prepared a note telling her I was there and would follow them until I figured out a way for her rescue. She did not recognize me because of my clothes and because my beard was close shaven. I looked too respectable to be me. Anyway, when she approached, I pretended to stumble on a loose board on the walkway and put the note in her hand. She was wise enough to grasp the note and did not look at it until it was safe. That is how I happen to be here today."

"Luca, I will never be able to thank you enough or recompense you enough for all that you have done for my children and me. I hope, one day, I can repay you for the trouble you have been put through."

"Lord, it was no trouble at all. Connie means a lot to me, and your other children also, of course."

When we returned to the location of the only doorway we knew about into the underworld, there were three more dead Ashkenazi soldiers laying on the ground, killed by Luca's mercenaries, their horses feeding nearby on grass sprouting from between rocks. I forced a priest to show us how to open the door on the pain of death if he didn't. He promptly revealed the hidden lever. Before I entered the cavern with my friends and family, I looked up at the high rocky cliff top and saw a dog that looked just like the one we followed in our search for the opening we were about to enter. The animal turned sideways for a moment and looked down on us, then turned and disappeared. I noted that the dog had no tail.

Chapter Seventeen

An Unsettling Dream and a New Danger

Upon waking in the morning, consider the privilege it is to be alive, to have the ability to think, to experience joy, and to feel love.
—*Marcus Aurelius*

Lest I forgot again, before entering back into the cavern, I took some moments to thank God for our rescue that, earlier, had seemed to be impossible. Maybe Pagiel was correct; maybe I would survive but, still, much had to be accomplished.

Luca, Cosimo, Connie, Gerald, and the seven other men who had been by my side for many weeks discussed what steps we would take next. In another corner of the large room, ten of Luca's men were guarding the seven priests. Connie knew the room the children were in but wasn't sure how to get there from where we stood. Gerald grabbed the High Priest's arm, drug him over to where we were and tied a rope around his neck that had once been on one of ours.

Gerald said, "High Priest...by the way, what is your name?"

He smelled of urine and fear and humility. My desire to

kill the man was still strong, and maybe I would, but not until we were at a safe place. Also, I had to try and convince him to change his life's ambition in the next few hours. Otherwise, I could never know when another pack of Ashkenazim might show up at my house one day and kill me or someone close to me. My quest was to stop their plans. Saving my family from capture wasn't part of the original plan, wasn't the reason I was going back into the lion's den.

"My name is Yoseph. It seems it is now my turn to beg, sir. For the sake of my people and my family, I beg of you to spare my life and the lives of my priests. I'll do whatever you ask of me."

"We will talk about that later but," I said, "right now, I want to retrieve my children, and you will help me do that. Come with us."

The priest took us on a convoluted route to the rooms dedicated to the High Priest and his immediate family. There, we met his wife and three youths in their teens, one boy of fifteen, and two girls, one and two years younger. The girls seemed pleasant enough, courteous, but frightened to meet topsiders. The son had a scowl, and I could see hate in his eyes. I should have watched him a little closer. We were their first aboveground people who were not Jews, they had ever met. In a spare room nearby, we found my children. Catherine Adele ran to me and cried, believing she would never see me again. Troy was playing on the floor with some toys the priests' children had given him. I will always believe my children, if they had not been recovered, were to become the priest's and his wife to raise and nurture. That thought made me hate the man a little bit less. It also complicated what I had to do with him.

My little man, my only boy left to me, reached his arms towards me, and said, "Poppa." For the first time in a long time, I wept. If only Dania and Jaleel could be there with me, and that thought brought me back to reality.

"Yoseph, you must come with me, and we must have a long and serious talk."

I remember turning around and heading for the door leading out of the priest's apartment. I remember a loud explosive sound, and, at almost the same time, I felt a searing hot pain in my upper body. Then, nothing.

When I opened my eyes again, I was lying in a bed, and Connie's head was laying on her arms next to my knees.

"My Connie," I softly said.

She raised her head quickly, as if I had startled her. Then a broad smile lit up her beautiful face. My daughter, the last child left from Anna's and my marriage. If Connie's hair was yellow/gold like her mother's, they could have looked like twins.

"Poppa!"

She hugged me, left to tell the others that I was still alive, and then, returned.

During those moments she was away, I thought about the dream, if it was a dream, I had before my eyes opened in that unknown bed, in an unknown room, somewhere far underground. It was a wonderful dream, because it answered the question haunting my mind for months, no, years, or at least it gave me a strong clue as to how to conclude my impossible task of stopping the Ashkenazim from committing a terrible mistake.

She returned with Luca and Cosimo, who had stood guard outside my door while I slept.

"How long have I been sleeping?"

When I tried to get up to get out of bed, I felt a sharp pain in my chest and back. I looked down and saw bandages wrapped around my upper body and remembered the sudden pain and noise before I fell asleep.

"As best I can tell in this place without windows to know when it is day or night, I would say either two or three days," Connie said.

"Felt like twenty days to me," said Luca. "I'm like a tree. I need sunshine now and then to survive. I don't know how these moles can tolerate living like this."

"Three days?!," I almost shouted. "What happened to me? Why am I bandaged like this."

I tried again to get up but was pushed back down by Connie.

"Just lay there. We have everything under control. The boy, the High Priest's son, shot you with one of their so-called gonnes. He was angry you were taking control out of his father's hands. The Jews have a very nice hospital with great healers, who are called chirurgeons here. One of them, Chadli, with others assisting him, opened you up to sew the holes in your left lung made by the lead ball. The ball had entered your back and exited the front of your chest, making holes in and out of that lung, as well as your body. Chadli cut open your chest, broke a rib to better reach your lung and sewed the holes closed. I watched it all to make sure he didn't finish what the boy started. I think he did a good job, and he has checked on you two or three times every day since. He should be here again soon. He takes his healing seriously. The hired men Luca brought with him are being used to secure certain areas. Two are always stationed outside the priests' room.

Enzo, Carlos, and Bennetto tried to take the highest army officer who is left to locate all the hidden entrances to this underground world, but he refused. They tried coercion, but with no luck. When you are well enough, you can try to get the point across to him that we won't take no for an answer. You have a talent for convincing people to cooperate."

"Where is the High Priest?"

"He's in a prison cell with his son. The Chief Priests are in the next room. We put them there until you can decide what to do with them."

"I will want to talk to the High Priest soon but, first, who is the commanding officer of their army?"

"He's dead," said Luca. "So is the next in command. They were killed with the other soldiers when my mercenaries attacked at your failed execution."

"Well, who is next in command?"

Cosimo explained, "It seems every person in this vast hole, ultimately, is in submission to the High Priest, including the army. The army does have their own leadership, but the religious leaders have overall authority down here, or that is how it is supposed to be, but it may not be the case any longer. The newest person in command of the military is a young man named Chaim. I can get him whenever you are ready to talk to him."

"I will want to talk to the High Priest and Chaim at the same time. Has anyone discovered where Pagiel is? Is he still alive?"

Connie smiled and said, "Yes, we found him. He was in one of the prison cells just across the hall and two rooms down from where the priests are kept. He is alive, shaken, but okay otherwise. He is eager to see you and, when you are stronger, you can talk to him. He has some things he wants to say to you."

While we were talking and catching up on what had happened over the past week, a tall stranger knocked at the door and walked up to me. Connie introduced him as my talented chirurgeon, Chadli.

"You appear to be still alive and, by the looks of you, healing nicely. I worried at first, that we might lose you, but you have a strong body and a strong will to live, I think."

When he smiled, I saw the glint of one gold tooth in the otherwise perfect set of very white teeth. The man who an ethereal old woman on a beach in Centumcellae had foretold would save my life.

"Thank you for your willingness to take care of me under the circumstances."

"No circumstances would prevent me from healing someone who needs healing. It is my calling and my pleasure, sir. I will change your bandages, and it would be best if you rested in peace this afternoon. In fact, the rest of the next week."

I fell asleep again and, when I woke up, Connie shoved a bowl of wonderful smelling soup in my face and told me to eat. I had not eaten in days and was terribly hungry and thirsty.

"Where am I, Connie?"

"You are in the High Priest's apartment, in his very own bedroom. He wasn't using it. His wife is rooming with their daughters across the great room. The wife, Hila, made this soup for you. She feels terrible because the son shot you. I think they could be nice people, just confused and easily fooled by wolves in sheep's clothing."

"I've got to get up. I can't stand to lay here any longer.

Please bring the High Priest and the new army commander to me. It's time I revealed what's going to happen next. I suppose I should tell you, also. Bring Luca, Cosimo, Gerald, Carlos, and Enzo, and I will tell you all first.

After telling my closest companions what was revealed to me in my dream and having a short discussion afterwards, the men left to retrieve the priest and the commander.

Connie said, "Are you sure about this Poppa? I mean, are you sure the dream was real enough to wager our future on it and the future of England and Europe? It sounds like it could work, I trust your judgment, but I don't know. I hope it will end this nightmare that has nearly destroyed us."

"I think the creature gave me good advice, but he or she just did not tell me how to do what was spoken to me. The people who speak to me in visions never give me specifics. I am left to interpret what they tell me."

We all gathered in the great room, and I then told the High Priest and the army's newest commander what was going to take place.

During my unconscious state after being shot, I dreamt I met something or someone. It was the most beautiful creature I had ever seen. The creature did not appear to be either a man or a woman. Maybe it was both; maybe it was neither. It was so beautiful, appeared so authoritative, that I started to kneel before it. I knew it wasn't God, but it seemed so perfect, so holy, so magnificent, that worship of it seemed like the right thing to do. It wouldn't let me do that, however. He, or it, said he was no more important than I, but he had a message for me. He said that I was not ready to go with him to wherever he was from, but that I had more work to do and, thus, I was to remain and, after recovering, finish the task I was given. Soon, he said, it would be time for my long rest. The creature told me the Ashkenazim must be exposed. To expose them would be to destroy their mission.

That was it. Nothing more. Like all the other visions I've had in my long life, they were all cryptic, leaving the interpretation up to me. It was maddening sometimes. After I awoke from my days of sleep, I meditated on the word "exposed" and concluded that the Ashkenazim must leave their world. All of them. Every colony. Evicted. Exposed to the aboveground world. Much easier said than accomplished, I reckoned.

The High Priest and the commander weren't buying what I said must happen.

The Priest was shaking his head, and the commander said, "What you are saying is impossible for us. We will not just give up our commitment and expose ourselves to the world on your word that it is the right thing to do. You are a fool to think we would take your word, a pagan gentile, for what we, as a chosen nation, should do." Then he laughed at the idea, which angered me.

"Soldier, you don't have a choice. Your priest knows that what he and his ancestors have told you is a lie. You, your army, all your people, are committing your lives to a fallacy. A mindset that will lead to your ultimate destruction."

"Cosimo, Carlos, Enzo, look for maps in this apartment that give a layout of this place. Tear the place apart if you must. If you can't find them here, keep looking elsewhere until you do. Get more men if you need them."

While I was talking to them, one of our men stuck his head inside our door and said, "We got trouble out here."

Connie got up and went outside to investigate.

"Yoseph, tell your army that you must do what I tell you. I've just about had it with you and your people, and I'm being reasonable with my request. You don't want to be around me when I stop being reasonable. A lot of dead or crippled people have made that mistake."

Connie came back in and said, "It was some of the soldiers, a dozen of them. They are demanding we send their commander out to give them orders on what they should do next."

"Luca, send your men to retrieve the Chief Priests and Yoseph's son. It's time to make my point understood. I've lost all patience with these people. Connie, send in one of those soldiers making demands of us."

She selected the most outspoken of the soldiers and brought him into the room.

"Soldier, what's your problem?"

"Sir, we don't know what is going on in here, but we think our commander and our High Priest are being held against their will and, if so, we will see to it they are released."

"Cosimo, have you found any maps yet?"

"Yes, some, but we are still looking for more that would give more details."

"Also, while you are looking, look for silver or gold that we can use, coins especially, but any kind will do. Maybe you can find the coins they took from me when we were captured, and my swords they took from me."

Whatever pain medicine I had been given was wearing off, and I needed more. The pain also made me more irritable. I looked at sheaves of maps and found one that revealed the locations of the entrances and another that showed where the armory was, the two most important pieces of information I wanted most.

The Chief Priests and the scowling son came in and the great room was getting crowded, since more guards were needed to ensure nothing got out of hand.

"Where is Pagiel? I need him," I said to no one in particular.

To the soldier, I said, "We have your leaders. You will leave here and tell the rest of your men that we have them, and they are to stand down. If any trouble comes from the army, we will have to use their priests as our shield and our protection. Do you understand what I am saying? I will not hesitate to kill any or all of them and anyone else who stands in our way to prevent your leadership's madness. Now, leave us."

"Luca, Connie, come with me. Yoseph can join his wife and children, but don't let Chaim join his men just yet, so that he doesn't start giving orders to take us by force."

We went into the bedroom I had been recovering in for some privacy while we made plans.

"Luca, I'm afraid a rebellion is about to happen amongst the army that will be too big for us to overcome. I'm not sure how long the army will stay at bay with us holding the priests and their commander. I'd like you to take Connie, my children, Pagiel, the priests, Yoseph's wife, and their daughters, and leave for Antioch. I still want you to bring Connie home. From Antioch, or even here in Tarsus, you can find a ship to return west. I will tell the priest you will release his family if he and his people give us what we want."

"No, Poppa. I can't do that, not knowing how this is going to turn out and how you heal. Also, we have no money for expenses. Luca had to spend it all on the men outside."

"I'm sure we can find enough gold around here, in this apartment alone, that will pay for your trip.

"Let me talk to the wife," Connie offered. "It's worth a try to see how much influence she has on her husband. I like her; she seems friendly. Maybe she can talk some sense into him. Also, some one of us should go to Tarsus, I think, and, if there is any kind of strong leadership there, a sheriff, a mayor, Mamluk chieftain, or someone who oversees the city, they must be informed about this place and their plans. Tell them about the entrances. If we must, we will expose the Ashkenazim against their will."

"Good ideas, Connie. Talk to the wife. Luca, send Cosimo and two of your men with him to Tarsus, and see if there is a strong leader of some kind that can help us. Also, send two or three of the men to find the armory. Look at the map; take it if you need to. If it isn't too late, we should try to secure it or blow it up. The writing is in Hebrew but Connie or Pagiel can help interpret it for you."

I called in the six Chief Priests into the bedroom to get their impression on what was taking place.

"Priests, you know why I am here, but to clarify my purpose, it is to stop the madness you people are trying to force onto an unsuspecting world. Adonai says he is opposed to it, and so are the visions I have received from yours and my God himself that clearly tell me that God is opposed to it. You have been forced all your lives to believe, or at least support, the idea that what you are doing is God's will. Now I want to hear from each of you that you will support me in my difficult task to persuade the High Priest, the army, and your people that you will no longer live the way you have been with the single-minded intention of killing masses of people. I cannot let you do it, and I will die in the effort to stop you, but you must know, you will die before I do, unless you help me. What will it be?"

A knock on the door. Pagiel opens it and peers in at me.

To the priests, I said, "Think about what I just said while I talk to my friend."

"Pagiel! My dear friend, come inside. We were just discussing how these priests are going to assist us."

"That's what I need to talk to you about, lord."

"It's great to see you again, my friend. I hope you can give me some good news, because I am in great need of it right now."

In another small room where only the two of us stood, Pagiel told me, "Lord, the men Luca brought with him, the very ones who saved you from execution, they can't be trusted. I believe the army, even as we speak, is offering them gold to betray you. You and those you trust must leave immediately or they will take us by force."

That was not what I wanted to hear. Despite the pain in my chest and back, I had to take flight with my closest companions, and with hostages, as well.

I called for Luca and said, "Luca," I whispered in his ear, "your men are betraying us for gold. We must leave immediately. You, Cosimo, Enzo, Carlos, Gerald, and the men who joined us in Rome, tie up all the priests and the boy so that they can't stray away from us. Bring Yoseph's wife and daughters also. They are going with us. We must leave now. Get Connie and tell her to bring the women. Hostages are our only hope."

The pain in my body was great, but the need to escape greater. We couldn't afford to use the lift to take us to the closest entrance. The army by then might have soldiers stationed by it. That meant I had to climb at least a hundred feet up carrying weapons and maps, while holding pressure on my chest wound. We made it as far as the closest stairs when a soldier yelled for us to stop. We kept going and he fired his gonne. Since I was the last in the line trying to reach the stairs, I was hit in the left arm. The pain was intense, but my focus was on escape, and I ran on. He could only shoot once, and he was not foolish enough to charge all of us with only a sword. He would run and tell his friends, I was sure.

One of the Chief Priests was near me, his hands tied behind his back. I pushed him up the stairs ahead of me. I gasped for breath as my lung leaked air with every step I took, drops of blood fell from my arm and a red rose bloomed on my chest bandage. Too much of that and I would lose my grasp on consciousness. *Please God*, I prayed, *help me make it to the top.*

I made it to the next floor. I heard men below me. Many footfalls on the steps. Everyone above me went to the next set of steps, and I was still the last of the crowd running for our lives. I looked behind me and saw a soldier point his cursed gonne at me and fire. The bullet grazed my left hip but missed the bone. The pain was agonizing, but still I limped upward. I had no other choice except to die. The man below me was replaced with another man holding another gonne. He fired but, by then, I had pulled one of the priests down beside me and he was hit in the back. I pushed him down the steps, and he rolled down into the crowd running towards me. They killed a priest. That was on them, and that was bad news for the priest but, also, very bad news for me. The priests evidently were not sacred enough for them not to kill and maybe not valuable enough for us to use them as bargaining power.

On the third set of stairs, I was running on my last reserve of strength. The crowd above me was slowing down, also, probably because the girls were getting exhausted, too. I thought of Catherine Adele and how frightened she must be. Who was carrying Troy, I wondered? I yelled at Luca and asked him if he still had any hand-bombs. The request was passed up to him, and he yelled back that he had one left.

"Pass it down to me."

I reached the next floor. I still had maybe another forty feet to climb. There was no way I could continue to run up the stairs. The wound in my hip was burning, and only sheer determination kept me putting one foot on the next stair riser. To die was to betray everyone who had followed me. One riser at a time. I grabbed another priest. They seem to be expendable, so I would use them, as I needed them to protect me from flying lead.

I was climbing steps, pushing the priest, bleeding, and gnashing my teeth while holding the hand-bomb under my damaged left arm while I struck my flint, trying to ignite the bomb's fuse. Men, several of them, were ten steps behind me racing towards us, but not shooting at us. By then, they must have gotten orders to capture me alive. I finally ignited the wick and tossed it at the closest of the pursuers. The sound was tremendous in the enclosed well of the stairs. The priest behind me yelled. He must have been hit by a piece of the metal. I pushed him ahead of me. He sat down and refused to budge. I left him to bleed, after giving him another wound, and weakly plodded on.

We made it to the floor leading to the one entrance we knew about. Someone pulled the lever that opened the hidden doorway. I had no idea if it was day or nighttime outdoors. When we emerged from the doorway, I could see there was maybe two hours, at the most, until dark. The nearby arena still held horses. Not enough for all of us. We would have to double up. Only a few still had saddles. The priests and Yoseph's family had never ridden a horse before. The horses panicked, and so were the hostages. For a moment, I stood outside panting and saw the chaos going on around me. It looked like foxes trying to herd one-legged chickens. Absolute turmoil as Luca, Cosimo, and others, were shouting at the priests to get on a horse, two each on a horse, and the remaining priests mewling like wounded pigs.

I yelled at Luca to get them on the horses or kill them, whichever they preferred. I told him to go to Tarsus and set up a defense system behind its walls and inform the person or persons in charge to prepare for hell to descend upon them. I instructed him to leave, and I would slow the pursuers down for as long as I could. I was going to die anyway. Pagiel was wrong. My life for theirs, at least for a while, was worth it to me. I was bleeding out of three, no, four wounds in my body, and God only knew how many pints of blood I had lost. My left arm was numb, and I knew the lead ball had broken the bone. My left boot was filling up with blood from my hip wound. I could not make it.

Luca and Cosimo did not listen to me but picked me up and sat me on a horse despite my protests. We rode away towards Tarsus, every step of my horse jarring my damaged arm, which was between ten and fifteen miles southwest. I did not know when we arrived, since I had passed out long before. While I was out, I did not die, I did not see Jesus, I did not see anyone or anything. I saw the back of my eyelids and that was all. I checked out of consciousness for a while. May God have mercy on our souls.

Chapter Eighteen
The Beginning of War

War is sweet for those who haven't experienced it.
—Pindar

When I opened my eyes, I looked at a ceiling covered in mosaics depicting Jesus shepherding a flock of sheep. I was confused and wondered if I were dead. When I tried to lift my head, my pains told me that I was still alive. I turned my head to my left and saw a woman dressed all in black, with a white cap, and I assumed she was a nun by her dress and her solemn and wrinkled face. When she saw me move, her deep wrinkles transformed her face, and a smile displayed precious little in the way of teeth.

"Where am I?"

I spoke to her in Latin, thinking she might understand me. She replied to me in Greek that I was in the basement of the Church of St. Paul.

When I turned my head to the right, I saw Eesha with her head and arms lying on my bed. She was asleep.

281

I wondered how long she had been there. In a little while, Connie came in.

"Poppa! You must stop scaring me!"

She hugged my neck and, when she removed herself, I felt tears on my cheek. I felt so bad I had put her through so much misery. Connie's hug woke Eesha, and she smiled at us, displaying her amazingly white teeth contrasted with her darker skin.

"Are the children, okay?" I asked Connie.

"They are fine. Kat is so worried about you. She asks me dozens of times a day how you are doing. Troy is okay, also. He is adapting well and so is Kat, but I fear we need to get them home before long. All this chaos is not good for them."

"Mine lord," Eesha said blinking sleep away, "happiest I am for you to wake up okay. Beside me was worried, worried, worried. Thank to you not dead like me fear."

I saw tears in her eyes. I touched her hand and told her thank you.

"Eesha has not left your side since she found out you were here. You must have made quiet an impression on her."

"How long have I been asleep?"

"Three days, total, this time. You woke up long enough, once, for the chirurgeon to give you drink. You've lost so much blood, Poppa. You must rest. The chirurgeons here are as efficient as Chadli was. Your arm was broken, and they splinted it. They also treated your hip by stitching the wound, it is not serious, but he did not reopen your chest. He wanted to but felt it would be too much for you after treating the other two injuries. Instead, he repaired the stitches on the outside of your body. I'm sure they will want to ask you about opening your chest to see why it is still bleeding. These

Muslims have extensive knowledge of medicine, as did the Ashkenazim. It seems that comparing what the Ashkenazim and the Muslims know, England is very deficient in the medical sciences. I wish we could bring some of the healers back home with us."

Home! Just the sound of the word made me homesick. I sorely missed the quiet, tranquil days when no one was trying to kill me.

"Connie, what's been happening? Have the Ashkenazim attacked? Where are the priests? Are our men, okay? Has anyone been harmed besides me?"

"There is much to tell, but I'm afraid, if I tell you everything, you will insist on getting up, and you cannot get up right now. Your wounds need to heal, and that will probably take weeks to do. I can see to it that things will be done that will suit your sense of the way things are to be done. Luca and Cosimo are doing a great job, and the Sultan Ismail, the local ruler here in Tarus, is helping us, also. He assures us that their walls will protect us until plans can be made to deal with the Ashkenazim. I have not told him all we know. I did not know how much you wanted us to say to others. I wanted to leave that up to you, but he is very curious about what's going on and about the danger we have brought to his city. Maybe tomorrow, you can talk to him, and I will tell you all that has happened since we left the caverns. We did lose one of the Chief Priests. He fell off his horse in our haste to escape the caverns, and other horses trampled him. For today, rest, eat, and let Sister Rosa make you comfortable. I'll let Kat come in to say high, then, rest. I insist."

As much as I wanted to hold a decision-making meeting, I couldn't stay awake and slept until the next day. I opened my eyes at mid-morning to see Catherine Adele and Eesha sitting next to me. I couldn't have asked for better faces to wake up to, except maybe for Dania.

"Let's go home, Poppa," Kat pleaded.

"As soon as it is possible, we will, my dear daughter."

We talked for a while; Sister Rosa brought me more chicken broth with small chunks of chicken to eat. Eesha just sat smiling and listened, absorbed in our conversation. I think everything since we met was so astounding to her that she could do nothing but marvel. I wondered if she had ever been loved by anyone. My daughter, Kat, and I talked until I finished my meal. Connie arrived soon after, bringing the sultan with her. He was a tall, handsome man, dark hair, dark eyes, and with a dark close-cropped beard that accented his good looks. He was younger than I expected, probably in his mid-forties, and vigorous.

"*As-Salam-u-Alaikum, Kaazim*," I said to him as he approached my bed.

He gave me a broad smile since I greeted him in his language and religion. He replied, "*Wa-Alaikumussalam wa-Rahmatullah.*"

"Your daughter tells me you are getting better, and your wounds are healing nicely. Our chirurgeons can do wonders nowadays. I don't want to tire you too much, knowing you need your rest, but I must ask for what reason you and your family and companions have entered my city and apparently, brought much trouble to us with you. When my people are endangered, I must know why, you see. They look to me for protection and, if I don't give them their expected protection, then, my position as their sultan becomes a little tenuous."

"I understand your concern. Let me fill you in as much

as I can and, when I am finished, I hope you will give us assistance, since it will be in your best interest to do so. If not, we will be on our way as soon as I can travel, with my deep gratitude for the help you have already given us."

I spent the next hour explaining all that I knew, bringing him up to date on our escape and arrival in his fortified city. Under the new circumstances we were in, I felt an obligation to tell him everything. I believed a considerable confrontation with the Jews was eminent. He needed to be aware of the Ashkenazim secrets and their plan to impose their will upon much of the known world, the impacts of which directly affected his city due to it being logistically close to the primary Jewish colony.

The more I revealed to him, the more the lines in his face deepened. He held his questions until I finished, and as was expected, he had many of them. The first being, "Is this all possible?" Indeed, it was possible, I assured him, and I had three wounds in my body to prove it to be so.

"I'm sorry to have brought this upon you and your people, sire. It is better you know now than when their army attacks in mass at some unknown time soon. Also, we know too much as well as having their priests. They will attack soon, I'm afraid."

"How many soldiers do you think they may have?"

"I believe there may be as many as ten thousand at this colony alone. They are armed with more than swords, also. They have weapons that use gun powder that are held in their hands, and they have cannons that can destroy your protective walls. They may have other advanced weapons that I don't know about. Somehow, we must convince them to stop their madness."

"Ten thousand?! I can bring together maybe one thousand among our people here, and we have some cannons ourselves, but ten thousand is too many. You said the caverns have entrances, and you have a map of them. Why can't we, using kegs of black powder, bring down the mountain on top of their entrances and seal them inside where they can no longer be a threat to us?"

"That would be a good way of stopping them for a while. I do believe that they have the machinery and capability that can eventually dig other tunnels out of their underground caverns. Also, they have five other colonies, with potentially ten thousand soldiers each in them. We don't know their entrances, except one in my country, and all of them must be stopped. Our only hope, as I see it, is to re-educate them into believing they have been mistaken all along in their thinking. Somewhere in this church, we are holding their leadership: one High Priest and three Chief Priests who are left. We also have in our custody the High Priest's family. I am hoping to convince the priests to call this focus of theirs off and rejoin civilization in the aboveground world. It will not be easy. They are very determined people with centuries of dogmatism towards a central goal: world domination and retribution for past wrongs done by anti-Jewish people. You are Muslim. I am Christian. It will be quite a challenge to convince the Jews to agree with us, I believe."

The sultan blew out a long breath. "Vekna Allah. Maza sinfal Allah. You have stirred up a viper's nest, my friend. My first thoughts are to send you and your people away but, if what you are saying is true, and they will eventually attack my city regardless, I must help you, even though I don't know how to do that just yet. I will summon my security chief and advisors. We will speak about this. It is quite possible that we will talk to you more about this tomorrow."

Pagiel knocked on my door as soon as the sultan left. Just one bit of good news I pleaded under my breath.

"Lord, do you wish to know what I have seen in my mind, that I believe is about to happen?"

I could tell by his face that I didn't want to know but, knew I must.

"Lord, our men, those we left behind because they were betraying us? They are all dead. The newest commander is ambitious and wants to impress his people. He has taken control of the colony. I have seen fire falling from the sky and the city devastated. Lord, we may be doomed! I'm not sure if the devastation is what will be or what could be. Either way, I think we are in trouble. I fear the priests' usefulness is not what you may have hoped for. Your wounds, lord?"

"What about my wounds Pagiel?"

"Lord, your chest wound will never completely heal. I'm sorry, my lord."

All of what he said was disappointing, but not surprising. My run of bad luck, if there is such a thing as luck, had been going downhill since I was first taken captive at the English colony. *I just want to get my family home; then, it would be okay for me to die,* I thought. My reasons for living had expired weeks earlier. How does one stop the tide of bad things happening? It seems it would be simpler to stop the ocean's waves from reaching the shore. I had opened the mythical Pandora's box, and all my efforts had not been able to put evil back into it.

Connie came in my room while Pagiel was still spouting gloom and despair and said there was a man with a flag of truce at the city gate. He wants to talk to us. Looks like one of the soldiers. There is a host, a very large host, of soldiers in the distance."

All this while, throughout the conversations, Eesha sat by me, as if to leave, she might not see me again. I wondered if rescuing her was going to be like I had adopted an abandoned and hungry puppy that would always be underfoot.

"Okay, let him come here, but I must sit in a chair. I don't want to negotiate from a point of view of weakness. Summon Yoseph, Sultan Ismail, Luca, Cosimo, along with yourself, for this parlay. Connie, please translate for Ismail."

The soldier, who said his name was Commander Chaim, and he emphasized the word "commander", had an air of arrogance, and I believed Pagiel was correct in his assessment that he was ambitious. My committee of advisors were in my room waiting when the little man came in, escorted by Enzo, Carlos, and Ferrante, their swords drawn in the event of attempted foul play by the visitor.

"You wish to speak to us," I said, seeing no need for small talk.

I have thought about this so many times in my tumultuous life, about my aversion to sneers. When a man sneers at me, something inside revolts, my pride is insulted and my anger spikes. All I want to do is peel the sneer off their face. If only my wounds weren't so painful, I might have done that and sent him back to his soldiers lacking a couple of lips. I have always struggled with overreaction to threats, whether physical or perceived attacks on my ego.

"Yes, I do have something to say to all of you. It is probable that by tomorrow at this time, you will all be dead unless you grant me my wishes."

"Pray tell, commander, what are your wishes, and are your wishes yours or your people's desires?"

"I am my people. Do not mistake my authority here. My first wish, my command, is that by tomorrow at sunrise, you turn yourself over to us. Also, all those who came with you and landed in Antioch must accompany you, as well as your daughter and the two other children. You must give back everything you took from the High Priest's apartment, specifically maps and all the gold and silver you took. Even your swords. All of it. I also must have the code the priest uses to communicate with the rest of our nation's colonies."

My anger kindled, and I said, "Why should we give into your demands? You have no authority here. If you do not do what we demand, your High Priest, his family, and the Chief Priests will suffer accordingly. I would not hesitate to use them to our advantage."

The arrogant and vile piece of human flesh laughed out loud.

I warned him, "Sir, you stand on shaky ground here. You will not scoff at what we say in here. Your flag of truce is not a ticket to do or say anything you wish. Be straight forward and dignified if you want to leave here intact."

"Of course," he said. The sneer, for the time being, was replaced with a red face and thin lips, because it was his turn for his pride to be wounded. "Let me let you in on a piece of news. I don't care about the High Priest, his family, or the Chief Priests. We can appoint as many of them as we wish and, from now on, they will do what we, the army, say, not the other way around, as has been the case. You can have them to do whatever you wish, but they will do you no good as shields. If you do not give into my demands, the city of Tarsus will be destroyed, along with every man, woman, priest, and child within."

His sneer returned.

I looked at the High Priest's face. I saw fear and anger. He looked at the soldier and then, at me and shook his head in disbelief.

"How dare you speak like that about us," Yoseph shouted. "I am the spiritual leader of the Ashkenazi nation, and they listen only to me. I give commands to our people from here to the island of England, not the army and certainly not you. You will surrender yourself to us for discipline, or I will see to it you are judged by the council of priests and, I assure you, you will be found guilty and stoned to death for your insolence and treason!"

Ignoring the priest's outburst, Commander Chaim looked at me, and said, "So, tomorrow at sunrise out where my army is posted, there you will bring yourself and your companions to us with all the things I mentioned. To emphasize I am serious and to give you a preview of what will happen if you don't comply, though at a much greater scale tomorrow, any moment now, fire and brimstone will descend upon this modern-day Sodom."

He turned around and walked out of my room, followed by Enzo, Carlos, and Ferrante.

There was silence in the room for a while. A long while. Finally, Ismail said, "Well, that was enlightening. All we must do is send you and your companions, those you brought into our city uninvited, out to this army and Tarsus' troubles will be over. If what you have told me is true, that no matter what happens tomorrow, they will still attack us anyway later, maybe we should settle our disagreement with them sooner than later. However, if you wish to voluntarily turn yourself over to that arrogant infidel, then I won't hold you back. I'm sorry if I seem heartless, but I don't know you or those people outside and I do not like being put in this position of choosing to give you refuge at the potential sacrifice of my city and my people just because that man is angry with you. Do you think he can destroy my city, my city that has stood here for thousands of years?"

"They may have that ability," I mused. "However, whether it be tomorrow or next year or five years from now, they intend on taking control of Tarsus and a thousand other such cities from the Euphrates River in Persia to my home in England. I'm deeply sorry for putting you at risk. We came here for protection and to buy us time to develop a plan on how to stop what they are about to do. Somehow, someway, we, that is, you and we, must find out how to stop them. I believe, even if me and my people turn ourselves over to Chaim, he will still destroy your city because, by now, he will know we told you everything. I have inadvertently triggered their long-awaited journey to domination. I don't blame you for being angry with me, but please help us stop them."

As soon as I finished speaking, Carlos rushed in and said we must see what was happening outside. I was in the church's basement and was still too weak to run up the stairs, but the rest left to see what Chaim's example of what must happen to us if we failed to give in to his demands. I could hear muffled explosions, shouts, and running footfalls. I cursed my wounds and my weakness. When my family needed me most, I did not have the strength to even pull my boots on. When I had my demons still, I would be completely healed within a week. Not so anymore.

Ever present in the room with me, Eesha said, "Lord, no one happy. Why not you happy? We trouble?"

"It's a long story, child, but don't worry. I will protect you if it is within my power to do so. You must know that there are some bad men outside who will try to do harm to us, but be of good cheer, Eesha. We will prevail and you will be safe with us."

I wanted to say, "I promise," but I knew better than to promise something that was out of my control to guarantee.

A long time later, Connie and the others came back, everyone except Sultan Ismail. Each of them with a forlorn look.

Connie said, "Poppa, men are floating over the city throwing hand-bombs down onto buildings, exploding on impact. They are also dropping fiery balls of something, igniting roofs of buildings and stables. They are also firing gonnes down onto people running for their lives. The men are standing in baskets suspended underneath a large floating object that allows them to drift over the city like birds, evidently propelled by the wind. There is only one of them, but what if they have many?"

Maybe Pagiel was right. Maybe we were doomed. I hung my head in dejection. Was it possible to defeat them? At every turn, the Ashkenazim was showing they had the upper hand. Pessimism tormented my mind. I simply couldn't give into their demands. I couldn't let them take Connie and my other children. Not my new friends, either. I managed, after they left, to get down on my knees and prayed. For an hour, I prayed until interrupted by the sultan.

"The Jews are a determined and skillful bunch of people, but so are my people. I have summoned assistance from my Islamic brothers from nearby cities. I propose to ignite explosive powder at all the entrances of their underground caverns, except one, so that we can better monitor their comings and goings through that one."

The High Priest came into the room at that point, as did Connie, Luca, Gerald, and Cosimo. Eesha, of course, was already in the room, not that she could offer much advice.

"Sir," Yoseph said, with a solemn resolve, "I must dispatch messages to all the other colonies immediately, if it isn't too late. I have the code that unmistakably identifies the message has originated with me, their High Priest. I will command them to do what you have wanted to accomplish all this time. I have just now witnessed the awful potential power that can be unleashed under the manipulation of an audacious and power-hungry demagogue. I haven't listened to you. I wish I had. I now recognize our divergence from the divine will of Adonai has been obscured by our pursuit of a government we thought would be blessed by him, a quest that inadvertently emboldened a man like Chaim, with insatiable appetites for dominion. My colony is now out of control, led by a motivated madman. Certainly, I knew we were not following Adonai's will; every High Priest knew that. We just wanted a government under his guidance and blessing, not appreciating what men thirsty for power would do. We can't have the kind of leadership we longed for in the world above with Chaim in power. Or someone like Chaim. How naïve we were! He has the army under his control, as well as all the weaponry developed over centuries. We priests are now powerless. For hundreds of years, we've been developing our plans, never believing a traitor, such as that lunatic, would even think of going against who we are, our base values that make us Ashkenazim, for his own gain. It seems we are no different than the gentiles we criticized for their pagan ways. I shall instruct our brethren to relinquish pursuing the plans we've long held against the gentiles. I shall go down in our history as the High Priest who failed his people. Moreover, I shall forewarn them of the insurrection in the Armenian colony, where a militant faction has brazenly defied their spiritual leadership, a leadership they now shun in favor of secular supremacy. I have, at long last, realized the profound misjudgments that have pervaded our collective consciousness for centuries. I will also ask the nearest colony in Adrianople to come to our assistance as soon as possible to fight against the rebellious band. My coded message can reach Adrianople in six days."

"Anyone disagree with what the priest is saying?" I asked them all.

None did. It was worth the attempt.

"Go, Yoseph, send the message, but how can you send a message to Adrianople so far away and they can receive it in six days? It must be many hundreds of miles across wilderness from here."

"No time to explain now, but I promise I will tell you later. I must prepare the message and instruct a carrier on how to proceed with the conveyance."

With that, Yoseph left, and, for the first time, I allowed the tiniest glimmer of hope to enter my mind, though knowing it would take days, if not weeks, for help to arrive from the north. Truly, the High Priest seemed to have been convinced of our message, and it took a madman's rebellion to get the point across to him. It seemed strange, but propitious, that, after their centuries of preparation, the first madman in their history, the first military leader, the first to openly rebel against the priests, happened just recently, instigated by our arrival. The killing of the former head general and the second in command opened the way for this rebellion to take place. Had Chaim been planning this from long ago or did he just see the opportunity for power and fame when his superiors were killed? Indeed, it was propitious that our destiny brought us to Armenia.

How long would it take for the Sultan's people to arrive? We only had until sunrise the next day before Chaim would unleash his army and their weaponry on us. We really needed help soon; days might be too late for Tarsus and its inhabitants.

"Sultan Ismail, concerning your earlier suggestion, if you still concur, send your men to blow up all the known entrances, except the one. The entrance we emerged from, one of my men can show you which one, leave it alone right now and monitor it from a safe distance. Send fifty men who can do the explosive charges. Be careful because the army might now be guarding them since we know their whereabouts. Let Cosimo go with your men; he will have a map showing their locations."

Isamail said, "I'll send a hundred to be sure. Their new commandant is young, arrogant, impetuous, and foolish. He should not have sent the floating weapon to scare us. Now we know where to set up our small cannons, the four pounders, on the windward side of the wall, and that we should bring water up from the sea to be prepared. My spies tell me they are preparing more of those floating weapons, which will be able to launch by tomorrow, I think. We can utilize our larger cannons, the twelve pounders, against the men when they attack on the other walls. We will be ready for them. They have yet to organize their army in setting up a proper siege. He gives away too much information, and they are too sure of themselves."

"The army," I said, "at least those we have fought so far, are inexperienced when it comes to man against man fighting. They rely too heavily on their gonnes and are easily defeated if it comes to fighting with swords. Also, bows and arrows can be quite effective against them since they are just as accurate as their gonnes when used by experienced bowmen. However, they can eventually throw as many as ten thousand at us. Even if Yoseph's message gets to Adrianople in six days, to get an army here can be as much as three weeks from now. Have you sent for your brethren yet?"

"My messenger left this morning. They will be here in two days. No more."

"Good," I said. "Also, it occurred to me that, if the enemy uses several of those floating things, I wonder if they might use them to not only drop fire and bombs down on your city, but they might land on buildings or drop from ropes for the purpose of opening one or more of the city gates. It might be wise to guard the inside of the gates as much as the outside of them."

When Yoseph had finished writing his message, he brought it to me to read. After my agreement, he put the coded message in Enzo's hands, who would join Pagiel, because Pagiel spoke the Hebrew language, and they would carry the command message to the distribution point with instructions for the Jews in the other colonies to permanently stand down, as well as for the closest colony to send military aid as soon as possible. Enzo, my most trusted man after Luca and Cosimo, would do whatever it took to find a way through the posted enemy's line and deliver the message that might be our best hope.

"Yoseph, how can your people get messages to each other so rapidly? Your people were always waiting for us at every seaport well ahead of us."

"The Mongol leader, the great khan, Genghis, set up an express post delivery system one hundred and fifty years ago. We adopted a similar way of sending messages the long distances that he used. Stations have been set up between our colonies every ten to fifteen miles, depending on terrain, where fresh horses are stabled, and men are housed. A message can be delivered a hundred miles a day easily, often more."

"Very wise of your people," I said. "Do you think the rabbis at the other colonies will approve of your message? The rabbi I met in England seemed very legalistic about the centuries' old plan to overtake the gentiles from England to Jerusalem. Our lives and the lives of hundreds of thousands of people depend on them believing your message."

"I have never had a rabbi disobey a command before, albeit this one is significantly more difficult for them to understand. I do think it is quite possible that the commander has already sent messages to prepare for war, but he does not, at least to my knowledge, have the identifying code used by my position. Chaim, by being the military leader in our colony, makes him superior in rank over the commanders in the other colonies. We will have to wait and see what the other commanders do. Never in our underground history has a military commander countermanded the High Priest. The two men you are sending would be able to tell us if Chaim has sent out a message. I know Chaim well enough. He was always a hothead who thought he was more important than he really was, but my former commander had always kept him in line before his death."

"Connie," I said, who was rarely some place other than by my side, "bring Yoseph to be with his family. I'm sure they have missed each other. Yoseph, please send the remaining Chief Priests to me. I would like a word with them. Yoseph, before you go, I have another question. We found the map showing all the entrances to your underground world. Is that map up to date? Are there any other openings we need to know about?"

"Poppa, you are doing too much. You need to rest more and talk and move less."

Eesha said, "Lord Poppa, I say you too rest now. You do too much while you sick. You do what Connie lady say."

Yoseph smiled. "We do have what you might call a 'sally port', an emergency port located halfway between two major entrances. My apartment has a secret doorway that opens to a tunnel that ends at the hidden portal. Only me and the Chief Priests are aware that it even exists. Not even today's army knows about it. I failed to mention it because I have used it only once in my life and had forgotten it. My wife and I were married shortly after I was appointed High Priest. We desired to have a little private time to ourselves without the prying eyes of priests and parents watching us. What a pleasant time that was, free and unfettered by responsibilities! Long before now, priests worried that a military commander might, to satiate his desire for power, stage a takeover of our people, thus, the secret tunnel was dug to provide safety and protection for the spiritual leadership. Their fears seem to have come true, haven't they? Could it be of some use, you think?"

"Could be. One more question. I wonder about the rest of your people. I believe the army makes up a sizeable percentage of your colony but, maybe, there are more who aren't in the military. What about your scientists, teachers, women, young adults not in the army, day-to-day workers, and farmers? How dedicated are they to the ideology of world domination that you have believed in for so long? Are they as dogmatic as the military, or do they just want to live and let live like most people in the world do? Is there a leader of the civilian population, like a mayor or a similar position? Someone besides the priests and the commanders of the army?"

"The people you mentioned have not the least interest in supremacy of any kind or any other intrigues outside their daily duties and interests. They are simple people who just want to eat, drink, have children, and provide for their families. Even our teachers rarely teach, and they are not required to, as that it is the right of the Jew to dominate the world. It is the military hierarchy who does that. When a child reaches the age of fifteen, such as my son, they begin their indoctrination into the army, and that might be why he shot you. Alas, he is not one of the elites who is exempt from the army due to intelligence. Those who are tested as the brightest when they become of age are removed from military service obligations, and become students of art, science, medicine, music, history, or machinery design. They are encouraged to excel, be creative, and are rewarded for coming up with fresh ideas and having a creative imagination. The others, who tested less intelligently, remain in the army until they are forty years old. Those who test lower than the military level of capabilities become workers in the mines, are used to expand our underground living spaces, work at underground farming departments, care for horses and other animals, and such things that do not require a great deal of intelligence. In other words, the commander was not among the brightest of our people. That might be a flaw in our historical plans to take over much of the world, but we depended heavily on valor and weaponry, as well as the army's loyalty to their spiritual leadership. To answer your question, it is the army that is the most dogmatic, but they have been pawns in the service of the priests over the centuries, respecting the priests as being Adonai's chosen leadership. Always before, to go against the will of the High Priest was the same as defying YHWA, and that was considered a very dangerous path to take. We priests are direct descendants of Levi, the patriarch chosen to provide the spiritual leadership since the days of Moses. There was always the promise, or the hope, that they would be the generation that would establish our nation as the premier race in the world, never worrying about ridicule or persecution again. Maybe it is our destiny to be the people who are to be bullied by the gentiles of the world because we killed the prophets. To answer your question about civilian leadership, there is no official leader of the people besides us priests and the army hierarchy, but there is an unofficial person. His name is Caleb. He is a rabbi, the only one in our colony. The other colonies have several but, because we have six Chief Priests and me, there is no need for more of them here, other than Caleb. His duty is to lead at, and maintain, our synagogue. He is the sabbath worship leader, except on one of our numerous days of feasts, such as Hanika. During those times, the priests preside. The people respect his compassionate leadership. He has a lot of influence on them and knows their moods. When I want to receive advice on the attitudes of the non-military people, I go to him. The non-military people of our community outnumber the military by four or five thousand at least."

Since waking up the day before, I had been given much broth and increasingly more meat and vegetables in my meals. Muslim healers believed that a loss of blood could be effectively cured by having the patient drink lots of liquids, primarily water, believing that the body was able to somehow convert water into blood. The idea made sense to me, so I drank as much as I could. I had spent countless hours studying under healers and reading Islamic authors on medicine during my early years of travel in the far east. Though I was opposed to their faith, I was impressed with their sciences, including medicine.

It was getting late in the day and, in another twelve to fourteen hours, the attack most probably would begin. If only I could have offered myself as a condition to release my family and friends to safety, but I could not, would not, sacrifice them. I would fight with what little strength I had left to defend their lives.

I heard distant explosions, like far off thunder, and believed the entrances were being blown up at the caverns. Still, there was the sally port. If my strength would recover quickly enough, I would enter that port and see what mischief I could cause. Maybe destroy the armory, maybe seek out more intelligence on their comings and goings. Maybe find out where the new commander slept at night and slit his throat.

Chapter Nineteen

Pagiel's Capture and the Battle Rages

Our wretched species is so made that those who walk on the well-trodden path always throw stones at those who are showing a new road.
— *Voltaire*

By nightfall that day, as many preparations that could be thought of were made. It was time to wait and see what destiny would bring to us the next morning at sunrise. The crew who went to destroy the entrance openings were successful, but at the expense of three of Ismail's men. The Ashkenazim had set two or three soldiers to guard each of them, and all of them were killed. With all the men Commander Chaim had at his disposal, he should have had more there. I hoped his lack of wisdom, prudence and battle experience would lead to his downfall. A man's arrogance would carry him only so far. By the time I laid down to try and sleep, Enzo and Pagiel had not returned. I believed they would have been back if things had gone smoothly. However, in war, things seldom go smoothly.

Before retiring, I had the luxury of spending an hour

with Catherine Adele and Troy. Eesha, for once, was not present. Gerald was trying to give her English lessons, I think. We spoke of their mother and what we might do when we returned home. Troy was walking, mostly running, and was learning new words every day. How was I to raise them without their mother? Pagiel's vision that I would succumb to my wounds eventually worried me about what would happen to them.

It was hours after midnight before I finally slept, and then, woke to the sound of rapid footsteps outside the walls of the church. I had managed to convince Connie that I needed to sleep on the ground floor, rather than the basement, so that I could more effectively monitor the impending battle soon to take place and offer some guidance on preparations and defense. The basement would have been safer, I know, especially if bombs were about to be dropping on us, but to not know what was going on outside would drive me crazy. Outside my window, the dark night was merging into the gray that occurs just before the sun rises above the eastern horizon. Roosters were crowing, dogs were barking, and I could hear a goat bleating in the distance. In less than half an hour, Commander Chaim's deadline would expire without his requests honored. Of course, he didn't think it would be and, in fact, he would have been very unhappy had I shown up with my companions. What fun would that be if he couldn't add his own light to the early morning sky with manmade explosives?

Connie came into my room and said everyone was just waiting for the Ashkenazim to make the first move. I wondered if the battle to take place momentarily was the beginning of the domination of our part of the world, a preliminary test to see if everything was ready for the ultimate battle to take place throughout the chosen area to war against, or if it was simply to extract me and my companions. Chaim had to know that my friends and I had already told Tarsus' leadership about their secrets. It stood to reason that he would want to kill all of us. That would effectively initiate the long-looked-for war with the aboveground world, Armageddon Phase One.

"Connie, has Enzo and Pagiel returned from delivering the message?"

"Not yet."

"They should have been back by now! Could they have been captured or killed?"

"We don't know that, Poppa. It's been less than a day."

"I know," I said, ashamed of my outburst. Stress, a strong desire to take a lead in the upcoming action, sitting around all day, and feeling responsible for all that was going on around me was taking its toll on my mental state. Eesha had come back in the room, and her constant presence and crazy questions were beginning to drag on my patience. The priest had discovered a merchant who could speak Bengali, but she would not stay with him and his family, choosing, instead to be wherever I was, her protector, or Gerald, who had taken some interest in her.

A loud boom shook the window next to my bed, followed by Connie running out to see what was happening. I was taking opium twice a day for the pain, and the chirurgeon healers were putting some herbs in my poultices to aid in the healing of my wounds. I believe they were working, and, in another week, they were to take out the stitches used to close the holes made by lead balls in my arm and hip. If I could just get some more strength in my legs, I would go up on the wall and direct the defense of the city. How could I leave that up to a man I didn't know?

"Where were Luca and Cosimo?" I yelled to an empty room, except for Eesha, of course.

"Connie!"

Enough, I said to myself and got up and limped slowly to the door leading outside.

"Lord sir, no, you do not go out! You rest now surely. You get in beeg trouble if you leave. Connie, I tell on you and she be big mad at you."

The loud boom I had heard was a cannon ball hitting the city wall. It was followed by reports from our cannons. I saw men running up and down the wall parapet, shouting instructions. Another ball hit the stone wall, sending shards of stone fragments in all directions, some of them hit two men, and they fell backwards from the impact. I heard another cannon bellow over to my right, and then, I saw the tops of the upside-down floating bags coming in our direction in the morning breeze. The sun was fully up now.

Suddenly, the tops of a dozen or more floating basket carriers appeared, and Tarsus' cannons were bellowing iron balls at them continuously. One by one, I saw the huge bags cave in and the baskets plummet, men screaming. They were floating low overhead in an obvious attempt to drop their deadly fire more accurately, or to drop men on ropes inside the city walls. They were easy targets, and like shooting at a ship floating in a pond. One basket leader did something to raise his carrier, but the cannon's angle couldn't be adjusted to permit it to shoot the intruder down. The basket floated high over the city, and flaming balls began dropping down on buildings, as well as fused hand-bombs. Some of the Tarsus men began shooting arrows at the basket, but to little effect. The fires were extinguished quickly, and the bombs did little damage, other than scare the residents near where the bombs fell. The basket floated on out towards the sea as it gathered altitude. It must be a suicide trip with no possible return. I saw no more of the floating weapons come our way that morning. So many of them were shot down, and none were able to drop any men into the city.

In the meantime, our cannons on the north wall continued to spew out iron balls at the enemy beyond, while the enemy's cannons unleashed their own balls against the walls our cannons sat upon. I found a broom handle and hobbled on my damaged hip, using only my right arm, towards the north wall to see if I could offer any advice and to better see what was happening beyond the wall. I had the cannoneers elevate the angle of their weapons to reach further into the troops massed around their cannons.

Every break in our parapet had a cannon. Men were firing, and others were sponging out the spent powder remnants before ramming down more powder charges, followed by iron balls. Another blast and the cycle repeated. All along the line, cannons were firing. Men were shouting because ears were deafened from the tremendous noise all around them. It was organized chaos. The smell of burnt powder, the coppery smell of blood, bile and vomit and feces and urine, all the smells emphasized that war had begun. The war called my name, it yelled to me to come, see, and offer assistance, so I went towards it, despite the pain in my chest and the potential consequences of my actions. The pain in my hip was forgotten and the fire in my blood was raging now, and I needed to be a part of the melee that was happening, to personally experience it. I had no sword on me, but I found one on a man who had fallen backwards off the wall. I wished I had Blind Justice. I heard Connie yelling at me, and Eesha's squeaky fussing, also, but I ignored them and limped on, shouting orders, giving directions, and offering praises where appropriate.

Far beyond the wall, across the open no-man's land, I saw a panorama of death, destruction, and turmoil. Their iron balls could be seen as they flew towards our position. Some went over our heads, crashing into homes and markets, some went against the stone walls we stood upon that were twelve feet thick. Beyond the enemy position, I saw men on horseback riding back and forth shouting orders. Many horses lay on their side, dead and disgorged. Men lay littered on the ground, also. None of the dead had been picked up by their own people, and none of the wounded were being attended to. All their focus was on destroying us. The smoke became thicker and more pungent with little wind to disperse it. Under a small canopy, I recognized Commander Chaim as he looked out upon the battle. I directed the closest cannoneer to me, to direct their aim at that figure. If my left arm wasn't damaged, I would give it my best to hit him with an arrow. I had only "ifs" in my quiver, though. It was not yet Chaim's time to die and all the cannon balls missed him by many yards.

I saw Ismail striding down the parapet shouting orders and giving encouragement, slapping some men on their backs, and calling out their name. He saw me and walked up to me with his hands behind his back like he was on a casual stroll enjoying the day and the world around him.

"Sir Troy," he said, "a fine day for a battle, isn't it? Just the right temperature. Shouldn't you be in bed somewhere?"

"Ismail, I couldn't let you get all the enjoyment of the battle. I just dropped by to see if I could offer some assistance, but it looks like you have everything under control."

As the morning wore on, very slowly, the cannon barrage began to let up. By then, I had returned to my bunk. I was very tired but satisfied that the battle was going well enough for us thus far. My biggest concern was where Enzo and Pagiel were. At the noon hour, Sister Rosa brought me a meal, not just broth, but meat and vegetables and cider. While I was eating, Luca, Cosimo, and Connie came in.

"Enzo has returned. He is getting something to eat and drink, and then, will come see you."

Enzo had returned. What implications did that have? Not Enzo and Pagiel. I lost my appetite. The cannon booms continued outside. Connie, Luca, and Cosimo stared, waiting for the explosion to come from me. I desperately wanted a sword and someone to swing it against. I clinched my teeth and waited. The silence in the room was louder than the cannons outside.

Soon Enzo came in and he explained to me and my confidants what had happened.

"We rode," he began, "until it became too dark to find landmarks, and made a cold camp in the hills. The next morning, we found the first relay station, just where Yoseph told me it was. I waited in a nearby dry creek bed and let Pagiel go alone, since he spoke the Jew's language, and I would be seen as a complication. I could see him ride up to the station, give them the pouch containing the message, talk to them for a little while, and then, he came back to where I lay hidden. All went well, it seemed. There was no indication that the army had arrived before us. We both saw the dispatch leave the station heading north. That was early yesterday morning. We felt good about accomplishing our task without confrontation. We rode all day back to Tarsus and cold camped again last night. We were relieved that we were almost back in the city."

"We rose early this morning and rode just a little way when we heard cannons and debated about how to return, the way we left the city or go by way of the sea gate. Figuring the north wall was under attack from the Ashkenazim, we thought best to ride west of the city and circle to the south where the sea gate faced the ports. Neither of us could understand the language of the other but, with hand signals, we communicated well enough."

"When we topped a hill, below us was a long line of what had to be soldiers, because they were all dressed in the same brown uniform, and all of them were either doing some activity around a cannon or watching the walls, as if waiting for orders. We had ridden into a hornets' nest of Jews. We then turned to ride west, away from the soldiers, when they spotted us. They began shooting those devilish weapons at us. I rode, kicking the side of my horse, and then, looked back. One of the shooters had shot at Pagiel, missed him, but hit his horse. When the horse fell, it pinned Pagiel's leg under it. A dozen soldiers were running towards him. I had little choice but to ride away. I'm sorry, lord, for failing to protect him like you would want me."

"It's okay, Enzo. You had no other choice. You would have been captured if you had tried to save him. We will do what we can, all that's possible, to get him back. I will not fail him."

"What are you going to do?" asked Connie. "What I want you to do is lay down and rest."

"Yes, master lord, rest your poor self," Eesha added. "You do Connie say."

"I'm going to get him back, and Luca and Cosimo are going to help me. If they will."

"Poppa, listen to me. If you don't rest and eat properly, I'm going to lose you, and where is that going to leave me and your other children? Momma always said you were a driven and a single focused man. I know what she meant. If you don't listen to me, I'm going to get some rope and have you tied down to your bunk."

"Me say that to you master lord again," said Eesha.

"Connie, he has been captured because of me. Now, please, send for Yoseph, Luca, and Cosimo, and I want you here, as well. We must make some plans. Eesha, don't you have some place you need to be? Go see if Gerald needs to say something to you."

When Yoseph returned, he was in a much better frame of mind than in earlier days, having spent the last two days with his wife and children. While he was getting cheerier, I was getting the opposite. My pain wasn't as bad as it was two days earlier, and my bleeding no longer soaked through my bandages, but I was weeks away from being completely healed. I had no time for healing any longer. It would have to come while I did what I had to do, or it would not. Regardless, there was work to be done.

Luca and Cosimo had increasingly become men I depended upon. They were young, strong, and loyal men. They were experienced at fighting, and they fought with their brains as well as with brawn. Both were good leaders, and so was Connie. I made a mental note to myself, that when I had the time, I would tell her once more how much she meant to me and how proud I was of her. Her common sense and leadership skills were equal to any man I knew. It was only that Luca and Cosimo had the physical strength that made the difference when it came to man-to-man fighting.

With the five of us in my recovery room, as Eesha had finally gone off somewhere, I talked to them about what I wanted to do next.

"Yoseph, you spoke of a sally port that no one knows about but you and the other priests. I need to know where that port is. It is impossible to enter the one remaining entrance since it will be too heavily guarded. I must get inside. Ismail's friends should be here in a day or two. Possibly the Adrianople colony will send an army in two or three weeks. Even then, there will be fighting and much killing, and the battles could linger for many weeks. In the meantime, Pagiel's safety is compromised. There may be a way to shorten this war if we can get inside the caverns and do two things. One, of course, is to see if we can free Pagiel. The other is to speak with the non-military people of the colony if that is possible. Specifically, to gain an audience with a man who the people will listen to."

"Yoseph, tell me more about Caleb. You said he has the respect of your people, the non-military people, at least. If we could get a message to him and convince him that the army is in rebellion against the best interests of his people and to his priests, do you think it possible they might reject the army's dissidence? Could they possibly join forces with us to overcome, or at least influence the mindset of the less radical soldiers? The civilian population, after all, have family members that make up a large part of the army. If we could get a message from you and give it to Caleb, do you think he would help us in our efforts to overcome Commander Chaim's perverse and mutinous actions?"

Yoseph studied his hands as if they held the answers to my questions. The cannons outside were growing still fewer in their reports. We looked at each other, waiting for him to respond, and I could see in Connie's mind and in the way she slowly shook her head that she might not like the way this conversation was going to end.

"Caleb is a good man, from a good family, going back many generations. I highly respect his wisdom, and I think he respects my leadership, as well. I also think he would closely evaluate whatever I had to say. He would question my turnaround and my perspective about our future, of course, but, if he were convinced it was truly my desire, he would honor it. He would give his life for the people and his life for me, too, I think."

"Okay," I said, "this could be a big break for us, so let's give this a try. My plan, then, is to enter the underground cavern through the hidden sally port, if Yoseph can remember where it is, find Caleb, and convince him that his High Priest wants him to influence the civilians that the army has acted on their own, rebelling against the wishes of the colony's spiritual leadership. A written message from Yoseph could outline what we want him to do. In due time, Yoseph will give him more detailed information about this new direction, but he must immediately do whatever subversive actions he can to thwart the work of an out-of-control Commander Chaim. Also, he must aid us in finding and releasing Pagiel. He may be in a cell in the same prison we were in."

"Who are you thinking will deliver this message to Caleb?" Connie asked.

"Of those in this room, besides Yoseph, I'm the only one who speaks Hebrew fluently, so it would have to be me. He probably can understand Arabic, since that seems to be the language of this aboveground territory, but I'd rather rely upon conversing with him using his native language. I hope that Luca and Cosimo would go with me to do any heavy work that needs doing, but that would be up to them to volunteer."

Luca and Cosimo acknowledged their agreement to go with me. Connie, however, was furious. She said she spoke enough Hebrew and Arabic to get by and she was healthy enough to run, if necessary, and climb stairs or obstacles, or even fight, whereas I was not able to do any of those things effectively in my current condition. I had only the use of one arm, I limped painfully, and did not have enough breath because of my damaged lung to climb stairs in a hurry. She had a strong argument.

Luca said, "Lord, Connie is right. You would be a burden if it came to fighting, and there most assuredly is going to be some. It is doubtful you can ride a horse to get to the sally port without a lot of pain. This tunnel cannot be an easy walk to negotiate, either. There will be many floors to climb, either up or down or both, and then, there is the ride back to consider, and it might be a hurried ride to escape. No, lord, you aren't ready. In three weeks maybe, but can we wait that long?"

Could I send my daughter to do my work? Was it pride or concern for her safety, or both? If something happened to her, I would surely fall on my sword and die a thousand miles from my home. Her mother would haunt my dreams at night.

If she and the others were successful, however, it could end all our nightmares.

"What do you think, Cosimo? Yoseph?"

They both agreed with Luca. I was outvoted by my family and friends. It was a humbling experience. I felt old and a little bit worthless.

"Yoseph, what about one of the Chief Priests? Are any of them trustworthy enough to go with Luca and Cosimo to serve as an interpreter, and to convince Caleb to warn the people about the army?"

He said, "I can vouch for their love and worship of Adonai. I can vouch for their dedication to the Ashkenazim, but they have not seen what I have seen. They know only that three of their closest friends have been killed, because they were taken hostage and removed from their homes by you, who they still consider their enemy. I cannot vouch for their understanding or appreciation of the predicament we are in. I can speak to them and try to convince at least one to assist if you would like. They, however, cannot communicate with Luca and Cosimo verbally."

"Yoseph," I quietly spoke, trying to mask my deepest feelings, "describe to us how to find this hidden entrance."

There was a half-moon that night. The mid-February air was chilly, promising the possibility of frost the next morning. I gave final instructions to the three who were to leave. I hugged Connie for a long time. I whispered into her ear that I loved her deeply, and that I was enormously proud to be her father. While Yoseph was with us, maybe to his dissatisfaction, I prayed with Connie, Luca, and Cosimo. We held hands and I prayed in the name of our savior, the very God/man Yoseph's ancestors had condemned, the Jew, Jesus Christ.

Chapter Twenty

Connie, Luca, and Cosimo Secretly Enter the Ashkenazim World

Success is not achieved by the impractical who merely contemplate, but by the individuals who face reality head-on and take purposeful action.
—Plato

I can see patches of ground outside my window as I look out upon my castle's garden. An early spring thaw has melted much of the snow that has blanketed my estate for the past month. Winter is lessening its grasp on my part of the world. Soon, I will be finishing my last story, my last winter's tale. So much of what I have written in this story had to do with me, what I did or what I saw. Now, it is time to record what my daughter did, her and her companions. What we did, what all of us did, happened nearly a year ago. If it weren't for the extraordinary efforts of people like Connie, Luca, Cosimo, and many others, our bodies would be lying and decaying amongst the forgotten hills and valleys of Armenia. So much happened after that final hug with my daughter that frosty morning, a little over a year ago. Here is what they told me after they returned from the secret sally port.

Luca held closely to his chest a leather pouch that contained the letter from Yoseph describing the mutinous behavior of Commander Chaim and his maniacal determination to disregard all spiritual leadership in favor of putting the Ashkenazi nation in jeopardy. The note gave instructions for Caleb to help us stop the effects of the army's rebellion. I read the note and gave my approval prior to three of our bravest leaving for the tunnel that would lead into the heart of Yoseph's underground world.

It was dark when they left by the sea gate. The night was quiet, and the enemy's cannons had stopped firing hours before. The half-moon had just risen above the tree line to the east when they rode away from me to the sea gate. I laid back down on my bed and tried to ride with them in my mind. It would take them two hours to reach the portal area, and another hour to feel their way around, probably, without using any form of light, other than the stars and a sliver of a moon, to find the wooden door covered by small rocks the size of one's hand. The pile of smaller rocks made finding the portal door possible, which existed among so many huge rocks. The work was complicated by having to find the right place and remove the rocks as silently as possible.

Once inside, they lit candles and, with Luca leading the way, Connie and Cosimo following, they walked quickly and, in most places, descended steps but, in others, climbed them, all of them steep. For an hour, they walked and climbed, convinced in their minds that it would not have been possible for me in my condition to go where they went.

Eventually, they reached a wooden door that, according

to Yoseph's instructions, was one that would gain them access to his bedroom chamber. On the other side of the door, however, was a wooden cabinet containing their clothes. It would have to be pushed out of the way and, to do that, it must be determined if anyone had taken up residence in Yoseph's old apartment which, by their laws, permitted only the current High Priest to reside.

They extinguished their candles and listened for sounds. It was close to midnight, so it was probable there would be no sounds if someone was asleep in the room. The three took counsel amongst themselves, and tempted fate by pushing the wardrobe outward just enough to see if the noise alerted anyone. Hearing nothing, they pushed more until there was space enough for Luca to squeeze out from behind the cabinet. Seeing and hearing nothing but his own breathing, Connie and Cosimo crept out, also. The apartment was empty of people and looked as it did when we abandoned it in our haste to depart the caverns.

There were lights outside the apartment door, as there were in every hall throughout the cavern system since no natural light existed underground. Their ability to provide light involving their extraordinary sparking system was efficient and remarkable. It also aided the three in negotiating halls and rooms and stairs that were necessary in their search for Caleb and Pagiel.

Using hand signals and whispers, they communicated. Luca held a drawing Yoseph made that would lead them to Caleb's apartment on another floor at a lower level. Yoseph said there was little chance they would meet anyone in the halls or stairs in the middle of the night. They had no need for patrols to keep their inhabitants safe, which is, sadly, not the case in our aboveground world where the night is festered with the worst of mankind prowling about looking for easy targets. Yoseph warned, however, that some departments are manned continuously and, there, they might find people wandering about.

Finding the first stairway, they descended to the next level, the level where Caleb's apartment lay. As they walked the hallways, some of which led to large rooms of varying uses, they walked with an air of confidence that they were supposed to be there, not like outsiders. One of the rooms was a break room, and several people were at tables eating a snack or meal. Connie waved and they walked on. Continuing beyond the break room, they came to a "T", and they took the right one, passing by a large room used for recreation. Beyond that room was another wide and long room used for growing plants and vegetables, and many people were tending them. Caring, planting, cutting, and packaging the vast strips of edible plants, they all went about their business dutifully, and paid no attention to the three interlopers. They saw lights over the plants, which had filters that augmented their growth, mimicking natural sunlight.

Luca was in the lead, with Connie in the middle, when a group of three men exited a side room and headed towards them. The hall was wide enough that they could easily pass by but, when they got even with Connie and her friends, they stopped.

"Are you three lost?" One of them asked. The three were dressed alike in brown clothing that Connie, Luca, and Cosimo recognized as the same garb the men wore who were laying siege to Tarsus.

Connie said, "We are looking for a healer. I am in a lot

of pain in my stomach, and my husband and his brother are taking me to find one. Can you direct us to where we might find a healer?"

"Your accent is strange. What is your name and what sector are you from? I haven't seen either of you before in this one."

"We have no time to be interrogated by you. We must find a healer right away if you don't mind."

The men and Connie had already concluded a confrontation was unavoidable at that point, and each began shifting their stance in preparation to neutralize the curious soldiers, if needed.

"You don't look like you are in pain. The three of you must come with us to our command post. Our superior will want to talk to you."

Luca grabbed the one doing all the talking and, with his arm around the man's neck, the other behind his head, he squeezed and broke the man's spine. Connie inserted her dagger in the neck of another while Cosimo broke the neck of the third. No sounds came from the soldiers, except the scuffling of their boots on the stone floor. The problem that faced them, then, was what to do with the bodies. Cosimo hurried to the room the soldiers had exited and found that it was a supply room. A light in the room shown down on shelving filled with various items that looked like clothing, blankets, and footwear. They hurriedly dragged the bodies into that room, knowing they would eventually be found but, maybe, not as soon as if they were still lying in the hallway. There was blood on the floor, and Cosimo grabbed an article of clothing from the supply room and tried to wipe it up.

Having memorized the location of Caleb's apartment,

which lay near the synagogue, they found it with no further problems. Since the underground world was synchronized with the aboveground world when it came to daylight versus nighttime, except for those departments that were staffed every hour of the day, it was considered nighttime for the rest, so that meant Caleb and his family were home, in bed and asleep.

When they reached the apartment, which was labeled, *Rabbi Caleb and family*, they tried the door latch and found it unlocked. Just as Yoseph had indicated, crime is virtually unknown among the Ashkenazim, and there was seldom a need for locks on doors.

The three entered the dark apartment, each lit a candle they had brought, and began the search for Caleb's bedroom. Finding part of the apartment that appeared to be where people slept, Luca stopped the other two and called out Caleb's name, not wanting to barge into his bedroom. He counted to ten and called out his name again. Directly, a door opened and a tall man with a long black beard with a few white strands came out, shielding his eyes from the candlelight.

"What! Who are you? What is going on here?"

"Are you Rabbi Caleb?" Connie asked.

"I am, and who are you?"

"Rabbi, my name is Connie, and this man is Luca, and this man is called Cosimo. They don't speak your language, so you will have to address me. We come from the aboveground world, and we are here on the behalf of your High Priest, Yoseph. He has an urgent message for you and your people. The army under the command of a man named Chaim has taken control of the military to satisfy his own ambition and, in defiance of the priests, has begun a siege of the nearby city of Tarsus. Chaim has refused to stand down at Yoseph's command. They also plan on executing the program of territorial domination spoken of for decades by your leadership. Many people have been killed already, both those in Tarsus and those of your own people. That program is now void. Please read this letter written by your High Priest to you explaining what he wishes for you to do."

The rabbi took the scroll, walked over to a lever, pulled it down, and immediately the room was filled with light coming from overhead fixtures in the ceiling. He read:

Rabbi Caleb:

The three people in your presence were sent by me. We desperately need your help in reaching out to the people of our nation. Our army is in rebellion and no longer under the priestly council's control. It has been brought to my, and the Chief Priests', attention that there is no longer any hope of a providential takeover of the lands we believed were due us. Lands that we have for centuries hoped to bring under Ashkenazim control. Our desire was to create a theocratic government spanning from Jerusalem to the great ocean to the west for the glory of Adonai. Commander Chaim has usurped control of our people, and they are now under his authority. He has militarily seized power and is attempting to seize control over the world above for his own glory, not Adonai. He is even now laying siege to the city of Tarsus, and the loss of life is enormous. That is not what Adonai, nor our forefathers, wanted. We must stop them. You have a son and daughter in the army. Most families have members in the army. They must exercise pressure on family members to revolt against

323

the unauthorized takeover by Commander Chaim. Use
your influence as the synagogue rabbi and the respect you
enjoy among the people to spread the word secretly and do
whatever you can to stop the military in their ill-conceived
and treasonous takeover.

In the name of Adonai,

Yoseph bar Judah, High Priest

"Can this be true?" Caleb asked. "Where are the priests?"

Connie explained where they were, and that the army was responsible for killing three of the Chief Priests, but the others were safe in the city. She filled in some of the details about how Chaim was bent on destroying Tarsus, about his determination to capture her family and friends in the city, because they all knew the army's goal of territorial dominance. She did not go into how the priests wound up in Tarsus, since that would just complicate things. While she was explaining all this, a loud horn went off outside the apartment. Three short blasts, a pause, then three more short blasts. That cycle continued for a long while.

"What do those horn blasts mean, Caleb?"

"It means all adults are summoned to the synagogue. It is the largest room in our caverns and has room for all of us. There must be an important announcement to be delivered. It is highly unusual to do this during our sleep period. Did anyone notice you on your way here? I must prepare and go to the synagogue."

"Caleb, will you help us? Will you speak to your people and make them understand that the army must be stopped?"

He sighed deeply, held up the scroll, and said he had no choice but to follow his High Priest's request. He told the three that he knew Chaim, never liked him, and could believe he wanted control, though Caleb never believed the man had enough intelligence to be a high commander.

"One more thing, Caleb. The other reason we are here is to search for and rescue, if we can, a man by the name of Pagiel. He is one of yours from another colony. Chaim captured him yesterday. We don't know where he is, but possibly, in your prison. Do you know where he might be, and have you heard of his capture?"

"No, I have not heard of Pagiel. If he was captured, then, I suppose he is in the prison chambers below. Now, please, I must get my wife and myself ready for the synagogue."

Luca said, "They must have found the bodies. There will be a search soon. That's probably what the announcement will be about. Every room, apartment, and hallway, in this god forsaken world will be searched. We better get down to the prison level and check it out."

When we exited Caleb's apartment, people were already filling the hall, presumably heading to the synagogue. The hordes of people were going the same direction we wanted, so we did not look too suspicious, especially since most of them were mainly asleep. When we reached a stair column, however, we peeled off and descended to the lower floors. Eighty steps, or so, we descended towards the prison level. Many people were climbing up while we were climbing down, and they gave curious looks at the one woman and two men who continued to descend. Once, one man asked, "Aren't you going the wrong way?" Maybe he was trying to be witty, or maybe he made a mental note of who the strangers were and their appearance.

They eventually reached the prison door that opened

onto a long hallway separating individual cell rooms. Some of them were simply rooms surrounded by vertical iron bars; others were stonewalled rooms. There were no guards. If there were any, they must have gone to the synagogue which, thankfully, the blaring horns had stopped announcing the call to attend. At each doorway, they called out Pagiel's name. There were six stone rooms on each side of the hallway, and three iron-barred cells on each side. The iron-barred cells only contained one person, and it wasn't Pagiel.

"Connie? Luca? Cosimo? Is that really you?"

"Pagiel!"

"Oh, it's great to see you again. Thank you for coming for me."

Then the realization hit them. No key. How were they to open the door? As strong as the two men were, muscles would not serve as a key.

"Stay here," Luca said. "I'll go look for something that will do."

Knowing they had a short time before the army's searches would begin, Luca raced upstairs, down halls, finding nothing that could serve as a key or battering ram or anything in between. Connie and Cosimo consoled Pagiel while they waited for Luca to return. After what seemed like hours, Luca burst through the door.

"Get ready; four soldiers are after me."

After saying that, he went behind the door. Connie and Cosimo drew their short swords and daggers in readiness, their hearts beating rapidly for what would happen next. The door swung open, hiding Luca, and the four men burst into the hall and stood in front of Connie and Cosimo.

"What are you doing here?!" they demanded. "Where

is the man who just came in the door? You, put down your swords or you will die."

Three of them pulled gonnes from their waist holster. The fourth man, apparently the leader, pointed to the floor and told them again to put down their weapons.

"And what if we don't?" Connie said, pointing her sword towards the speaker. He made the fatal mistake of thinking, because she was a woman, that she would not be experienced in sword play. He reached for her arm, only to feel six inches of steel enter his gut. When she pushed the blade into the man, Luca stepped up behind two of them and, with both his blades, thrust them into the men's backs. Cosimo put his dagger point to the throat of a fourth man.

"Now," said Connie, "you drop your weapons or bleed like your friends."

The man was fool enough to think he was fast enough to raise his gonne in time, but Cosimo was just a little faster, and the man paid the ultimate price for his mistake when the dagger slid so quietly across his neck. Unfortunately, neither of the four soldiers had keys to the cells, so it remained a question of how to get Pagiel out of his room.

Luca, ever resourceful, picked up one of the gonnes, told everyone to stand back, including Pagiel, aimed and fired the device at the lock's mechanism. The ball made a huge dent in the cover plate but did nothing to open the lock. Luca picked up another and repeated the firing of lead balls. Again, the shot only created more of a dent, but enough that the cover plate opened a little bit more. He asked for Connie's short sword, which he used to pry off the plate to reveal the locking bolt underneath. The bolt still would not move sideways to release the door. With one more try at firing the last available gonne, Luca placed the end of the barrel next to a gear that would rotate the bolt sideways if it were allowed to turn. This time, firing the gonne at the gear, shattering it. The bolt was free to move but was still stuck due to it being damaged from one of the previous firings. Again, Luca used the sword to pry the bolt away from the slot within the door jam. It moved, but not enough. He continued to pry the bolt with all his considerable strength, and it moved more. He hollered at Pagiel to begin kicking at the door from his side or use his body weight and throw himself against his side of the jammed door.

"Hit it hard, Pagiel. Hit it again. Once more Pagiel."

When the bolt moved just enough to allow the door to move outwards, Pagiel was free.

"No time to celebrate; we must be going."

Approximately a hundred steps led up to the priest's apartment level. They took the first thirty or so steps two at a time, and then ran the next thirty quickly. The next thirty slower, and then, they had to rest and catch their breath for just a few moments. Then on they went for the next ten, and those, they took slower and quieter.

The synagogue meeting must have adjourned. The hall outside the living quarters of the priests were filled with citizens and soldiers going back to their posts or apartments to try and get more sleep. The number of soldiers in the hall made the three outsiders believe the search for intruders or below ground murderers was commencing. What if Rabbi Caleb had tried to give out a message at the meeting and he was arrested, Connie wondered. She decided she would worry about that possibility once they were safe. Escape was their immediate hurdle to overcome.

One at a time, the four joined in the rush of people returning to duty or homes as if they were one of the lemmings racing to the sea cliff. Reaching the door that said, *"High Priest, Yoseph, and family,"* they went inside, shut and, that time, locked the door. Quickly, they entered the tunnel, pulled the wardrobe cabinet back in its place, lit candles and, as fast as the tunnel floor and steps would permit, they raced towards the sallyport exit. When they opened the doorway, it was still dark. They found their horses nearby and began their return to the city's sea gate. Pagiel sat behind Connie, and they rode away with his arms around her waist.

By the time they got near the city walls, it was still quite dark, the moon just setting, indicating that dawn was not very far away. City lights were their primary means of knowing which direction to take, but that wasn't the only way. They could see dozens of fires burning outside the city's eastern wall in curious metal boxes that were tended to by a hundred or more men. When they got within half a mile of the activity, they saw there was a lot of commotion surrounding the fire boxes. Curious, they investigated and found many more of the enormous floating bags that were being prepared for flight. They discovered that each bag was made from huge canvas sheets, like what was used as ship sails, covered in a sheen that reflected firelight emitted from a metal box at the base of every bag. A fire was inside the box, and men were shoveling coal into it, making a large flame, forcing hot air into the base of the canvas openings. The sheen, they surmised, must have been from a treatment that prevented air from escaping through the fabric's tiny webbing. They found that the secret to the floating carriers was hot air! Hot air always rises! The heated air allowed the bags, inflated with the hot air, to carry the baskets loaded with men and their equipment. It was ingenious! The only drawback was that the inflatables couldn't be steered, but relied upon the direction of the wind to carry them in whatever direction the breeze brought them.

With the eastern wall filled with army activities and the northern wall besieged with cannonade, they knew there would be no way to approach the city from those directions. They also discovered the seaside wall were seeing an increasing number of soldiers arriving between the wharves and the wall, who were busy setting up cannons on that side. They assumed it would be the same on the western wall, as well. A total besiegement of the city. They were expected to enter the sea gate on their return, since they had left from there. It was no longer a safe option. In fact, they didn't see an option. That was not true; there was one option. A stupid, outlandish, and impossible option, proposed by Luca, was to highjack one of the vessels and fly over the city walls and settle down in it.

Connie said, "Luca, even if we could get into one, what is going to happen when we try to float down? We will be shot just as if we were the enemy. No, I believe we will have to find a place and wait until a better option arrives. Ismail's men should be arriving soon, maybe."

While the cover of darkness still hid them, they observed what the soldiers were doing. Already, floating vessels were lifting off, and the early breezes blowing towards the sea were delivering them high up and over the walls. Too dark to aim with their cannons effectively, the city defenses were helpless in stopping them, though they tried. Additionally, the bags flew much higher until they got past the eastern wall cannonade arrayed along the parapet. Then they began their descent to better aim their hand-bombs and flaming projectiles at buildings within the city walls guided by the many lights glowing among homes where people were beginning to stir. The army had learned from the previous disaster, when most of them were shot down, that they were too easy a target flying so low and in daylight. Men were loading into their baskets, ropes, bags of coal, hand-bombs, and straw-covered balls covered with a wet, black, sticky substance. They watched as a pilot of one of the vessels increased the intensity of the coal fire and, when he had the canvas inflated sufficiently, it began to rise.

Fascinated, they watched one vessel after another ascend into the black night. At least three dozen of them. Then they saw a curious sight. Three inflated bags were tethered together and, when they rose, below the baskets was an object they guessed was about two feet in diameter by eight or ten feet long, suspended between the overhead vessels. They didn't know what it was, but one thing they knew for sure: it looked ominous.

The eastern sky was growing lighter, and birds had begun to chirp, and to stay there watching the vessels floating away put them in grave danger of being spotted. They turned their horses and began riding towards the east in hopes of finding a place to hide themselves until it was possible to enter the city. They knew that Ismail's friends' arrival could take anywhere from a day to a week or more.

They had not ridden very far when the night was lit up like a tremendous bolt of lightning. The sound that came next, though, was louder than any thunder they had ever heard.

While the four were watching the floating objects rising into the dark sky, I was awake and kneeling over my night bucket. I coughed so hard that I spat blood, confirming that I had not been ready to venture into the bowels of the caverns. The stitches must have been pulled loose in my lung, I imagined. Not good. I had laid back down on my cot when I saw the same blinding light Connie and the others saw. Almost at the same time came the sound and, with the sound, came a million pieces of colored glass flying into my room from the southern wall of the church building. The ground shook so tremendously that I thought, at first, that a volcano erupted nearby, followed by an earthquake. Outside the now open window frames, I could hear hundreds of voices wailing and yelling, and many people running every which way. I began to assume it was a hand-bomb, but there was no hand-bomb that powerful. The children! Are they okay, I wondered?

Using my stick like a crutch, I limped across the sanctuary and into their room. Thankfully, their room was windowless and were spared the flying glass. They asked what had happened and why my face was bleeding. The glass in my room must have peppered my face with little flying pieces. My white beard very easily showed blood. First, a lead ball dug a scar across my face, and then, the blast sent glass against it. *I will no longer be pretty if the Jews don't stop pelting me with lead and glass*, I thought.

Enzo, Branca, and Mattia were outside in the sanctuary calling my name, so I kissed the children and went to hear what they had to report.

"Lord," said Branca, "the big blast; it destroyed a hundred buildings at least! Thousands may be dead, and it isn't over. When it exploded, gases must have been released, because the wind was blowing a yellowish cloud downwind, and people who breathed the yellow air were suffocating. They are dying. The bomb is still killing people. I've never heard of such destruction before. What can we do?"

Fight or die. That's all we can do, I thought. Where were Connie and the others, I began to wonder after the shock of the explosion left me?

While I was fretting over where they were, Ismail arrived to tell me that his cousin was spotted by one of his spies two miles east of the city. We talked about the bomb, and he was obviously worried that there might be others of those. He warned that the body count would be incredible. Rescuers were digging through rubble already, but the yellow air had been dispersed by the wind. The temperature was cold, and people trapped in the rubble would be prone, especially if wounded, to sickness or death.

Chapter Twenty-One

An Ultimatum from the Ashkenazi Army

Death of a thousand capable people does not cause as much harm as it does if one fool becomes the master.
—Rumi

The sultan's cousin, Emir Rashid, arrived with nearly a thousand men on horseback. It was enough to disperse any of the enemies on the eastern side of the city wall. After clearing away the Ashkenazim on that side, they attacked the soldiers on the southern wall and, since they had not yet finished entrenching themselves and setting up their cannons, they were routed and fled without much trouble. The Jews were too heavily entrenched and armed to attack on the northern side. That would take more planning and more effort, more men, and more lives lost. Ismail was still too concerned about the hundreds in the city who had been killed by the big bomb to attempt an attack on the entrenched soldiers just yet. Some of those in the city center and downwind of there, affected by the yellow cloud, were members of his and his wife's family. His countenance was one of sadness, mixed with fury. I feared his hatred might extend to me and my companions for bringing this destruction upon his city.

Around noon, Connie, Luca, Cosimo, and Pagiel arrived at the sea gate under a flag of truce or parlay, and they were promptly let in. By that time, I wondered again, if Pagiel had wished he had never become acquainted with me. So many bad things had happened to him since we "rescued" him from his English colony prison cell. Of course, he would probably have been stoned to death so, maybe I was still worthy to be his friend in his eyes.

It was reported to Ismail that the Jews were constructing wooden structures along their northern skirmish line, and the object of these structures was yet unknown.

A message from the Ashkenazim arrived midafternoon that day. The messenger wasn't Commander Chaim this time. It was a strikingly beautiful young woman dressed in the army's drab brown uniform, baggy enough to conceal her womanly figure. No veil, no scarf, nothing covered her face or head. She held in her hands a brief message scrawled on a parchment that said:

To the occupants of Tarsus:

You have until sunset today to deliver the following people to the Ashkenazim military leader, Commander Chaim:

The man called Troy,

The woman called Connie,

Mercenaries: Luca, Cosimo, and the man seen riding with Pagiel.

The Jew, Pagiel,

City leader, Sultan Ismail

Additionally, the Ashkenazim commander demands that, by sunset, all gates leading into the city of Tarsus are to be opened, permitting the entrance of the army of the Ashkenazim without obstruction or harm. To ignore these demands will lead to the complete destruction of Tarsus.

Signed: Commander Chaim.

I read the message, written in Hebrew, aloud in the languages they could readily understand. Arabic for Ismail, Hebrew for Pagiel, and Italian for Luca and Cosimo.

The lovely messenger bearing the parchment said, "I have also been instructed to warn you that the bomb that was unleashed upon your city this morning, it was just one of many at our disposal."

"Anything else?"

"Yes, Commander Chaim also instructed me to tell you that, in two days' time, he will have five times the number of soldiers at his disposal than you see right now. Also, in a fortnight, he can have twice that number available to assault your city with violence you can't conceive. Those are his words."

In the room, with the messenger and myself, was Ismail, Yoseph, Connie, Luca, Cosimo, and Ismail's cousin, the Emir Rashid. All of us, including myself, looked worried. If they had multiple bombs like we experienced that morning, the city could not stand. I was ready to sacrifice myself, but not Connie, and I knew Ismail was too furious and too prideful to give in to the weasel Chaim. We were in a deadlock.

"Well," I said, "evidently, they know Pagiel has been removed from their prison and they must know who removed

337

him. I wonder if Chaim knows you have given Yoseph's message to Rabbi Caleb?"

As soon as I spoke those words, it occurred to me that I said them in front of Chaim's messenger. I could not take them back nor could I now allow her to leave with that knowledge.

Yoseph said, "I can't believe Caleb would volunteer names unless he was severely tortured, or a family member was threatened with torture. I wouldn't put it past Chaim, however. Apparently, none of the spiritual leaders of our nation are of any value to him. Adonai will deal with him. If not today, then, the day of judgment, he will."

"Well, is there anything else you wish to tell us?" I asked the lady messenger, still angry with myself for revealing too much. As if she had read my mind, she said further.

"I have knowledge, shared with me, that it was a prisoner in one of the cells that informed the military who the three were who broke Pagiel out of his cell. Their names were spoken in his presence, and he used that information to gain his freedom. As to the man called Enzo, he was seen with Pagiel when he was captured."

"Thank you for that admission," said Yoseph.

"Anything else?"

"Yes, I wish to seek asylum with you. I wish not to return to my people."

After some time of hesitation, while I absorbed what she said, while I celebrated the news, I interpreted her statement for the rest and, by the look on everyone's faces, they were as shocked as I was.

"Are you serious, and if so, why," asked Connie, who could understand Hebrew, "and who are you?"

"My name is Leah. I'm Commander Chaim's sister. I hate

him. He's cruel, mad, and he is determined to continue with his deranged mission to be the sovereign leader of all our people, as well as take control of all the people above ground if that is even possible. He is obsessed with power and is gloating over the opportunity that has fallen into his grasp. He is willing to kill anyone who gets in his way. He has long wanted to be known as a king of sorts. I don't want to ever see him again. He's been a mean and vile person ever since I can remember. I've longed to escape his spitefulness and influence. Even our parents are afraid of his lunacy. He would easily kill them if it would gain him anything."

After my translation, we all looked at each other for input on what to say about the bizarre admission. I wondered if she might do us a great favor by returning and sticking a dagger in his neck. That might be hoping for too much, and maybe too much to ask of her. It was an option and one, I believed, each of the others harbored, as well. Her willingness to stay with us saved us from my slip of the tongue and the subsequent effort to detain her.

Those of us in the room held a quick discussion and agreed that, if she wished to stay with us, it was okay and, just maybe, she could advise us on defensive aspects, knowing her brother and whatever plans she had overheard. It was agreed to accept her desire for asylum.

"Leah," I said, "you are welcome here but just know, that your brother has warned that he will destroy the city. None of us will turn ourselves over to Chaim by sunset. It will not be possible to ensure you, or us, will survive your brother's destruction of this city."

"I understand. You owe me nothing. I just want away from my brother, his insanity, and away from that underground world I've been forced to exist in all my life. I want to live free, even if it's only for hours instead of years."

"Connie, after our meeting, would you find a place for Leah to sleep, and someone to get her anything she might need while here?"

"There are still some boats at the wharves for any of you who wish to take one and leave, but I'm staying and will protect my people for as long as I breathe," said Ismail. None of us cared to leave. None of us wished to be viewed as cowards, least of all, me. Ismail would not even consider having his immediate family leave the city. Even knowing that death, or a worse ending, was likely for all of us. I wondered about the emir. This wasn't his fight; he was just fulfilling an obligation.

Ismail suggested, "What if we blast closed the only remaining entrance to the caverns? It could buy us a few weeks at least before the rest of Chaim's army can join him and, by then, hopefully, the Adrianople army will have arrived to give us relief."

"That's a great idea, but I would like to give it one more day before we attempt to do that," I said. "If Caleb can convince the civilian people to rebel against the army, or at least weaken their resolve, they will need to be able to exit their underground habitat. If we have not heard from them in a day, we will have to do that, Ismail. To hope Caleb will be able to convince his people to rebel against Chaim in just another day would be asking for a miracle, but hope is all we have right now."

"Emir," I asked, "will you and your men stay and fight with us? I would understand it if you left under these circumstances."

"I stand with my cousin until the end. We must come

up with a plan, though. I can't stay and do nothing. Between Ismail's and my men, we have a little less than two thousand men who can still hold a sword and fight. The enemy out there may have about the same amount, maybe a little more, but they have superior weapons. It's time to outthink them, rather than outfight them. If their boast is true that, in two days, they can have five times more men, we must do something drastic between now and the next two days. I believe that, sometime within those two days, we should take the initiative and attack the enemy. My people can circle around and attack the enemy from behind while my cousin advances in the front. It will cost many lives of course, but I think we can prevail if it is a surprise attack."

Yoseph said, "I still believe Adrianople will arrive with an army. We have that hope yet. I don't believe they can make it before another ten days, however. I think our best hope right now is Caleb. I believe in him, and his ability to convince people to listen to reason. If he hasn't been discovered, and possibly killed, I think he will greatly negate the effectiveness of the army. I just don't know how long it will take for him to do something that will help. Sunset today is just a few hours away. Neither Caleb nor the army from Adrianople can provide us any help by sunset today, I'm afraid."

"Ismail," I said. "Is it possible that we can get some volunteers from among your men, especially if they can speak Hebrew, to infiltrate the Ashkenazim line? To do some reconnaissance, to at least find out what they are doing, and maybe even sabotage their weaponry, if possible? Also, if any are willing, they can take the uniforms from the soldiers that were killed descending from those floating vessels yesterday as disguises. It will be dangerous, and some may be killed, but it may give us some valuable information for planning purposes to use against them."

"A few of my people can speak Hebrew," Rashid said. "Ismail and I will see to it immediately."

"Also, Ismail, I think it wise to organize response teams to be ready to fight fires that will come from future explosions, if you haven't already done so."

Nothing else to do but wait for sunset and see what will happen. Meanwhile, the sounds of hammering and sawing told us that the building of unknown structures continued beyond the north wall. Connie asked Leah if she knew, but she said that kind of information wasn't given to people of her status or rank. Being Chaim's sister gave her no advantages. Also, being a woman in her world made her value as a person less than a man. That observation always baffled me about the status of women in the world. I had spent much time in Africa, Japan, Mongolia, and even Israel. In those countries, women were dealt with as inferior to men and thus were not allowed to contribute towards any worthwhile decisions in life and are treated as if they are slaves to their fathers, brothers, or husbands. Plutarch, the widely respected and well-read Greek philosopher, said women were "deceitful, savage, sexually insatiable, frivolous, and gossips." He believed women were inferior to men in every way. Any man who loved his wives and knew his wives as well as I did mine, knew Plutarch was a fool. Connie, for instance, was equal to or greater than any man alive that I knew.

The sound of shouting and hammering continued across the vacant field. The unknown was always scary, and the new structures must be another example of their ingenious secret weaponry designed to overwhelm their opponents. How could we defeat such ingenuity in the hands of a madman?

Sunset came. It seemed much too early for the sun to sink below the western horizon that day but, sink, it did. An hour went by with nothing happening and it was growing dark. I began to think they were waiting for darkness, and then, send more floaters with bombs. It was foolish of us not to think about that scenario. We should have had two hundred men well east of the city lying in wait to attack the soldiers if they sent floaters up like they did the night before. It was probably too late by the time any of us thought of it. Many lights could be seen amongst their northern siege line as the building process continued. I was so curious that I was forced to climb the steps up to the parapet again. I had to see for myself what was happening. Maybe we could begin firing our cannons at them once more, at least towards the new structures. Ismail had warned me they were getting low on powder and iron balls and that was another worry for us.

Before I began the climb up the steps, Luca said a scouting party was organized. Seven men, including Gerald, left the sea gate and were on their way north.

"Gerald," I said. "Why did he go? You should have stopped him."

"He said he wanted to do something besides sitting around all day not being used. I think he wanted to prove to you he was his father's son."

Exasperated, I climbed the steps. At the top, I could see the many lights around the structures, and I immediately knew what they were. I had never seen one personally, only sketches, but there was no mistaking the configuration. They were trebuchets. My heart sank. When they were completed, they could hurl their bombs easily over the city walls as many times, with as many bombs, as they wished. Far more dangerous than catapults, they could sling heavy objects, such as spherical metal bombs, at us, and it looked as though they would be ready to begin by the next morning. We were doomed!

I climbed down the steps and returned to the church. I called for a meeting among the usual members and told them what I saw. Little was said. Our heads hung down and we each entertained our own thoughts. We cleaned our fingernails, scratched our itches, inspected our boots, blew out our breath, and prayed to our gods, but could find no words to speak. We all would probably die the next morning, and nothing could be done about it, except to initiate a suicide attack, as the emir suggested. It galled me to think Chaim would win. If only I was healthier! If I were, I would infiltrate their line after dark, find his sleeping quarters, and remove his head from his body. Or die trying. I would not ask Luca or Cosimo to do that, even though they were as capable as I was before being wounded. We needed a break! We were well overdue for one. God, please help us!

Chapter Twenty-Two
Rabbi Caleb

If you realize that all things change, there is nothing you will try to hold on to. If you are not afraid of dying, there is nothing you cannot achieve.
—*Lao Tzu*

Caleb read the message given to him, written by his High Priest, several times, trying to squeeze more information out of it, trying to get inside his priest's mind. All his fifty years of life, he had been indoctrinated with the promise that his people would leave their underground world one day and take what Adonai truly meant to give them. Not just some vast land mass, but much, much more, with many more opportunities for him and his people. He dreamed his people would see to it that the temple would be rebuilt on the holy mountain of Mariah. He knew the Torah said nothing about the land to the west. He was one of the leaders who is permitted to read it and had done so daily for decades. He simply trusted the insight and wisdom of what his superiors said, his high and chief priests. He had studied the Mishna, the Midrash, and the Torah diligently since he was thirteen years old. The Talmud was ambiguous about the boundaries of the land promised to his people, at least it was in the case with the Talmud kept and studied by the Ashkenazim. Could the Ashkenazim be wrong in the eyes of his God, though? He often wondered if the Jews who lived and walked the streets of Jerusalem had a different Talmud. The Talmud was not Holy Scripture, though, it was a compilation written by very learned and highly respected men. It was only an interpretation of Scripture made by fallible and mortal men. However, he knew his people wanted to take control of the aboveground peoples, not just because their priests said it was due them, but also because it was in retribution for centuries of persecution by those gentile peoples.

There were enough questions in his mind to wonder if the note from Yoseph was completely legitimate. Could the note have been written under duress? The most pressing question in his mind, though, wasn't whether their Talmud was accurately interpreting the Torah, but the rebellion of the military and the rejection of their spiritual leadership. Yoseph's message stated the army had rebelled, but was it the truth? If it was true, he could not allow the army to disregard Adonai's instructions. He gave the instructions to his prophets and priests, not army commanders. There were enough current activities taking place within his world that gave him pause, such as, the recent colony-wide meeting in the synagogue the night before, hosted by and conducted by the military, to believe the note had legitimacy. There were also calls for his two children to begin preparation for required military exercises. That was too ominous to believe the timing was coincidental. Then there was Chaim, who he knew to be belligerent and egotistical, and it would not be surprising to Caleb if Chaim was doing what the note from Yoseph had said he was. He reluctantly decided he would do whatever he could to disregard the military leadership in favor of his godly priests. His moral code gave him no other choice.

Caleb sent messages to the heads of every department in his colony. Messages were sent to the directors of hydra planting, mining, food distribution and preparation, animal procurement and care, primary, secondary, and advanced education, scientific research, the treasury, aboveground intelligence, each department of maintenance, waste management, water control, construction, and all the rest of non-military branches. All of them were to tell no one of their summons, not even their families. They were to meet him in the synagogue at the appointed hour. From there, he would provide them with information, discuss their opinions and, as a group, make decisions. Then he would have them disseminate the decisions and instructions quietly to the civilian population.

When Caleb was sure all department heads were present, he had the synagogue door bolted shut, something that, as far as he knew, had never been done before.

Caleb began the clandestine meeting by saying, "I have been your rabbi for the past twenty-three years. You all know me, and I hope you respect my position as your rabbi but, mostly, I hope you know me as one of your friends. I was given a message, not many hours ago, that affects all of us. Every single man, woman, and child in our world. Maybe each of you have heard rumors that our military has begun operations aboveground. Maybe some of you have a family member taking part in that or have been summoned to take part. The rumors are true. Right now, the army, under the control of Commander Chaim bar Joram, is attacking the city of Tarsus not many miles from here. Commander Chaim has taken unauthorized control of the army and, by extension, our whole colony. This is in violation of our laws and our Chief and High Priests commands. The military has commenced a program of regional domination. Regardless of what you have been taught about our Ashkenazim destiny, the army has taken upon itself to conduct an operation without any spiritual guidance or approval. That means they are acting against not only our belief system, but against Adonai himself. They are seeking to establish a military rulership of the aboveground world, not a spiritual renewal of the people, as our priests had desired."

He then read the message given to him from Yoseph.

Caleb also read from the book of Isaiah: "I have spread out My hands all day long to a rebellious people, who walk in the way, which is not good, following their own thoughts, a people who continually provoke Me to My face."

"Do you understand the terrible implications of what is happening? Ten thousand men and women, who are my and your family members, have been deceived to fulfill the ambition of one rebellious mad man. If we don't stop him using our family for his own personal desires, many will die, killed in fighting a war that can't be won. In fact, as I understand it, many have already been killed. Our ancestors have fought against Adonai's wishes before and have always lost. What can we do to stop the madness? I ask you for suggestions on how we can prevent our sons and daughters, our husbands, and wives, from being killed for no purpose other than to inflate the ego of a deluded and rebellious lunatic."

There was silence among the audience for a while, then

mumblings began, as the large crowd tried to digest the information they had just heard, and then express their take on the situation, on what was said to them. It was a momentous situation in their world where everything was always routine. No one had ever in their lifetime rebelled against the priests. It just wasn't done. They were all god-fearing people. The law was final. What the priests said was final. They lived under a long list of strict moral laws well beyond what the Ten Commandments dictated. Rebellion was forbidden. Thou shalt not rebel was their eleventh commandment.

A professor, department head of advanced education, said, "It is my understanding that we have but one recourse. That recourse is to rebel against the rebellion. The army has no jurisdiction, no authority over the heads of families. We simply need to say to our children or family members that they are no longer obligated to serve the commander. It is our duty and our right to say that. Some of our family members may already be involved in the war aboveground, but many, maybe even most, are still with us. Let us demand, as is our right as parents, to say no to the army leadership, unless or until the priests say otherwise. After all, the fifth commandment teaches us that our children must honor and obey their parents. It says nothing about obeying an army commander, rather than their parents."

Caleb asked the crowd, "Anybody disagree with what Professor Perez just said?"

There were a few others who asked questions, and they were discussed. Most of them were dealing with the Ashkenazi interpretation of the Torah. Some wanted more assurance that they were not violating their laws but, in the end, there was general agreement with the professor's argument.

"Then it is agreed by all that we will instruct our family members to reject the call to duty in the army until our priests tell us otherwise. All who agree with this plan, raise their hand."

"Let's go from here then and carry out this decision. You must, as soon as it is possible, meet with those under your guidance and tell them our decision. If anyone suffers repercussions from this decision, inform me promptly. There could be some single-minded family members in the army who might feel more of an obligation towards their commanders than their parents or priests, for instance. If so, let me know as soon as you hear of it. Before we leave, let us pray."

The word went throughout the colony, and ideas such as what was revealed, like gossip among all peoples of the world, traveled very quickly. It was especially rapid among the Ashkenazim because they were a people who were not used to controversy or conflicting ideas or ideology. Not many hours elapsed before every reasoning person had heard the news and was astounded. A new world was emerging. Change. Change was something that never happened, but change had come.

Chapter Twenty-Three

If it Weren't for Bad News, There Would be No News at All.

Hiraeth: (n.) a deep spiritual sense of longing, a yearning for that which has past, a sense of homesickness tinged with grief or sorrow over the lost or departed. It is the echo of the lost places of our soul's past and our grief for them.

I waited for the break to come. Surely God was watching so, surely, he was going to intervene and help. It was totally dark now. Just Connie and I stood outside Saint Paul's church and looked at the darkened sky, thinking at any moment flaming objects would be flying over the walls. The suspense was terrible, but I knew the explosions would be more terrible. It had rained earlier, but it had stopped, leaving only a chill in its place. I told Connie that, if it were possible, I would go ask Caleb what was happening in his world. Tomorrow evening, I would be forced to send some men to seal in the Ashkenazim in their underground habitation for as long as it took for them to tunnel out. I didn't want to do that and cut off a possible course of help until there was no other choice, but I couldn't let thousands more of Chaim's people emerge as more enemies to confront. They would be the blind being led by the blind.

To let us know they were still out there, cannons from our enemy resumed. No response came from our side. We needed to save powder. Where did the Jews get so much powder? I waited for some word from Gerald and the others who left to infiltrate the enemy line. The only duties I was capable of were to worry and wait. I agonized over what may befall us the next morning when the trebuchets were completed. My primary job as a father was to protect my family. I wondered how I could do that with bombs falling all around. I should have demanded they leave on a ship. For months "should" and "if" came up often in my thoughts. I would someday have to give an account for my poor showing as a father, having put my family in so much harm that I could have prevented. If I were seventeen again, knowing what I know now, would I have left my family and endure a long series of events that would lead to this fateful day? Too complex of a question to answer with a simple yes or a no, I concluded. No control over the past, only today and tomorrow. Maybe not even then.

There was nothing I could do to stop the chain of events unfolding, so I told Connie good night, hugged Catherine Adele, and Troy, said goodnight to Eesha, and laid down. As soon as I laid my head down, a coughing fit occurred, and I spat more blood in my night bucket. I decided then, it was time to talk to Pagiel. I didn't want to try and sleep anyway. Too much on my mind. He usually came to me if he had a vision of importance but, sometimes, he held back things he knew would upset me. I found him talking to Luca, Cosimo, and Leah.

"I'm Leah's interpreter," Pagiel volunteered. He said it with a smile, and I knew he was hiding something, but I was too obtuse to read its' meaning.

"Pagiel, can I talk to you a moment?"

"How are you fairing, Pagiel?"

"Lord, I'm doing alright; just a little anxious about what's coming."

"That's what I want to talk to you about. I have learned to trust your insight, your feelings for what will happen. Since you very well might know what's coming, is there anything I need to know? Maybe something that can help me plan or prepare for the days ahead? Something that might help me protect my family?"

He was sitting down at the time I asked. He crossed his legs, then, uncrossed them. He looked out the door we had entered as if he wished he could get up and leave through it. Another cannonball hit the north wall, otherwise, the silence was real enough to feel. I had the sinking feeling he saw something, and the something was not good news. I wouldn't recognize good news any longer even if it hit me in the face.

"Pagiel..."

"Lord, I believe we are going to be alright. I have seen enough to know your family will be alright. Don't fret over them."

"That's a huge relief, but what else?"

"The Adrianople army is on the way, and they will be here at the end of next week. Chaim will be defeated; I'm sure of it. Caleb, too, is working to help us. I don't know exactly how, but Chaim will not succeed. You will be able to return to England, Lord."

"That's all great to hear, but what are you not telling me, Pagiel? I can tell by the look on your face there is more you know about that will happen."

Who likes hearing bad news? It seemed to me, in my quiet

hours before sleep finally comes, ever since the Ashkenazim captured me in England, things had gotten steadily worse. I had spent the last months depressed or angry or both. If you sow thorns, you will reap thorns.

"Lord, something will happen to Gerald tonight. I think he will live, but not without severe injuries. You will not recover from your chest wounds. They will slowly kill you, maybe in a year, maybe less, maybe a little more, but the damage is too great for you to live longer. It hurts me to tell you, lord. You are my best friend. I had never had a friend until I met you. You saved my life, lord. I wish I could die instead of you."

He wept. I sat down next to him. I tried to think of something to say to make him feel better. I knew I was dying and had gotten over the idea by then. I discovered, while sitting next to him, that my heart was less hard, less filled with grief and hatred and anger. I didn't want to spend my last days hating. If I could survive the battles to come, and the Lord allowed me to return to my England home, I would be a loving family man with the time I had left. Do my very best to make wise decisions, the very best I am capable of. Maybe it was too little, too late, but I would end my legacy on a positive note. I had always believed I would die in battle or ambushed in a dark alley by an enemy, not killed by a fifteen-year-old disgruntled boy shooting me in the back. How ironic. Gerald, my only grandchild still living, must be in trouble, and there was nothing I could do to go to his aid. I could only wait and fret. I should not have allowed him to leave our city walls.

"Pagiel, my friend, I am honored that you think of me as your best friend. That is the best news I've heard in a very long time. It's enough to know I have friends like you, and that you believe I will be able to return to my home and spend the rest of my time in peace. What more can I ask for?"

Another cannon ball hit the parapet, and people yelling, spoiled our moment. I patted him on his back and returned to my cot. I had much to think about. I mostly wondered what would happen to Gerald. Two weeks ago, I would be, right now, preparing to search for him and go out amongst the enemy to defend him with my swords. That was then, and now, I had only the use of one arm, and it hurt to walk, even breathe.

To my surprise, I fell asleep quickly. Maybe it was because I had been purged of hate that the murder of Dania, Jaleel, and Carl had given birth to. I awakened by what seemed to be a loud blast. It wasn't a dream, and it didn't sound as if it were inside the city. Another Ashkenazi super weapon, maybe? Not long after, Connie came into my room and found me sitting on the side of my cot coughing into my night bucket.

"Poppa, what's wrong? There is blood on your beard. I'm going to get the chirurgeon."

"No, wait. Why did you come to see me? It's still dark out. What was that explosion I heard?"

"Something happened outside the walls. Sentries report an explosion took place among the Ashkenazi siege line and there are fires. We don't know yet what has happened, but it appears that two or more of the trebuchets have been damaged or destroyed. We thought you would want to know. Now, I'm going for the chirurgeon."

Half an hour later, the sultan's best healer arrived and examined me. My left arm was healing properly, and I soon would not need the splints to hold the bone in place. The holes in my upper arm, made by the lead ball entering and exiting, were healing well. My arm had withered and lost some muscle strength, I'm sure, but no longer had much pain. My hip still hurt some, mostly when I walked and when I sat down, but my chest wound was the most serious. The chirurgeon wanted to cut me open again and see why I was spitting out blood. He surmised the two holes in my left lung had their stitches come loose before it was completely healed. He blamed the lack of rest and too much moving around as the reason for the failed stitching that had led to bleeding and intense coughing spells. Being cut open again had no appeal to me. Besides, according to Pagiel, it would serve no purpose, so I declined the offer. I spent the next hour arguing with Connie for the reasons I had declined and refuting all her insistences that I let the healer operate. We were still arguing the pros and cons of doing the procedure when the sultan entered my room. At least for the moment, Connie was forced to stop her pleading and listen to the sultan.

"Some of my men who were sent to the enemy's siege line have returned. They have reported some success in their efforts, and you will be interested in what they have to say. The team leader, Malik, can fill you in on what happened."

Chapter Twenty-Four

"He was the bravest man I have ever met."

War is created by people too old to fight for those too young to die
—African proverb.

Malik, the son of Hassan said, "As-salamu alakum" when he came to me, and I responded with "Wa-alakum as-salam".

"Sit down, Malik, and tell me the news." By the time he began to relate his story, Connie had retrieved Luca and Cosimo. Connie interpreted the Arabic language to her friends as he spoke."

"We left the city under the cover of darkness the evening before. There were the six of us, men loyal to the Sultan Ismail, plus the man, Gerald. I believe he is your grandson. I was appointed the scouting team leader. We traveled, wearing soldier's clothes we had removed from dead men killed in the fighting on the previous night. We traveled on foot, and Gerald brought up the rear. He spoke little and we all minimized all sounds as much as possible. Truthfully, I

357

did not want your grandson with us, because I did not know his usefulness or his dedication to what we had to do. I was afraid he was too young and inexperienced for the task we were going on. I was also afraid he would give us away if he got frightened.

"We made it successfully to the outer perimeter of the enemy's line. At the outer edge of the line, no one could tell us from other soldiers because of the darkness. There were several sentries, but they were not observant, and we killed them easily and quietly, taking their strange weapons with us, even though we did not know how to use them. Beyond that, however, there were many more campfires and, amongst the campfires, sat the wooden structures they were building. There were many oil lamps burning at all the devices being built, but only one had men working. Most men, though, who weren't in their tents, were eating, laughing, and paying little attention to any of us.

"Once we got closer to the middle of the siege line, we got a better look at the tall wooden things they were building. It looked as if three of them were completed. No work was being done on them. One was only partially completed, though, and a small crew was all over it, as if they were in a hurry to finish.

"Not far away, sitting near the center of two of the structures, was a wagon filled with what looked like large iron balls. I estimated them to be about three feet across. Beyond it, and between the other two structures, was another wagon filled with more black iron balls. We figured them to be bombs and, most likely, would be used by the completed structures to send against our walls or into the city.

"The seven of us, finding a place to talk quietly and away from the soldiers, talked about how to sabotage the weapons they were building. There were hundreds of campfires and tents, and we knew the seven of us could not kill enough of the infidels to make any difference. It was decided that two of my men each would go to the three completed structures and, using the enemy's own oil lamps, set them afire. Four of my men had already left, and Amaar and I were about to leave to go to the third one, so I looked around to tell Gerald to keep watch for any more sentries. When I looked for Gerald, he was not there. He must have slipped away while I was giving instructions to my men. I was angry with him at first for leaving us when I wanted him to stand watch. I saw, then, because the light was the brightest in that area, Gerald climbing up on the nearest wagon containing the load of bombs. None of the soldiers seemed to have noticed him standing alone on top of the wagon. He looked like any other soldier, I guess.

"I saw him crouching down and placing or pouring something on the black spheres. I saw him jump down on the back side of the wagon and run. Then, I thought he could be about to set off an explosion, so I grabbed Amaar's arm and told him to run. We had run only a few yards when I heard the largest explosion I have ever heard. We were hit by a sudden and strong blast of hot air, and it knocked us down into a small depression, and that may have saved our lives, because the blast also carried pieces of metal, wood, and other debris in the wake of the violent rushing wind. My hearing was gone, as was Amaar's. When I looked up, I saw a huge ball of fire rising and fading away into blackness. Men from all over were rushing towards the explosion to see what had happened. Very little light remained after the fire ball rose, but I saw enough to know the wagon was destroyed and the two closest wooden structures were, as well. A third appeared damaged severely and on fire, leaving only one of them left, and it was not finished.

"Many men were scattered about, some on fire. Many tents were on fire, as well. We saw dozens of dead men and pieces of dead men laying everywhere. My two men, who had gone to the furthest structure, survived the blast, but two others, I think, were killed by the explosion. I hadn't seen Gerald since he leapt off the wagon, which was soon followed by a huge blast. Four of us made it back here while all the confusion was taking place. Maybe I should have stayed to see for sure what happened to my men and Gerald, but I was sure they could not have survived the blast.

"I had doubts about the character of your grandson. I now know he was the bravest man I have ever met. I'm sorry for your loss, sir."

Chapter Twenty-Five

Caleb's Arrival

*Love of power, operating through greed and through personal
ambition, was the cause of all these evils.*
—Thucydides

I thanked Malik for his report, what they had accomplished, and for their bravery. The pain in my heart had now exceeded the pain in my chest. My life was continuing to turn against me, and I felt helpless to stop the avalanche of bad things suffocating my life. One by one, everyone left my room, except Eesha and Connie.

Eesha sat in a corner of the room and wept. I do not know if she cried for Gerald or for me. Probably it was for both of us.

Connie said, "Poppa, I am so sorry. At least we know Gerald was a brave man who would have made Carl so proud."

Just words. She was speaking to me words that had for me no value, no comfort. Words are created by air from our lungs, forced out through our voice box. Simple air that became words could not give me any solace, could not give back what was gone. Maybe in the next life, but not in this one. Words could not restore what was lost no more than I could relive yesterday. Hope too, was lost, for me in this life. Hope is what makes us different than animals. Different from monkeys who sit on tree limbs picking lice out of their hair and eating them. If it weren't for hope, we might as well be picking and eating lice. The weight of seeing so many of my family who had died during the last few months, because of me, was drowning me in a pool of self-pity. It was so strange to me how much my life had changed in a matter of a few months. What had I said or done to cause all the anguish I felt?

I had a mental picture of me sitting in a tree scratching my naked butt and eating lice when a loud explosion happened nearby. I vaguely thought the fourth trebuchet must be working now. Ismail should concentrate his cannons on that one launcher of death. Even stupid men would know to do that.

The sun was high now, though it couldn't be seen. Too many clouds, too much smoke. Too many people were screaming, and too many people running around with no one to tell them what to do. I turned around and went back to my room, alone this time, and spat blood into a clay jar, laid down and stared at the ceiling, wondering at any moment if it would fall on me.

I finally drifted off to sleep, then awoke. It must have been only a short sleep because another explosion erupted. We are doomed, I thought, and then, I went back to sleep.

"Poppa, wake up. Poppa!"

I looked at the face of my daughter. The one whose face showed she still had hope. I tried to focus on her eyes, to search for what lay in her soul.

"Poppa! Wake up!"

I did not want to wake up. What was there to wake up to? Well, I summoned the last scraps of manhood that hadn't died with the rest of my family and asked, "Yes, what do you want, Connie?"

"You need to get up if you can and come see this. Outside, come on, get up."

For her, my dear, sweet, loyal Connie, I got up. She was the one who fussed at me every time I moved around and now, she was insisting I get up, so, I got up. I leaned on her strong shoulders like she used to do on mine when she was just a child. We walked over to the steps that led to the top of the parapet. My hip hurt, but the comfort of her strong shoulders helping to hold me up made the climb not an ordeal, but one that gave new life to my flagging resolve.

At the top of the parapet, I saw smoke rising from the siege line where the three destroyed trebuchets were now only a black smudge. I stared at the line and wondered why the last remaining bomb-launcher wasn't slinging death balls at us.

Connie said, "Can't you see them? Look to the northeast. Can you see them?"

My eyes focused on a scene of thousands of little somethings coming our way. Fifty or seventy-five abreast maybe, little moving figures walking towards us. As far as I could see, the little figures stretched like ants coming over the hill. I turned to Connie standing next to me. She looked at me with a grand smile, and there was that hopeful look on her face again.

"Rabbi Caleb must be leading his people to confront the commander," she said.

Her enthusiasm was contagious. Could it possibly be

true? Were the Jews coming to join the army or where they going to stop the army from killing us? I hoped they were going to save us. I hoped they would. Even I, the one who had given up all hope, hoped it would be good news. There is that fragile and fleeting word again: hope.

We watched the vast, massed hoard move like a living and sun-speckled river that had escaped its banks and was flowing in our direction. More people joined us on the parapet. Some on top were yelling at people below, describing what they saw. Luca and Cosimo came up and stood next to us as we eagerly watched to see what would happen next.

It was maybe half an hour before the front of the human river reached the siege line. The river did not stop, though, but continued to flow, and eventually surrounded the siege line. There were thousands of them. Ten, fifteen thousand, maybe more, much more. Branches of the living and undulating river flowed towards the east and west, enveloping the lines of soldiers who were stationed to prevent any of the people of Tarsus from escaping. Thousands upon thousands upon thousands of Jews were down below. Every capable Ashkenazim who could walk must have left the only home they had ever known to confront Commander Chaim, most of them having never seen the sun before, never felt a breeze on their skin. Maybe they were there to support him; we still weren't sure.

It must have been an hour, maybe not that long, but it seemed much longer, that a half dozen men broke off the mass of people and began walking towards the city's north gate. When they got within seventy-five yards, Connie recognized one of the men. It was Rabbi Caleb. He was holding a flag of truce in his right hand.

Ismail and half dozen of his men walked out to speak with him. They spoke for a long while. When they finished, each group returned to their respective sides.

"Help me down the steps, Connie."

The seed of hope began to take root in me. I once embraced "joi de vie", maybe I would again.

By the time Connie, Luca, Cosimo, and I reached the ground, Ismail and his men entered the gate. People gathered around to hear what was to be said. Hundreds of people were crowding and pushing to hear about their fate.

"Everyone," Ismail shouted, "listen. Quiet. The man I just spoke to was Rabbi Caleb. He said the siege was over! He gave me his word that his people are sorry for what has happened to our city, that the man responsible for the damage will be tried for his crimes and will never again be allowed to cause such death and destruction, not here, not anywhere. The rabbi promises to give restitution to the families who have lost loved ones and to the damages done to our city. He assures me that the priests will support him in his promise. We will talk more in the next few days but, for now, all the soldiers around our city will be recalled. He expresses his deepest regret for the pain and suffering caused by one of their people."

Everyone shouted their joy and thanksgiving for the war's end. I looked at Connie and our companions and we all smiled. Could it all be over? The months of fighting, running, and dying be over now? I know everything under the sun must eventually come to an end, but it didn't seem this one would. If Caleb and his people had come a day earlier, maybe Gerald would still be alive. "Maybe" and "why" were two words that had no business being thought of that day, so I set them aside, and gave thanks for the end of the deadly confrontation.

We returned to the church and told everyone there the news. The High Priest, the Chief Priest, Pagiel, Catherine Adele, Troy, and the rest of my mercenary friends who had been through so much with me. We all were happy, smiling, hugging each other, and all of us talking at the same time. Eesha was jumping up and down like a child, clapping her hands. I don't know if she knew what was going on, but she was caught up in the enthusiasm everyone was displaying. Little Troy was celebrating also, even though he didn't know what he was celebrating, either. He jumped up and down and clapped his chubby hands together like Eesha, as if the world was a grand place to live in, and so, it was now.

I studied Yoseph's face to see if I saw any jealousy of Caleb, or obstinacy over what he had promised Ismail. I saw only happiness and an expression of contentment, so I hoped he and the priests would support the rabbi's promise as they forged a peace with the people of Tarsus.

As if our joy that the end of the war had ended wasn't enough to celebrate, a most amazing and very unexpected thing happened to make our happiness complete. One of the sultan's fighting men came into our room with a message.

"Sire, there are some Jews at the gate who have injured men with them. They are carrying two of our men, the two that we thought had been killed by the big blast. They are badly injured and have been brought to the chirurgeons for aid. They also have a man they say is not one of theirs and is not one of our people. Maybe it's one of yours. He's unconscious and can't tell us who he is. He has also been brought to a chirurgeon. If you wish, you can see if you know him."

For long moments we said nothing, but all of us held thoughts that were too delicate to speak out loud in fear that uttering them would destroy our new-found hopes. Connie said she would go with the messenger to see who it was they had brought. Gerald's name was never mentioned. The news, however, stopped our few moments of celebrating an end of long months of trials. Not because we were sad, or our joy had diminished by the messenger, but because we, at least I, didn't want to put a curse on what my deepest hope had just become. Long moments went by with very few words being spoken. Even Eesha was quiet. Troy looked at the adults and wondered why everyone had suddenly become quiet.

Soon, Connie came into the room, and I studied her face for clues as to what she might say. I held my breath and expected to hear more bad news, ripping the scab off my mental wounds.

"It's him," she said with the slightest of smiles. "It's Gerald." Then I let my breath out. "He's alive, but badly wounded, and is still unconscious. Some assistants are cleaning him up right now. Two of the chirurgeons are working on the wounds of their men first. I don't know the extent of his injuries until he is examined by a chirurgeon. I know that his legs are broken because both lay at odd angles. It's good he is unconscious because, otherwise, he would be in great pain. I'm going back and stay there until I know more."

When she left, I dared to hope for Gerald's life. Now that he was back and still alive, for him to die would be to grieve all over again over his death. *Please Lord God*, I begged, *let him live!* The news that it was Gerald made the rest of my companions feel lighthearted again, and they began conversing with each other, and were happy the way things were turning out. Everyone but Eesha. Maybe she understood enough English to know Gerald was badly injured, and maybe she felt enough compassion for him that it made her sad.

"Eesha," I said to her, "what are you thinking? What makes you sad?"

"My heart hurt, lord. Gerald like me. I not mean that. I mean he I like. He nice me to me. Him, you, my life now. I want life to fall down on him, lord. I want him feel good. Him not good, make me feel not good. What be happen to me?"

"I understand," I told her. "He means a lot to both of us. I pray he will recover completely, and we can all go to our homes."

"No," she said, "I not go home back again. This not home here, also. What be happen to Eesha?"

What was I to do with her? Taking her back to England wasn't what I wanted to do. I wanted her to stay in Tarsus and let it become her new home, but I felt the beginnings of pressure to bring her to England against my better judgment.

Over the next three days, there were long meetings held between the Sultan's men and the Jews. High Priest Yoseph, the highest-ranking person among the Ashkenazim, represented his people, along with the three remaining Chief Priests and Rabbi Caleb. I sat in on all the meetings, even though I held no position in either group but, since I was the reason for the war to have happened in the first place, I insisted on being present. Connie was with me throughout the meetings and gave me assistance during my coughing spells.

It was decided that the Ashkenazim would emerge from their underground habitation and, with the sultan's authorization, purchase land to inhabit and farm throughout Armenia. In doing so, they would also be a tax base for the sultan and his people, and those monies would be used to rebuild the city of Tarsus and its walls. It was also agreed that the Jews would share all discoveries made by their scientists with the leadership of the city of Tarsus. A pact was signed by both sides agreeing to never again war with each other. Each party recognized the complication of differing religious worldviews between them and promised that neither would interfere with the way the other party worshipped. Nothing was committed to paper concerning the vast geography of the underground world below their feet. No doubt, there would be many Ashkenazim, especially the older ones, who would elect to stay belowground, since it was the only world, they knew. It may take many generations for them to eventually leave the underworld for life amongst the natural world above.

Three days after that, the army from Adrianople arrived. They were no longer needed to quell the fighting, but it was a meaningful meeting that took place between them and the Armenian colony. Yoseph stood by his word to all of us and made them swear allegiance anew to his spiritual leadership. The armies of all the colonies extending to England would stand down as a fighting unit and would serve only as a police and defensive force. Many thousands of Ashkenazim Jews would be released into the world, and a protection force was justifiably needed. Persecution would not be tolerated. No colony would be permitted to retain the old way of life of making plans to emerge aboveground to take over surrounding governments. It was also agreed that representatives of each colony would meet annually to discuss ways to keep their faiths pure and their people safe from prejudiced, curious, and skeptical people of the outside world. Regular communication was sent out, bearing witness to what was decided with the city of Tarsus and the Adrianople contingent, to all the network of colonies. The

Ashkenazim Jews would meld into the world inhabited by the Sephardic Jews.

I knew that it would take decades for the transition to be complete. Before the Ashkenazim would be accepted, if ever they were. I knew I would never see the completion of all that had to take place. Maybe Catherine Adele and Troy might.

I was able to give my thanks to Rabbi Caleb personally for what he did. He was a good man, and it was his leadership that ultimately stopped the war between the above and belowground worlds who were separated not only by geography, but ideology, as well.

We stayed on in Tarsus for another month, hoping Gerald and I would become stronger for the long trip back to England. My hip and arm were as healed as they ever would be and, while my lungs would never heal, travel would most probably not make them any worse. Gerald awoke two days after he was brought to Tarsus' chirurgeons. He had two badly broken legs and a broken left arm, and many cuts and holes caused by flying debris that required stitches. When he was awake and strong enough to talk, he told me what had happened that night he saved us from the trebuchets rain of death.

"While Malik was giving instructions to his men, which left me out of his plan, I had an idea of my own on how to either destroy the bombs and weapons, or damage them long enough to buy some time until help could arrive. I doubted I would survive what I was about to do, but I wanted you to be proud of me, Poppa. As I got closer to the wagon holding the bombs, I saw that almost all the Ashkenazim were either asleep or focused on their conversations around campfires. I was ignored as I approached the first wagon containing the large metal balls. Next to the numerous cannons, lay cannon balls, sponges, ramrods, and powder charges. I took two charges and an oil lantern over to the first wagon, approaching it from behind, hidden from the nearby soldiers where I couldn't be seen by those still awake. When I climbed up on the wagon, I stuffed the two powder charges between openings among the bombs. I was also able to knock out and remove a bung from one of the sphere's fill-hole. Then I poured lamp oil over the balls leading up to the powder charges. Using another oil lamp I retrieved, I placed it next to the powder and bombs wet with the oil I had poured out. Leaping off the backside of the wagon, I stepped back about thirty feet and fired the gonne I had taken from a dead sentry. I only had one chance. If I had missed the lamp glass, I would have been discovered and taken prisoner or killed on the spot. *Lord, please guide my hand and my aim,* I thought to myself. Then I pulled the trigger.

"There were just maybe two or three heartbeats between me pulling that trigger and when the world went dark. During those heartbeats, I turned and ran away from the wagon, but it wasn't long before the blast's terrific gust of wind hit me from behind in my haste to get away. I do not know what happened, or why I wasn't killed from flying metal pieces. Maybe I fell into a ditch while running or some other depression that saved me because the terrain was uneven. The last thing I remember was hearing the oil lamp's glass shattering. It wasn't until I woke up back in Tarsus that I discovered I still lived."

I let him know that not only was Connie and I proud of him, but his father surely would have been, also.

After a month had passed and Gerald was able to withstand being transported with not too much pain, it came time for all of us to leave for England. To Eesha's credit, since Gearld needed her more than me, she stayed by his side and waited on him all day, every day, so it appeared she would find her new home with us. It became time, also, for decisions to be made among my mercenary friends on where they would go and how much silver I owed them. As for me, I did get a little better but the coughing never left me.

At the end of March 1363, we were fortunate enough to find a merchant ship in the Tarsus harbor that accepted fifteen of us as passengers, including Eesha, and brought us to Constantinople. We were anxious to get home, so we gambled we could find a ship heading west from there. The Mediterranean, unlike many parts of the world, was blessed with better winter and early spring weather than most seaports, and we were privileged to find a ship that would take us to Venice. In two months, we arrived in Southampton on the southern coast of England.

Chapter Twenty-Six

Home

A man can be himself only so long as he is alone; and if he does not love solitude, he will not love freedom; for it is only when he is alone that he is really free.
—Arthur Schopenhauer

I will die. You will die. We will all die, and the universe will carry on without care. All that we have is that shout into the wind — how we live. How we go. And how we stand before we fall.
—Pierce Brown

When we arrived in Southampton, our group consisted of, besides myself, Connie, my two young children, Pagiel, Luca, Leah, and Eesha. Cosimo, Enzo, and Carlos chose to return to their wives and family after we docked at Centumcellae. Branca, Mattia, Luigi, Ferrante, and Benetto also chose to return to their families in Rome. I had to make a short journey to the Roman bank to withdraw a great deal of silver to pay my friends what was due them. It was difficult to see them leave us after all we had been through. I would miss their presence and their friendship, especially Cosimo and Enzo. They had put their lives at risk for my sake. Luca had no family, so he decided to travel with us back to England. He made great progress in learning English during the two months of travel it took us to return. Eesha, too, made progress in putting her words in the proper order. Pagiel had nowhere else to go. He hinted at maybe re-establishing some relationships with those he knew in the English colony now that he was no longer considered a hunted escaped prisoner.

Yes, Leah came with us to England, also. Much to my surprise, there was an almost immediate spark or connection that took place without me knowing it between Pagiel and Leah. Gentle Pagiel, an unassuming and humble man who loved nature and children, fell deep into the almost mystical aura of Leah. She was an astoundingly beautiful, olive skinned, young woman, despite living out of sunlight for all her life. The two of them seemed so very different, but they fell maddingly in love with each other, and she chose to leave her people, and the embarrassment of being the sister of Chaim, and come to England with us.

I was very anxious to see how the English colony had taken to the new edict demanded by the Armenian colony and how their transformation into aboveground English inhabitants was going. On the travels back to England, I thought about my promise to Francois. My promise that I would evict his family from his estate. I made that promise in a state of anger and grief. Would I commit to that promise and require his wife and family to leave? Every time I had a coughing fit, I reaffirmed, yes, I would take ownership of the estate in payment for the hell Francois caused me. I left Carl, Dania, and Jaleel buried in foreign soil because of Francois.

We purchased a wagon to transport Gerald, who lay on blankets in the back, because he was not ready to sit on a horse yet. It took us two weeks to journey from Southampton to Goodrich Castle. I feared that our pursuers might have burned my home, and I was greatly relieved when I found it still intact. Connie and Luca spent five days there with me, cleaning up the damage the Ashkenazim caused in my home in their search for me many months earlier. The dead bodies of my servants were still in the kitchen, their spilled blood forever staining the stone floor. The two children of my husband-and-wife servants were not found when we arrived, and I assumed some neighbors had taken them in. Connie was very anxious to return to London to take back control of the trading company where she was the president. Luca promised to escort her there to ensure her safety. I thanked him for his service and his consideration for Connie's safety.

What would Gerald do? He had turned twenty-one years of age during our return home. He once was the adventurous type, shunning the kind of work his father and aunt did because he thought it was too dull. He would never be able to walk without the assistance of a cane or crutches. His bones never healed properly. Connie urged him to work with her, to learn what his father did, and he reluctantly agreed to try it. He needed an income, and Connie would see that he got one.

When Connie and Luca rode away, taking Gerald and Eesha with them, I was left in my ancient castle alone with Catherine Adele, Troy, Pagiel, and Leah. Much had to be done. None of us could cook, not even Leah. I would have to look for new servants. Some for around our home, and some to plant and harvest my crops. So much to do and little time to do it.

After days of taking care of business around the castle, hiring house servants and a cook, I had yet to visit my safe place. My lovely, tranquil, go to place where I needed mental rest and to absorb the healing comfort that only nature can give me. My forest habitat. Things were back to normal again. At least the new normal was.

It was a beautiful, warm day in June. Mid-morning. The morning dew sparkled across the lawn, and the tight wrappings of buds were slowly opening to reveal a wondrous display of vibrant colored flowers. The garden needed much attention. There was no wife, no matriarchy, to see that it achieved the beauty it once had.

I entered the forest and walked upon the once beaten down path, that meandered amongst the giant trees that had never felt the cold iron of an axe before. The path hadn't welcomed the feet of a man in a long time and was covered in brown, crisp leaves. Many of the giant trees were hundreds of years old. Much older than even I was. Giant beeches, sycamores, oaks, chestnuts, and pines stood at attention as I walked by, acknowledging me as their lord, but greeted me as a friend and protector. The breeze blowing amongst the leaves and needles whispered to me, "welcome home". In the distance, I heard my very best confidant mummering and singing, because I once again came to keep it company as it ran rapidly across smooth and round rocks. It would whisper secrets to me also, as I sat and watched it titter on through the forest until it reached a lake for a pause in its rush, and then, pick up speed again on its final journey to the broad River Wye beyond my estate.

To my great surprise and astonishment, when I got to my favorite spot by the brook, I saw a man sitting at the base of the old elm tree where I always sat. I stopped for a moment to make sure that what I was seeing was real. I started to approach the man and ask why he was on my land when he spoke to me without turning around.

"Hello, Troy. I've been waiting for you. Come, let's talk."

"Who are you?" I asked, bewildered at how he knew me, and why he was sitting where only I was allowed to sit.

He stood up and turned around and I saw nothing about him I recognized. He was neither remarkable in his appearance nor had a memorable face. He looked ordinary, except for his eyes that were an amazing shade of light blue. If I were to guess his heritage, I would guess he was Jewish, because of his dark hair, olive skin, and the shape of his nose, but I have never known a Jew with such blue eyes.

"I am the King of Salem," he said in such a way that I took it to mean he was serious.

"Kind of Salem?" I asked with not a little bit of derision. "The only King of Salem I've ever heard about is known as Melchisedec. Are you Melchisedec?"

"It is as you say."

He then reached out his right hand, as if to shake hands with me. I hesitated for just a moment, somewhat frightened, because I thought him to be a little mad. I doubted very much the man was king of anything or that he could be the one who has no father or mother, no beginning or end of days, the one called Melchisedec. He continued to hold his hand out waiting for me to take it so, reluctantly, I did. I felt a slight tingling in my hands, not just my right hand, but both.

"So, if you are Melchisedec, I can't help but wonder if it has come my time to face my destiny, and begin payment for all the sins and wrongs I have committed? Must I go with you today?"

"Not yet," he said. "You have one more thing to do."

"No, please, I can't. I'm worn out and my wounds will not heal. I cannot leave and go on another dangerous undertaking in my condition, not physically or mentally. Haven't I done enough of those? The last one cost me the lives of three of my family, as well as my health. What have I received in return for my sacrifices?"

All the while I spoke, he looked at me with those sad blue eyes. They were the light blue of an August sky. I saw compassion in them, but I got the impression from his countenance that he would not take no for an answer.

"Troy, you misunderstand me. I'm not asking you to leave your home to go anywhere, or to endanger you or your family. You have earned your rest. You have been given privileges to invest until your master returns to see how you have increased those abilities for good purposes. Some would have invested them in themselves for the personal return it would bring without benefit to others. You were tested to see if you were worthy of redemption. Worthy of glorification. Worthy to take your place among God's greatest leaders. I'm here to make you aware that your sacrifices have been noted and have been found worthy of your long due rewards, but, like I said, you have one more thing to do."

I was so shocked that my knees betrayed me, and my legs gave out. I fell to the ground on my hands and knees. Could what he was saying be true? Had I officially passed life's greatest test?

"Troy," he continued, "all I am asking you to do is to return to your parlor and write this story down for the ages to know what happened and what almost happened. Never again until the end of days shall man come so close to annihilation due to God's anger. Write the story so that the few who read it will know the truth. Man must never forget the sacrifices paid by so many, especially by you. For the past hundred and fifty years, your sanctifying struggles against evil forces prepared you for what you did these past months. Write your story. Then you may find your rest."

When he had spoken those last words, he smiled for the first time since we met, turned, and walked back down the path and, once he passed over a rise in the trail, was seen no more. That very day, I began writing down all the things that had happened since I found that journal belonging to Francois Laurent. I wrote feverishly for weeks on end. Weeks turned into months. My last quest.

Trails and trials.

My life can be summed up in those two words. I have been on more adventures than I can count. All of them filled with trials that sometimes seemed unsurmountable. Somehow, I overcame each of them. Each time, I learned more about life. I left my life and my family at the age of seventeen to find knowledge and wealth, never knowing that wasn't what I was really looking for. I found both, and won and lost wealth several times, and won again vast quantities of gold and silver. They gave me some comfort and the ability to accomplish things I had wished for, but they did not satisfy me. They did not, because I had a hole in my heart for something greater than things, things I was unable to accomplish for myself.

Every man has a hole in his heart that must be filled with something. Mammon cannot do it for anyone. I had seen more of the world than any man or woman could ever see in the many decades I lived. So many trails. So many trials. I had visited with popes, kings, emperors, chieftains, as well as humble priests and abbots. I had gazed at the faces of angels and the Lord of Lords himself. Having done that, there still was that one thing missing in my life.

I had finally found what it was I was looking for. I found it sitting next to a brook. I found peace at last.

The old elm tree roots would cradle me once again, and its high limbs provided shade as it had a thousand times before. Geese honked at me from above, letting me know they were back from unknown lands in the south. I smiled and leaned my head back against the mass of the elm and let the waters sing a lullaby to me. I dozed off. Then, I let the arms of what I longed for, what had filled the vacant hole in my life, surround me.

Peace.

At last.

The End

Epilogue

Let no one weep for me or celebrate my funeral with mourning; for I still live, as I pass to and fro through the mouths of men.
—Quintus Ennius

Connie, my dear, strong daughter, made it safely back to London and rebuilt the East Asia Trading Company back to its former profitability, and established satellite offices throughout southern England. It came as no surprise to anyone when she announced that she was going to marry Luca. Their marriage ceremony took place in the garden behind my castle. It was a beautiful thing to behold. They married the summer we returned from Armenia. Two weeks later, Catherine Adele and Troy went to live with them, and they became Luca and Connie's adopted children. It was sad to see them ride away, to give them away. I loved them so much, but my health was declining, and it was best they leave while I could still hug them and see them off. They became the kind of family any father would want them to be. Every year they visit my castle and lay garlands on my headstone.

381

Before Connie and Luca left to return to London, I made time to tell her what she really meant to me; that she was the bravest of us all. I told Luca how much I had depended on him and how he had fulfilled all my expectations and more. I spent a few uncomfortable moments hugging the big man. I created a will that would, among other things, bequeath my beloved Goodrich Castle to Connie and Luca. Catherine Adele and Troy would always have the place to come home to.

Pagiel married beautiful Leah. They now live in a large estate that once belonged to a French nobleman of Jewish descent. Francois' wife and daughter were evicted from the big house, and now live in a small servant's home on the property with permission from Pagiel. They will live there until they desire to leave, or they die. It will be their choice. Pagiel and Leah would eventually have seven children, all girls, all beautiful. Leah never learned how to cook. They live off the income I bequeathed them. They live an unadventurous life, but a very happy one.

Gerald recovered, except for a pronounced limp, and set about learning all he could from Connie. He first left England a young, impetuous, and immature young man, but returned a much wiser and thoughtful adult. A near death experience caused a change in him that would serve him well as long as he lived. He had a great helper, too. Eesha never left his side. Gerald had a choice of sending her away or marrying her. He chose to make her his wife. She still amuses everyone with her version of the "England words".

Commander Chaim was given a trial presided over by the High Priest and four Chief Priests. Rabbi Caleb became the fourth Chief Priest. Chaim was found guilty of sedition, treason, blasphemy, and rebellion and sentenced to death.

In accordance with Jewish custom, he was stoned to death. He was buried in an unmarked grave, and its location has been lost to history. High Priest, Yoseph bar Judah's son, the one who shot the lead ball that would eventually kill me, became an embittered man. Life aboveground did not suit him. Some say he died from too much rum; some say he died from remorse.

The English Ashkenazim colony learned of the new edict from Armenia long before my party reached Southampton. The counsel of rabbis made the decision to leave it up to their citizens to leave and live aboveground or choose to remain underground. The majority chose to live as they always had been. Some left, but many of those returned, not liking the weather and hardships found in the new world on the surface. The known was more comfortable and safer than the strange world above where there were few ways of earning a living, where a king controlled their lives, where taxes were expected, where there was too much rain or snow, and the ways of the world were inferior to the world in which they lived underground. To them, the English people were distasteful and lacked the hygiene, education, camaraderie, resourcefulness, and courtesy enjoyed by their fellow Jews belowground. However, the secrecy of their location and existence was over.

I never learned what the colonies in Charolais, Rouen, Castile, Milan, or even Adrianople decided to do, and very little of what happened to Britannia after all their entire view of the world was turned upside down by Yoseph's decree. I would not live long enough to learn if persecutions continued toward the Ashkenazim. They deserved the right to be citizens of the world just like my family and me, and free of

383

societal prejudices. Yoseph told me before I left Tarsus there was an old Hebrew saying that went, "Ha-Nekhtom May-Eed Ahl Ee-sa-toe", meaning "the finished product testifies to its ingredients". He promised me that never again would his people assume the misguided endeavor to take what was not theirs to take. He explained that the Ashkenazim were good, moral people dedicated to service and worship of their god. He apologized for misleading them that resulted in the army's compulsion to take control of the masses for personal gain. He did not fathom the depths of human depravity, that Jew or gentile were capable of. Now, he knows, and it became a mission of his to educate his people against the very sins the Torah spoke against.

I never learned what happened to the rest of my mercenary friends who left us at port in Centumcellae, either. They were good men, and I hoped the silver I gave them permitted them to retire from fighting, and live in peace the rest of their lives, and never have to draw blood again. The journey's expenses from the time I and my two companions escaped from prison in the Britania Colony, to our return home to my castle, drained my wealth by about twenty percent. It was of little matter, as I still had more than I could spend, and the silver I spent was for a good cause.

As for me, well, I found my peace at last. When I sat down for the last time next to that great elm tree whose roots sip from the nameless stream on my estate and, when I let the music of the laughing water lull me into a deep and everlasting sleep, I found the kind of peace that transcends what few mortals are given in life.

Everyone has a legacy. Not everyone has one to be proud of. I was pleased with mine, and I give credit for that to my wives for raising our children well. My legacy will never end, I think. What I've done, what I have achieved through the amazing gifts I have been given, the lives I have been a big part of, will be in the mouths of my descendants to tell and retell until the end of time.

Beyond my closed eyelids, I could see clearer than I had ever seen before. I saw the stream I was resting next to. It was so clear; it was like polished gold whose surface rippled and undulated past me in the brightest of sunlight. On the other side of the living water, I saw people I knew! I saw Veronica, Susan, Anna, and Jaleel. I saw Carl, Abbot Peter, and Father Matthias. What a sight it was to see those whom I loved or revered. They beckoned me to come.

I went.

Peace.

At last.

Jerry B. Sanders was born and raised in south Louisiana and is an avid outdoorsman. After retiring as an engineer from a major U.S. oil company, Sanders discovered his love of writing and now spends his time between hunting, travelling, and writing. His fascination with medieval England, the writings of Bernard Cornwell and Ken Follet, and the many adaptations of Robin Hood and King Arthur have inspired and influenced his work. *Between Heaven and Hell* is a trilogy infused with Sanders' strong sense of duty and deep love for his family, paying tribute to his father in the form of the main protagonist, Troy Kensington. He now lives in Tahlequah, Oklahoma with his wife Cordelia.